Jack London

John Griffith London (born John Griffith Chaney; January 12, 1876 – November 22, 1916) was an American novelist, journalist, and social activist. A pioneer in the world of commercial magazine fiction, he was one of the first writers to become a worldwide celebrity and earn a large fortune from writing. He was also an innovator in the genre that would later become known as science fiction. His most famous works include The Call of the Wild and White Fang, both set in the Klondike Gold Rush, as well as the short stories "To Build a Fire", "An Odyssey of the North", and "Love of Life". He also wrote about the South Pacific in stories such as "The Pearls of Parlay" and "The Heathen". London was part of the radical literary group "The Crowd" in San Francisco and a passionate advocate of unionization, socialism, and the rights of workers. He wrote several powerful works dealing with these topics, such as his dystopian novel The Iron Heel, his non-fiction exposé The People of the Abyss, and The War of the Classes. (Source: Wikipedia)

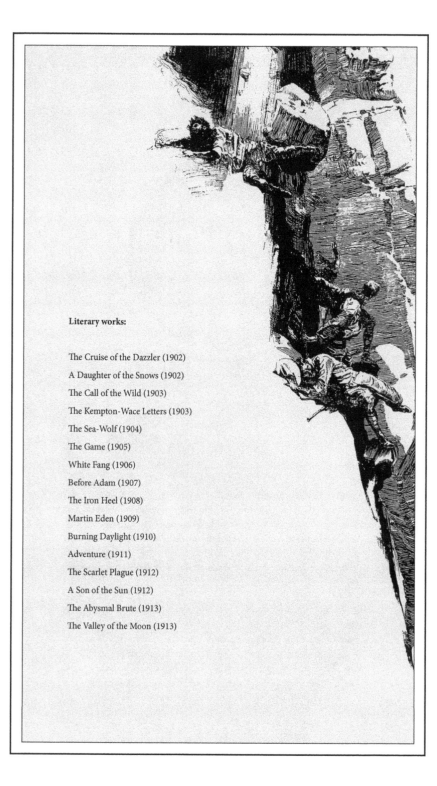

Literary works:

The Cruise of the Dazzler (1902)

A Daughter of the Snows (1902)

The Call of the Wild (1903)

The Kempton-Wace Letters (1903)

The Sea-Wolf (1904)

The Game (1905)

White Fang (1906)

Before Adam (1907)

The Iron Heel (1908)

Martin Eden (1909)

Burning Daylight (1910)

Adventure (1911)

The Scarlet Plague (1912)

A Son of the Sun (1912)

The Abysmal Brute (1913)

The Valley of the Moon (1913)

THE
WORKS
OF
JACK LONDON

VOL. 17 (OF 17)

THEFT

WHEN GOD LAUGHS
AND OTHER STORIES

WHITE FANG

An Imprint of Moon Classics LLC

A Wholly Owned Subsidiary of Queenior LLC

A Melodragon Company

Copyright © 2020

First Printing: 2020

ISBN 978-1-6627-2124-3 (Paperback)

ISBN 978-1-6627-2125-0 (Hardcover)

Published by Moon Classics

www.moonclassics.com

Contents

THE
WORKS
OF
JACK LONDON
VOL. 17 (OF 17)

THEFT

Time of Play, To-Day, in Washington, D. C.

It Occurs in Twenty Hours

CHARACTERS

Margaret Chalmers

Howard Knox

Thomas Chalmers

Master Thomas Chalmers

Ellery Jackson Hubbard

Anthony Starkweather

Mrs Starkweather

Connie Starkweather

Felix Dobleman

Linda Davis

Julius Rutland

John Gieford

Matsu Sakari

Dolores Ortega

Senator Dowsett Mrs Dowsett

Housekeeper, Servs

Wife of Senator Chalmers

A Congressman from Oregon

A United States Senator and several times millionaire

Son of Margaret and Senator Chalmers

A Journalist

A great magnate, and father of Margaret Chalmers

His wife

Their younger daughter

Secretary to Anthony Starkweather

Maid to Margaret Chalmers

Episcopalian Minister

Labor Agitator

Secretary of Japanese Embassy

Wife of Peruvian Minister

Agents, etc

ACTORS' DESCRIPTION OF CHARACTERS

Margaret Chalmers. Twenty-seven years of age; a strong, mature woman, but quite feminine where her heart or sense of beauty are concerned. Her eyes are wide apart. Has a dazzling smile, which she knows how to use on occasion. Also, on occasion, she can be firm and hard, even cynical An intellectual woman, and at the same time a very womanly woman, capable of sudden tendernesses, flashes of emotion, and abrupt actions. She is a finished product of high culture and refinement, and at the same time possesses robust vitality and instinctive right-promptings that augur well for the future of the race.

Howard Knox. He might have been a poet, but was turned politician. Inflamed with love for humanity. Thirty-five years of age. He has his vision, and must follow it. He has suffered ostracism because of it, and has followed his vision in spite of abuse and ridicule. Physically, a well-built, powerful man. Strong-featured rather than handsome. Very much in earnest, and, despite his university training, a trifle awkward in carriage and demeanor, lacking in social ease. He has been elected to Congress on a reform ticket, and is almost alone in fight he is making. He has no party to back him, though he has a following of a few independents and insurgents.

Thomas Chalmers. Forty-five to fifty years of age. Iron-gray mustache. Slightly stout. A good liver, much given to Scotch and soda, with a weak heart. Is liable to collapse any time. If anything, slightly lazy or lethargic in his emotional life. One of the "owned" senators representing a decadent New England state, himself master of the state political machine. Also, he is nobody's fool. He possesses the brain and strength of character to play his part. His most distinctive feature is his temperamental opportunism.

Master Thomas Chalmers. Six years of age. Sturdy and healthy despite his grandmother's belief to the contrary.

Ellery Jackson Hubbard. Thirty-eight to forty years of age. Smooth-shaven. A star journalist with a national reputation; a large, heavy-set man, with large head, large hands—everything about him is large. A man radiating prosperity, optimism and selfishness. Has no morality whatever. Is a conscious individualist, cold-blooded, pitiless, working only for himself, and believing in nothing but himself.

Anthony Starkweather. An elderly, well preserved gentleman, slenderly built, showing all the signs of a man who has lived clean and has been almost an ascetic. One to whom the joys of the flesh have had little meaning. A cold, controlled man whose one passion is for power. Distinctively a man of power. An eagle-like man, who, by keenness of brain and force of character, has carved out a fortune of hundreds of millions. In short, an industrial and financial magnate of the first water and of the finest type to be found in the United States. Essentially a moral man, his rigid New England morality has suffered a sea change and developed into the morality of the master-man of affairs, equally rigid, equally uncompromising, but essentially Jesuitical in that he believes in doing wrong that right may come of it. He is absolutely certain that civilization and progress rest on his shoulders and upon the shoulders of the small group of men like him.

Mrs. Starkweather. Of the helpless, comfortably stout, elderly type. She has not followed her husband in his moral evolution. She is the creature of old customs, old prejudices, old New England ethics. She is rather confused by the modern rush of life.

Connie Starkweather. Margaret's younger sister, twenty years old. She is nothing that Margaret is, and everything that Margaret is not. No essential evil in her, but has no mind of her own—hopelessly a creature of convention. Gay, laughing, healthy, buxom—a natural product of her care-free environment.

Feux Dobleman. Private secretary to Anthony Starkweather. A young man of correct social deportment, thoroughly and in all things just the sort of private secretary a man like Anthony Starkweather would have. He is a weak-souled creature, timorous, almost effeminate.

16

Linda Davis. Maid to Margaret. A young woman of twenty-five or so, blond, Scandinavian, though American-born. A cold woman, almost featureless because of her long years of training, but with a hot heart deep down, and characterized by an intense devotion to her mistress. Wild horses could drag nothing from her where her mistress is concerned.

Junus Rutland. Having no strong features about him, the type realizes itself.

John Gifford. A labor agitator. A man of the people, rough-hewn, narrow as a labor-leader may well be, earnest and sincere. He is a proper, better type of labor-leader.

Matsu Sakari. Secretary of Japanese Embassy. He is the perfection of politeness and talks classical book-English. He bows a great deal.

Dolores Ortega. Wife of Peruvian Minister; bright and vivacious, and uses her hands a great deal as she talks, in the Latin-American fashion.

Senator Dowsett. Fifty years of age; well preserved.

Mrs. Dowsett. Stout and middle-aged.

ACT I. A ROOM IN THE HOUSE OF SENATOR CHALMERS

Scene. *In Senator Chalmers' home. It is four o'clock in the afternoon, in a modern living room with appropriate furnishings. In particular, in front, on left, a table prepared for the serving of tea, all excepting the tea urn itself. At rear, right of center, is main entrance to the room. Also, doorways at sides, on left and right. Curtain discloses Chalmers and Hubbard seated loungingly at the right front.*

Hubbard

(*After an apparent pause for cogitation.*) I can't understand why an old wheel-horse like Elsworth should kick over the traces that way.

Chalmers

Disgruntled. Thinks he didn't get his fair share of plums out of the Tariff Committee. Besides, it's his last term. He's announced that he's going to retire.

Hubbard

(*Snorting contemptuously, mimicking an old man's pompous enunciation.*) "A Resolution to Investigate the High Cost of Living!"—old Senator Elsworth introducing a measure like that! The old buck!—— How are you going to handle it?

Chalmers

It's already handled.

Hubbard

Yes?

Chalmers

(*Pulling his mustache.*) Turned it over to the Committee to Audit and Control the Contingent Expenses of the Senate.

Hubbard

(*Grinning his appreciation.*) And you're chairman. Poor old Elsworth. This way to the lethal chamber, and the bill's on its way.

Chalmers

Elsworth will be retired before it's ever reported. In the meantime, say after a decent interval, Senator Hodge will introduce another resolution to investigate the high cost of living. It will be like Elsworth's, only it won't.

Hubbard

(*Nodding his head and anticipating.*) And it will go to the Committee on Finance and come back for action inside of twenty-four hours.

Chalmers

By the way, I see *Cartwright's Magazine* has ceased muck-raking.

Hubbard

Cartwrights never did muck-rake—that is, not the big Interests— only the small independent businesses that didn't advertise.

Chalmers

Yes, it deftly concealed its reactionary tendencies.

Hubbard

And from now on the concealment will be still more deft. I've gone into it myself. I have a majority of the stock right now.

Chalmers

I thought I had noticed a subtle change in the last two numbers.

Hubbard

(*Nodding.*) We're still going on muck-raking. We have a splendid series on Aged Paupers, demanding better treatment and more sanitary conditions. Also we are going to run "Barbarous Venezuela" and show up thoroughly the rotten political management of that benighted country.

20

Chalmers

(*Nods approvingly, and, after a pause.*) And now concerning Knox. That's what I sent for you about. His speech comes off tomorrow per schedule. At last we've got him where we want him.

Hubbard

I have the ins and outs of it pretty well. Everything's arranged. The boys have their cue, though they don't know just what's going to be pulled off; and this time to-morrow afternoon their dispatches will be singing along the wires.

Chalmers

(*Firmly and harshly.*) This man Knox must be covered with ridicule, swamped with ridicule, annihilated with ridicule.

Hubbard

It is to laugh. Trust the great American people for that. We'll make those little Western editors sit up. They've been swearing by Knox, like a little tin god. Roars of laughter for them.

Chalmers

Do you do anything yourself?

Hubbard

Trust me. I have my own article for Cartwright's blocked out. They're holding the presses for it. I shall wire it along hot-footed to-morrow evening. Say——?

Chalmers

(*After a pause.*) Well?

Hubbard

Wasn't it a risky thing to give him his chance with that speech?

21

Chalmers

It was the only feasible thing. He never has given us an opening. Our service men have camped on his trail night and day. Private life as unimpeachable as his public life. But now is our chance. The gods have given him into our hands. That speech will do more to break his influence—

Hubbard

(*Interrupting.*) Than a Fairbanks cocktail.

(*Both laugh.*) But don't forget that this Knox is a live wire. Somebody might get stung. Are you sure, when he gets up to make that speech, that he won't be able to back it up?

Chalmers

No danger at all.

Hubbard

But there are hooks and crooks by which facts are sometimes obtained.

Chalmers

(*Positively.*) Knox has nothing to go on but suspicions and hints, and unfounded assertions from the yellow press.

(*Man-servant enters, goes to tea-table, looks it over, and makes slight rearrangements.*) (*Lowering his voice.*) He will make himself a laughing stock. His charges will turn into boomerangs. His speech will be like a sheet from a Sunday supplement, with not a fact to back it up. (*Glances at Servant.*) We'd better be getting out of here. They're going to have tea.

(*The Servant, however, makes exit.*) Come to the library and have a high-ball. (*They pause as Hubbard speaks.*)

Hubbard

(*With quiet glee.*) And to-morrow Ali Baba gets his.

22

Chalmers

Ali Baba?

Hubbard

That's what your wife calls him—Knox.

Chalmers

Oh, yes, I believe I've heard it before. It's about time he hanged himself, and now we've given him the rope.

Hubbard

(*Sinking voice and becoming deprecatingly confidential.*)

Oh, by the way, just a little friendly warning, Senator Chalmers. Not so fast and loose up New York way. That certain lady, not to be mentioned—there's gossip about it in the New York newspaper offices. Of course, all such stories are killed. But be discreet, be discreet If Gherst gets hold of it, he'll play it up against the Administration in all his papers.

(*Chalmers, who throughout this speech is showing a growing resentment, is about to speak, when voices are heard without and he checks himself.*)

(*Enter. Mrs. Starkweather, rather flustered and imminently in danger of a collapse, followed by Connie Starkweather, fresh, radiant, and joyous.*)

Mrs. Starkweather

(*With appeal and relief.*)

Oh——Tom!

(*Chalmers takes her hand sympathetically and protectingly.*)

Connie

(*Who is an exuberant young woman, bursts forth.*) Oh, brother-in-law! Such excitement! That's what's the matter with mother. We ran into a go-cart. Our chauffeur was not to blame. It was the woman's fault. She tried to cross just as we were turning the corner. But we hardly grazed it. Fortunately the baby was not hurt—only spilled. It was ridiculous. *(Catching sight of Hubbard.)* Oh, there you are, Mr. Hubbard. How de do.

(Steps half way to meet him and shakes hands with him.) (Mrs. Starkweather looks around helplessly for a chair, and Chalmers conducts her to one soothingly.)

Mrs. Starkweather

Oh, it was terrible! The little child might have been killed. And such persons love their babies, I know.

Connie

(To Chalmers.) Has father come? We were to pick him up here. Where's Madge?

Mrs. Starkweather

(Espying Hubbard, faintly.) Oh, there is Mr. Hubbard.

(Hubbard comes to her and shakes hands.) I simply can't get used to these rapid ways of modern life. The motor-car is the invention of the devil. Everything is *too* quick. When I was a girl, we lived sedately, decorously. There was time for meditation and repose. But in this age there is time for nothing. How Anthony keeps his head is more than I can understand. But, then, Anthony is a wonderful man.

Hubbard

I am sure Mr. Starkweather never lost his head in his life.

Chalmers

Unless when he was courting you, mother.

Mrs. Starkweather

(A trifle grimly.) I'm not so sure about that.

Connie

24

(*Imitating a grave, business-like enunciation.*) Father probably conferred first with his associates, then turned the affair over for consideration by his corporation lawyers, and, when they reported no flaws, checked the first spare half hour in his notebook to ask mother if she would have him.

(*They laugh.*) And looked at his watch at least twice while he was proposing.

Mrs. Starkweather

Anthony was not so busy then as all that.

Hubbard

He hadn't yet taken up the job of running the United States.

Mrs. Starkweather

I'm sure I don't know what he is running, but he is a very busy man—business, politics, and madness; madness, politics, and business.

(*She stops breathlessly and glances at tea-table.*) Tea. I should like a cup of tea. Connie, I shall stay for a cup of tea, and then, if your father hasn't come, we'll go home. (*To Chalmers.*) Where is Tommy?

Chalmers

Out in the car with Madge.

(*Glances at tea-table and consults watch.*) She should be back now.

Connie

Mother, you mustn't stay long. I have to dress.

Chalmers

Oh, yes, that dinner.

(*Yawns.*) I wish I could loaf to-night.

Connie

25

(*Explaining to Hubbard.*) The Turkish Charge d'Affaires—I never can remember his name. But he's great fun—a positive joy. He's giving the dinner to the British Ambassador.

Mrs. Starkweather

(*Starting forward in her chair and listening intently.*) There's Tommy, now.

(*Voices of Margaret Chalmers and of Tommy heard from without. Hers is laughingly protesting, while Tommy's is gleefully insistent.*) (*Margaret and Tommy appear and pause just outside door, holding each other's hands, facing each other, too immersed in each other to be aware of the presence of those inside the room. Margaret and Tommy are in street costume.*)

Tommy

(*Laughing.*)

But mama.

Margaret

(*Herself laughing, but shaking her head.*) No. Tommy First—

Margaret

No; you must run along to Linda, now, mother's boy. And we'll talk about that some other time.

(*Tommy notices for the first time that there are persons in the room. He peeps in around the door and espies Mrs. Starkweather. At the same moment, impulsively, he withdraws his hands and runs in to Mrs. Starkweather.*)

Tommy

(*Who is evidently fond of his grandmother.*) Grandma!

(*They embrace and make much of each other.*)

(*Margaret enters, appropriately greeting the others—a kiss* (maybe) *to Connie, and a slightly cold handshake to Hubbard.*)

Margaret

(*To Chalmers.*) Now that you're here, Tom, you mustn't run away.

(*Greets Mrs. Starkweather.*)

Mrs. Starkweather

(*Turning Tommy's face to the light and looking at it anxiously.*) A trifle thin, Margaret.

Margaret

On the contrary, mother——

Mrs. Starkweather

(*To Chalmers.*) Don't you think so, Tom?

Connie

(*Aside to Hubbard.*) Mother continually worries about his health.

Hubbard

A sturdy youngster, I should say.

Tommy

(*To Chalmers.*) I'm an Indian, aren't I, daddy?

Chalmers

(*Nodding his head emphatically.*) And the stoutest-hearted in the tribe.

(*Linda appears in doorway, evidently looking for Tommy, and Chalmers notices her.*) There's Linda looking for you, young stout heart.

Margaret

Take Tommy, Linda. Run along, mother's boy.

Tommy

Come along, grandma. I want to show you something.

(*He catches Mrs. Starkweather by the hand. Protesting, but highly pleased, she allows him to lead her to the door, where he extends his other hand to Linda. Thus, pausing in doorway, leading a woman by either hand, he looks back at Margaret.*) (*Roguishly.*) Remember, mama, we're going to scout in a little while.

Margaret

(*Going to Tommy, and bending down with her arms around him.*) No, Tommy. Mama has to go to that horrid dinner to-night. But to-morrow we'll play.

(*Tommy is cast down and looks as if he might pout.*) Where is my little Indian now?

Hubbard

Be an Indian, Tommy.

Tommy

(*Brightening up.*)

All right, mama. To-morrow.——if you can't find time to-day.

(*Margaret kisses him.*) (*Exit Tommy, Mrs. Starkweather, and Linda, Tommy leading them by a hand in each of theirs.*)

Chalmers

(*Nodding to Hubbard, in low voice to Hubbard and starting to make exit to right.*) That high-ball.

(*Hubbard disengages himself from proximity of Connie, and starts to follow.*)

Connie

(*Reproachfully.*) If you run away, I won't stop for tea.

28

Margaret

Do stop, Tom. Father will be here in a few minutes.

Connie

A regular family party.

Chalmers

All right. We'll be back. We're just going to have a little talk.

(*Chalmers and Hubbard make exit to right.*) (*Margaret puts her arm impulsively around Connie—a sheerly spontaneous act of affection—kisses her, and at same time evinces preparation to leave.*)

Margaret

I've got to get my things off. Won't you wait here, dear, in case anybody comes? It's nearly time.

(*Starts toward exit to rear, but is stopped by Connie.*) Madge.

(*Margaret immediately pauses and waits expectantly, smiling, while Connie is hesitant.*)

I want to speak to you about something, Madge. You don't mind?

(*Margaret, still smiling, shakes her head.*) Just a warning. Not that anybody could believe for a moment, there is anything wrong, but——

Margaret

(*Dispelling a shadow of irritation that has crossed her face.*)

If it concerns Tom, don't tell me, please. You know he does do ridiculous things at times. But I don't let him worry me any more; so don't worry me about him.

(*Connie remains silent, and Margaret grows curious.*) Well?

Connie

It's not about Tom—

(*Pauses.*) It's about you.

Margaret

Oh.

Connie

I don't know how to begin.

Margaret

By coming right out with it, the worst of it, all at once, first.

Connie

It isn't serious at all, but—well, mother is worrying about it. You know how old-fashioned she is. And when you consider our position— father's and Tom's, I mean—it doesn't seem just right for you to be seeing so much of such an enemy of theirs. He has abused them dreadfully, you know. And there's that dreadful speech he is going to give to-morrow. You haven't seen the afternoon papers. He has made the most terrible charges against everybody—all of us, our friends, everybody.

Margaret

You mean Mr. Knox, of course. But he wouldn't harm anybody, Connie, dear.

Connie

(*Bridling,*) Oh, he wouldn't? He as good as publicly called father a thief.

Margaret

When did that happen? I never heard of it.

Connie

Well, he said that the money magnates had grown so unprincipled, sunk so low, that they would steal a mouse from a blind kitten.

30

Margaret

I don't see what father has to do with that.

Connie

He meant him just the same.

Margaret

You silly goose. He couldn't have meant father. Father? Why, father wouldn't look at anything less than fifty or a hundred millions.

Connie

And you speak to him and make much of him when you meet him places. You talked with him for half an hour at that Dugdale reception. You have him here in your own house—Tom's house—when he's such a bitter enemy of Tom's. (*During the foregoing speech, Anthony Starkweather makes entrance from rear. His face is grave, and he is in a brown study, as if pondering weighty problems. At sight of the two women he pauses and surveys them. They are unaware of his presence.*)

Margaret

You are wrong, Connie. He is nobody's enemy. He is the truest, cleanest, most right-seeking man I have ever seen.

Connie

(*Interrupting.*) He is a trouble-maker, a disturber of the public peace, a shallow-pated demagogue—

Margaret

(*Reprovingly.*)

Now you're quoting somebody—— father, I suppose. To think of him being so abused—poor, dear Ali Baba—

Starkweather

(*Clearing his throat in advertisement of his presence.*) A-hem.

(*Margaret and Connie turn around abruptly and discover him.*)

Margaret

And Connie Father!

(*Both come forward to greet him, Margaret leading.*)

Starkweather

(*Anticipating, showing the deliberate method of the busy man saving time by eliminating the superfluous.*) Fine, thank you. Quite well in every particular. This Ali Baba? Who is Ali Baba?

(*Margaret looks amused reproach at Connie.*)

Connie

Mr. Howard Knox.

Starkweather

And why is he called Ali Baba?

Margaret

That is my nickname for him. In the den of thieves, you know. You remember your Arabian Nights.

Starkweather

(*Severely.*) I have been wanting to speak to you for some time, Margaret, about that man. You know that I have never interfered with your way of life since your marriage, nor with your and Tom's housekeeping arrangements. But this man Knox. I understand that you have even had him here in your house—

Margaret

(*Interrupting.*) He is very liable to be here this afternoon, any time, now.

(*Connie displays irritation at Margaret.*)

Starkweather

(*Continuing imperturbably.*) *Your* house—*you*, my daughter, and the wife of Senator Chalmers. As I said, I have not interfered with you since your marriage. But this Knox affair transcends household arrangements. It is of political importance. The man is an enemy to our class, a firebrand. Why do you have him here?

Margaret

Because I like him. Because he is a man I am proud to call "friend." Because I wish there were more men like him, many more men like him, in the world. Because I have ever seen in him nothing but the best and highest. And, besides, it's such good fun to see how one virtuous man can so disconcert you captains of industry and arbiters of destiny. Confess that you are very much disconcerted, father, right now. He will be here in a few minutes, and you will be more disconcerted. Why? Because it is an affair that transcends family arrangements. And it is your affair, not mine.

Starkweather

This man Knox is a dangerous character—one that I am not pleased to see any of my family take up with. He is not a gentleman.

Margaret

He is a self-made man, if that is what you mean, and he certainly hasn't any money.

Connie

(*Interrupting.*) He says that money is theft—at least when it is in the hands of a wealthy person.

Starkweather

He is uncouth—ignorant.

Margaret

33

I happen to know that he is a graduate of the University of Oregon.

Starkweather

(*Sneeringly.*) A cow college. But that is not what I mean. He is a demagogue, stirring up the wild-beast passions of the people.

Margaret

Surely you would not call his advocacy of that child labor bill and of the conservation of the forest and coal lands stirring up the wild-beast passions of the people?

Starkweather

(*Wearily.*) You don't understand. When I say he is dangerous it is because he threatens all the stabilities, because he threatens us who have made this country and upon whom this country and its prosperity rest.

(*Connie, scenting trouble, walks across stage away from them.*)

Margaret

The captains of industry—the banking magnates and the mergers?

Starkweather

Call it so. Call it what you will. Without us the country falls into the hands of scoundrels like that man Knox and smashes to ruin.

Margaret

(*Reprovingly.*) Not a scoundrel, father.

Starkweather

He is a sentimental dreamer, a hair-brained enthusiast. It is the foolish utterances of men like him that place the bomb and the knife in the hand of the assassin.

Margaret

He is at least a good man, even if he does disagree with you on political and industrial problems. And heaven knows that good men are rare enough these days.

Starkweather

I impugn neither his morality nor his motives—only his rationality. Really, Margaret, there is nothing inherently vicious about him. I grant that. And it is precisely that which makes him such a power for evil.

Margaret

When I think of all the misery and pain which he is trying to remedy—I can see in him only a power for good. He is not working for himself but for the many. That is why he has no money. You have heaven alone knows how many millions—you don't; you have worked for yourself.

Starkweather

I, too, work for the many. I give work to the many. I make life possible for the many. I am only too keenly alive to the responsibilities of my stewardship of wealth.

Margaret

But what of the child laborers working at the machines? Is that necessary, O steward of wealth? How my heart has ached for them! How I have longed to do something for them—to change conditions so that it will no longer be necessary for the children to toil, to have the playtime of childhood stolen away from them. Theft—that is what it is, the playtime of the children coined into profits. That is why I like Howard Knox. He calls theft theft. He is trying to do something for those children. What are you trying to do for them?

Starkweather

Sentiment. Sentiment. The question is too vast and complicated, and you cannot understand. No woman can understand. That is why you run to sentiment. That is what is the matter with this Knox—sentiment. You can't run a government of ninety millions of people on sentiment, nor on abstract ideas of justice and right.

Margaret

But if you eliminate justice and right, what remains?

Starkweather

This is a practical world, and it must be managed by practical men— by thinkers, not by near-thinkers whose heads are addled with the half-digested ideas of the French Encyclopedists and Revolutionists of a century and a half ago.

(*Margaret shows signs of impatience—she is not particularly perturbed by this passage-at-arms with her father, and is anxious to get off her street things.*)

Don't forget, my daughter, that your father knows the books as well as any cow college graduate from Oregon. I, too, in my student days, dabbled in theories of universal happiness and righteousness, saw my vision and dreamed my dream. I did not know then the weakness, and frailty, and grossness of the human clay. But I grew out of that and into a man. Some men never grow out of that stage. That is what is the trouble with Knox. He is still a dreamer, and a dangerous one.

(*He pauses a moment, and then his thin lips shut grimly. But he has just about shot his bolt.*)

Margaret

What do you mean?

Starkweather

He has let himself in to give a speech to-morrow, wherein he will be called upon to deliver the proofs of all the lurid charges he has made against the Administration—against us, the stewards of wealth if you please. He will be unable to deliver the proofs, and the nation will laugh. And that will be the political end of Mr. Ali Baba and his dream.

Margaret

It is a beautiful dream. Were there more like him the dream would come true. After all, it is the dreamers that build and that never die. Perhaps you will find that he is not so easily to be destroyed. But I can't stay and argue with you, father. I simply must go and get my things off.

(*To Connie.*) You'll have to receive, dear. I'll be right back.

(*Julius Rutland enters. Margaret advances to meet him, shaking his hand.*) You must forgive me for deserting for a moment.

Rutland

(*Greeting the others.*) A family council, I see.

Margaret

(*On way to exit at rear.*) No; a discussion on dreams and dreamers. I leave you to bear my part.

Rutland

(*Bowing.*) With pleasure. The dreamers are the true architects. But—a—what is the dream and who is the dreamer?

Margaret

(*Pausing in the doorway.*) The dream of social justice, of fair play and a square deal to everybody. The dreamer—Mr. Knox.

(*Rutland is so patently irritated, that Margaret lingers in the doorway to enjoy.*)

Rutland

That man! He has insulted and reviled the Church—my calling. He—

Connie

(*Interrupting.*) He said the churchmen stole from God. I remember he once said there had been only one true Christian and that He died on the Cross.

Margaret

He quoted that from Nietzsche.

Starkweather

(*To Rutland, in quiet glee.*) He had you there.

Rutland

(*In composed fury.*) Nietzsche is a blasphemer, sir. Any man who reads Nietzsche or quotes Nietzsche is a blasphemer. It augurs ill for the future of America when such pernicious literature has the vogue it has.

Margaret

(*Interrupting, laughing.*) I leave the quarrel in your hands, sir knight. Remember—the dreamer and the dream. (*Margaret makes exit.*)

Rutland

(*Shaking his head.*) I cannot understand what is coming over the present generation. Take your daughter, for instance. Ten years ago she was an earnest, sincere lieutenant of mine in all our little charities.

Starkweather

Has she given charity up?

Connie

It's settlement work, now, and kindergartens.

Rutland

(*Ominously.*) It's writers like Nietzsche, and men who read him, like Knox, who are responsible.

(*Senator Dowsett and Mrs. Dowsett enter from rear.*)

(*Connie advances to greet them. Rutland knows Mrs. Dowsett, and Connie introduces him to Senator Dowsett.*)

(In the meantime, not bothering to greet anybody, evincing his own will and way, Starkweather goes across to right front, selects one of several chairs, seats himself, pulls a thin note-book from inside coat pocket, and proceeds to immerse himself in contents of same.) *(Dowsett and Rutland pair and stroll to left rear and seat themselves, while Connie and Mrs. Dowsett seat themselves at tea-table to left front. Connie rings the bell for Servant.)*

Mrs. Dowsett

(Glancing significantly at Starkweather, and speaking in a low voice.) That's your father, isn't it? I have so wanted to meet him.

Connie

(Softly.) You know he's peculiar. He is liable to ignore everybody here this afternoon, and get up and go away abruptly, without saying good-bye.

Mrs. Dowsett

(Sympathetically.) Yes, I know, a man of such large affairs. He must have so much on his mind. He is a wonderful man—my husband says the greatest in contemporary history—more powerful than a dozen presidents, the King of England, and the Kaiser, all rolled into one.

(Servant enters with tea urn and accessories, and Connie proceeds to serve tea, all accompanied by appropriate patter—"Two lumps?" "One, please." "Lemon;" etc.)

(Rutland and Dowsett come forward to table for their tea, where they remain.)

(Connie, glancing apprehensively across at her father and debating a moment, prepares a cup for him and a small plate with crackers, and hands them to Dowsett, who likewise betrays apprehensiveness.)

Connie

Take it to father, please, senator.

(Note:—*Throughout the rest of this act, Starkweather is like a being apart, a king sitting on his throne. He divides the tea function with Margaret. Men come up to him and speak with him. He sends for men. They come and go at his bidding. The whole attitude, perhaps unconsciously on his part, is that wherever he may be he is master. This attitude is accepted by all the others; forsooth, he is indeed a great man and master. The only one who is not really afraid of him is Margaret; yet she gives in to him in so far as she lets him do as he pleases at her afternoon tea.*) (*Dowsett carries the cup of tea and small plate across stage to Starkweather. Starkweather does not notice him at first.*)

Connie

(*Who has been watching.*) Tea, father, won't you have a cup of tea?

(*Through the following scene between Starkweather and Dowsett, the latter holds cup of tea and crackers, helplessly, at a disadvantage. At the same time Rutland is served with tea and remains at the table, talking with the two women.*)

Starkweather

(*Looking first at Connie, then peering into cup of tea. He grunts refusal, and for the first time looks up into the other man's face. He immediately closes note-book down on finger to keep the place.*) Oh, it's you. Dowsett.

(*Painfully endeavoring to be at ease.*) A pleasure, Mr. Starkweather, an entirely unexpected pleasure to meet you here. I was not aware you frequented frivolous gatherings of this nature.

Starkweather

(*Abruptly and peremptorily.*) Why didn't you come when you were sent for this morning?

Dowsett

I was sick—I was in bed.

Starkweather

That is no excuse, sir. When you are sent for you are to come. Understand? That bill was reported back. Why was it reported back? You told Dobleman you would attend to it.

Dowsett

It was a slip up. Such things will happen.

Starkweather

What was the matter with that committee? Have you no influence with the Senate crowd? If not, say so, and I'll get some one who has.

Dowsett

(*Angrily.*) I refuse to be treated in this manner, Mr. Starkweather. I have some self-respect—

(*Starkweather grunts incredulously.*) Some decency—

(*Starkweather grunts.*) A position of prominence in my state. You forget, sir, that in our state organization I occupy no mean place.

Starkweather

(*Cutting him off so sharply that Dowsett drops cup and saucer.*) Don't you show your teeth to me. I can make you or break you. That state organization of yours belongs to me.

(*Dowsett starts—he is learning something new. To hide his feelings, he stoops to pick up cup and saucer.*) Let it alone! I am talking to you.

(*Dowsett straightens up to attention with alacrity.*) (*Connie, who has witnessed, rings for Servant.*) I bought that state organization, and paid for it. You are one of the chattels that came along with the machine. You were made senator to obey my orders. Understand? Do you understand?

Dowsett

(*Beaten.*) I—I understand.

Starkweather

That bill is to be killed.

Dowsett

Yes, sir.

Starkweather

Quietly, no headlines about it.

(*Dowsett nods.*) Now you can go.

(*Dowsett proceeds rather limply across to join group at tea-table.*) (*Chalmers and Hubbard enter from right, laughing about something. At sight of Starkweather they immediately become sober.*) (*No hands are shaken. Starkweather barely acknowledges Hubbard's greeting.*)

Starkweather

Tom, I want to see you.

(*Hubbard takes his cue, and proceeds across to tea-table.*)

(*Enter Servant. Connie directs him to remove broken cup and saucer. While this is being done, Starkweather remains silent. He consults note-book, and Chalmers stands, not quite at ease, waiting the other's will. At the same time, patter at tea-table. Hubbard, greeting others and accepting or declining cup of tea.*)

(*Servant makes exit*).

Starkweather

(*Closing finger on book and looking sharply at Chalmers.*) Tom, this affair of yours in New York must come to an end. Understand?

Chalmers

(*Starting.*) Hubbard has been talking.

Starkweather

No, it is not Hubbard. I have the reports from other sources.

42

Chalmers

It is a harmless affair.

Starkweather

I happen to know better. I have the whole record. If you wish, I can give you every detail, every meeting. I know. There is no discussion whatever. I want no more of it.

Chalmers

I never dreamed for a moment that I was—er—indiscreet.

Starkweather

Never forget that every indiscretion of a man in your position is indiscreet. We have a duty, a great and solemn duty to perform. Upon our shoulders rest the destinies of ninety million people. If we fail in our duty, they go down to destruction. Ignorant demagogues are working on the beast-passions of the people. If they have their way, they are lost, the country is lost, civilization is lost. We want no more Dark Ages.

Chalmers

Really, I never thought it was as serious as all that.

Starkweather

(*Shrugging shoulders and lifting eyebrows.*) After all, why should you? You are only a cog in the machine. I, and the several men grouped with me, am the machine. You are a useful cog—too useful to lose—

Chalmers

Lose?—Me?

Starkweather

I have but to raise my hand, any time—do you understand?—any time, and you are lost. You control your state. Very well. But never forget that to-morrow, if I wished, I could buy your whole machine out from under you. I know you cannot change yourself, but, for the sake of the big issues at stake, you must be careful, exceedingly careful. We are compelled to work with weak tools. You are a good liver, a flesh-pot man. You drink too much. Your heart is weak.—Oh, I have the report of your doctor. Nevertheless, don't make a fool of yourself, nor of us. Besides, do not forget that your wife is my daughter. She is a strong woman, a credit to both of us. Be careful that you are not a discredit to her.

Chalmers

All right, I'll be careful. But while we are—er—on this subject, there's something I'd like to speak to you about.

(*A pause, in which Starkweather waits non-committally.*) It's this man Knox, and Madge. He comes to the house. They are as thick as thieves.

Starkweather

Yes?

Chalmers

(*Hastily.*) Oh, not a breath of suspicion or anything of that sort, I assure you. But it doesn't strike me as exactly appropriate that your daughter and my wife should be friendly with this fire-eating anarchist who is always attacking us and all that we represent.

Starkweather

I started to speak with her on that subject, but was interrupted.

(*Puckers brow and thinks.*) You are her husband. Why don't you take her in hand yourself?

(*Enters Mrs. Starkweather from rear, looking about, bowing, then locating Starkweather and proceeding toward him.*)

Chalmers

What can I do? She has a will of her own—the same sort of a will that you have. Besides, I think she knows about my—about some of my—indiscretions.

Starkweather

(*Slyly.*)

Harmless indiscretions?

(*Chalmers is about to reply, but observes Mrs. Starkweather approaching.*)

Mrs. Starkweather

(*Speaks in a peevish, complaining voice, and during her harrangue Starkweather immerses himself in notebook.*) Oh, there you are, Anthony. Talking politics, I suppose. Well, as soon as I get a cup of tea we must go. Tommy is not looking as well as I could wish. Margaret loves him, but she does not take the right care of him. I don't know what the world is coming to when mothers do not know how to rear their offspring. There is Margaret, with her slum kindergartens, taking care of everybody else's children but her own. If she only performed her church duties as eagerly! Mr. Rutland is displeased with her. I shall give her a talking to—only, you'd better do it, Anthony. Somehow, I have never counted much with Margaret. She is as set in doing what she pleases as you are. In my time children paid respect to their parents. This is what comes of speed. There is no time for anything. And now I must get my tea and run. Connie has to dress for that dinner.

(*Mrs. Starkweather crosses to table, greets others characteristically and is served with tea by Connie.*)

(*Chalmers waits respectfully on Starkweather.*)

Starkweather

(*Looking up from note-book.*) That will do, Tom.

(*Chalmers is just starting across to join others, when voices are heard outside rear entrance, and Margaret enters with Dolores Ortega, wife of the Peruvian Minister, and Matsu Sakari, Secretary of Japanese Legation—both of whom she has met as they were entering the house.*)

(*Chalmers changes his course, and meets the above advancing group. He knows Dolores Ortega, whom he greets, and is introduced to Sakari.*)

(*Margaret passes on among guests, greeting them, etc. Then she displaces Connie at tea-table and proceeds to dispense tea to the newcomers.*)

(*Groups slowly form and seat themselves about stage as follows: Chalmers and Dolores Ortega; Rutland, Dowsett, Mrs. Starkweather; Connie, Mr. Dowsett, and Hubbard.*)

(*Chalmers carries tea to Dolores Ortega.*)

(*Sakari has been lingering by table, waiting for tea and pattering with Margaret, Chalmers, etc.*)

Margaret

(*Handing cup to Sakari.*) I am very timid in offering you this, for I am sure you must be appalled by our barbarous methods of making tea.

Sakari

(*Bowing.*) It is true, your American tea, and the tea of the English, are quite radically different from the tea in my country. But one learns, you know. I served my apprenticeship to American tea long years ago, when I was at Yale. It was perplexing, I assure you—at first, only at first I really believe that I am beginning to have a—how shall I call it?—a tolerance for tea in your fashion.

Margaret

You are very kind in overlooking our shortcomings.

Sakari

(*Bowing.*) On the contrary, I am unaware, always unaware, of any shortcomings of this marvelous country of yours.

Margaret

(*Laughing.*) You are incorrigibly gracious, Mr. Sakari. (*Knox appears at threshold of rear entrance and pauses irresolutely for a moment*)

Sakari

46

(*Noticing Knox, and looking about him to select which group he will join.*) If I may be allowed, I shall now retire and consume this—tea.

(*Joins group composed of Connie, Mrs. Dowsett, and Hubbard.*)

(*Knox comes forward to Margaret, betraying a certain awkwardness due to lack of experience in such social functions. He greets Margaret and those in the group nearest her.*)

Knox

(*To Margaret.*) I don't know why I come here. I do not belong. All the ways are strange.

Margaret

(*Lightly, at the same time preparing his tea.*) The same Ali Baba—once again in the den of the forty thieves. But your watch and pocket-book are safe here, really they are.

(*Knox makes a gesture of dissent at her facetiousness.*) Now don't be serious. You should relax sometimes. You live too tensely.

(*Looking at Starkweather.*) There's the arch-anarch over there, the dragon you are trying to slay.

(*Knox looks at Starkweather and is plainly perplexed.*) The man who handles all the life insurance funds, who controls more strings of banks and trust companies than all the Rothschilds a hundred times over—the merger of iron and steel and coal and shipping and all the other things—the man who blocks your child labor bill and all the rest of the remedial legislation you advocate. In short, my father.

Knox

(*Looking intently at Starkweather.*) I should have recognized him from his photographs. But why do you say such things?

Margaret

Because they are true.

(*He remains silent.*) Now, aren't they? (*She laughs.*) Oh, you don't need to answer. You know the truth, the whole bitter truth. This *is* a den of thieves. There is Mr. Hubbard over there, for instance, the trusty journalist lieutenant of the corporations.

Knox

(*With an expression of disgust.*) I know him. It was he that wrote the Standard Oil side of the story, after having abused Standard Oil for years in the pseudo-muck-raking magazines. He made them come up to his price, that was all. He's the star writer on *Cartwright's*, now, since that magazine changed its policy and became subsidizedly reactionary. I know him—a thoroughly dishonest man. Truly am I Ali Baba, and truly I wonder why I am here.

Margaret

You are here, sir, because I like you to come.

Knox

We do have much in common, you and I.

Margaret

The future.

Knox

(*Gravely, looking at her with shining eyes.*) I sometimes fear for more immediate reasons than that.

(*Margaret looks at him in alarm, and at the same time betrays pleasure in what he has said.*) For you.

Margaret

(*Hastily.*) Don't look at me that way. Your eyes are flashing. Some one might see and misunderstand.

Knox

(*In confusion, awkwardly.*) I was unaware that I—that I was looking at you——in any way that——

Margaret

I'll tell you why you are here. Because I sent for you.

Knox

(*With signs of ardor.*) I would come whenever you sent for me, and go wherever you might send me.

Margaret

(*Reprovingly.*)

Please, please—— It was about that speech. I have been hearing about it from everybody—rumblings and mutterings and dire prophecies. I know how busy you are, and I ought not to have asked you to come. But there was no other way, and I was so anxious.

Knox

(*Pleased.*) It seems so strange that you, being what you are, affiliated as you are, should be interested in the welfare of the common people.

Margaret

(*Judicially.*) I do seem like a traitor in my own camp. But as father said a while ago, I, too, have dreamed my dream. I did it as a girl—Plato's *Republic*, Moore's *Utopia*—I was steeped in all the dreams of the social dreamers.

(*During all that follows of her speech, Knox is keenly interested, his eyes glisten and he hangs on her words.*)

And I dreamed that I, too, might do something to bring on the era of universal justice and fair play. In my heart I dedicated myself to the cause of humanity. I made Lincoln my hero-he still is. But I was only a girl, and where was I to find this cause?—how to work for it? I was shut in by a thousand restrictions, hedged in by a thousand conventions. Everybody laughed at me when I expressed the thoughts that burned in me. What could I do? I was only a woman. I had neither vote nor right of utterance. I must remain silent.

I must do nothing. Men, in their lordly wisdom, did all. They voted, orated, governed. The place for women was in the home, taking care of some lordly man who did all these lordly things.

Knox

You understand, then, why I am for equal suffrage.

Margaret

But I learned—or thought I learned. Power, I discovered early. My father had power. He was a magnate—I believe that is the correct phrase. Power was what I needed. But how? I was a woman. Again I dreamed my dream—a modified dream. Only by marriage could I win to power. And there you have the clew to me and what I am and have become. I met the man who was to become my husband. He was clean and strong and an athlete, an outdoor man, a wealthy man and a rising politician. Father told me that if I married him he would make him the power of his state, make him governor, send him to the United States Senate. And there you have it all.

Knox

Yes?—— Yes?

Margaret

I married. I found that there were greater forces at work than I had ever dreamed of. They took my husband away from me and molded him into the political lieutenant of my father. And I was without power. I could do nothing for the cause. I was beaten. Then it was that I got a new vision. The future belonged to the children. There I could play my woman's part. I was a mother. Very well. I could do no better than to bring into the world a healthy son and bring him up to manhood healthy and wholesome, clean, noble, and alive. Did I do my part well, through him the results would be achieved. Through him would the work of the world be done in making the world healthier and happier for all the human creatures in it. I played the mother's part. That is why I left the pitiful little charities of the church and devoted myself to settlement work and tenement house reform, established

50

my kindergartens, and worked for the little men and women who come so blindly and to whom the future belongs to make or mar.

Knox

You are magnificent. I know, now, why I come when you bid me come.

Margaret

And then you came. You were magnificent. You were my knight of the windmills, tilting against all power and privilege, striving to wrest the future from the future and realize it here in the present, now. I was sure you would be destroyed. Yet you are still here and fighting valiantly. And that speech of yours to-morrow—

Chalmers

(*Who has approached, bearing Dolores Ortega's cup.*) Yes, that speech. How do you do, Mr. Knox.

(*They shake hands.*) A cup of tea, Madge. For Mrs. Ortega. Two lumps, please.

(*Margaret prepares the cup of tea.*) Everybody is excited over that speech. You are going to give us particular fits, to-morrow, I understand.

Knox

(*Smiling.*) Really, no more than is deserved.

Chalmers

The truth, the whole truth, and nothing but the truth?

Knox

Precisely.

(*Receiving back cup of tea from Margaret.*)

Chalmers

Believe me, we are not so black as we're painted. There are two sides to this question. Like you, we do our best to do what is right. And we hope, we still hope, to win you over to our side.

(*Knox shakes his head with a quiet smile.*)

Margaret

Oh, Tom, be truthful. You don't hope anything of the sort. You know you are hoping to destroy him.

Chalmers

(*Smiling grimly.*) That is what usually happens to those who are not won over.

(*Preparing to depart with cup of tea; speaking to Knox.*) You might accomplish much good, were you with us. Against us you accomplish nothing, absolutely nothing.

(*Returns to Dolores Ortega.*)

Margaret

(*Hurriedly.*) You see. That is why I was anxious—why I sent for you. Even Tom admits that they who are not won over are destroyed. This speech is a crucial event. You know how rigidly they rule the House and gag men like you. It is they, and they alone, who have given you opportunity for this speech? Why?—Why?

Knox

(*Smiling confidently.*) I know their little scheme. They have heard my charges. They think I am going to make a firebrand speech, and they are ready to catch me without the proofs. They are ready in every way for me. They are going to laugh me down. The Associated Press, the Washington correspondents—all are ready to manufacture, in every newspaper in the land, the great laugh that will destroy me. But I am fully prepared, I have—

Margaret

The proofs?

Knox

Yes.

Margaret

Now?

Knox

They will be delivered to me to-night—original documents, photographs of documents, affidavits—

Margaret

Tell me nothing. But oh, do be careful! Be careful!

Mrs. Dowsett

(*Appealing to Margaret.*) Do give me some assistance, Mrs. Chalmers. (*Indicating Sakari.*) Mr. Sakari is trying to make me ridiculous.

Margaret

Impossible.

Mrs. Dowsett

But he is. He has had the effrontery—

Chalmers

(*Mimicking Mrs. Dowsett.*) Effrontery!—O, Sakari!

Sakari

The dear lady is pleased to be facetious.

Mrs. Dowsett

He has had the effrontery to ask me to explain the cause of high prices. Mr. Dowsett says the reason is that the people are living so high.

Sakari

Such a marvelous country. They are poor because they have so much to spend.

Chalmers

Are not high prices due to the increased output of gold?

Mrs. Dowsett

Mr. Sakari suggested that himself, and when I agreed with him he proceeded to demolish it. He has treated me dreadfully.

Rutland

(*Clearing his throat and expressing himself with ponderous unction.*) You will find the solution in the drink traffic. It is liquor, alcohol, that is undermining our industry, our institutions, our faith in God—everything. Yearly the working people drink greater quantities of alcohol. Naturally, through resulting inefficiency, the cost of production is higher, and therefore prices are higher.

Dowsett

Partly so, partly so. And in line with it, and in addition to it, prices are high because the working class is no longer thrifty. If our working class saved as the French peasant does, we would sell more in the world market and have better times.

Sakari

(*Bowing.*) As I understand it then, the more thrifty you are the more you save, and the more you save the more you have to sell, the more you sell, the better the times?

Dowsett

Exactly so. Exactly.

Sakari

The less you sell, the harder are the times?

Dowsett

Just so.

Sakari

Then if the people are thrifty, and buy less, times will be harder?

Dowsett

(*Perplexed.*) Er—it would seem so.

Sakari

Then it would seem that the present bad times are due to the fact that the people are thrifty, rather than not thrifty?

(*Dowsett is nonplussed, and Mrs. Dowsett throws up her hands in despair.*)

Mrs. Dowsett

(*Turning to Knox.*) Perhaps you can explain to us, Mr. Knox, the reason for this terrible condition of affairs.

(*Starkweather closes note-book on finger and listens.*) (*Knox smiles, but does not speak.*)

Dolores Ortega

Please do, Mr. Knox. I am so dreadfully anxious to know why living is so high now. Only this morning I understand meat went up again.

(*Knox hesitates and looks questioningly at Margaret.*)

Hubbard

I am sure Mr. Knox can shed new light on this perplexing problem.

Chalmers

Surely you, the whirlwind of oratorical swords in the House, are not timid here—among friends.

Knox

(*Sparring.*) I had no idea that questions of such nature were topics of conversation at affairs like this.

Starkweather

(*Abruptly and imperatively.*) What causes the high prices?

Knox

(*Equally abrupt and just as positive as the other was imperative.*) *Theft!*

(*It is a sort of a bombshell he has exploded, but they receive it politely and smilingly, even though it has shaken them up.*)

Dolores Ortega

What a romantic explanation. I suppose everybody who has anything has stolen it.

Knox

Not quite, but almost quite. Take motorcars, for example. This year five hundred million dollars has been spent for motor-cars. It required men toiling in the mines and foundries, women sewing their eyes out in sweat-shops, shop girls slaving for four and five dollars a week, little children working in the factories and cotton-mills—all these it required to produce those five hundred millions spent this year in motor-cars. And all this has been stolen from those who did the work.

Mrs. Starkweather

I always knew those motor-cars were to blame for terrible things.

Dolores Ortega

But Mr. Knox, I have a motor-car.

Knox

Somebody's labor made that car. Was it yours?

Dolores Ortega

Mercy, no! I bought it—— and paid for it.

Knox

Then did you labor at producing something else, and exchange the fruits of that labor for the motor-car?

(*A pause.*)

You do not answer. Then I am to understand that you have a motor-car which was made by somebody else's labor and for which you gave no labor of your own. This I call theft. You call it property. Yet it is theft.

Starkweather

(*Interrupting Dolores Ortega who was just about to speak.*)

But surely you have intelligence to see the question in larger ways than stolen motor-cars. I am a man of affairs. I don't steal motor-cars.

Knox

(*Smiling.*) Not concrete little motor-cars, no. You do things on a large scale.

Starkweather

Steal?

Knox

(*Shrugging his shoulders.*) If you will have it so.

Starkweather

I am like a certain gentleman from Missouri. You've got to show me.

Knox

And I'm like the man from Texas. It's got to be put in my hand.

Starkweather

I shift my residence at once to Texas. Put it in my hand that I steal on a large scale.

Knox

Very well. You are the great financier, merger, and magnate. Do you mind a few statistics?

Starkweather

Go ahead.

Knox

You exercise a controlling interest in nine billion dollars' worth of railways; in two billion dollars' worth of industrial concerns; in one billion dollars' worth of life insurance groups; in one billion dollars' worth of banking groups; in two billion dollars' worth of trust companies. Mind you, I do not say you own all this, but that you exercise a controlling interest. That is all that is necessary. In short, you exercise a controlling interest in such a proportion of the total investments of the United States, as to set the pace for all the rest. Now to my point. In the last few years seventy billions of dollars have been artificially added to the capitalization of the nation's industries. By that I mean water—pure, unadulterated water. You, the merger, know what water means. I say seventy billions. It doesn't matter if we call it forty billions or eighty billions; the amount, whatever it is, is a huge one. And what does seventy billions of water mean? It means, at five per cent, that three billions and a half must be paid for things this year, and every year, more than things are really worth. The people who labor have to pay this. There is theft for you. There is high prices for you. Who put in the water? Who gets the theft of the water? Have I put it in your hand?

Starkweather

Are there no wages for stewardship?

Knox

Call it any name you please.

Starkweather

Do I not make two dollars where one was before? Do I not make for more happiness than was before I came?

Knox

Is that any more than the duty any man owes to his fellowman?

Starkweather

Oh, you unpractical dreamer. (*Returns to his note-book.*)

Rutland

(*Throwing himself into the breach.*) Where do I steal, Mr. Knox?—I who get a mere salary for preaching the Lord's Word.

Knox

Your salary comes out of that water I mentioned. Do you want to know who pays your salary? Not your parishioners. But the little children toiling in the mills, and all the rest—all the slaves on the wheel of labor pay you your salary.

Rutland

I earn it.

Knox

They pay it.

Mrs. Dowsett

Why, I declare, Mr. Knox, you are worse than Mr. Sakari. You are an anarchist.

(*She simulates shivering with fear.*)

Chalmers

(*To Knox.*) I suppose that's part of your speech to-morrow.

Dolores Ortega

(*Clapping her hands.*) A rehearsal! He's trying it out on us!

Sakari

How would you remedy this—er—this theft?

(*Starkweather again closes note-book on finger and listens as Knox begins to speak.*)

Knox

Very simply. By changing the governmental machinery by which this household of ninety millions of people conducts its affairs.

Sakari

I thought—I was taught so at Yale—that your governmental machinery was excellent, most excellent.

Knox

It is antiquated. It is ready for the scrap-heap. Instead of being our servant, it has mastered us. We are its slaves. All the political brood of grafters and hypocrites have run away with it, and with us as well. In short, from the municipalities up, we are dominated by the grafters. It is a reign of theft.

Hubbard

But any government is representative of its people. No people is worthy of a better government than it possesses. Were it worthier, it would possess a better government.

(*Starkweather nods his head approvingly.*)

Knox

That is a lie. And I say to you now that the average morality and desire for right conduct of the people of the United States is far higher than that of the government which misrepresents it. The people are essentially worthy of a better government than that which is at present in the hands of the politicians, for the benefit of the politicians and of the interests the politicians represent. I wonder, Mr. Sakari, if you have ever heard the story of the four aces.

Sakari

I cannot say that I have.

Knox

Do you understand the game of poker?

Sakari

(*Considering.*) Yes, a marvelous game. I have learned it—at Yale. It was very expensive.

Knox

Well, that story reminds me of our grafting politicians. They have no moral compunctions. They look upon theft as right—eminently right. They see nothing wrong in the arrangement that the man who deals the cards should give himself the best in the deck. Never mind what he deals himself, they'll have the deal next and make up for it.

Dolores Ortega

But the story, Mr. Knox. I, too, understand poker.

Knox

It occurred out in Nevada, in a mining camp. A tenderfoot was watching a game of poker, He stood behind the dealer, and he saw the dealer deal himself four aces from the bottom of the deck.

(*From now on, he tells the story in the slow, slightly drawling Western fashion.*) The tenderfoot went around to the player on the opposite side of the table.

"Say," he says, "I just seen the dealer give himself four aces off the bottom."

The player looked at him a moment, and said, "What of it?"

"Oh, nothing," said the tenderfoot, "only I thought you might want to know. I tell you I seen the dealer give himself four aces off the bottom."

"Look here, Mister," said the player, "you'd better get out of this. You don't understand the game. It's HIS deal, ain't it?"

Margaret

(*Arising while they are laughing.*) We've talked politics long enough. Dolores, I want you to tell me about your new car.

Knox

(*As if suddenly recollecting himself.*) And I must be going.

(*In a low voice to Margaret.*) Do I have to shake hands with all these people?

Margaret

(*Shaking her head, speaking low.*) Dear delightful Ali Baba.

Knox

(*Glumly.*) I suppose I've made a fool of myself.

Margaret

(*Earnestly.*) On the contrary, you were delightful. I am proud of you.

(*As Knox shakes hands with Margaret, Sakari arises and comes forward*).

Sakari

I, too, must go. I have had a charming half hour, Mrs. Chalmers. But I shall not attempt to thank you.

(*He shakes hands with Margaret.*)

(*Knox and Sakari proceed to make exit to rear.*)

(*Just as they go out, Servant enters, carrying card-tray, and advances toward Starkweather.*)

(*Margaret joins Dolores Ortega and Chalmers, seats herself with them, and proceeds to talk motor-cars.*)

(*Servant has reached Starkweather, who has taken a telegram from tray, opened it, and is reading it.*)

Starkweather

Damnation!

Servant

I beg your pardon, sir.

Starkweather

Send Senator Chalmers to me, and Mr. Hubbard.

Servant

Yes, sir.

(*Servant crosses to Chalmers and Hubbard, both of whom immediately arise and cross to Starkweather.*)

(*While this is being done, Margaret reassembles the three broken groups into one, seating herself so that she can watch Starkweather and his group across the stage.*)

(*Servant lingers to receive a command from Margaret.*)

(*Chalmers and Hubbard wait a moment, standing, while Starkweather rereads telegram.*)

Starkweather

(*Standing up.*) Dobleman has just forwarded this telegram. It's from New York—from Martinaw. There's been rottenness. My papers and letter-files have been ransacked. It's the confidential stenographer who has been tampered with—you remember that middle-aged, youngish-oldish woman, Tom? That's the one.—Where's that servant?

63

(*Servant is just making exit.*) Here! Come here!

(*Servant comes over to Starkweather.*) Go to the telephone and call up Dobleman. Tell him to come here.

Servant

(*Perplexed.*) I beg pardon, sir.

Starkweather

(*Irritably.*) My secretary. At my house. Dobleman. Tell him to come at once.

(*Servant makes exit.*)

Chalmers

But who can be the principal behind this theft?

(*Starkweather shrugs his shoulders.*)

Hubbard

A blackmailing device most probably. They will attempt to bleed you—

Chalmers

Unless—

Starkweather

(*Impatiently.*) Yes?

Chalmers

Unless they are to be used to-morrow in that speech of Knox.

(*Comprehension dawns on the faces of the other two men.*)

Mrs. Starkweather

(*Who has arisen.*) Anthony, we must go now. Are you ready? Connie has to dress.

Starkweather

I am not going now. You and Connie take the car.

Mrs. Starkweather

You mustn't forget you are going to that dinner.

Starkweather

(*Wearily.*) Do I ever forget?

(*Servant enters and proceeds toward Starkweather, where he stands waiting while Mrs. Starkweather finishes the next speech. Starkweather listens to her with a patient, stony face.*)

Mrs. Starkweather

Oh, these everlasting politics! That is what it has been all afternoon—high prices, graft, and theft; theft, graft, and high prices. It is terrible. When I was a girl we did not talk of such things. Well, come on, Connie.

Mrs. Dowsett

(*Rising and glancing at Dowsett.*) And we must be going, too.

(*During the following scene, which takes place around Starkweather, Margaret is saying good-bye to her departing guests.*)

(*Mrs. Starkweather and Connie make exit.*)

(*Dowsett and Mrs. Dowsett make exit.*)

(*The instant Mrs. Dowsett's remark puts a complete end to Mrs. Starkweather's speech, Starkweather, without answer or noticing his wife, turns and interrogates Servant with a glance.*)

Servant

Mr. Dobleman has already left some time to come here, sir.

Starkweather

Show him in as soon as he comes.

Servant

Yes, sir.

(*Servant makes exit.*)

(*Margaret, Dolores Ortega, and Rutland are left in a group together, this time around tea-table, where Margaret serves Rutland another cup of tea. From time to time Margaret glances curiously at the serious group of men across the stage.*)

(*Starkweather is thinking hard with knitted brows. Hubbard is likewise pondering.*)

Chalmers

If I were certain Knox had those papers I would take him by the throat and shake them out of him.

Starkweather

No foolish talk like that, Tom. This is a serious matter.

Hubbard

But Knox has no money. A Starkweather stenographer comes high.

Starkweather

There is more than Knox behind this. (*Enter Dobleman, walking quickly and in a state of controlled excitement.*)

Dobleman

(*To Starkweather.*) You received that telegram, sir?

(*Starkweather nods.*) I got the New York office—Martinaw—right along afterward, by long distance. I thought best to follow and tell you.

Starkweather

What did Martinaw say?

Dobleman

The files seem in perfect order.

Starkweather

Thank God!

(*During the following speech of Dobleman, Rutland says good-bye to Margaret and Dolores Ortega and makes exit.*)

(*Margaret and Dolores Ortega rise a minute afterward and go toward exit, throwing curious glances at the men but not disturbing them.*)

(*Dolores Ortega makes exit.*)

(*Margaret pauses in doorway a moment, giving a final anxious glance at the men, and makes exit.*)

Dobleman

But they are not. The stenographer, Miss Standish, has confessed. For a long time she has followed the practice of taking two or three letters and documents at a time away from the office. Many have been photographed and returned. But the more important ones were retained and clever copies returned. Martinaw says that Miss Standish herself does not know and cannot tell which of the ones she returned are genuine and which are copies.

Hubbard

Knox never did this.

Starkweather

Did Martinaw say whom Miss Standish was acting for?

Dobleman

Gherst.

(*The alarm on the three men's faces is patent.*)

Starkweather

Gherst!

(*Pauses to think.*)

Hubbard

Then it is not so grave after all. A yellow journal sensation is the best Gherst can make of it. And, documents or not, the very medium by which it is made public discredits it.

Starkweather

Trust Gherst for more ability than that. He will certainly exploit them in his newspapers, but not until after Knox has used them in his speech. Oh, the cunning dog! Never could he have chosen a better mode and moment to strike at me, at the Administration, at everything. That is Gherst all over. Playing to the gallery. Inducing Knox to make this spectacular exposure on the floor of the House just at the critical time when so many important bills are pending.

(*To Dobleman.*)

Did Martinaw give you any idea of the nature of the stolen documents?

Dobleman

(*Referring to notes he has brought.*) Of course I don't know anything about it, but he spoke of the Goodyear letters—

(*Starkweather betrays by his face the gravity of the information.*)

the Caledonian letters, all the Black Rider correspondence. He mentioned, too, (*Referring to notes.*) the Astonbury and Glutz letters. And there were others, many others, not designated.

Starkweather

This is terrible!

(*Recollecting himself.*)

Thank you, Dobleman. Will you please return to the house at once. Get New York again, and fullest details. I'll follow you shortly. Have you a machine?

Dobleman

A taxi, sir.

Starkweather

All right, and be careful.

(*Dobleman makes exit*)

Chalmers

I don't know the import of all these letters, but I can guess, and it does seem serious.

Starkweather

(*Furiously.*) Serious! Let me tell you that there has been no exposure like this in the history of the country. It means hundreds of millions of dollars. It means more—the loss of power. And still more, it means the mob, the great mass of the child-minded people rising up and destroying all that I have labored to do for them. Oh, the fools! The fools!

Hubbard

(*Shaking his head ominously.*) There is no telling what may happen if Knox makes that speech and delivers the proofs.

Chalmers

It is unfortunate. The people are restless and excited as it is. They are being constantly prodded on by the mouthings of the radical press, of the muck-raking magazines and of the demagogues. The people are like powder awaiting the spark.

Starkweather

This man Knox is no fool, if he *is* a dreamer. He is a shrewd knave. He is a fighter. He comes from the West—the old pioneer stock. His father drove an ox-team across the Plains to Oregon. He knows how to play his cards, and never could circumstances have placed more advantageous cards in his hands.

Chalmers

And nothing like this has ever touched you before.

Starkweather

I have always stood above the muck and ruck—clear and clean and unassailable. But this—this is too much! It is the spark. There is no forecasting what it may develop into.

Chalmers

A political turnover.

Starkweather

(*Nodding savagely.*) A new party, a party of demagogues, in power. Government ownership of the railways and telegraphs. A graduated income tax that will mean no less than the confiscation of private capital.

Chalmers

And all that mass of radical legislation—the Child Labor Bill, the new Employers' Liability Act, the government control of the Alaskan coal fields, that interference with Mexico. And that big power corporation you have worked so hard to form.

Starkweather

It must not be. It is an unthinkable calamity. It means that the very process of capitalistic development is hindered, stopped. It means a setback of ten years in the process. It means work, endless work, to overcome the setback. It means not alone the passage of all this radical legislation with the consequent disadvantages, but it means the fingers of the mob clutching at our grip of control. It means anarchy. It means ruin and misery for all the blind fools and led-cattle of the mass who will strike at the very sources of their own existence and comfort.

(*Tommy enters from left, evidently playing a game, in the course of which he is running away. By his actions he shows that he is pursued. He intends to cross stage, but is stopped by sight of the men. Unobserved by them, he retraces his steps and crawls under the tea-table.*)

Chalmers

Without doubt, Knox is in possession of the letters right now.

Starkweather

There is but one thing to do, and that is—get them back.

(*He looks questioningly at the two men.*)

(*Margaret enters from left, in flushed and happy pursuit of Tommy—for it is a game she is playing with him. She startles at sight of the three men, whom she first sees as she gains the side of the tea-table, where she pauses abruptly, resting one hand on the table.*)

Hubbard

I'll undertake it.

Starkweather

There is little time to waste. In twenty hours from now he will be on the floor making his speech. Try mild measures first. Offer him inducements—any inducement. I empower you to act for me. You will find he has a price.

Hubbard

And if not?

Starkweather

Then you must get them at any cost.

Hubbard

(*Tentatively.*) You mean—?

Starkweather

I mean just that. But no matter what happens, I must never be brought in. Do you understand?

Hubbard

Thoroughly.

Margaret

(*Acting her part, and speaking with assumed gayety.*) What are you three conspiring about? (*All three men are startled.*)

Chalmers

We are arranging to boost prices a little higher.

Hubbard

And so be able to accumulate more motorcars.

Starkweather

(*Taking no notice of Margaret and starting toward exit to rear.*) I must be going. Hubbard, you have your work cut out for you. Tom, I want you to come with me.

Chalmers

(*As the three men move toward exit.*) Home?

Starkweather

Yes, we have much to do.

Chalmers

Then I'll dress first and follow you.

(*Turning to Margaret.*) Pick me up on the way to that dinner.

(*Margaret nods. Starkweather makes exit without speaking. Hub-bard says good-bye to Margaret and makes exit, followed by Chalmers.*)

(*Margaret remains standing, one hand resting on table, the other hand to her breast. She is thinking, establishing in her mind the connection between Knox and what she has overheard, and in process of reaching the conclusion that Knox is in danger.*)

(*Tommy, having vainly waited to be discovered, crawls out dispiritedly, and takes Margaret by the hand. She scarcely notices him.*)

Tommy

(*Dolefully.*) Don't you want to play any more? (*Margaret does not reply*). I was a good Indian.

Margaret

(*Suddenly becoming aware of herself and breaking down. She stoops and clasps Tommy in her arms, crying out, in anxiety and fear, and from love of her boy.*) Oh, Tommy! Tommy!

Curtain

ACT II. Rooms of Howard Knox at Hotel Waltham

Scene. Sitting room of Howard Knox—dimly lighted. Time, eight o'clock in the evening.

Entrance from hallway at side to right. At right rear is locked door leading to a room which dees not belong to Knox's suite. At rear center is fireplace. At left rear door leading to Knox's bedroom. At left are windows facing on street. Near these windows is a large library table littered with books, magazines, government reports, etc. To the right of center, midway forward, is a Hat-top desk. On it is a desk telephone. Behind it, so that one sitting in it faces audience, is revolving desk-chair. Also, on desk, are letters in their envelopes, etc. Against clear wall-spaces are bookcases and filing cabinets. Of special note is bookcase, containing large books, and not more than five feet high, which is against wall between fireplace and door to bedroom.

Curtain discloses empty stage.

(After a slight interval, door at right rear is shaken and agitated. After slight further interval, door is opened inward upon stage. A Man's head appears, cautiously looking around).

(Man enters, turns up lights, is followed by second Man. Both are clad decently, in knock-about business suits and starched collars, cuffs, etc. They are trim, deft, determined men).

(Following upon them, enters Hubbard. He looks about room, crosses to desk, picks up a letter, and reads address).

Hubbard

This is Knox's room all right

First Man

Trust us for that.

Second Man

We were lucky the guy with the whiskers moved out of that other room only this afternoon.

First Man

His key hadn't come down yet when I engaged it.

Hubbard

Well, get to work. That must be his bedroom.

(*He goes to door of bedroom, opens, and peers in, turns on electric lights of bedroom, turns them out, then turns back to men.*) You know what it is—a bunch of documents and letters. If we find it there is a clean five hundred each for you, in addition to your regular pay.

(*While the conversation goes on, all three engage in a careful search of desk, drawers, filing cabinets, bookcases, etc.*)

Second Man

Old Starkweather must want them bad.

Hubbard

Sh-h. Don't even breathe his name.

Second Man

His nibs is damned exclusive, ain't he?

First Man

I've never got a direct instruction from him, and I've worked for him longer than you.

Second Man

Yes, and you worked for him for over two years before you knew who was hiring you.

Hubbard

(*To First Man.*) You'd better go out in the hall and keep a watch for Knox. He may come in any time.

(*First Man produces skeleton keys and goes to door at right. The first key opens it. Leaving door slightly ajar, he makes exit.*)

(*Desk telephone rings and startles Hubbard.*)

Second Man

(*Grinning at Hubbard's alarm.*)

It's only the phone.

Hubbard

(*Proceeding with search.*) I suppose you've done lots of work for Stark—

Second Man

(*Mimicking him.*) Sh-h. Don't breathe his name.

(*Telephone rings again and again, insistently, urgently.*)

Hubbard

(*Disguising his voice.*) Hello—Yes.

(*Shows surprise, seems to recognize the voice, and smiles knowingly.*)

No, this is not Knox. Some mistake. Wrong number—

(*Hanging up receiver and speaking to Second Man in natural voice.*) She did hang up quick.

Second Man

You seemed to recognize her.

Hubbard

No, I only thought I did.

(*A pause, while they search.*)

Second Man

I've never spoken a word to his nibs in my life. And I've drawn his pay for years too.

Hubbard

What of it?

Second Man

(*Complainingly.*) He don't know I exist.

Hubbard

(*Pulling open a desk drawer and examining contents.*)

The pay's all right, isn't it?

Second Man

It sure is, but I guess I earn every cent of it. (*First Man enters through door at right He moves hurriedly but cautiously. Shuts door behind him, but neglects to re-lock it.*)

First Man

Somebody just left the elevator and is coming down the hall.

(*Hubbard, First Man, and Second Man, all start for door at right rear.*)

(*First Man pauses and looks around to see if room is in order. Sees desk-drawer which Hubbard has neglected to close, goes back and closes it.*)

(*Hubbard and Second Man make exit.*)

(*First Man turns lights low and makes exit.*)

(*Sound of locking door is heard.*)

(*A pause.*)

(A knocking at door to right. A pause. Then door opens and Gifford enters. He turns up lights, strolls about room, looks at watch, and sits down in chair near right of fireplace.) (Sound of key in lock of door to right.) (Door opens, and Knox enters, key in hand. Sees Gifford.)

Knox

(Advancing to meet him at fireplace and shaking hands.) How did you get in?

Gifford

I let myself in. The door was unlocked.

Knox

I must have forgotten it.

Gifford

(Drawing bundle of documents from inside breast pocket and handing them to Knox.) Well, there they are.

Knox

(Fingering them curiously.) You are sure they are originals? *(Gifford nods.)*

I can't take any chances, you know. If Gherst changed his mind after I gave my speech and refused to show the originals—such things have happened.

Gifford

That's what I told him. He was firm on giving duplicates, and for awhile it looked as if my trip to New York was wasted. But I stuck to my guns. It was originals or nothing with you, I said, and he finally gave in.

Knox

(Holding up documents.) I can't tell you what they mean to me, nor how grateful—

Gifford

(*Interrupting.*) That's all right. Don't mention it. Gherst is wild for the chance. It will do organized labor a heap of good. And you are able to say your own say at the same time. How's that compensation act coming on?

Knox

(*Wearily.*) The same old story. It will never come before the House. It is dying in committee. What can you expect of the Committee of Judiciary?—composed as it is of ex-railroad judges and ex-railroad lawyers.

Gifford

The railroad brotherhoods are keen on getting that bill through.

Knox

Well, they won't, and they never will until they learn to vote right. When will your labor leaders quit the strike and boycott and lead your men to political action?

Gifford

(*Holding out hand.*) Well, so long. I've got to trot, and I haven't time to tell you why I think political action would destroy the trade union movement.

(*Knox tosses documents on top of low bookcase between fireplace and bedroom door, and starts to shake hands.*) You're damn careless with those papers. You wouldn't be if you knew how much Gherst paid for them.

Gifford

You don't appreciate that other crowd. It stops at nothing.

Knox

I won't take my eyes off of them. And I'll take them to bed with me to-night for safety. Besides, there is no danger. Nobody but you knows I have them.

Gifford

(*Proceeding toward door to right.*) I'd hate to be in Starkweather's office when he discovers what's happened. There'll be some bad half hours for somebody. (*Pausing at door.*) Give them hell to-morrow, good and plenty. I'm going to be in a gallery. So long. (*Makes exit.*)

(*Knox crosses to windows, which he opens, returns to desk, seats himself in revolving chair, and begins opening his correspondence.*) (*A knock at door to right.*)

Knox

Come in.

(*Hubbard enters, advances to desk, but does not shake hands. They greet each other, and Hubbard sits down in chair to left of desk.*) (*Knox, still holding an open letter, re-volves chair so as to face his visitor. He waits for Hubbabd to speak.*)

Hubbard

There is no use beating about the bush with a man like you. I know that. You are direct, and so am I. You know my position well enough to be assured that I am empowered to treat with you.

Knox

Oh, yes; I know.

Hubbard

What we want is to have you friendly.

Knox

That is easy enough. When the Interests become upright and honest—

Hubbard

Save that for your speech. We are talking privately. We can make it well worth your while—

Knox

(*Angrily.*) If you think you can bribe me—

Hubbard

(*Suavely.*) Not at all. Not the slightest suspicion of it. The point is this. You are a congressman. A congressman's career depends on his membership in good committees. At the present you are buried in the dead Committee on Coinage, Weights, and Measures. If you say the word you can be appointed to the livest committee—

Knox

(*Interrupting.*) You have these appointments to give?

Hubbard

Surely. Else why should I be here? It can be managed.

Knox

(*Meditatively.*) I thought our government was rotten enough, but I never dreamed that House appointments were hawked around by the Interests in this fashion.

Hubbard

You have not given your answer.

Knox

You should have known my answer in advance.

Hubbard

There is an alternative. You are interested in social problems. You are a student of sociology. Those whom I represent are genuinely interested in you. We are prepared, so that you may pursue your researches more deeply—we are prepared to send you to Europe. There, in that vast sociological laboratory, far from the jangling strife of politics, you will have every opportunity to study. We are prepared to send you for a period of ten years. You will receive ten thousand dollars a year, and, in addition, the day your steamer leaves New York, you will receive a lump sum of one hundred thousand dollars.

Knox

And this is the way men are bought

Hubbard

It is purely an educational matter.

Knox

Now it is you who are beating about the bush.

Hubbard

(*Decisively.*) Very well then. What price do you set on yourself?

Knox

You want me to quit—to leave politics, everything? You want to buy my soul?

Hubbard

More than that. We want to buy those documents and letters.

Knox

(*Showing a slight start.*) What documents and letters?

Hubbard

You are beating around the bush in turn. There is no need for an honest man to lie even—

Knox

(*Interrupting.*) To you.

Hubbard

(*Smiling.*) Even to me. I watched you closely when I mentioned the letters. You gave yourself away. You knew I meant the letters stolen by Gherst from Starkweather's private files—the letters you intended using to-morrow.

Knox

Intend using to-morrow.

Hubbard

Precisely. It is the same thing. What is the price? Set it.

Knox

I have nothing to sell. I am not on the market.

Hubbard

One moment. Don't make up your mind hastily. You don't know with whom you have to deal. Those letters will not appear in your speech to-morrow. Take that from me. It would be far wiser to sell for a fortune than to get nothing for them and at the same time not use them.

(*A knock at door to right startles Hubbard.*)

Knox

(*Intending to say, "Come in"*) Come—

Hubbard

(*Interrupting.*) Hush. Don't. I cannot be seen here.

Knox

(*Laughing.*) You fear the contamination of my company. (*The knock is repeated.*)

Hubbard

(*In alarm, rising, as Knox purses his lips to bid them enter.*) Don't let anybody in. I don't want to be seen here—with you. Besides, my presence will not put you in a good light.

Knox

(*Also rising, starting toward door.*) What I do is always open to the world. I see no one whom I should not permit the world to know I saw.

(*Knox starts toward door to open it.*) (*Hubbabd, looking about him in alarm, flees across stage and into bedroom, closing the door. During all the following scene, Hubbard, from time to time, opens door, and peers out at what is going on.*)

Knox

(*Opening door, and recoiling.*) Margaret! Mrs. Chalmers!

(*Margaret enters, followed by Tommy and Linda. Margaret is in evening dress covered by evening cloak.*)

Margaret

(*Shaking hands with Knox.*) Forgive me, but I had to see you. I could not get you on the telephone. I called and called, and the best I could do was to get the wrong number.

Knox

(*Recovering from his astonishment.*) Yes. I am glad.

(*Seeing Tommy.*) Hello, Tommy.

(*Knox holds out his hand, and Tommy shakes it gravely. Linda stays in back-ground. Her face is troubled.*)

Tommy

How do you do?

Margaret

There was no other way, and it was so necessary for me to warn you. I brought Tommy and Linda along to chaperon me.

(*She looks curiously around room, specially indicating filing cabinets and the stacks of government reports on table.*) Your laboratory.

Knox

Ah, if I were only as great a sociological wizard as Edison is a wizard in physical sciences.

Margaret

But you are. You labor more mightily than you admit—or dare to think. Oh, I know you—better than you do yourself.

Tommy

Do you read all those books?

Knox

Yes, I am still going to school and studying hard. What are you going to study to be when you grow up?

(*Tommy meditates but does not answer.*)

President of these great United States?

Tommy

(*Shaking his head.*) Father says the President doesn't amount to much.

Knox

Not a Lincoln?

(*Tommy is in doubt.*)

Margaret

But don't you remember what a great good man Lincoln was? You remember I told you?

Tommy

(*Shaking his head slowly.*) But I don't want to be killed.—I'll tell you what!

Knox

What?

Tommy

I want to be a senator like father. He makes them dance.

(*Margaret is shocked, and Knox's eyes twinkle.*)

Knox

Makes whom dance?

Tommy

(*Puzzled.*) I don't know.

(*With added confidence.*) But he makes them dance just the same.

(*Margaret makes a signal to Linda to take Tommy across the room.*)

Linda

(*Starting to cross stage to left.*) Come, Tommy. Let us look out of the window.

Tommy

I'd rather talk with Mr. Knox.

Margaret

Please do, Tommy. Mamma wants to talk to Mr. Knox.

(*Tommy yields, and crosses to right, where he joins Linda in looking out of the window.*)

Margaret

You might ask me to take a seat

Knox

Oh! I beg pardon.

(*He draws up a comfortable chair for her, and seats himself in desk-chair, facing her.*)

Margaret

I have only a few minutes. Tom is at father's, and I am to pick him up there and go on to that dinner, after I've taken Tommy home.

Knox

But your maid?

Margaret

Linda? Wild horses could not drag from her anything that she thought would harm me. So intense is her fidelity that it almost shames me. I do not deserve it. But this is not what I came to you about.

(*She speaks the following hurriedly.*) After you left this afternoon, something happened. Father received a telegram. It seemed most important. His secretary followed upon the heels of the telegram. Father called Tom and Mr. Hubbard to him and they held a conference. I think they have discovered the loss of the documents, and that they believe you have them. I did not hear them mention your name, yet I am absolutely certain that they were talking about you. Also, I could tell from father's face that something was terribly wrong. Oh, be careful! Do be careful!

Knox

There is no danger, I assure you.

Margaret

But you do not know them. I tell you-you do not know them. They will stop at nothing—at nothing. Father believes he is right in all that he does.

Knox

I know. That is what makes him so formidable. He has an ethical sanction.

Margaret

(*Nodding.*) It is his religion.

Knox

And, like any religion with a narrow-minded man, it runs to mania.

Margaret

He believes that civilization rests on him, and that it is his sacred duty to preserve civilization.

Knox

I know. I know.

Margaret

But you? But you? You are in danger.

Knox

No; I shall remain in to-night. To-morrow, in the broad light of midday, I shall proceed to the House and give my speech.

Margaret

(*Wildly.*) Oh, if anything should happen to you!

Knox

(*Looking at her searchingly.*) You do care?

(*Margaret nods, with eyes suddenly downcast.*) For Howard Knox, the reformer? Or for me, the man?

Margaret

(*Impulsively.*) Oh, why must a woman forever remain quiet? Why should I not tell you what you already know?—what you must already know? I do care for you—for man and reformer, both—for—

(*She is aflame, but abruptly ceases and glances across at Tommy by the window, warned instinctively that she must not give way to love in her child's presence.*)

Linda! Will you take Tommy down to the machine—

Knox

(*Alarmed, interrupting, in low voice.*) What are you doing?

Margaret

(*Hushing Knox with a gesture.*) I'll follow you right down.

(*Linda and Tommy proceed across stage toward the right exit.*)

Tommy

(*Pausing before Knox and gravely extending his hand.*) Good evening, Mr. Knox.

Knox

(*Awkwardly.*) Good evening, Tommy. You take my word for it, and look up this Lincoln question.

Tommy

I shall. I'll ask father about it.

Margaret

(*Significantly.*) You attend to that, Linda. Nobody must know—this.

(*Linda nods.*)

(*Linda and Tommy make exit to right.*)

(*Margaret, seated, slips back her cloak, revealing herself in evening gown, and looks at Knox sumptuously, lovingly, and willingly.*)

Knox

(*Inflamed by the sight of her.*) Don't! Don't! I can't stand it. Such sight of you fills me with madness.

(*Margaret laughs low and triumphantly.*) I don't want to think of you as a woman. I must not. Allow me.

89

(He rises and attempts to draw cloak about her shoulders, but she resists him. Yet does he succeed in partly cloaking her.)

Margaret

I want you to see me as a woman. I want you to think of me as a woman. I want you mad for me.

(She holds out her arms, the cloak slipping from them.)

I want—don't you see what I want?——

(Knox sinks back in chair, attempting to shield his eyes with his hand.)

(Slipping cloak fully back from her again.)

Look at me.

Knox

(Looking, coming to his feet, and approaching her, with extended arms, murmuring softly.) Margaret. Margaret.

(Margaret rises to meet him, and they are clasped in each other's arms.)

(Hubbard, peering forth through door, looks at them with an expression of cynical amusement. His gaze wan-ders, and he sees the documents, within arm's reach, on top of bookcase. He picks up documents, holds them to the light of stage to glance at them, and, with triumphant expression on face, disappears and closes door.)

Knox

(Holding Margaret from him and looking at her.) I love you. I do love you. But I had resolved never to speak it, never to let you know.

Margaret

Silly man. I have known long that you loved me. You have told me so often and in so many ways. You could not look at me without telling me.

Knox

You saw?

Margaret

How could I help seeing? I was a woman. Only, with your voice you never spoke a word. Sit down, there, where I may look at you, and let me tell you. I shall do the speaking now.

(*She urges him back into the desk-chair, and reseats herself.*) (*She makes as if to pull the cloak around 'her.*) Shall I?

Knox

(*Vehemently.*) No, no! As you are. Let me feast my eyes upon you who are mine. I must be dreaming.

Margaret

(*With a low, satisfied laugh of triumph.*) Oh, you men! As of old, and as forever, you must be wooed through your senses. Did I display the wisdom of an Hypatia, the science of a Madam Curie, yet would you keep your iron control, throttling the voice of your heart with silence. But let me for a moment be Lilith, for a moment lay aside this garment constructed for the purpose of keeping out the chill of night, and on the instant you are fire and aflame, all voluble with love's desire.

Knox

(*Protestingly.*) Margaret! It is not fair!

Margaret

I love you—and—you?

Knox

(*Fervently and reverently.*) I love you.

Margaret

Then listen. I have told you of my girlhood and my dreams. I wanted to do what you are so nobly doing. And I did nothing. I could do nothing.

I was not permitted. Always was I compelled to hold myself in check. It was to do what you are doing, that I married. And that, too, failed me. My husband became a henchman of the Interests, my own father's tool for the perpetuation of the evils against which I desired to fight.

(*She pauses.*) It has been a long fight, and I have been very tired, for always did I confront failure. My husband—I did not love him. I never loved him. I sold myself for the Cause, and the cause profited nothing. (*Pause.*) Often, I have lost faith—faith in everything, in God and man, in the hope of any righteousness ever prevailing. But again and again, by what you are doing, have you awakened me. I came to-night with no thought of self. I came to warn you, to help the good work on. I remained—thank God!—I remained to love you—and to be loved by you. I suddenly found myself, looking at you, very weary. I wanted you—you, more than anything in the world.

(*She holds out her arms.*) Come to me. I want you—now.

(*Knox, in an ecstacy, comes to her. He seats himself on the broad arm of the chair and is drawn into her arms.*)

Knox

But I have been tired at times. I was very tired to-night—and you came. And now I am glad, only glad.

Margaret

I have been wanton to-night. I confess it. I am proud of it. But it was not—professional. It was the first time in my life. Almost do I regret—almost do I regret that I did not do it sooner—it has been crowned with such success. You have held me in your arms—your arms. Oh, you will never know what that first embrace meant to me. I am not a clod. I am not iron nor stone. I am a woman—a warm, breathing woman—.

(*She rises, and draws him to his feet.*)

Kiss me, my dear lord and lover. Kiss me. (*They embrace.*)

Knox

(*Passionately, looking about him wildly as if in search of something.*) What shall we do?

(*Suddenly releasing her and sinking back in his own chair almost in collapse.*) No. It cannot be. It is impossible. Oh, why could we not have met long ago? We would have worked together. What a comradeship it would have been.

Margaret

But it is not too late.

Knox

I have no right to you.

Margaret

(*Misunderstanding.*) My husband? He has not been my husband for years. He has no rights. Who, but you whom I love, has any rights?

Knox

No; it is not that.

(*Snapping his fingers.*) That for him.

(*Breaking down.*) Oh, if I were only the man, and not the reformer! If I had no work to do!

Margaret

(*Coming to the back of his chair and caressing his hair.*) We can work together.

Knox

(*Shaking his head under her fingers.*) Don't! Don't!

(*She persists, and lays her cheek against his.*) You make it so hard. You tempt me so.

(He rises suddenly, takes her two hands in his, leads her gently to her chair, seats her, and reseats himself in desk-chair.) Listen. It is not your husband. But I have no right to you. Nor have you a right to me.

Margaret

(Interrupting, jealously.) And who but I has any right to you?

Knox

(Smiling sadly.) No; it is not that. There is no other woman. You are the one woman for me. But there are many others who have greater rights in me than you. I have been chosen by two hundred thousand citizens to represent them in the Congress of the United States. And there are many more—

(He breaks off suddenly and looks at her, at her arms and shoulders.) Yes, please. Cover them up. Help me not to forget.

(Margaret does not obey.) There are many more who have rights in me—the people, all the people, whose cause I have made mine. The children— there are two million child laborers in these United States. I cannot betray them. I cannot steal my happiness from them. This afternoon I talked of theft. But would not this, too, be theft?

Margaret

(Sharply.) Howard! Wake up! Has our happiness turned your head?

Knox

(Sadly.) Almost—and for a few wild moments, quite. There are all the children. Did I ever tell you of the tenement child, who when asked how he knew when spring came, answered: When he saw the saloons put up their swing doors.

Margaret

(Irritated.) But what has all that to do with one man and one woman loving?

94

Knox

Suppose we loved—you and I; suppose we loosed all the reins of our love. What would happen? You remember Gorki, the Russian patriot, when he came to New York, aflame with passion for the Russian revolution. His purpose in visiting the land of liberty was to raise funds for that revolution. And because his marriage to the woman he loved was not of the essentially legal sort worshiped by the shopkeepers, and because the newspapers made a sensation of it, his whole mission was brought to failure. He was laughed and derided out of the esteem of the American people. That is what would happen to me. I should be slandered and laughed at. My power would be gone.

Margaret

And even if so—what of it? Be slandered and laughed at. We will have each other. Other men will rise up to lead the people, and leading the people is a thankless task. Life is so short. We must clutch for the morsel of happiness that may be ours.

Knox

Ah, if you knew, as I look into your eyes, how easy it would be to throw everything to the winds. But it would be theft.

Margaret

(*Rebelliously.*) Let it be theft. Life is so short, dear. We are the biggest facts in the world—to each other.

Knox

It is not myself alone, nor all my people. A moment ago you said no one but I had any right to you. You were wrong. Your child—

Margaret

(*In sudden pain, pleadingly.*) Don't!

Knox

I must. I must save myself—and you. Tommy has rights in you. Theft again. What other name for it if you steal your happiness from him?

Margaret

(*Bending her head forward on her hand and weeping.*) I have been so lonely—and then you—you came, and the world grew bright and warm—a few short minutes ago you held me—in your arms—a few short minutes ago and it seemed my dream of happiness had come true—and now you dash it from me—

Knox

(*Struggling to control himself now that she is no longer looking at him.*) No; I ask you to dash it from yourself. I am not too strong. You must help me. You must call your child to your aid in helping me. I could go mad for you now—

(*Rising impulsively and coming to her with arms outstretched to clasp her.*) Right now—

Margaret

(*Abruptly raising her head, and with one outstretched arm preventing the embrace.*) Wait.

(*She bows her head on her hand for a moment, to think and to win control of herself.*)

(*Lifting her head and looking at him.*) Sit down—please.

(*Knox reseats himself.*)

(A pause, during which she looks at him and loves him.) Dear, I do so love you—

(*Knox loses control and starts to rise.*) No! Sit there. I was weak. Yet I am not sorry. You are right. We must forego each other. We cannot be thieves, even for love's sake. Yet I am glad that this has happened—that I have lain in your arms and had your lips on mine. The memory of it will be sweet always.

(*She draws her cloak around her, and rises.*)

(*Knox rises.*) You are right. The future belongs to the children. There lies duty—yours, and mine in my small way. I am going now. We must not see each other ever again. We must work—and forget. But remember, my heart goes with you into the fight. My prayers will accompany every stroke.

(*She hesitates, pauses, draws her cloak thoroughly around her in evidence of departure.*) Dear—will you kiss me—once—one last time? (*There is no passion in this kiss, which is the kiss of renunciation. Margaret herself terminates the embrace.*)

(*Knox accompanies her silently to the door and places hand on knob.*) I wish I had something of you to have with me always—a photograph, that little one, you remember, which I liked so. (*She nods.*) Don't run the risk of sending it by messenger. Just mail it ordinarily.

Margaret

I shall mail it to-morrow. I'll drop it in the box myself.

Knox

(*Kissing her hand.*) Good-bye.

Margaret

(*lingeringly.*) But oh, my dear, I am glad and proud for what has happened. I would not erase a single line of it.

(*She indicates for Knox to open door, which he does, but which he immediately closes as she continues speaking.*) There must be immortality. There must be a future life where you and I shall meet again. Good-bye.

(*They press each other's hands.*)

(*Exit Margaret.*)

(*Knox stands a moment, staring at closed door, turns and looks about him indecisively, sees chair in which Margaret sat, goes over to it, kneels down, and buries his face.*)

(*Door to bedroom opens slowly and Hubbard peers out cautiously. He cannot see Knox.*)

Hubbard

(*Advancing, surprised.*) What the deuce? Everybody gone?

Knox

(*Startled to his feet.*) Where the devil did you come from?

Hubbard

(*Indicating bedroom.*) In there. I was in there all the time.

Knox

(*Endeavoring to pass it off.*) Oh, I had forgotten about you. Well, my callers are gone.

Hubbard

(*Walking over close to him and laughing at him with affected amusement.*) Honest men are such dubs when they do go wrong.

Knox

The door was closed all the time. You would not have dared to spy upon me.

Hubbard

There was something familiar about the lady's voice.

Knox

You heard!—what did you hear?

Hubbard

Oh, nothing, nothing—a murmur of voices—and the woman's—I could swear I have heard her voice before.

(*Knox shows his relief.*) Well, so long.

(*Starts to move toward exit to right.*) You won't reconsider your decision?

Knox

(*Shaking his head.*)

Hubbard

(*Pausing, open door in hand, and laughing cynically.*) And yet it was but a moment ago that it seemed I heard you say there was no one whom you would not permit the world to know you saw.

(*Starting.*) What do you mean?

Hubbard

Good-bye.

(*Hubbard makes exit and closes door.*) (*Knox wanders aimlessly to his desk, glances at the letter he was reading of which had been interrupted by Hubbard's entry of first act, suddenly recollects the package of documents, and walks to low bookcase and looks on top.*)

Knox

(*Stunned.*) The thief!

(*He looks about him wildly, then rushes like a madman in pursuit of Hubbard, making exit to right and leaving the door Hying open.*) (*Empty stage for a moment.*)

Curtain

ACT III. A Room in the Washington House of Anthony Starkweather

Scene. The library, used as a sort of semi-office by Starkweather at such times when he is in Washington. Door to right; also, door to right rear. At left rear is an alcove, without hangings, which is dark. To left are windows. To left, near windows, a flat-top desk, with desk-chair and desk-telephone. Also, on desk, conspicuously, is a heavy dispatch box. At the center rear is a large screen. Extending across center back of room are heavy, old-fashioned bookcases, with swinging glass doors. The bookcases narrow about four feet from the floor, thus forming a ledge. Between left end of bookcases and alcove at left rear, high up on wall, hangs a large painting or steel engraving of Abraham Lincoln. In design and furnishings, it is a simple chaste room, coldly rigid and slightly old-fashioned.

It is 9:30 in the morning of the day succeeding previous act.

Curtain discloses Starkweather seated at desk, and Dobleman, to right of desk, standing.

Starkweather

All right, though it is an unimportant publication. I'll subscribe.

Dobleman

(*Making note on pad.*) Very well, sir. Two thousand.

(*He consults his notes.*) Then there is *Vanderwater's Magazine.* Your subscription is due.

Starkweather

How much?

Dobleman

You have been paying fifteen thousand.

Starkweather

It is too much. What is the regular subscription?

Dobleman

A dollar a year.

Starkweather

(*Shaking his head emphatically.*) It is too much.

Dobleman

Professor Vanderwater also does good work with his lecturing. He is regularly on the Chautauqua Courses, and at that big meeting of the National Civic Federation, his speech was exceptionally telling.

Starkweather

(*Doubtfully, about to give in.*) All right—

(*He pauses, as if recollecting something.*) (*Dobleman has begun to write down the note.*) No. I remember there was something in the papers about this Professor Vanderwater—a divorce, wasn't it? He has impaired his authority and his usefulness to me.

Dobleman

It was his wife's fault.

Starkweather

It is immaterial. His usefulness is impaired. Cut him down to ten thousand. It will teach him a lesson.

Dobleman

Very good, sir.

Starkweather

And the customary twenty thousand to *Cartwrights.*

Dobleman

(*Hesitatingly.*) They have asked for more. They have enlarged the magazine, reorganized the stock, staff, everything.

Starkweather

Hubbard's writing for it, isn't he?

Dobleman

Yes, sir. And though I don't know, it is whispered that he is one of the heavy stockholders.

Starkweather

A very capable man. He has served me well. How much do they want?

Dobleman

They say that Nettman series of articles cost them twelve thousand alone, and that they believe, in view of the exceptional service they are prepared to render, and are rendering, fifty thousand—

Starkweather

(*Shortly.*) All right. How much have I given to University of Hanover this year?

Dobleman

Seven—nine millions, including that new library.

Starkweather

(*Sighing.*) Education does cost. Anything more this morning?

Dobleman

(*Consulting notes.*) Just one other—Mr. Rutland. His church, you know, sir, and that theological college. He told me he had been talking it over with you. He is anxious to know.

Starkweather

He's very keen, I must say. Fifty thousand for the church, and a hundred thousand for the college—I ask you, candidly, is he worth it?

Dobleman

The church is a very powerful molder of public opinion, and Mr. Rutland is very impressive. (*Running over the notes and producing a clipping.*) This is what he said in his sermon two weeks ago: "God has given to Mr. Starkweather the talent for making money as truly as God has given to other men the genius which manifests itself in literature and the arts and sciences."

Starkweather

(*Pleased.*) He says it well.

Dobleman

(*Producing another clipping.*) And this he said about you in last Sunday's sermon: "We are to-day rejoicing in the great light of the consecration of a great wealth to the advancement of the race. This vast wealth has been so consecrated by a man who all through life has walked in accord with the word, The love of Christ constraineth me.'"

Starkweather

(*Meditatively.*) Dobleman, I have meant well. I mean well. I shall always mean well. I believe I am one of those few men, to whom God, in his infinite wisdom, has given the stewardship of the people's wealth. It is a high trust, and despite the abuse and vilification heaped upon me, I shall remain faithful to it.

(*Changing his tone abruptly to businesslike briskness.*) Very well. See that Mr. Rutland gets what he has asked for.

Dobleman

Very good, sir. I shall telephone him. I know he is anxious to hear.

(*Starting to leave the room.*) Shall I make the checks out in the usual way?

Starkweather

Yes: except the Rutland one. I'll sign that myself. Let the others go through the regular channels. We take the 2:10 train for New York. Are you ready?

Dobleman

(*Indicating dispatch box.*) All, except the dispatch box.

Starkweather

I'll take care of that myself.

(*Dobleman starts to make exit to left, and Starkweather, taking notebook from pocket, glances into it, and looks up.*)

Dobleman.

Dobleman

(*Pausing.*) Yes, sir.

Starkweather

Mrs. Chalmers is here, isn't she?

Dobleman

Yes, sir. She came a few minutes ago, with her little boy. They are with Mrs. Starkweather.

Starkweather

Please tell Mrs. Chalmers I wish to see her.

Dobleman

Yes, sir.

(*Dobleman makes exit.*) (*Maidservant enters from right rear, with card tray.*)

Starkweather

(*Examining card.*) Show him in.

(*Maidservant makes exit right rear*). (*Pause, during which Starkweather consults notebook.*) (Maidservant re-enters, showing in Hubbard.)

(*Hubbard advances to desk.*) (*Starkweather is so glad to see him that he half rises from his chair to shake hands.*)

Starkweather

(*Heartily.*) I can only tell you that what you did was wonderful. Your telephone last night was a great relief. Where are they?

Hubbard

(*Drawing package of documents from inside breast pocket and handing them over.*) There they are—the complete set. I was fortunate.

Starkweather

(*Opening package and glancing at a number of the documents while he talks.*) You are modest, Mr. Hubbard.—It required more—than fortune.—It required ability—of no mean order.—The time was short.—You had to think—and act—with too great immediacy to be merely fortunate.

(*Hubbard bows, while Starkweather rearranges package.*)

There is no need for me to tell you how I appreciate your service. I have increased my subscription to Cartwright's to fifty thousand, and I shall speak to Dobleman, who will remit to you a more substantial acknowledgment than my mere thanks for the inestimable service you have rendered.

(*Hubbard bows.*)

You—ah—you have read the documents?

Hubbard

I glanced through them. They were indeed serious. But we have spiked Knox's guns. Without them, that speech of his this afternoon becomes a farce—a howling farce. Be sure you take good care of them.

(*Indicating documents, which Starkweather still holds.*) Gherst has a long arm.

Starkweather

He cannot reach me here. Besides, I go to New York to-day, and I shall carry them with me. Mr. Hubbard, you will forgive me—

(*Starting to pack dispatch box with papers and letters lying on desk.*) I am very busy.

Hubbard

(*Taking the hint.*) Yes, I understand. I shall be going now. I have to be at the Club in five minutes.

Starkweather

(*In course of packing dispatch box, he sets certain packets of papers and several medium-sized account books to one side in an orderly pile. He talks while he packs, and Hubbard waits.*) I should like to talk with you some more—in New York. Next time you are in town be sure to see me. I am thinking of buying the *Parthenon Magazine,* and of changing its policy. I should like to have you negotiate this, and there are other important things as well. Good day, Mr. Hubbard. I shall see you in New York—soon.

(*Hubbard and Starkweather shake hands.*)

(*Hubbard starts to make exit to right rear.*)

(*Margaret enters from right rear.*)

(*Starkweather goes on packing dispatch box through following scene.*)

Hubbard

Mrs. Chalmers.

(*Holding out hand, which Margaret takes very coldly, scarcely inclining her head, and starting to pass on.*) (*Speaking suddenly and savagely.*) You needn't be so high and lofty, Mrs. Chalmers.

Margaret

(*Pausing and looking at him curiously as if to ascertain whether he has been drinking.*) I do not understand.

Hubbard

You always treated me this way, but the time for it is past. I won't stand for your superior goodness any more. You really impressed me with it for a long time, and you made me walk small. But I know better now. A pretty game you've been playing—you, who are like any other woman. Well, you know where you were last night. So do I.

Margaret

You are impudent.

Hubbard

(*Doggedly.*) I said I knew where you were last night. Mr. Knox also knows where you were. But I'll wager your husband doesn't.

Margaret

You spy!

(*Indicating her father.*) I suppose you have told—him.

Hubbard

Why should I?

Margaret

You are his creature.

Hubbard

If it will ease your suspense, let me tell you that I have not told him. But I do protest to you that you must treat me with more—more kindness.

(*Margaret makes no sign but passes on utterly oblivious of him.*)
(*Hubbard stares angrily at her and makes exit*) (*Starkweather, who is finishing*

packing, puts the documents last inside box, and closes and locks it. To one side is the orderly stack of the several account books and packets of papers.)

Starkweather

Good morning, Margaret. I sent for you because we did not finish that talk last night. Sit down.

(*She gets a chair for herself and sits down.*)

You always were hard to manage, Margaret. You have had too much will for a woman. Yet I did my best for you. Your marriage with Tom was especially auspicious—a rising man, of good family and a gentleman, eminently suitable—

Margaret

(*Interrupting bitterly.*) I don't think you were considering your daughter at all in the matter. I know your views on woman and woman's place. I have never counted for anything with you. Neither has mother, nor Connie, when business was uppermost, and business always is uppermost with you. I sometimes wonder if you think a woman has a soul. As for my marriage—you saw that Tom could be useful to you. He had the various distinctive points you have mentioned. Better than that he was pliable, capable of being molded to perform your work, to manipulate machine politics and procure for you the legislation you desired. You did not consider what kind of a husband he would make for your daughter whom you did not know. But you gave your daughter to him—sold her to him—because you needed him—

(*Laughs hysterically.*) In your business.

Starkweather

(*Angrily.*) Margaret! You must not speak that way. (*Relaxing.*)

Ah, you do not change. You were always that way, always bent on having your will—

Margaret

108

Would to God I had been more successful in having it.

Starkweather

(*Testily.*) This is all beside the question. I sent for you to tell you that this must stop—this association with a man of the type and character of Knox—a dreamer, a charlatan, a scoundrel—

Margaret

It is not necessary to abuse him.

Starkweather

It must stop—that is all. Do you understand? It must stop.

Margaret

(*Quietly.*) It has stopped. I doubt that I shall ever see him again. He will never come to my house again, at any rate. Are you satisfied?

Starkweather

Perfectly. Of course, you know I have never doubted you—that—that way.

Margaret

(*Quietly.*) How little you know women. In your comprehension we are automatons, puppets, with no hearts nor heats of desire of our own, with no springs of conduct save those of the immaculate and puritanical sort that New England crystallized a century or so ago.

Starkweather

(*Suspiciously.*) You mean that you and this man—?

Margaret

I mean nothing has passed between us. I mean that I am Tom's wife and Tommy's mother. What I did mean, you have no more understood than you understand me—or any woman.

Starkweather

(*Relieved.*) It is well.

Margaret

(*Continuing.*) And it is so easy. The concept is simple. A woman is human. That is all. Yet I do believe it is news to you.

(*Enters Dobleman from right carrying a check in his hand. Starkweather, about to speak, pauses.*) (*Dobleman hesitates, and Starkweather nods for him to advance.*)

Dobleman

(*Greeting Margaret, and addressing Starkweather.*) This check. You said you would sign it yourself.

Starkweather

Yes, that is Rutland's. (*Looks for pen.*)

(*Dobleman offers his fountain pen.*) No; my own pen.

(*Unlocks dispatch box, gets pen, and signs check. Leaves dispatch box open.*) (*Dobleman takes check and makes exit to right.*)

Starkweather

(*Picking up documents from top of pile in open box.*)

This man Knox. I studied him yesterday. A man of great energy and ideals. Unfortunately, he is a sentimentalist. He means right—I grant him that. But he does not understand practical conditions. He is more dangerous to the welfare of the United States than ten thousand anarchists. And he is not practical. (*Holding up documents.*)

Behold, stolen from my private files by a yellow journal sneak thief and turned over to him. He thought to buttress his speech with them this afternoon. And yet, so hopelessly unpractical is he, that you see they are already back in the rightful owner's hands.

Margaret

Then his speech is ruined?

Starkweather

Absolutely. The wheels are all ready to turn. The good people of the United States will dismiss him with roars of laughter—a good phrase, that: Hubbard's, I believe.

(*Dropping documents on the open cover of dispatch box, picking up the pile of several account books and packets of papers, and rising.*) One moment. I must put these away.

(*Starkweather goes to alcove at left rear. He presses a button and alcove is lighted by electricity, discovering the face of a large safe. During the following scene he does not look around, being occupied with working the combination, opening the safe, putting away account books and packets of papers, and with examining other packets which are in safe.*)

(*Margaret looks at documents lying on open cover of dispatch box and glancing quickly about room, takes a sudden resolution. She seizes documents, makes as if to run wildly from the room, stops abruptly to reconsider, and changes her mind. She looks about room for a hiding place, and her eyes rest on portrait of Lincoln. Moving swiftly, picking up a light chair on the way, she goes to corner of bookcase nearest to portrait, steps on chair, and from chair to ledge of bookcase where, clinging, she reaches out and up and drops documents behind portrait. Stepping quickly down, with handkerchief she wipes ledge on which she has stood, also the seat of the chair. She carries chair back to where she found it, and reseats herself in chair by desk.*) (*Starkweather locks safe, emerges from alcove, turns off alcove lights, advances to desk chair, and sits down. He is about to close and lock dispatch box when he discovers documents are missing. He is very quiet about it, and examines contents of box care-fully.*)

Starkweather

(*Quietly.*) Has anybody been in the room?

Margaret

No.

Starkweather

(*Looking at her searchingly.*) A most unprecedented thing has occurred. When I went to the safe a moment ago, I left these documents on the cover of the dispatch box. Nobody has been in the room but you. The documents are gone. Give them to me.

Margaret

I have not been out of the room.

Starkweather

I know that. Give them to me.

(*A pause.*) You have them. Give them to me

Margaret

I haven't them.

Starkweather

That is a lie. Give them to me.

Margaret

(*Rising.*) I tell you I haven't them—

Starkweather

(*Also rising.*) That is a lie.

Margaret

(*Turning and starting to cross room.*) Very well, if you do not believe me—

Starkweather

(*Interrupting.*) Where are you going?

Margaret

Home.

Starkweather

(*Imperatively.*) No, you are not. Come back here.

(*Margaret comes back and stands by chair.*) You shall not leave this room. Sit down.

Margaret

I prefer to stand.

Starkweather

Sit down.

(*She still stands, and he grips her by arm, forcing her down into chair.*) Sit down. Before you leave this room you shall return those documents. This is more important than you realize. It transcends all ordinary things of life as you have known it, and you will compel me to do things far harsher than you can possibly imagine. I can forget that you are a daughter of mine. I can forget that you are even a woman. If I have to tear them from you, I shall get them. Give them to me.

(*A pause.*) What are you going to do?

(*Margaret shrugs her shoulders.*) What have you to say?

(*Margaret again shrugs her shoulders.*) What have you to say?

Margaret

Nothing.

Starkweather

(*Puzzled, changing tactics, sitting down, and talking calmly.*) Let us talk this over quietly. You have no shred of right of any sort to those documents. They are mine. They were stolen by a sneak thief from my private files. Only this morning—a few minutes ago—did I get them back. They are mine, I tell you. They belong to me. Give them back.

Margaret

I tell you I haven't them.

Starkweather

You have got them about you, somewhere, concealed in your breast there. It will not save you. I tell you I shall have them. I warn you. I don't want to proceed to extreme measures. Give them to me.

(*He starts to press desk-button, pauses, and looks at her.*) Well?

(*Margaret shrugs her shoulders.*) (*He presses button twice.*) I have sent for Dobleman. You have one chance before he comes. Give them to me.

Margaret

Father, will you believe me just this once? Let me go. I tell you I haven't the documents. I tell you that if you let me leave this room, I shall not carry them away with me. I tell you this on my honor. Do you believe me? Tell me that you do believe me.

Starkweather

I do believe you. You say they are not on you. I believe you. Now tell me where they are—you have them hidden somewhere—(*Glancing about room.*)—And you can go at once.

(*Dobleman enters from right and advances to desk. Starkweather and Margaret remains silent.*)

Dobleman

You rang for me.

Starkweather

(*With one last questioning glance at Margaret, who remains impassive.*) Yes, I did. Have you been in that other room all the time?

114

Dobleman

Yes, sir.

Starkweather

Did anybody pass through and enter this room?

Dobleman

No, sir.

Starkweather

Very well. We'll see what the maid has to say.

(*He presses button once.*) Margaret, I give you one last chance.

Margaret

I have told you that if I leave this room, I shall not take them with me.

(*Maid enters from right rear and advances.*)

Starkweather

Has anybody come into this room from the hall in the last few minutes?

Maid

No, sir; not since Mrs. Chalmers came in.

Starkweather

How do you know?

Maid

I was in the hall, sir, dusting all the time.

Starkweather

That will do.

(*Maid makes exit to right rear.*) Dobleman, a very unusual thing has occurred.

Mrs. Chalmers and I have been alone in this room. Those letters stolen by Gherst had been returned to me by Hubbard but the moment before. They were on my desk. I turned my back for a moment to go to the safe. When I came back they were gone.

Dobleman

(*Embarrassed.*) Yes, sir.

Starkweather

Mrs. Chalmers took them. She has them now.

Dobleman

(*Attempts to speak, stammers.*) Er—er—yes, sir

Starkweather

I want them back. What is to be done?

(*Dobleman remains in hopeless confusion.*) Well!

Dobleman

(*Speaking hurriedly and hopefully.*) S-send for Mr. Hubbard. He got them for you before.

Starkweather

A good suggestion. Telephone for him. You should find him at the Press Club.

(*Dobleman starts to make exit to right.*) Don't leave the room. Use this telephone. (*Indicating desk telephone.*) (*Dobleman moves around to left of desk and uses telephone standing up.*) From now on no one leaves the room. If my daughter can be guilty of such a theft, it is plain I can trust no one—no one.

Dobleman

116

(*Speaking in transmitter.*) Red 6-2-4. Yes, please.

(*Waits.*)

Starkweather

(*Rising.*) Call Senator Chalmers as well. Tell him to come immediately.

Dobleman

Yes, sir—immediately.

Starkweather

(*Starting to cross stage to center and speaking to Margaret.*) Come over here.

(*Margaret follows. She is obedient, frightened, very subdued—but resolved.*)

Why have you done this? Were you truthful when you said there was nothing between you and this man Knox?

Margaret

Father; don't discuss this before the—

(*Indicating Dobleman.*)—the servants.

Starkweather

You should have considered that before you stole the documents.

(*Dobleman, in the meantime, is telephoning in a low voice.*)

Margaret

There are certain dignities—

Starkweather

(*Interrupting.*) Not for a thief.

(*Speaking intensely and in a low voice.*) Margaret, it is not too late. Give them back, and no one shall know.

117

(*A pause, in which Margaret is silent, in the throes of indecision.*)

Dobleman

Mr. Hubbard says he will be here in three minutes. Fortunately, Senator Chalmers is with him.

(*Starkweather nods and looks at Margaret.*) (*Door at left rear opens, and enter Mrs. Starkweather and Connie. They are dressed for the street and evidently just going out.*)

Mrs. Starkweather

(*Speaking in a rush.*) We are just going out, Anthony. You were certainly wrong in making us attempt to take that 2:10 train. I simply can't make it. I know I can't. It would have been much wiser—

(*Suddenly apprehending the strain of the situation between Starkweather and Margaret.*)—Why, what is the matter?

Starkweather

(*Patently disturbed by their entrance, speaking to Dobleman, who has finished with the telephone.*) Lock the doors.

(*Dobleman proceeds to obey.*)

Mrs. Starkweather

Mercy me! Anthony! What has happened?

(*A pause.*) Madge! What has happened?

Starkweather

You will have to wait here a few minutes, that is all.

Mrs. Starkweather

But I must keep my engagements. And I haven't a minute to spare.

(*Looking at Dobleman locking doors.*) I do not understand.

Starkweather

(*Grimly,*) You will, shortly. I can trust no one any more. When my daughter sees fit to steal—

Mrs. Starkweather

Steal!—Margaret! What have you been doing now?

Margaret

Where is Tommy?

(*Mrs. Starkwater is too confounded to answer, and can only stare from face to face.*) (*Margaret looks her anxiety to Connie.*)

Connie

He is already down in the machine waiting for us. You are coming, aren't you?

Starkweather

Let him wait in the machine. Margaret will come when I get done with her.

(*A knock is heard at right rear.*) (*Starkweather looks at Dobleman and signifies that he is to open door.*)

(*Dobleman unlocks door, and Hubbabd and Chalmers enter. Beyond the shortest of nods and recognitions with eyes, greetings are cut short by the strain that is on all. Dobleman relocks door.*)

Starkweather

(*Plunging into it.*) Look here, Tom. You know those letters Gherst stole. Mr. Hubbard recovered them from Knox and returned them to me this morning. Within five minutes Margaret stole them from me—here, right in this room. She has not left the room. They are on her now. I want them.

Chalmers

(*Who is obviously incapable of coping with his wife, and who is panting for breath, his hand pressed to his side.*) Madge, is this true?

Margaret

I haven't them. I tell you I haven't them.

Starkweather

Where are they, then?

(*She does not answer.*)

If they are in the room we can find them. Search the room. Tom, Mr. Hubbard, Dobleman. They must be recovered at any cost.

(*While a thorough search of the room is being made, Mrs. Starkweather, overcome, has Connie assist her to seat at left. Margaret also seats herself, in same chair at desk.*)

Chalmers

(*Pausing from search, while others continue.*) There is no place to look for them. They are not in the room. Are you sure you didn't mislay them?

Starkweather

Nonsense. Margaret took them. They are a bulky package and not easily hidden. If they aren't in the room, then she has them on her.

Chalmers

Madge, give them up.

Margaret

I haven't them.

(*Chalmers, stepping suddenly up to her, starts feeling for the papers, running his hands over her dress.*)

Margaret

(*Springing to her feet and striking him in the face with her open palm.*) How dare you!

(*Chalmers recoils, Mrs. Starkweather is threatened with hysteria and is calmed by the frightened Connie, while Starkweather looks on grimly.*)

Hubbard

(*Giving up search of room.*) Possibly it would be better to let me retire, Mr. Starkweather.

Starkweather

No; those papers are here in this room. If nobody leaves there will be no possible chance for the papers to get out of the room. What would you recommend doing, Hubbard?

Hubbard

(*Hesitatingly.*) Under the circumstances I don't like to suggest—

Starkweather

Go on.

Hubbard

First, I would make sure that she—er—Mrs. Chalmers has taken them.

Starkweather

I have made that certain.

Chalmers

But what motive could she have for such an act?

(*Hubbard looks wise.*)

Starkweather

(*To Hubbard.*) You know more about this than would appear. What is it?

Hubbard

I'd rather not. It is too—

(*Looks significantly at Mrs. Starkweather and Connie.*)—er—delicate.

Starkweather

This affair has gone beyond all delicacy. What is it?

Margaret

No! No!

(*Chalmers and Starkweather look at her with sudden suspicion.*)

Starkweather

Go on, Mr. Hubbard.

Hubbard

I'd—I'd rather not.

Starkweather

(*Savagely.*) I say go on.

Hubbard

(*With simulated reluctance.*) Last night—I saw—I was in Knox's rooms—

Margaret

(*Interrupting.*) One moment; please. Let him speak, but first send Connie away.

Starkweather

No one shall leave this room till the documents are produced. Margaret, give me the letters, and Connie can leave quietly, and even will Hubbard's lips remain sealed. They will never breathe a word of whatever shameful thing his eyes saw. This I promise you.

(*A pause, wherein he waits vainly for Margaret to make a decision.*) Go on, Hubbard.

Margaret

(*Who is terror-stricken, and has been wavering.*) No! Don't! I'll tell. I'll give you back the documents.

(*All are expectant She wavers again, and steels herself to resolution.*) No; I haven't them. Say all you have to say.

Starkweather

You see. She has them. She said she would give them back.

(*To Hubbard.*) Go on.

Hubbard

Last night—

Connie

(*Springing up.*) I won't stay!

(*She rushes to left rear and finds door locked.*) Let me out! Let me out!

Mrs. Starkweather

(*Moaning and lying back in chair, legs stretched out and giving preliminary twitches and jerks of hysteria.*) I shall die! I shall die! I know I shall die!

Starkweather

(*Sternly, to Connie.*) Go back to your mother.

Connie

(*Returning reluctantly to side of Mrs. Starkweather, sitting down beside her, and putting fingers in her own ears.*) I won't listen! I won't listen!

Starkweather

(*Sternly.*) Take your fingers down.

Hubbard

Hang it all, Chalmers, I wish I were out of this. I don't want to testify.

Starkweather

Take your fingers down.

(*Connie reluctantly removes her fingers.*) Now, Hubbard.

Hubbard

I protest. I am being dragged into this.

Chalmers

You can't help yourself now. You have cast black suspicions on my wife.

Hubbard

All right. She—Mrs. Chalmers visited Knox in his rooms last night.

Mrs. Starkweather

(*Bursting out.*) Oh! Oh! My Madge! It is a lie! A lie! (*Kicks violently with her legs.*) (*Connie soothes her.*)

Chalmers

You've got to prove that, Hubbard. If you have made any mistake it will go hard with you.

Hubbard

(*Indicating Margaret.*) Look at her. Ask her.

(*Chalmers looks at Margaret with growing suspicion.*)

Margaret

Linda was with me. And Tommy. I had to see Mr. Knox on a very important matter. I went there in the machine. I took Linda and Tommy right into Mr. Knox's room.

Chalmers

(*Relieved.*) Ah, that puts a different complexion on it.

Hubbard

That is not all. Mrs. Chalmers sent the maid and the boy down to the machine and remained.

Margaret

(*Quickly.*) But only for a moment

Hubbard

Much longer—much, much longer. I know how long I was kicking my heels and waiting.

Margaret

(*Desperately.*) I say it was but for a moment—a short moment.

Starkweather

(*Abruptly, to Hubbard.*) Where were you?

Hubbard

In Knox's bedroom. The fool had forgotten all about me. He was too delighted with his—er—new visitor.

Starkweather

You said you saw.

Hubbard

The bedroom door was ajar. I opened it.

Starkweather

What did you see?

Margaret

(*Appealing to Hubbard.*) Have you no mercy? I say it was only a moment.

(*Hubbard shrugs his shoulders.*)

Starkweather

We'll settle the length of that moment Tommy is here, and so is the maid. Connie, Margaret's maid is here, isn't she? (Connie does not answer.) Answer me!

Connie

Yes.

Starkweather

Dobleman, ring for a maid and tell her to fetch Tommy and Mrs. Chalmer's maid.

(*Dobleman goes to desk and pushes button once.*)

Margaret

No! Not Tommy!

Starkweather

(*Looking shrewdly at Margaret, to Dobleman.*) Mrs. Chalmer's maid will do.

(*A knock is heard at left rear. Dobleman opens door and talks to maid. Closes door.*)

Starkweather

Lock it.

(*Dobleman locks door.*)

Chalmers

(*Coming over to Margaret.*) So you, the immaculate one, have been playing fast and loose.

Margaret

You have no right to talk to me that way, Tom—

Chalmers

I am your husband.

Margaret

You have long since ceased being that.

Chalmers

What do you mean?

Margaret

I mean just what you have in mind about yourself right now.

Chalmers

Madge, you are merely conjecturing. You know nothing against me.

Margaret

I know everything—and without evidence, if you please. I am a woman. It is your atmosphere. Faugh! You have exhaled it for years. I doubt not that proofs, as you would call them, could have been easily obtained. But I was not interested. I had my boy. When he came, I gave you up, Tom. You did not seem to need me any more.

Chalmers

And so, in retaliation, you took up with this fellow Knox.

Margaret

No, no. It is not true, Tom. I tell you it is not true.

Chalmers

You were there, last night, in his rooms, alone—how long we shall soon find out—

(*Knock is heard at left rear. Dobleman proceeds to unlock door.*) And now you have stolen your father's private papers for your lover.

Margaret

He is not my lover.

Chalmers

But you have acknowledged that you have the papers. For whom, save Knox, could you have stolen them?

(*Linda enters. She is white and strained, and looks at Margaret for some cue as to what she is to do.*)

Starkweather

That is the woman.

(*To Linda.*) Come here.

127

(*Linda advances reluctantly.*) Where were you last night? You know what I mean.

(*She does not speak.*) Answer me.

Linda

I don't know what you mean, sir—unless—

Starkweather

Yes, that's it. Go on.

Linda

But I don't think you have any right to ask me such questions. What if I—if I did go out with my young man—

Starkweather

(*To Margaret.*) A very faithful young woman you've got.

(*Briskly, to the others.*) There's nothing to be got out of her. Send for Tommy. Dobleman, ring the bell.

(*Dobleman starts to obey.*)

Margaret

(*Stopping Dobleman.*) No, no; not Tommy. Tell them, Linda.

(*Linda looks appealingly at her.*)

(*Kindly.*) Don't mind me. Tell them the truth.

Chalmers

(*Breaking in.*) The whole truth.

Margaret

Yes, Linda, the whole truth.

(*Linda, looking very woeful, nerves herself for the ordeal.*)

Starkweather

Never mind, Dobleman.

(*To Linda.*) Very well. You were at Mr. Knox's rooms last night, with your mistress and Tommy.

Linda

Yes, sir.

Starkweather

Your mistress sent you and Tommy out of the room.

Linda

Yes, sir.

Starkweather

You waited in the machine.

Linda

Yes, sir.

Starkweather

(*Abruptly springing the point he has been working up to.*) How long?

(*Linda perceives the gist of the questioning just as she is opening her mouth to reply, and she does not speak.*)

Margaret

(*With deliberate calmness of despair.*) Half an hour—an hour—any length of time your shameful minds dictate. That will do, Linda. You can go.

Starkweather

No, you don't. Stand over there to one side.

(*To the others.*) The papers are in this room, and I shall keep my mind certain on that point.

Hubbard

I think I have shown the motive.

Connie

You are a beast!

Chalmers

You haven't told what you saw.

Hubbard

I saw them in each other's arms—several times. Then I found the stolen documents where Knox had thrown them down. So I pocketed them and closed the door.

Chalmers

How long after that did they remain together?

Hubbard

Quite a time, quite a long time.

Chalmers

And when you last saw them?

Hubbard

They were in each other's arms—quite enthusiastically, I may say, in each other's arms. (*Chalmers is crushed.*)

Margaret

(*To Hubbard.*) You coward.

(*Hubbard smiles.*)

(*To Starkweather.*) When are you going to call off this hound of yours?

Starkweather

When I get the papers. You see what you've been made to pay for them already. Now listen to me closely. Tom, you listen, too. You know the value of these letters. If they are not recovered they will precipitate a turn-over that means not merely money but control and power. I doubt that even you would be re-elected. So what we have heard in this room must be forgotten—absolutely forgotten. Do you understand?

Chalmers

But it is adultery.

Starkweather

It is not necessary for that word to be mentioned. The point is that everything must be as it was formerly.

Chalmers

Yes, I understand.

Starkweather

(*To Margaret.*) You hear. Tom will make no trouble. Now give me the papers. They are mine, you know.

Margaret

It seems to me the people, who have been lied to, and cajoled, and stolen from, are the rightful owners, not you.

Starkweather

Are you doing this out of love for this—this man, this demagogue?

Margaret

For the people, the children, the future.

Starkweather

Faugh! Answer me.

Margaret

(*Slowly.*) Almost I do not know. Almost I do not know.

(*A knock is heard at left rear. Dobleman answers.*)

Dobleman

(*Looking at card Maid has given him, to Starkweather.*) Mr. Rutland.

Starkweather

(*Making an impatient gesture, then abruptly changing his mind, speaking grimly.*) Very well. Bring him in. I've paid a lot for the Church, now we'll see what the Church can do for me.

Connie

(*Impulsively crossing stage to Margaret, putting arms around her, and weeping.*)

Please, please, Madge, give up the papers, and everything will be hushed up. You heard what father said. Think what it means to me if this scandal comes out. Father will hush it up. Not a soul will dare to breathe a word of it. Give him the papers.

Margaret

(*Kissing her, shaking head, and setting her aside.*) No; I can't. But Connie, dearest—

(*Connie pauses.*) It is not true, Connie. He—he is not my lover. Tell me that you believe me.

Connie

(*Caressing her.*) I do believe you. But won't you return the papers—for my sake?

(A knock at door.)

Margaret

I can't.

(*Enter Rutland.*)

(*Connie returns to take care of Mrs. Starkweather.*)

Rutland

(*Advances beamingly upon Starkweather.*) My, what a family gathering. I hastened on at once, my dear Mr. Starkweather, to thank you in person, ere you fled away to New York, for your generously splendid—yes, generously splendid—contribution—

(*Here the strained situation dawns upon him, and he remains helplessly with mouth open, looking from one to another.*)

Starkweather

A theft has been committed, Mr. Rutland. My daughter has stolen something very valuable from me—a package of private papers, so important—well, if she succeeds in making them public I shall be injured to such an extent financially that there won't be any more generously splendid donations for you or anybody else. I have done my best to persuade her to return what she has stolen. Now you try. Bring her to a realization of the madness of what she is doing.

Rutland

(*Quite at sea, hemming and hawing.*) As your spiritual adviser, Mrs. Chalmers—if this be true—I recommend—I suggest—I—ahem—I entreat—

Margaret

Please, Mr. Rutland, don't be ridiculous. Father is only making a stalking horse out of you. Whatever I may have done, or not done, I believe I am doing right. The whole thing is infamous. The people have been lied to and robbed, and you are merely lending yourself to the infamy of perpetuating the lying and the robbing. If you persist in obeying my father's orders—yes, orders—you will lead me to believe that you are actuated by desire for more of those generously splendid donations. (*Starkweather sneers.*)

Rutland

(*Embarrassed, hopelessly at sea.*) This is, I fear—ahem—too delicate a matter, Mr. Starkweather, for me to interfere. I would suggest that it be advisable for me to withdraw—ahem—

Starkweather

(*Musingly.*) So the Church fails me, too.

(*To Rutland.*) No, you shall stay right here.

Margaret

Father, Tommy is down in the machine alone. Won't you let me go?

Starkweather

Give me the papers.

(Mrs. Starkweather rises and totters across to Margaret, moaning and whimpering.)

Mrs. Starkweather

Madge, Madge, it can't be true. I don't believe it. I know you have not done this awful thing. No daughter of mine could be guilty of such wickedness. I refuse to believe my ears—

(Mrs. Starkweather sinks suddenly on her knees before Margaret, with clasped hands, weeping hysterically.)

Starkweather

(Stepping to her side.) Get up.

(Hesitates and thinks.) No; go on. She might listen to you.

Margaret

(Attempting to raise her mother.) Don't, mother, don't. Please get up.

(Mrs. Starkweather resists her hysterically.) You don't understand, mother. Please, please, get up.

Mrs. Starkweather

Madge, I, your mother, implore you, on my bended knees. Give up the papers to your father, and I shall forget all I have heard. Think of the family name. I don't believe it, not a word of it; but think of the shame and disgrace. Think of me. Think of Connie, your sister. Think of Tommy. You'll have your father in a terrible state. And you'll kill me. (Moaning and rolling her head.)

I'm going to be sick. I know I am going to be sick.

Margaret

(Bending over mother and raising her, while Connie comes across stage to help support mother.) Mother, you do not understand. More is at stake than the good name of the family or—(*Looking at Rutland.*)—God. You speak of Connie and Tommy. There are two millions of Connies and Tommys working as child laborers in the United States to-day. Think of them. And besides,

mother, these are all lies you have heard. There is nothing between Mr. Knox and me. He is not my lover. I am not the—the shameful thing—these men have said I am.

Connie

(*Appealingly.*) Madge.

Margaret

(*Appealingly.*) Connie. Trust me. I am right. I know I am right.

(*Mrs. Starkweather, supported by Connie, moaning incoherently, is led back across stage to chair.*)

Starkweather

Margaret, a few minutes ago, when you told me there was nothing between you and this man, you lied to me—lied to me as only a wicked woman can lie.

Margaret

It is clear that you believe the worst.

Starkweather

There is nothing less than the worst to be believed. Besides, more heinous than your relations with this man is what you have done here in this room, stolen from me, and practically before my very eyes. Well, you have crossed your will with mine, and in affairs beyond your province. This is a man's game in which you are attempting to play, and you shall take the consequences. Tom will apply for a divorce.

Margaret

That threat, at least, is without power.

Starkweather

And by that means we can break Knox as effectually as by any other. That is one thing the good stupid people will not tolerate in a chosen representative. We will make such a scandal of it—

Mrs. Starkweather

(*Shocked.*) Anthony!

Starkweather

(*Glancing irritably at his wife and continuing.*) Another thing. Being proven an adulterous woman, morally unfit for companionship with your child, your child will be taken away from you.

Margaret

No, no. That cannot be. I have done nothing wrong. No court, no fair-minded judge, would so decree on the evidence of a creature like that.

(*Indicating Hubbard.*)

Hubbard

My evidence is supported. In an adjoining room were two men. I happen to know, because I placed them there. They were your father's men at that. There is such a thing as seeing through a locked door. They saw.

Margaret

And they would swear to—to anything.

Hubbard

I doubt not they will know to what to swear.

Starkweather

Margaret, I have told you some, merely some, of the things I shall do. It is not too late. Return the papers, and everything will be forgotten.

Margaret

You would condone this—this adultery. You, who have just said that I was morally unfit to have my own boy, will permit me to retain him. I had never dreamed, father, that your own immorality would descend to such vile depths. Believing this shameful thing of me, you will forgive and forget it all for the sake of a few scraps of paper that stand for money, that stand for a license to rob and steal from the people. Is this your morality—money?

Starkweather

I have my morality. It is not money. I am only a steward; but so highly do I conceive the duties of my stewardship—

Margaret

(*Interrupting, bitterly.*) The thefts and lies and all common little sins like adulteries are not to stand in the way of your high duties—that the end hallows the means.

Starkweather

(*Shortly.*) Precisely.

Margaret

(*To Rutland.*) There is Jesuitism, Mr. Rutland. I would suggest that you, as my father's spiritual adviser—

Starkweather

Enough of this foolery. Give me the papers.

Margaret

I haven't them.

Starkweather

What's to be done, Hubbard?

Hubbard

She has them. She has as much as acknowledged that they are not elsewhere in the room. She has not been out of the room. There is nothing to do but search her.

Starkweather

Nothing else remains to be done. Dobleman, and you, Hubbard, take her behind the screen. Strip her. Recover the papers.

(*Dobleman is in a proper funk, but Hubbard betrays no unwillingness.*)

Chalmers

No; that I shall not permit. Hubbard shall have nothing to do with this.

Margaret

137

It is too late, Tom. You have stood by and allowed me to be stripped of everything else. A few clothes do not matter now. If I am to be stripped and searched by men, Mr. Hubbard will serve as well as any other man. Perhaps Mr. Rutland would like to lend his assistance.

Connie

Oh, Madge! Give them up.

(*Margaret shakes her head.*)

(*To Starkweather.*) Then let me search her, father.

Starkweather

You are too willing. I don't want volunteers. I doubt that I can trust you any more than your sister.

Connie

Let mother, then.

Starkweather

(*Sneering.*) Margaret could smuggle a steamer-trunk of documents past her.

Connie

But not the men, father! Not the men!

Starkweather

Why not? She has shown herself dead to all shame.

(*Imperatively.*) Dobleman!

Dobleman

(*Thinking his time has come, and almost dying.*) Y-y-yes, sir.

Starkweather

Call in the servants.

Mrs. Starkweather

(*Crying out in protest.*) Anthony!

138

Starkweather

Would you prefer her to be searched by the men?

Mrs. Starkweather

(*Subsiding.*) I shall die, I shall die. I know I shall die.

Starkweather

Dobleman. Ring for the servants.

(*Dobleman, who has been hesitant, crosses to desk and pushes button, then returns toward door.*) Send in the maids and the housekeeper.

(*Linda, blindly desiring to be of some assistance, starts impulsively toward Margaret.*) Stand over there—in the corner.

(*Indicating right front.*)

(*Linda pauses irresolutely and Margaret nods to her to obey and smiles encouragement. Linda, protesting in every fiber of her, goes to right front.*)

(*A knock at right rear and Dobleman unlocks door, confers with maid, and closes and locks door.*)

Starkweather

(*To Margaret.*) This is no time for trifling, nor for mawkish sentimentality. Return the papers or take the consequences.

(*Margaret makes no answer.*)

Chalmers

You have taken a hand in a man's game, and you've got to play it out or quit. Give up the papers.

(*Margaret remains resolved and impassive.*)

Hubbard

(*Suavely.*) Allow me to point out, my dear Mrs. Chalmers, that you are not merely stealing from your father. You are playing the traitor to your class.

139

Starkweather

And causing irreparable damage.

Margaret

(*Firing up suddenly and pointing to Lincoln's portrait*) I doubt not he caused irreparable damage when he freed the slaves and preserved the Union. Yet he recognized no classes. I'd rather be a traitor to my class than to him.

Starkweather

Demagoguery. Demagoguery.

(*A knock at right rear. Dobleman opens door. Enter Mrs. Middleton who is the housekeeper, followed by two Housemaids. They pause at rear. Housekeeper to the fore and looking expectantly at Starkweather. The Maids appear timid and frightened.*)

Housekeeper

Yes, sir.

Starkweather

Mrs. Middleton, you have the two maids to assist you. Take Mrs. Chalmers behind that screen there and search her. Strip all her clothes from her and make a careful search. (*Maids show perturbation.*)

Housekeeper

(*Self-possessed.*) Yes, sir. What am I to search for?

Starkweather

Papers, documents, anything unusual. Turn them over to me when you find them.

Margaret

(*In a sudden panic.*) This is monstrous! This is monstrous!

Starkweather

So is your theft of the documents monstrous.

Margaret

(*Appealing to the other men, ignoring Rutland and not considering Dobleman at all.*)

You cowards! Will you stand by and permit this thing to be done? Tom, have you one atom of manhood in you?

Chalmers

(*Doggedly.*) Return the papers, then.

Margaret

Mr. Rutland—

Rutland

(*Very awkwardly and oilily.*) My dear Mrs. Chalmers. I assure you the whole circumstance is unfortunate. But you are so palpably in the wrong that I cannot interfere—(*Margaret turns from him in withering scorn.*)—That I cannot interfere.

Dobleman

(*Breaking down unexpectedly.*) I cannot stand it. I leave your employ, sir. It is outrageous. I resign now, at once. I cannot be a party to this.

(*Striving to unlock door.*) I am going at once. You brutes! You brutes!

(*Breaks into convulsive sobbings.*)

Chalmers

Ah, another lover, I see.

Dobleman manages to unlock door and starts to open it.)

Starkweather

You fool! Shut that door!

(*Dobleman hesitates.*) Shut it!

(*Dobleman obeys.*) Lock it!

(*Dobleman obeys.*)

Margaret

(*Smiling wistfully, benignantly.*) Thank you, Mr. Dobleman.

(*To Starkweather.*) Father, you surely will not perpetrate this outrage, when I tell you, I swear to you—

Starkweather

(*Interrupting.*) Return the documents then.

Margaret

I swear to you that I haven't them. You will not find them on me.

Starkweather

You have lied to me about Knox, and I have no reason to believe you will not lie to me about this matter.

Margaret

(*Steadily.*) If you do this thing you shall cease to be my father forever. You shall cease to exist so far as I am concerned.

Starkweather

You have too much of my own will in you for you ever to forget whence it came. Mrs. Middleton, go ahead.

(*Housekeeper, summoning Maids with her eyes, begins to advance on Margaret.*)

Connie

(*In a passion.*) Father, if you do this I shall never speak to you again.

(*Breaks down weeping.*) (*Mrs. Starkweather, during following scene, has mild but continuous shuddering and weeping hysteria.*)

Starkweather

(*Briskly, looking at watch.*) I've wasted enough time on this. Mrs. Middleton, proceed.

Margaret

(*Wildly, backing away from Housekeeper.*) I will not tamely submit. I will resist, I promise you.

Starkweather

Use force, if necessary.

(*The Maids are reluctant, but Housekeeper commands them with her eyes to close in on Margaret, and they obey.*)

(*Margaret backs away until she brings up against desk.*)

Housekeeper

Come, Mrs. Chalmers.

(*Margaret stands trembling, but refuses to notice Housekeeper.*) (*Housekeeper places hand on Margaret's arm.*)

Margaret

(*Violently flinging the hand off, crying imperiously.*) Stand back!

(*Housekeeper instinctively shrinks back, as do Maids. But it is only for the moment. They close in upon Margaret to seise her.*)

(*Crying frantically for help.*) Linda! Linda!

(*Linda springs forward to help her mistress, but is caught and held struggling by Chalmers, who twists her arm and finally compels her to become quiet.*)

(*Margaret, struggling and resisting, is hustled across stage and behind screen, the Maids warming up to their work. One of them emerges from behind screen for the purpose of getting a chair, upon which Margaret is evidently forced to sit. The screen is of such height, that occasionally, when standing up and struggling, Margaret's bare arms are visible above the top of it. Muttered exclamations are heard, and the voice of Housekeeper trying to persuade Margaret to sub-mit.*)

Margaret

(*Abruptly, piteously.*) No! No!

(*The struggle becomes more violent, and the screen is overturned, disclosing Margaret seated on chair, partly undressed, and clutching an envelope in her hand which they are trying to force her to relinquish.*)

143

Mrs. Starkweather

(*Crying wildly.*) Anthony! They are taking her clothes off!

(*Renewed struggle of Linda with Chalmers at the sight.*)

(*Starkweather, calling Rutland to his assistance, stands screen up again, then, as an afterthought, pulls screen a little further away from Margaret.*)

Margaret

No! No!

(*Housekeeper appears triumphantly with envelope in her hand and hands it to Hubbard.*)

Hubbard

(Immediately.) That's not it.

(*Glances at address and starts.*) It's addressed to Knox.

Starkweather

Tear it open. Read it.

(*Hubbard tears envelope open.*) (*While this is going on, struggle behind screen is suspended.*)

Hubbard

(*Withdrawing contents of envelope.*) It is only a photograph—of Mrs. Chalmers.

(*Reading.*) "For the future—Margaret."

Chalmers

(*Thrusting Linda back to right front and striding up to Hubbard.*) Give it to me. (*Hubbard passes it to him, and he looks at it, crumples it in his hand, and grinds it under foot.*)

Starkweather

That is not what we wanted, Mrs. Middleton. Go on with the search.

(*The search goes on behind the screen without any further struggling.*)

144

(*A pause, during which screen is occasionally agitated by the searchers removing Margaret's garments.*)

Housekeeper

(*Appearing around corner of screen.*) I find nothing else, sir.

Starkweather

Is she stripped?

Housekeeper

Yes, sir.

Starkweather

Every stitch?

Housekeeper

(*Disappearing behind screen instead of answering for a pause, during which it is patent that the ultimate stitch is being removed, then reappearing.*) Yes, sir.

Starkweather

Nothing?

Housekeeper

Nothing.

Starkweather

Throw out her clothes—everything.

(*A confused mass of feminine apparel is tossed out, falling near Dobleman's feet, who, in consequence, is hugely mortified and embarrassed.*)

(*Chalmers examines garments, then steps behind screen a moment, and reappears.*)

Chalmers

Nothing.

(*Chalmers, Starkweather, and Hubbard gaze at each other dumbfoundedly.*)

(*The two Maids come out from behind screen and stand near door to right rear.*)

(*Starkweather is loath to believe, and steps to Margaret's garments and overhauls them.*)

Starkweather

(*To Chalmers, looking inquiringly toward screen.*) Are you sure?

Chalmers

Yes; I made certain. She hasn't them.

Starkweather

(*To Housekeeper.*) Mrs. Middleton, examine those girls.

Housekeeper

(Passing hands over dresses of Maids.) No, sir.

Margaret

(*From behind screen, in a subdued, spiritless voice.*) May I dress—now?

(*Nobody answers.*) It—it is quite chilly.

(*Nobody answers.*) Will you let Linda come to me, please?

(*Starkweather nods savagely to Linda, to obey.*) (*Linda crosses to garments, gathers them up, and disappears behind screen.*)

Starkweather

(*To Housekeeper.*)

You may go.

(*Exit Housekeeper and the two Maids.*)

Dobleman

(*Hesitating, after closing door.*) Shall I lock it?

(*Starkweather does not answer, and Dobleman leaves door unlocked.*)

Connie

(*Rising.*) May I take mother away?

(*Starkweather, who is in a brown study, nods.*) (*Connie assists Mrs. Starkweather to her feet.*)

Mrs. Starkweather

(*Staggering weakly, and sinking back into chair.*) Let me rest a moment, Connie. I'll be better. (*To Starkweather, who takes no notice.*) Anthony, I am going to bed. This has been too much for me. I shall be sick. I shall never catch that train to-day.

(*Shudders and sighs, leans head back, closes eyes, and Connie fans her or administers smelling salts.*)

Chalmers

(*To Hubbard.*) What's to be done?

Hubbard

(*Shrugging shoulders.*) I'm all at sea. I had just left the letters with him, when Mrs. Chalmers entered the room. What's become of them? She hasn't them, that's certain.

Chalmers

But why? Why should she have taken them?

Hubbard

(*Dryly, pointing to crumpled photograph on floor.*) It seems very clear to me.

Chalmers

You think so? You think so?

Hubbard

I told you what I saw last night at his rooms. There is no other explanation.

Chalmers

(*Angrily.*) And that's the sort he is—vaunting his moral superiority—mouthing phrases about theft—our theft—and himself the greatest thief of all, stealing the dearest and sacredest things—

(*Margaret appears from behind screen, pinning on her hat. She is dressed, but somewhat in disarray, and Linda follows, pulling and touching and arranging. Margaret pauses near to Rutland, but does not seem to see him.*)

Rutland

(*Lamely.*) It is a sad happening—ahem—a sad happening. I am grieved, deeply grieved. I cannot tell you, Mrs. Chalmers, how grieved I am to have been compelled to be present at this—ahem—this unfortunate—

(*Margaret withers him with a look and he awkwardly ceases.*)

Margaret

After this, father, there is one thing I shall do—

Chalmers

(Interrupting.) Go to your lover, I suppose.

Margaret

(*Coldly.*) Have it that way if you choose.

Chalmers

And take him what you have stolen—

Starkweather

(*Arousing suddenly from brown study.*) But she hasn't them on her. She hasn't been out of the room. They are not in the room. Then where are they?

(*During the following, Margaret goes to the door, which Dobleman opens. She forces Linda to go out and herself pauses in open door to listen.*)

Hubbard

(*Uttering an exclamation of enlightenment, going rapidly across to window at left and raising it.*) It is not locked. It moves noiselessly. There's the explanation.

148

(*To Starkweather.*) While you were at the safe, with your back turned, she lifted the window, tossed the papers out to somebody waiting—

(*He sticks head and shoulders out of window, peers down, then brings head and shoulders back.*)—No; they are not there. Somebody was waiting for them.

Starkweather

But how should she know I had them? You had only just recovered them?

Hubbard

Didn't Knox know right away last night that I had taken them? I took the up-elevator instead of the down when I heard him running along the hall. Trust him to let her know what had happened. She was the only one who could recover them for him. Else why did she come here so immediately this morning? To steal the package, of course. And she had some one waiting outside. She tossed them out and closed the window—

(*He closes window.*)—You notice it makes no sound.—and sat down again—all while your back was turned.

Starkweather

Margaret, is this true?

Margaret

(*Excitedly.*) Yes, the window. Why didn't you think of it before? Of course, the window. He—somebody was waiting. They are gone now—miles and miles away. You will never get them. They are in his hands now. He will use them in his speech this afternoon. (*Laughs wildly.*)

(*Suddenly changing her tone to mock meekness, subtle with defiance.*) May I go—now?

(*Nobody answers, and she makes exit.*) (*A moments pause, during which Starkweather, Chalmers, and Hubbard look at each other in stupefaction.*)

Curtain

ACT IV

Scene. *Same as Act I. It is half past one of same day. Curtain discloses Knox seated at right front and waiting. He is dejected in attitude.*

(Margaret enters from right rear, and advances to him. He rises awkwardly and shakes hands. She is very calm and self-possessed.)

Margaret

I knew you would come. Strange that I had to send for you so soon after last night—

(With alarm and sudden change of manner.) What is the matter? You are sick. Your hand is cold.

(She warms it in both of her hands.)

Knox

It is flame or freeze with me.

(Smiling.) And I'd rather flame.

Margaret

(Becoming aware that she is warming his hand.)

Sit down and tell me what is the matter.

(Leading him by the hand she seats him, at the same time seating herself.)

Knox

(Abruptly.) After you left last night, Hubbard stole those documents back again.

Margaret

(Very matter-of-fact.) Yes; he was in your bedroom while I was there.

Knox

(Startled.) How do you know that? Anyway, he did not know who you were.

Margaret

Oh yes he did.

Knox

(*Angrily.*) And he has dared——?

Margaret

Yes; not two hours ago. He announced the fact before my father, my mother, Connie, the servants, everybody.

Knox

(*Rising to his feet and beginning to pace perturbedly up and down.*) The cur!

Margaret

(*Quietly.*) I believe, among other things, I told him he was that myself.

(*She laughs cynically.*) Oh, it was a pretty family party, I assure you. Mother said she didn't believe it—but that was only hysteria. Of course she believes it—the worst. So does Connie—everybody.

Knox

(*Stopping abruptly and looking at her horror-stricken.*) You don't mean they charged——?

Margaret

No; I don't mean that. I mean more. They didn't charge. They accepted it as a proven fact that I was guilty. That you were my—lover.

Knox

On that man's testimony?

Margaret

He had two witnesses in an adjoining room.

Knox

(*Relieved.*) All the better. They can testify to nothing more than the truth, and the truth is not serious. In our case it is good, for we renounced each other.

Margaret

You don't know these men. It is easy to guess that they have been well trained. They would swear to anything.

(*She laughs bitterly.*) They are my father's men, you know, his paid sleuth-hounds.

Knox

(*Collapsing in chair, holding head in hands, and groaning.*) How you must have suffered. What a terrible time, what a terrible time! I can see it all—before everybody—your nearest and dearest. Ah, I could not understand, after our parting last night, why you should have sent for me today. But now I know.

Margaret

No you don't, at all.

Knox

(*Ignoring her and again beginning to pace back and forth, thinking on his feet.*) What's the difference? I am ruined politically. Their scheme has worked out only too well. Gifford warned me, you warned me, everybody warned me. But I was a fool, blind—with a fool's folly. There is nothing left but you now.

(*He pauses, and the light of a new thought irradiates his face.*) Do you know, Margaret, I thank God it has happened as it has. What if my usefulness is destroyed? There will be other men—other leaders. I but make way for another. The cause of the people can never be lost. And though I am driven from the fight, I am driven to you. We are driven together. It is fate. Again I thank God for it.

(*He approaches her and tries to clasp her in his arms, but she steps back.*)

Margaret

(*Smiling sadly.*) Ah, now you flame. The tables are reversed. Last night it was I. We are fortunate that we choose diverse times for our moods—else there would be naught but one sweet melting mad disaster.

Knox

But it is not as if we had done this thing deliberately and selfishly. We have renounced. We have struggled against it until we were beaten. And now we are driven together, not by our doing but Fate's. After this affair this morning there is nothing for you but to come to me. And as for me, despite my best, I am finished. I have failed. As I told you, the papers are stolen. There will be no speech this afternoon.

Margaret

(*Quietly.*) Yes there will.

Knox

Impossible. I would make a triple fool of myself. I would be unable to substantiate my charges.

Margaret

You will substantiate them. What a chain of theft it is. My father steals from the people. The documents that prove his stealing are stolen by Gherst. Hubbard steals them from you and returns them to my father. And I steal them from my father and pass them back to you.

Knox

(*Astounded.*) You?—You?—

Margaret

Yes; this very morning. That was the cause of all the trouble. If I hadn't stolen them nothing would have happened. Hubbard had just returned them to my father.

Knox

(*Profoundly touched.*) And you did this for me—?

Margaret

Dear man, I didn't do it for you. I wasn't brave enough. I should have given in. I don't mind confessing that I started to do it for you, but it soon grew so terrible that I was afraid. It grew so terrible that had it been for you alone I should have surrendered. But out of the terror of it all I caught a wider vision, and all that you said last night rose before me. And I knew that you were right. I thought of all the people, and of the little children. I did it for them, after all. You speak for them. I stole the papers so that you could use them in speaking for the people. Don't you see, dear man?

(*Changing to angry recollection.*) Do you know what they cost me? Do you know what was done to me, to-day, this morning, in my father's house? I was shamed, humiliated, as I would never have dreamed it possible. Do you know what they did to me? The servants were called in, and by them I was stripped before everybody—my family, Hubbard, the Reverend Mr. Rutland, the secretary, everybody.

Knox

(*Stunned.*) Stripped—you?

Margaret

Every stitch. My father commanded it

Knox

(*Suddenly visioning the scene.*) My God!

Margaret

(*Recovering herself and speaking cynically, with a laugh at his shocked face.*) No; it was not so bad as that. There was a screen.

(*Knox appears somewhat relieved.*) But it fell down in the midst of the struggle.

Knox

But in heaven's name why was this done to you?

Margaret

Searching for the lost letters. They knew I had taken them.

(*Speaking gravely.*)

So you see, I have earned those papers. And I have earned the right to say what shall be done with them. I shall give them to you, and you will use them in your speech this afternoon.

Knox

I don't want them.

Margaret

(*Going to bell and ringing.*) Oh yes you do. They are more valuable right now than anything else in the world.

Knox

(*Shaking his head.*) I wish it hadn't happened.

Margaret

(*Returning to him, pausing by his chair, and caressing his hair.*) What?

Knox

This morning—your recovering the letters. I had adjusted myself to their loss, and the loss of the fight, and the finding of—you.

(*He reaches up, draws down her hand, and presses it to his lips.*) So—give them back to your father.

(*Margaret draws quickly away from him.*) (*Enter Man-servant at right rear.*)

Margaret

Send Linda to me.

(*Exit Man-servant.*)

Knox

What are you doing?

Margaret

(*Sitting down.*) I am going to send Linda for them. They are still in my father's house, hidden, of all places, behind Lincoln's portrait. He will guard them safely, I know.

Knox

(*With fervor.*) Margaret! Margaret! Don't send for them. Let them go. I don't want them.

(*Rising and going toward her impulsively.*) (*Margaret rises and retreats, holding him off.*) I want you—you—you.

(*He catches her hand and kisses it. She tears it away from him, but tenderly.*)

Margaret

(*Still retreating, roguishly and tenderly.*) Dear, dear man, I love to see you so. But it cannot be.

(*Looking anxiously toward right rear.*) No, no, please, please sit down.

(*Enter Linda from right rear. She is dressed for the street.*)

Margaret

(*Surprised.*) Where are you going?

Linda

Tommy and the nurse and I were going down town. There is some shopping she wants to do.

Margaret

Very good. But go first to my father's house. Listen closely. In the library, behind the portrait of Lincoln—you know it? (*Linda nods.*)

You will find a packet of papers. It took me five seconds to put it there. It will take you no longer to get it. Let no one see you. Let it appear as though you had brought Tommy to see his grandmother and cheer her up. You know she is not feeling very well just now. After you get the papers, leave Tommy there and bring them immediately back to me. Step on a chair to the ledge of the bookcase, and reach behind the portrait. You should be back inside fifteen minutes. Take the car.

Linda

Tommy and the nurse are already in it, waiting for me.

Margaret

Be careful. Be quick.

(*Linda nods to each instruction and makes exit.*)

Knox

(*Bursting out passionately.*) This is madness. You are sacrificing yourself, and me. I don't want them. I want you. I am tired. What does anything matter except love? I have pursued ideals long enough. Now I want you.

Margaret

(*Gravely.*) Ah, there you have expressed the pith of it. You will now forsake ideals for me—(*He attempts to interrupt.*) No, no; not that I am less than an ideal. I have no silly vanity that way. But I want you to remain ideal, and you can only by going on—not by being turned back. Anybody can play the coward and assert they are fatigued. I could not love a coward. It was your strength that saved us last night. I could not have loved you as I do, now, had you been weak last night. You can only keep my love—

Knox

(*Interrupting, bitterly.*) By foregoing it—for an ideal. Margaret, what is the biggest thing in the world? Love. There is the greatest ideal of all.

Margaret

(*Playfully.*) Love of man and woman?

Knox

What else?

Margaret

(*Gravely.*) There is one thing greater—love of man for his fellowman.

Knox

Oh, how you turn my preachments back on me. It is a lesson. Nevermore shall I preach. Henceforth—

Margaret

Yes.

(*Chalmers enters unobserved at left, pauses, and looks on.*)

Knox

Henceforth I love. Listen.

Margaret

You are overwrought. It will pass, and you will see your path straight before you, and know that I am right. You cannot run away from the fight.

Knox

I can—and will. I want you, and you want me—the man's and woman's need for each other. Come, go with me—now. Let us snatch at happiness while we may.

(*He arises, approaches her, and gets her hand in his. She becomes more complaisant, and, instead of repulsing him, is willing to listen and receive.*) As I have said, the fight will go on just the same. Scores of men, better men, stronger men, than I, will rise to take my place. Why do I talk this way? Because I love you, love you, love you. Nothing else exists in all the world but love of you.

Margaret

(*Melting and wavering.*) Ah, you flame, you flame.

(*Chalmers utters an inarticulate cry of rage and rushes forward at Knox*)

(*Margaret and Knox are startled by the cry and discover Chalmer's presence.*)

Margaret

(*Confronting Chalmers and thrusting him slightly back from Knox, and continuing to hold him off from Knox.*) No, Tom, no dramatics, please. This excitement of yours is only automatic and conventional. You really don't mean it. You don't even feel it. You do it because it is expected of you and because it is your training. Besides, it is bad for your heart. Remember Dr. West's warning—

(*Chalmers, making an unusually violent effort to get at Knox, suddenly staggers weakly back, signs of pain on his face, holding a hand convulsively clasped over his heart. Margaret catches him and supports him to a chair, into which he collapses.*)

Chalmers

(*Muttering weakly.*) My heart! My heart!

Knox

(*Approaching.*) Can I do anything?

Margaret

(*Calmly.*) No; it is all right. He will be better presently.

(*She is bending over Chalmers, her hand on his wrist, when suddenly, as a sign he is recovering, he violently flings her hand off and straightens up.*)

Knox

(*Undecidedly.*) I shall go now.

Margaret

No. You will wait until Linda comes back. Besides, you can't run away from this and leave me alone to face it.

Knox

(*Hurt, showing that he will stay.*) I am not a coward.

Chalmers

(*In a stifled voice that grows stronger.*) Yes; wait I have a word for you.

(*He pauses a moment, and when he speaks again his voice is all right.*)

(*Witheringly.*) A nice specimen of a reformer, I must say. You, who babbled yesterday about theft. The most high, righteous and noble Ali Baba, who has come into the den of thieves and who is also a thief.

(*Mimicking Margaret.*) "Ah, you flame, you flame!"

(*In his natural voice.*) I should call you; you thief, you thief, you wife-stealer, you.

Margaret

(*Coolly.*) I should scarcely call it theft.

Chalmers

(*Sneeringly.*) Yes; I forgot. You mean it is not theft for him to take what already belongs to him.

Margaret

Not quite that—but in taking what has been freely offered to him.

Chalmers

You mean you have so forgotten your womanhood as to offer—

Margaret

Just that. Last night. And Mr. Knox did himself the honor of refusing me.

Knox

(*Bursting forth.*) You see, nothing else remains, Margaret.

Chalmers

(*Twittingly.*) Ah, "Margaret."

Knox

(*Ignoring him.*) The situation is intolerable.

Chalmers

(*Emphatically*). It is intolerable. Don't you think you had better leave this house? Every moment of your presence dishonors it.

Margaret

Don't talk of honor, Tom.

Chalmers

I make no excuses for myself. I fancy I never fooled you very much. But at any rate I never used my own house for such purposes.

Knox

(*Springing at him.*) You cur!

Margaret

(*Interposing.*) No; don't. His heart.

Chalmers

(*Mimicking Margaret.*) No dramatics, please.

Margaret

(*Plaintively, looking from one man to the other.*) Men are so strangely and wonderfully made. What am I to do with the pair of you? Why won't you reason together like rational human beings?

Chalmers

(*Bitterly gay, rising to his feet.*) Yes; let us come and reason together. Be rational. Sit down and talk it over like civilized humans. This is not the stone age. Be reassured, Mr. Knox. I won't brain you. Margaret—

(*Indicating chair,*) Sit down. Mr. Knox—

(*Indicating chair.*) Sit down.

(*All three seat themselves, in a triangle.*) Behold the problem—the ever ancient and ever young triangle of the playwright and the short story writer—two men and a woman.

Knox

True, and yet not true. The triangle is incomplete. Only one of the two men loves the woman.

Chalmers

Yes?

Knox

And I am that man.

Chalmers

I fancy you're right.

(*Nodding his head.*) But how about the woman?

Margaret

She loves one of the two men.

Knox

And what are you going to do about it?

Chalmers

(*Judicially.*) She has not yet indicated the man.

(*Margaret is about to indicate Knox.*) Be careful, Madge. Remember who is Tommy's father.

Margaret

Tom, honestly, remembering what the last years have been can you imagine that I love you?

Chalmers

I'm afraid I've not—er—not flamed sufficiently.

Margaret

You have possibly spoken nearer the truth than you dreamed. I married you, Tom, hoping great things of you. I hoped you would be a power for good—

Chalmers

Politics again. When will women learn they must leave politics alone?

Margaret

And also, I hoped for love. I knew you didn't love me when we married, but I hoped for it to come.

Chalmers

And—er—may I be permitted to ask if you loved me?

Margaret

No; but I hoped that, too, would come.

Chalmers

It was, then, all a mistake.

Margaret

Yes; yours, and mine, and my father's.

Knox

We have sat down to reason this out, and we get nowhere. Margaret and I love each other. Your triangle breaks.

Chalmers

It isn't a triangle after all. You forget Tommy.

Knox

(*Petulantly.*) Make it four-sided, then, but let us come to some conclusion.

Chalmers

(*Reflecting.*) Ah, it is more than that. There is a fifth side. There are the stolen letters which Madge has just this morning restolen from her father. Whatever settlement takes place, they must enter into it.

(*Changing his tone.*) Look here, Madge, I am a fool. Let us talk sensibly, you and Knox and I. Knox, you want my wife. You can have her—on one consideration. Madge, you want Knox. You can have him on one consideration, the same consideration. Give up the letters and we'll forget everything.

Margaret

Everything?

Chalmers

Everything. Forgive and forget You know.

Margaret

You will forgive my—I—this—this adultery?

Chalmers

(*Doggedly.*) I'll forgive anything for the letters. I've played fast and loose with you, Madge, and I fancy your playing fast and loose only evens things up. Return the letters and you can go with Knox quietly. I'll see to that. There won't be a breath of scandal. I'll give you a divorce. Or you can stay on with me if you want to. I don't care. What I want is the letters. Is it agreed?

163

(*Margaret seems to hesitate.*)

Knox

(Pleadingly.) Margaret.

Margaret

Chalmers

(*Testily.*) Am I not giving you each other? What more do you want? Tommy stays with me. If you want Tommy, then stay with me, but you must give up the letters.

Margaret

I shall not go with Mr. Knox. I shall not give up the letters. I shall remain with Tommy.

Chalmers

So far as I am concerned, Knox doesn't count in this. I want the letters and I want Tommy. If you don't give them up, I'll divorce you on statutory grounds, and no woman, so divorced, can keep her child. In any event, I shall keep Tommy.

Margaret

(*Speaking steadily and positively.*) Listen, Tom; and you, too, Howard. I have never for a moment entertained the thought of giving up the letters. I may have led you to think so, but I wanted to see just how low, you, Tom, could sink. I saw how low you—all of you—this morning sank. I have learned—much. Where is this fine honor, Tom, which put you on a man-killing rage a moment ago? You'll barter it all for a few scraps of paper, and forgive and forget adultery which does not exist—

(*Chalmers laughs skeptically.*)—though I know when I say it you will not believe me. At any rate, I shall not give up the letters. Not if you do take Tommy away from me. Not even for Tommy will I sacrifice all the people. As I told you this morning, there are two million Tommys, child-laborers all, who cannot be sacrificed for Tommy's sake or anybody's sake.

(*Chalmers shrugs his shoulders and smiles in ridicule.*)

Knox

Surely, Margaret, there is a way out for us. Give up the letters. What are they?—only scraps of paper. Why match them against happiness—our happiness?

Margaret

But as you told me yourself, those scraps of paper represent the happiness of millions of lives. It is not our happiness that is matched against some scraps of paper. It is our happiness against millions of lives—like ours. All these millions have hearts, and loves, and desires, just like ours.

Knox

But it is a great social and cosmic process. It does not depend on one man. Kill off, at this instant, every leader of the people, and the process will go on just the same. The people will come into their own. Theft will be unseated. It is destiny. It is the process. Nothing can stop it.

Margaret

But it can be retarded.

Knox

You and I are no more than straws in relation to it. We cannot stop it any more than straws can stop an ocean tide. We mean nothing—except to each other, and to each other we mean all the world.

Margaret

(*Sadly and tenderly.*) All the world and immortality thrown in.

Chalmers

(*Breaking in.*) Nice situation, sitting here and listening to a strange man woo my wife in terms of sociology and scientific slang.

(*Both Margaret and Knox ignore him.*)

Knox

Dear, I want you so.

Margaret

(*Despairingly.*) Oh! It is so hard to do right!

Knox

(*Eagerly.*) He wants the letters very badly. Give them up for Tommy. He will give Tommy for them.

Chalmers

No; emphatically no. If she wants Tommy she can stay on; but she must give up the letters. If she wants you she may go; but she must give up the letters.

Knox

(*Pleading for a decision.*) Margaret.

Margaret

Howard. Don't tempt me and press me. It is hard enough as it is.

Chalmers

(*Standing up.*) I've had enough of this. The thing must be settled, and I leave it to you, Knox. Go on with your love-making. But I won't be a witness to it. Perhaps I—er—retard the—er—the flame process. You two must make up your minds, and you can do it better without me. I am going to get a drink and settle my nerves. I'll be back in a minute.

(*He moves toward exit to right.*) She will yield, Knox. Be warm, be warm.

(*Pausing in doorway.*) Ah, you flame! Flame to some purpose. (*Exit Chalmers.*)

(*Knox rests his head despairingly on his hand, and Margaret, pausing and looking at him sadly for a moment, crosses to him, stands beside him, and caresses his hair.*)

Margaret

It is hard, I know, dear. And it is hard for me as well.

Knox

It is so unnecessary.

Margaret

No, it is necessary. What you said last night, when I was weak, was wise. We cannot steal from my child—

Knox

But if he gives you Tommy? Margaret

(*Shaking her head.*) Nor can we steal from any other woman's child—from all the children of all the women. And other things I heard you say, and you were right. We cannot live by ourselves alone. We are social animals. Our good and our ill—all is tied up with all humanity.

Knox

(*Catching her hand and caressing it.*) I do not follow you. I hear your voice, but I do not know a word you say. Because I am loving your voice—and you. I am so filled with love that there is no room for anything else. And you, who yesterday were so remote and unattainable, are so near and possible, so immediately possible. All you have to do is to say the word, one little word. Say it.—Say it.

(*He carries her hand to his lips and holds it there.*)

Margaret

(*Wistfully.*) I should like to. I should like to. But I can't.

Knox

You must.

Margaret

There are other and greater things that say must to me. Oh, my dear, have you forgotten them? Things you yourself have spoken to me—the great stinging things of the spirit, that are greater than you and I, greater even than our love.

Knox

I exhaust my arguments—but still I love you.

Margaret

And I love you for it.

(*Chalmers enters from right, and sees Margaret still caressing Knox's hair.*)

Chalmers

(*With mild elation, touched with sarcasm.*) Ah, I see you have taken my advice, and reached a decision.

(*They do not answer. Margaret moves slowly away and seats herself.*) (*Knox remains with head bowed on hand.*) No?

(*Margaret shakes her head.*) Well, I've thought it over, and I've changed my terms. Madge, go with Knox, take Tommy with you.

(*Margaret wavers, but Knox, head bowed on hand, does not see her.*) There will be no scandal. I'll give you a proper divorce. And you can have Tommy.

Knox

(*Suddenly raising his head, joyfully, pleadingly.*) Margaret!

(*Margaret is swayed, but does not speak.*)

Chalmers

You and I never hit it off together any too extraordinarily well, Madge; but I'm not altogether a bad sort. I am easy-going. I always have been easy-going. I'll make everything easy for you now. But you see the fix I am in. You love another man, and I simply must regain those letters. It is more important than you realize.

Margaret

(*Incisively.*) You make me realize how important those letters are.

Knox

Give him the letters, Margaret

168

Chalmers

So she hasn't turned them over to you yet?

Margaret

No; I still have them.

Knox

Give them to him.

Chalmers

Selling out for a petticoat. A pretty reformer.

Knox

(*Proudly.*)

A better lover.

Margaret

(*To Chalmers.*)

He is weak to-day. What of it? He was strong last night. He will win back his strength again. It is human to be weak. And in his very weakness now, I have my pride, for it is the weakness of love. God knows I have been weak, and I am not ashamed of it. It was the weakness of love. It is hard to stifle one's womanhood always with morality. (*Quickly.*)

But do not mistake, Tom. This of mine is no conventional morality. I do not care about nasty gossipy tongues and sensation-mongering sheets; nor do I care what any persons of all the persons I know, would say if I went away with Mr. Knox this instant. I would go, and go gladly and proudly with him, divorce or no divorce, scandal or scandal triple-fold—if—if no one else were hurt by what I did. (*To Knox.*)

Howard, I tell you that I would go with you now, in all willingness and joy, with May-time and the songs of all singing birds in my heart—were it not for the others. But there is a higher morality. We must not hurt those others. We dare not steal our happiness from them. The future belongs to them, and we must not, dare not, sacrifice that future nor give it in pledge for our own happiness. Last night I came to you. I was weak—yes; more than that—I was ignorant. I did not know, even as late as last night, the monstrous vileness, the consummate wickedness of present-day conditions. I learned that today, this morning, and now. I learned that the morality of the Church was a pretense. Far deeper than it, and vastly more powerful, was the morality of the dollar. My father, my family, my husband, were willing to condone what they believed was my adultery. And for what? For a few scraps of paper that to them represented only the privilege to plunder, the privilege to steal from the people.

(*To Chalmers.*) Here are you, Tom, not only willing and eager to give me into the arms of the man you believe my lover, but you throw in your boy—your child and mine—to make it good measure and acceptable. And for what? Love of some woman?—any woman? No. Love of humanity? No. Love of God? No. Then for what? For the privilege of perpetuating your stealing from the people—money, bread and butter, hats, shoes, and stockings—for stealing all these things from the people.

(*To Knox.*) Now, and at last, do I realize how stern and awful is the fight that must be waged—the fight in which you and I, Howard, must play our parts and play them bravely and uncomplainingly—you as well as I, but I even more than you. This is the den of thieves. I am a child of thieves. All my family is composed of thieves. I have been fed and reared on the fruits of thievery. I have been a party to it all my life. Somebody must cease from this theft, and it is I. And you must help me, Howard.

Chalmers

(Emitting a low long whistle.) Strange that you never went into the suffragette business. With such speech-making ability you would have been a shining light.

Knox

(*Sadly.*) The worst of it is, Margaret, you are right. But it is hard that we cannot be happy save by stealing from the happiness of others. Yet it hurts, deep down and terribly, to forego you. (*Margaret thanks him with her eyes.*)

Chalmers

(*Sarcastically.*) Oh, believe me, I am not too anxious to give up my wife. Look at her. She's a pretty good woman for any man to possess.

Margaret

Tom, I'll accept a quiet divorce, marry Mr. Knox, and take Tommy with me—on one consideration.

Chalmers

And what is that?

Margaret

That I retain the letters. They are to be used in his speech this afternoon.

Chalmers

No they're not.

Margaret

Whatever happens, do whatever worst you can possibly do, that speech will be given this afternoon. Your worst to me will be none too great a price for me to pay.

Chalmers

No letters, no divorce, no Tommy, nothing.

Margaret

Then will you compel me to remain here. I have done nothing wrong, and I don't imagine you will make a scandal.

(*Enter Linda at right rear, pausing and looking inquiringly.*) There they are now.

(*To Linda.*) Yes; give them to me.

(*Linda, advancing, draws package of documents from her breast. As she is handing them to Margaret, Chalmers attempts to seise them.*)

Knox

(*Springing forward and thrusting Chalmers back.*) That you shall not!

171

(*Chalmers is afflicted with heart-seizure, and staggers.*)

Margaret

(*Maternally, solicitously.*) Tom, don't! Your heart! Be careful!

(*Chalmers starts to stagger toward bell*) Howard! Stop him! Don't let him ring, or the servants will get the letters away from us. (*Knox starts to interpose, but Chalmers, growing weaker, sinks into a chair, head thrown back and legs out straight before him.*) Linda, a glass of water.

(*Linda gives documents to Margaret, and makes running exit to right rear.*) (*Margaret bends anxiously over Chalmers.*) (*A pause.*)

Knox

(*Touching her hand.*) Give them to me.

(*Margaret gives him the documents, which he holds in his hand, at the same time she thanks him with her eyes.*) (*Enter Linda with glass of water, which she hands to Margaret.*) (*Margaret tries to place the glass to Chalmer's lips.*)

Chalmers

(*Dashing the glass violently from her hand to the floor and speaking in smothered voice.*) Bring me a whiskey and soda.

(*Linda looks at Margaret interrogatively. Margaret is undecided what to say, shrugs her shoulders in helplessness, and nods her head.*)

(*Linda makes hurried exit to right.*)

Margaret

(*To Knox.*) You will go now and you will give the speech.

Knox

(*Placing documents in inside coat pocket.*) I will give the speech.

Margaret

And all the forces making for the good time coming will be quickened by your words. Let the voices of the millions be in it.

(*Chalmers, legs still stretched out, laughs cynically.*)

172

You know where my heart lies. Some day, in all pride and honor, stealing from no one, hurting no one, we shall come together—to be together always.

Knox

(*Drearily.*) And in the meantime?

Margaret

We must wait

Knox

(*Decidedly.*) We will wait.

Chalmers

(*Straightening up.*) For me to die? eh?

(*During the following speech Linda enters from right with whiskey and soda and gives it to Chalmers, who thirstily drinks half of it. Margaret dismisses Linda with her eyes, and Linda makes exit to right rear.*)

Knox

I hadn't that in mind, but now that you mention it, it seems to the point. That heart of yours isn't going to carry you much farther. You have played fast and loose with it as with everything else. You are like the carter who steals hay from his horse that he may gamble. You have stolen from your heart. Some day, soon, like the horse, it will quit We can afford to wait. It won't be long.

Chalmers

(*After laughing incredulously and sipping his whiskey.*) Well, Knox, neither of us wins. You don't get the woman. Neither do I. She remains under my roof, and I fancy that is about all. I won't divorce her. What's the good? But I've got her tied hard and fast by Tommy. You won't get her.

(*Knox, ignoring hint, goes to right rear and pauses in doorway.*)

Margaret

Work. Bravely work. You are my knight. Go.

173

(*Knox makes exit.*)

(*Margaret stands quietly, face averted from audience and turned toward where Knox was last to be seen.*)

Chalmers

Madge.

(*Margaret neither moves nor answers.*) I say, Madge.

(*He stands up and moves toward her, holding whiskey glass in one hand.*) That speech is going to make a devil of a row. But I don't think it will be so bad as your father says. It looks pretty dark, but such things blow over. They always do blow over. And so with you and me. Maybe we can manage to forget all this and patch it up somehow.

(*She gives no sign that she is aware of his existence.*) Why don't you speak? (Pause.)

(He touches her arm.) Madge.

Margaret

(*Turning upon him in a blaze of wrath and with unutterable loathing.*)

Don't touch me!

(*Chalmers recoils.*)

Curtain

WHEN GOD LAUGHS AND
OTHER STORIES

WHEN GOD LAUGHS (with compliments to Harry Cowell)

"The gods, the gods are stronger; time
Falls down before them, all men's knees
Bow, all men's prayers and sorrows climb
Like incense toward them; yea, for these
Are gods, Felise."

Carquinez had relaxed finally. He stole a glance at the rattling windows, looked upward at the beamed roof, and listened for a moment to the savage roar of the south-easter as it caught the bungalow in its bellowing jaws. Then he held his glass between him and the fire and laughed for joy through the golden wine.

"It is beautiful," he said. "It is sweetly sweet. It is a woman's wine, and it was made for gray-robed saints to drink."

"We grow it on our own warm hills," I said, with pardonable California pride. "You rode up yesterday through the vines from which it was made."

It was worth while to get Carquinez to loosen up. Nor was he ever really himself until he felt the mellow warmth of the vine singing in his blood. He was an artist, it is true, always an artist; but somehow, sober, the high pitch and lilt went out of his thought-processes and he was prone to be as deadly dull as a British Sunday—not dull as other men are dull, but dull when measured by the sprightly wight that Monte Carquinez was when he was really himself.

From all this it must not be inferred that Carquinez, who is my dear friend and dearer comrade, was a sot. Far from it. He rarely erred. As I have said, he was an artist. He knew when he had enough, and enough, with him, was equilibrium—the equilibrium that is yours and mine when we are sober.

His was a wise and instinctive temperateness that savoured of the Greek. Yet he was far from Greek. "I am Aztec, I am Inca, I am Spaniard," I have heard him say. And in truth he looked it, a compound of strange and ancient races, what with his swarthy skin and the asymmetry and primitiveness of his features. His eyes, under massively arched brows, were wide apart and black with the blackness that is barbaric, while before them was perpetually falling down a great black mop of hair through which he gazed like a roguish satyr from a thicket. He invariably wore a soft flannel shirt under his velvet-corduroy jacket, and his necktie was red. This latter stood for the red flag (he had once lived with the socialists of Paris), and it symbolized the blood and brotherhood of man. Also, he had never been known to wear anything on his head save a leather-banded sombrero. It was even rumoured that he had been born with this particular piece of headgear. And in my experience it was provocative of nothing short of sheer delight to see that Mexican sombrero hailing a cab in Piccadilly or storm-tossed in the crush for the New York Elevated.

As I have said, Carquinez was made quick by wine—"as the clay was made quick when God breathed the breath of life into it," was his way of saying it. I confess that he was blasphemously intimate with God; and I must add that there was no blasphemy in him. He was at all times honest, and, because he was compounded of paradoxes, greatly misunderstood by those who did not know him. He could be as elementally raw at times as a screaming savage; and at other times as delicate as a maid, as subtle as a Spaniard. And—well, was he not Aztec? Inca? Spaniard?

And now I must ask pardon for the space I have given him. (He is my friend, and I love him.) The house was shaking to the storm, as he drew closer to the fire and laughed at it through his wine. He looked at me, and by the added lustre of his eye, and by the alertness of it, I knew that at last he was pitched in his proper key.

"And so you think you've won out against the gods?" he demanded.

"Why the gods?"

"Whose will but theirs has put satiety upon man?" he cried.

"And whence the will in me to escape satiety?" I asked triumphantly.

"Again the gods," he laughed. "It is their game we play. They deal and shuffle all the cards... and take the stakes. Think not that you have escaped by fleeing from the mad cities. You with your vine-clad hills, your sunsets and your sunrises, your homely fare and simple round of living!

"I've watched you ever since I came. You have not won. You have surrendered. You have made terms with the enemy. You have made confession that you are tired. You have flown the white flag of fatigue. You have nailed up a notice to the effect that life is ebbing down in you. You have run away from life. You have played a trick, shabby trick. You have balked at the game. You refuse to play. You have thrown your cards under the table and run away to hide, here amongst your hills."

He tossed his straight hair back from his flashing eyes, and scarcely interrupted to roll a long, brown, Mexican cigarette.

"But the gods know. It is an old trick. All the generations of man have tried it... and lost. The gods know how to deal with such as you. To pursue is to possess, and to possess is to be sated. And so you, in your wisdom, have refused any longer to pursue. You have elected surcease. Very well. You will become sated with surcease. You say you have escaped satiety! You have merely bartered it for senility. And senility is another name for satiety. It is satiety's masquerade. Bah!"

"But look at me!" I cried.

Carquinez was ever a demon for haling ones soul out and making rags and tatters of it.

He looked me witheringly up and down.

"You see no signs," I challenged.

"Decay is insidious," he retorted. "You are rotten ripe."

181

I laughed and forgave him for his very deviltry. But he refused to be forgiven.

"Do I not know?" he asked. "The gods always win. I have watched men play for years what seemed a winning game. In the end they lost."

"Don't you ever make mistakes?" I asked.

He blew many meditative rings of smoke before replying.

"Yes, I was nearly fooled, once. Let me tell you. There was Marvin Fiske. You remember him? And his Dantesque face and poet's soul, singing his chant of the flesh, the very priest of Love? And there was Ethel Baird, whom also you must remember."

"A warm saint," I said.

"That is she! Holy as Love, and sweeter! Just a woman, made for love; and yet—how shall I say?—drenched through with holiness as your own air here is with the perfume of flowers. Well, they married. They played a hand with the gods—"

"And they won, they gloriously won!" I broke in.

Carquinez looked at me pityingly, and his voice was like a funeral bell.

"They lost. They supremely, colossally lost."

"But the world believes otherwise," I ventured coldly.

"The world conjectures. The world sees only the face of things. But I know. Has it ever entered your mind to wonder why she took the veil, buried herself in that dolorous convent of the living dead?"

"Because she loved him so, and when he died..."

Speech was frozen on my lips by Carquinez's sneer.

"A pat answer," he said, "machine-made like a piece of cotton-drill. The world's judgment! And much the world knows about it. Like you, she fled from life. She was beaten. She flung out the white flag of fatigue. And no beleaguered city ever flew that flag in such bitterness and tears.

"Now I shall tell you the whole tale, and you must believe me, for I know. They had pondered the problem of satiety. They loved Love. They knew to the uttermost farthing the value of Love. They loved him so well that they were fain to keep him always, warm and a-thrill in their hearts. They welcomed his coming; they feared to have him depart.

"Love was desire, they held, a delicious pain. He was ever seeking easement, and when he found that for which he sought, he died. Love denied was Love alive; Love granted was Love deceased. Do you follow me? They saw it was not the way of life to be hungry for what it has. To eat and still be hungry—man has never accomplished that feat. The problem of satiety. That is it. To have and to keep the sharp famine-edge of appetite at the groaning board. This was their problem, for they loved Love. Often did they discuss it, with all Love's sweet ardours brimming in their eyes; his ruddy blood spraying their cheeks; his voice playing in and out with their voices, now hiding as a tremolo in their throats, and again shading a tone with that ineffable tenderness which he alone can utter.

"How do I know all this? I saw—much. More I learned from her diary. This I found in it, from Fiona Macleod: 'For, truly, that wandering voice, that twilight-whisper, that breath so dewy-sweet, that flame-winged lute-player whom none sees but for a moment, in a rainbow-shimmer of joy, or a sudden lightning-flare of passion, this exquisite mystery we call Amor, comes, to some rapt visionaries at least, not with a song upon the lips that all may hear, or with blithe viol of public music, but as one wrought by ecstasy, dumbly eloquent with desire.'

"How to keep the flame-winged lute-player with his dumb eloquence of desire? To feast him was to lose him. Their love for each other was a great love. Their granaries were overflowing with plenitude; yet they wanted to keep the sharp famine-edge of their love undulled.

"Nor were they lean little fledglings theorizing on the threshold of Love. They were robust and realized souls. They had loved before, with others, in the days before they met; and in those days they had throttled Love with caresses, and killed him with kisses, and buried him in the pit of satiety.

"They were not cold wraiths, this man and woman. They were warm human. They had no Saxon soberness in their blood. The colour of it was sunset-red. They glowed with it. Temperamentally theirs was the French joy in the flesh. They were idealists, but their idealism was Gallic. It was not tempered by the chill and sombre fluid that for the English serves as blood. There was no stoicism about them. They were Americans, descended out of the English, and yet the refraining and self-denying of the English spirit-groping were not theirs.

"They were all this that I have said, and they were made for joy, only they achieved a concept. A curse on concepts! They played with logic, and this was their logic.—But first let me tell you of a talk we had one night. It was of Gautier's Madeline de Maupin. You remember the maid? She kissed once, and once only, and kisses she would have no more. Not that she found kisses were not sweet, but that she feared with repetition they would cloy. Satiety again! She tried to play without stakes against the gods. Now this is contrary to a rule of the game the gods themselves have made. Only the rules are not posted over the table. Mortals must play in order to learn the rules.

"Well, to the logic. The man and the woman argued thus: Why kiss once only? If to kiss once were wise, was it not wiser to kiss not at all? Thus could they keep Love alive. Fasting, he would knock forever at their hearts.

"Perhaps it was out of their heredity that they achieved this unholy concept. The breed will out and sometimes most fantastically. Thus in them did cursed Albion array herself a scheming wanton, a bold, cold-calculating, and artful hussy. After all, I do not know. But this I know: it was out of their inordinate desire for joy that they forewent joy.

"As he said (I read it long afterward in one of his letters to her): 'To hold you in my arms, close, and yet not close. To yearn for you, and never to have you, and so always to have you.' And she: 'For you to be always just beyond my reach. To be ever attaining you, and yet never attaining you, and for this to last forever, always fresh and new, and always with the first flush upon us.

"That is not the way they said it. On my lips their love-philosophy is mangled. And who am I to delve into their soul-stuff? I am a frog, on the dank edge of a great darkness, gazing goggle-eyed at the mystery and wonder of their flaming souls.

"And they were right, as far as they went. Everything is good... as long as it is unpossessed. Satiety and possession are Death's horses; they run in span.

"'And time could only tutor us to eke

Our rapture's warmth with custom's afterglow.'

"They got that from a sonnet of Alfred Austin's. It was called 'Love's Wisdom.' It was the one kiss of Madeline de Maupin. How did it run?

"'Kiss we and part; no further can we go;

And better death than we from high to low

Should dwindle, or decline from strong to weak.'

"But they were wiser. They would not kiss and part. They would not kiss at all, and thus they planned to stay at Love's topmost peak. They married. You were in England at the time. And never was there such a marriage. They kept their secret to themselves. I did not know, then. Their rapture's warmth did not cool. Their love burned with increasing brightness. Never was there anything like it. The time passed, the months, the years, and ever the flame-winged lute-player grew more resplendent.

"Everybody marvelled. They became the wonderful lovers, and they were greatly envied. Sometimes women pitied her because she was childless; it is the form the envy of such creatures takes.

"And I did not know their secret. I pondered and I marvelled. As first I had expected, subconsciously I imagine, the passing of their love. Then I became aware that it was Time that passed and Love that remained. Then I became curious. What was their secret? What were the magic fetters with which they bound Love to them? How did they hold the graceless elf? What elixir of eternal love had they drunk together as had Tristram and Iseult of old time? And whose hand had brewed the fairy drink?

"As I say, I was curious, and I watched them. They were love-mad. They lived in an unending revel of Love. They made a pomp and ceremonial of it. They saturated themselves in the art and poetry of Love. No, they were not neurotics. They were sane and healthy, and they were artists. But they had accomplished the impossible. They had achieved deathless desire.

"And I? I saw much of them and their everlasting miracle of Love. I puzzled and wondered, and then one day—"

Carquinez broke off abruptly and asked, "Have you ever read, 'Love's Waiting Time'?"

I shook my head.

"Page wrote it—Curtis Hidden Page, I think. Well, it was that bit of verse that gave me the clue. One day, in the window-seat near the big piano— you remember how she could play? She used to laugh, sometimes, and doubt whether it was for them I came, or for the music. She called me a 'music-sot' once, a 'sound-debauchee.' What a voice he had! When he sang I believed in immortality, my regard for the gods grew almost patronizing and I devised ways and means whereby I surely could outwit them and their tricks.

"It was a spectacle for God, that man and woman, years married, and singing love-songs with a freshness virginal as new-born Love himself, with a ripeness and wealth of ardour that young lovers can never know. Young lovers were pale and anaemic beside that long-married pair. To see them, all fire and flame and tenderness, at a trembling distance, lavishing caresses of eye and voice with every action, through every silence—their love driving them toward each other, and they withholding like fluttering moths, each to the other a candle-flame, and revolving each about the other in the mad gyrations of an amazing orbit-flight! It seemed, in obedience to some great law of physics, more potent than gravitation and more subtle, that they must corporeally melt each into each there before my very eyes. Small wonder they were called the wonderful lovers.

"I have wandered. Now to the clue. One day in the window-seat I found a book of verse. It opened of itself, betraying long habit, to 'Love's Waiting Time.' The page was thumbed and limp with overhandling, and there I read:—

> *"So sweet it is to stand but just apart,*
>
> *To know each other better, and to keep*
>
> *The soft, delicious sense of two that touch...*
>
> *O love, not yet!... Sweet, let us keep our love*
>
>
> *Wrapped round with sacred mystery awhile,*
>
> *Waiting the secret of the coming years,*
>
> *That come not yet, not yet... sometime...*
>
> > *not yet...*
>
>
> *Oh, yet a little while our love may grow!*
>
> *When it has blossomed it will haply die.*
>
> *Feed it with lipless kisses, let it sleep,*
>
> *Bedded in dead denial yet some while...*
>
> *Oh, yet a little while, a little while.'*

"I folded the book on my thumb and sat there silent and without moving for a long time. I was stunned by the clearness of vision the verse had imparted to me. It was illumination. It was like a bolt of God's lightning in the Pit. They would keep Love, the fickle sprite, the forerunner of young life—young life that is imperative to be born!

"I conned the lines over in my mind—'Not yet, sometime'—'O Love, not yet'—'Feed it with lipless kisses, let it sleep.' And I laughed aloud, ha, ha! I saw with white vision their blameless souls. They were children. They did not understand. They played with Nature's fire and bedded with a naked sword. They laughed at the gods. They would stop the cosmic sap. They had invented a system, and brought it to the gaming-table of life, and expected to win out. 'Beware!' I cried. 'The gods are behind the table. They make new rules for every system that is devised. You have no chance to win.'

"But I did not so cry to them. I waited. They would learn that their system was worthless and throw it away. They would be content with whatever happiness the gods gave them and not strive to wrest more away.

"I watched. I said nothing. The months continued to come and go, and still the famine-edge of their love grew the sharper. Never did they dull it with a permitted love-clasp. They ground and whetted it on self-denial, and sharper and sharper it grew. This went on until even I doubted. Did the gods sleep? I wondered. Or were they dead? I laughed to myself. The man and the woman had made a miracle. They had outwitted God. They had shamed the flesh, and blackened the face of the good Earth Mother. They had played with her fire and not been burned. They were immune. They were themselves gods, knowing good from evil and tasting not. 'Was this the way gods came to be?' I asked myself. 'I am a frog,' I said. 'But for my mud-lidded eyes I should have been blinded by the brightness of this wonder I have witnessed. I have puffed myself up with my wisdom and passed judgment upon gods.'

"Yet even in this, my latest wisdom, I was wrong. They were not gods. They were man and woman—soft clay that sighed and thrilled, shot through with desire, thumbed with strange weaknesses which the gods have not."

Carquinez broke from his narrative to roll another cigarette and to laugh harshly. It was not a pretty laugh; it was like the mockery of a devil, and it rose over and rode the roar of the storm that came muffled to our ears from the crashing outside world.

"I am a frog," he said apologetically. "How were they to understand? They were artists, not biologists. They knew the clay of the studio, but they did not know the clay of which they themselves were made. But this I will say—they played high. Never was there such a game before, and I doubt me if there will ever be such a game again.

"Never was lovers' ecstasy like theirs. They had not killed Love with kisses. They had quickened him with denial. And by denial they drove him on till he was all aburst with desire. And the flame-winged lute-player fanned them with his warm wings till they were all but swooning. It was the very delirium of Love, and it continued undiminished and increasing through the weeks and months.

"They longed and yearned, with all the fond pangs and sweet delicious agonies, with an intensity never felt by lovers before nor since.

"And then one day the drowsy gods ceased nodding. They aroused and looked at the man and woman who had made a mock of them. And the man and woman looked into each other's eyes one morning and knew that something was gone. It was the flame-winged one. He had fled, silently, in the night, from their anchorites' board.

"They looked into each other's eyes and knew that they did not care. Desire was dead. Do you understand? Desire was dead. And they had never kissed. Not once had they kissed. Love was gone. They would never yearn and burn again. For them there was nothing left—no more tremblings and flutterings and delicious anguishes, no more throbbing and pulsing, and sighing and song. Desire was dead. It had died in the night, on a couch cold and unattended; nor had they witnessed its passing. They learned it for the first time in each other's eyes.

"The gods may not be kind, but they are often merciful. They had twirled the little ivory ball and swept the stakes from the table. All that remained was the man and woman gazing into each other's cold eyes. And then he died. That was the mercy. Within the week Marvin Fiske was dead—you remember the accident. And in her diary, written at this time, I long afterward read Mitchell Kennerly's:—

"'There was not a single hour

We might have kissed and did not kiss.'"

"Oh, the irony of it!" I cried out.

And Carquinez, in the firelight a veritable Mephistopheles in velvet jacket, fixed me with his black eyes.

"And they won, you said? The world's judgment! I have told you, and I know. They won as you are winning, here in your hills."

"But you," I demanded hotly; "you with your orgies of sound and sense, with your mad cities and madder frolics—bethink you that you win?"

He shook his head slowly. "Because you with your sober bucolic regime, lose, is no reason that I should win. We never win. Sometimes we think we win. That is a little pleasantry of the gods."

THE APOSTATE

"Now I wake me up to work;

I pray the Lord I may not shirk.

If I should die before the night,

I pray the Lord my work's all right.

Amen."

"If you don't git up, Johnny, I won't give you a bite to eat!"

The threat had no effect on the boy. He clung stubbornly to sleep, fighting for its oblivion as the dreamer fights for his dream. The boy's hands loosely clenched themselves, and he made feeble, spasmodic blows at the air. These blows were intended for his mother, but she betrayed practised familiarity in avoiding them as she shook him roughly by the shoulder.

"Lemme 'lone!"

It was a cry that began, muffled, in the deeps of sleep, that swiftly rushed upward, like a wail, into passionate belligerence, and that died away and sank down into an inarticulate whine. It was a bestial cry, as of a soul in torment, filled with infinite protest and pain.

But she did not mind. She was a sad-eyed, tired-faced woman, and she had grown used to this task, which she repeated every day of her life. She got a grip on the bedclothes and tried to strip them down; but the boy, ceasing his punching, clung to them desperately. In a huddle, at the foot of the bed, he still remained covered. Then she tried dragging the bedding to the floor. The boy opposed her. She braced herself. Hers was the superior weight, and the boy and bedding gave, the former instinctively following the latter in order to shelter against the chill of the room that bit into his body.

As he toppled on the edge of the bed it seemed that he must fall head-first to the floor. But consciousness fluttered up in him. He righted himself and for a moment perilously balanced. Then he struck the floor on his feet. On the instant his mother seized him by the shoulders and shook him. Again his fists struck out, this time with more force and directness. At the same time his eyes opened. She released him. He was awake.

"All right," he mumbled.

She caught up the lamp and hurried out, leaving him in darkness.

"You'll be docked," she warned back to him.

He did not mind the darkness. When he had got into his clothes, he went out into the kitchen. His tread was very heavy for so thin and light a boy. His legs dragged with their own weight, which seemed unreasonable because they were such skinny legs. He drew a broken-bottomed chair to the table.

"Johnny," his mother called sharply.

He arose as sharply from the chair, and, without a word, went to the sink. It was a greasy, filthy sink. A smell came up from the outlet. He took no notice of it. That a sink should smell was to him part of the natural order, just as it was a part of the natural order that the soap should be grimy with dish-water and hard to lather. Nor did he try very hard to make it lather. Several splashes of the cold water from the running faucet completed the function. He did not wash his teeth. For that matter he had never seen a toothbrush, nor did he know that there existed beings in the world who were guilty of so great a foolishness as tooth washing.

"You might wash yourself wunst a day without bein' told," his mother complained.

She was holding a broken lid on the pot as she poured two cups of coffee. He made no remark, for this was a standing quarrel between them, and the one thing upon which his mother was hard as adamant. "Wunst" a day it was compulsory that he should wash his face. He dried himself on a greasy towel, damp and dirty and ragged, that left his face covered with shreds of lint.

"I wish we didn't live so far away," she said, as he sat down. "I try to do the best I can. You know that. But a dollar on the rent is such a savin', an' we've more room here. You know that."

He scarcely followed her. He had heard it all before, many times. The range of her thought was limited, and she was ever harking back to the hardship worked upon them by living so far from the mills.

"A dollar means more grub," he remarked sententiously. "I'd sooner do the walkin' an' git the grub."

He ate hurriedly, half chewing the bread and washing the unmasticated chunks down with coffee. The hot and muddy liquid went by the name of coffee. Johnny thought it was coffee—and excellent coffee. That was one of the few of life's illusions that remained to him. He had never drunk real coffee in his life.

In addition to the bread, there was a small piece of cold pork. His mother refilled his cup with coffee. As he was finishing the bread, he began to watch if more was forthcoming. She intercepted his questioning glance.

"Now, don't be hoggish, Johnny," was her comment. "You've had your share. Your brothers an' sisters are smaller'n you."

He did not answer the rebuke. He was not much of a talker. Also, he ceased his hungry glancing for more. He was uncomplaining, with a patience that was as terrible as the school in which it had been learned. He finished his coffee, wiped his mouth on the back of his hand, and started to rise.

"Wait a second," she said hastily. "I guess the loaf kin stand you another slice—a thin un."

There was legerdemain in her actions. With all the seeming of cutting a slice from the loaf for him, she put loaf and slice back in the bread box and conveyed to him one of her own two slices. She believed she had deceived him, but he had noted her sleight-of-hand. Nevertheless, he took the bread shamelessly. He had a philosophy that his mother, because of her chronic sickliness, was not much of an eater anyway.

She saw that he was chewing the bread dry, and reached over and emptied her coffee cup into his.

"Don't set good somehow on my stomach this morning," she explained.

A distant whistle, prolonged and shrieking, brought both of them to their feet. She glanced at the tin alarm-clock on the shelf. The hands stood at half-past five. The rest of the factory world was just arousing from sleep. She drew a shawl about her shoulders, and on her head put a dingy hat, shapeless and ancient.

"We've got to run," she said, turning the wick of the lamp and blowing down the chimney.

They groped their way out and down the stairs. It was clear and cold, and Johnny shivered at the first contact with the outside air. The stars had not yet begun to pale in the sky, and the city lay in blackness. Both Johnny and his mother shuffled their feet as they walked. There was no ambition in the leg muscles to swing the feet clear of the ground.

After fifteen silent minutes, his mother turned off to the right.

"Don't be late," was her final warning from out of the dark that was swallowing her up.

He made no response, steadily keeping on his way. In the factory quarter, doors were opening everywhere, and he was soon one of a multitude that pressed onward through the dark. As he entered the factory gate the whistle blew again. He glanced at the east. Across a ragged sky-line of housetops a pale light was beginning to creep. This much he saw of the day as he turned his back upon it and joined his work gang.

He took his place in one of many long rows of machines. Before him, above a bin filled with small bobbins, were large bobbins revolving rapidly. Upon these he wound the jute-twine of the small bobbins. The work was simple. All that was required was celerity. The small bobbins were emptied so rapidly, and there were so many large bobbins that did the emptying, that there were no idle moments.

He worked mechanically. When a small bobbin ran out, he used his left hand for a brake, stopping the large bobbin and at the same time, with thumb and forefinger, catching the flying end of twine. Also, at the same time, with his right hand, he caught up the loose twine-end of a small bobbin. These various acts with both hands were performed simultaneously and swiftly. Then there would come a flash of his hands as he looped the weaver's knot and released the bobbin. There was nothing difficult about weaver's knots. He once boasted he could tie them in his sleep. And for that matter, he sometimes did, toiling centuries long in a single night at tying an endless succession of weaver's knots.

Some of the boys shirked, wasting time and machinery by not replacing the small bobbins when they ran out. And there was an overseer to prevent this. He caught Johnny's neighbour at the trick, and boxed his ears.

"Look at Johnny there—why ain't you like him?" the overseer wrathfully demanded.

Johnny's bobbins were running full blast, but he did not thrill at the indirect praise. There had been a time... but that was long ago, very long ago. His apathetic face was expressionless as he listened to himself being held up as a shining example. He was the perfect worker. He knew that. He had been told so, often. It was a commonplace, and besides it didn't seem to mean anything to him any more. From the perfect worker he had evolved into the perfect machine. When his work went wrong, it was with him as with the machine, due to faulty material. It would have been as possible for a perfect nail-die to cut imperfect nails as for him to make a mistake.

And small wonder. There had never been a time when he had not been in intimate relationship with machines. Machinery had almost been bred into him, and at any rate he had been brought up on it. Twelve years before, there had been a small flutter of excitement in the loom room of this very mill. Johnny's mother had fainted. They stretched her out on the floor in the midst of the shrieking machines. A couple of elderly women were called from their looms. The foreman assisted. And in a few minutes there was one more soul in the loom room than had entered by the doors. It was Johnny, born with the pounding, crashing roar of the looms in his ears, drawing with his first breath the warm, moist air that was thick with flying lint. He had coughed that first day in order to rid his lungs of the lint; and for the same reason he had coughed ever since.

The boy alongside of Johnny whimpered and sniffed. The boy's face was convulsed with hatred for the overseer who kept a threatening eye on him from a distance; but every bobbin was running full. The boy yelled terrible oaths into the whirling bobbins before him; but the sound did not carry half a dozen feet, the roaring of the room holding it in and containing it like a wall.

Of all this Johnny took no notice. He had a way of accepting things. Besides, things grow monotonous by repetition, and this particular happening he had witnessed many times. It seemed to him as useless to oppose the overseer as to defy the will of a machine. Machines were made to go in certain ways and to perform certain tasks. It was the same with the overseer.

But at eleven o'clock there was excitement in the room. In an apparently occult way the excitement instantly permeated everywhere. The one-legged boy who worked on the other side of Johnny bobbed swiftly across the floor to a bin truck that stood empty. Into this he dived out of sight, crutch and all. The superintendent of the mill was coming along, accompanied by a young man. He was well dressed and wore a starched shirt—a gentleman, in Johnny's classification of men, and also, "the Inspector."

He looked sharply at the boys as he passed along. Sometimes he stopped and asked questions. When he did so, he was compelled to shout at the top of his lungs, at which moments his face was ludicrously contorted with the strain of making himself heard. His quick eye noted the empty machine alongside of Johnny's, but he said nothing. Johnny also caught his eye, and he stopped abruptly. He caught Johnny by the arm to draw him back a step from the machine; but with an exclamation of surprise he released the arm.

"Pretty skinny," the superintendent laughed anxiously.

"Pipe stems," was the answer. "Look at those legs. The boy's got the rickets—incipient, but he's got them. If epilepsy doesn't get him in the end, it will be because tuberculosis gets him first."

Johnny listened, but did not understand. Furthermore he was not interested in future ills. There was an immediate and more serious ill that threatened him in the form of the inspector.

"Now, my boy, I want you to tell me the truth," the inspector said, or shouted, bending close to the boy's ear to make him hear. "How old are you?"

"Fourteen," Johnny lied, and he lied with the full force of his lungs. So loudly did he lie that it started him off in a dry, hacking cough that lifted the lint which had been settling in his lungs all morning.

"Looks sixteen at least," said the superintendent.

"Or sixty," snapped the inspector.

"He's always looked that way."

"How long?" asked the inspector, quickly.

"For years. Never gets a bit older."

"Or younger, I dare say. I suppose he's worked here all those years?"

"Off and on—but that was before the new law was passed," the superintendent hastened to add.

"Machine idle?" the inspector asked, pointing at the unoccupied machine beside Johnny's, in which the part-filled bobbins were flying like mad.

"Looks that way." The superintendent motioned the overseer to him and shouted in his ear and pointed at the machine. "Machine's idle," he reported back to the inspector.

They passed on, and Johnny returned to his work, relieved in that the ill had been averted. But the one-legged boy was not so fortunate. The sharp-eyed inspector haled him out at arms length from the bin truck. His lips were quivering, and his face had all the expression of one upon whom was fallen profound and irremediable disaster. The overseer looked astounded, as though for the first time he had laid eyes on the boy, while the superintendent's face expressed shock and displeasure.

"I know him," the inspector said. "He's twelve years old. I've had him discharged from three factories inside the year. This makes the fourth."

He turned to the one-legged boy. "You promised me, word and honour, that you'd go to school."

The one-legged boy burst into tears. "Please, Mr. Inspector, two babies died on us, and we're awful poor."

"What makes you cough that way?" the inspector demanded, as though charging him with crime.

And as in denial of guilt, the one-legged boy replied: "It ain't nothin'. I jes' caught a cold last week, Mr. Inspector, that's all."

In the end the one-legged boy went out of the room with the inspector, the latter accompanied by the anxious and protesting superintendent. After that monotony settled down again. The long morning and the longer afternoon wore away and the whistle blew for quitting time. Darkness had already fallen when Johnny passed out through the factory gate. In the interval the sun had made a golden ladder of the sky, flooded the world with its gracious warmth, and dropped down and disappeared in the west behind a ragged sky-line of housetops.

Supper was the family meal of the day—the one meal at which Johnny encountered his younger brothers and sisters. It partook of the nature of an encounter, to him, for he was very old, while they were distressingly young. He had no patience with their excessive and amazing juvenility. He did not understand it. His own childhood was too far behind him. He was like an old and irritable man, annoyed by the turbulence of their young spirits that was to him arrant silliness. He glowered silently over his food, finding compensation in the thought that they would soon have to go to work. That would take the edge off of them and make them sedate and dignified—like him. Thus it was, after the fashion of the human, that Johnny made of himself a yardstick with which to measure the universe.

During the meal, his mother explained in various ways and with infinite repetition that she was trying to do the best she could; so that it was with relief, the scant meal ended, that Johnny shoved back his chair and arose. He debated for a moment between bed and the front door, and finally went out the latter. He did not go far. He sat down on the stoop, his knees drawn up and his narrow shoulders drooping forward, his elbows on his knees and the palms of his hands supporting his chin.

As he sat there, he did no thinking. He was just resting. So far as his mind was concerned, it was asleep. His brothers and sisters came out, and with other children played noisily about him. An electric globe at the corner lighted their frolics. He was peevish and irritable, that they knew; but the spirit of adventure lured them into teasing him. They joined hands before him, and, keeping time with their bodies, chanted in his face weird and uncomplimentary doggerel. At first he snarled curses at them—curses he had learned from the lips of various foremen. Finding this futile, and remembering his dignity, he relapsed into dogged silence.

His brother Will, next to him in age, having just passed his tenth birthday, was the ringleader. Johnny did not possess particularly kindly feelings toward him. His life had early been embittered by continual giving over and giving way to Will. He had a definite feeling that Will was greatly in his debt and was ungrateful about it. In his own playtime, far back in the dim past, he had been robbed of a large part of that playtime by being compelled to take care of Will. Will was a baby then, and then, as now, their mother had spent her days in the mills. To Johnny had fallen the part of little father and little mother as well.

Will seemed to show the benefit of the giving over and the giving way. He was well-built, fairly rugged, as tall as his elder brother and even heavier. It was as though the life-blood of the one had been diverted into the other's veins. And in spirits it was the same. Johnny was jaded, worn out, without resilience, while his younger brother seemed bursting and spilling over with exuberance.

The mocking chant rose louder and louder. Will leaned closer as he danced, thrusting out his tongue. Johnny's left arm shot out and caught the other around the neck. At the same time he rapped his bony fist to the other's nose. It was a pathetically bony fist, but that it was sharp to hurt was evidenced by the squeal of pain it produced. The other children were uttering frightened cries, while Johnny's sister, Jennie, had dashed into the house.

He thrust Will from him, kicked him savagely on the shins, then reached for him and slammed him face downward in the dirt. Nor did he release him till the face had been rubbed into the dirt several times. Then the mother arrived, an anaemic whirlwind of solicitude and maternal wrath.

"Why can't he leave me alone?" was Johnny's reply to her upbraiding. "Can't he see I'm tired?"

"I'm as big as you," Will raged in her arms, his face a mass of tears, dirt, and blood. "I'm as big as you now, an' I'm goin' to git bigger. Then I'll lick you—see if I don't."

"You ought to be to work, seein' how big you are," Johnny snarled. "That's what's the matter with you. You ought to be to work. An' it's up to your ma to put you to work."

"But he's too young," she protested. "He's only a little boy."

"I was younger'n him when I started to work."

Johnny's mouth was open, further to express the sense of unfairness that he felt, but the mouth closed with a snap. He turned gloomily on his heel and stalked into the house and to bed. The door of his room was open to let in warmth from the kitchen. As he undressed in the semi-darkness he could hear his mother talking with a neighbour woman who had dropped in. His mother was crying, and her speech was punctuated with spiritless sniffles.

"I can't make out what's gittin' into Johnny," he could hear her say. "He didn't used to be this way. He was a patient little angel.

"An' he is a good boy," she hastened to defend. "He's worked faithful, an' he did go to work too young. But it wasn't my fault. I do the best I can, I'm sure."

Prolonged sniffling from the kitchen, and Johnny murmured to himself as his eyelids closed down, "You betcher life I've worked faithful."

The next morning he was torn bodily by his mother from the grip of sleep. Then came the meagre breakfast, the tramp through the dark, and the pale glimpse of day across the housetops as he turned his back on it and went in through the factory gate. It was another day, of all the days, and all the days were alike.

And yet there had been variety in his life—at the times he changed from one job to another, or was taken sick. When he was six, he was little mother and father to Will and the other children still younger. At seven he went into the mills—winding bobbins. When he was eight, he got work in another mill. His new job was marvellously easy. All he had to do was to sit down with a little stick in his hand and guide a stream of cloth that flowed past him. This stream of cloth came out of the maw of a machine, passed over a hot roller, and went on its way elsewhere. But he sat always in one place, beyond the reach of daylight, a gas-jet flaring over him, himself part of the mechanism.

He was very happy at that job, in spite of the moist heat, for he was still young and in possession of dreams and illusions. And wonderful dreams he dreamed as he watched the steaming cloth streaming endlessly by. But there was no exercise about the work, no call upon his mind, and he dreamed less and less, while his mind grew torpid and drowsy. Nevertheless, he earned two dollars a week, and two dollars represented the difference between acute starvation and chronic underfeeding.

But when he was nine, he lost his job. Measles was the cause of it. After he recovered, he got work in a glass factory. The pay was better, and the work demanded skill. It was piecework, and the more skilful he was, the bigger wages he earned. Here was incentive. And under this incentive he developed into a remarkable worker.

It was simple work, the tying of glass stoppers into small bottles. At his waist he carried a bundle of twine. He held the bottles between his knees so that he might work with both hands. Thus, in a sitting position and bending over his own knees, his narrow shoulders grew humped and his chest was contracted for ten hours each day. This was not good for the lungs, but he tied three hundred dozen bottles a day.

The superintendent was very proud of him, and brought visitors to look at him. In ten hours three hundred dozen bottles passed through his hands. This meant that he had attained machine-like perfection. All waste movements were eliminated. Every motion of his thin arms, every movement of a muscle in the thin fingers, was swift and accurate. He worked at high tension, and the result was that he grew nervous. At night his muscles twitched in his sleep, and in the daytime he could not relax and rest. He remained keyed up and his muscles continued to twitch. Also he grew sallow and his lint-cough grew worse. Then pneumonia laid hold of the feeble lungs within the contracted chest, and he lost his job in the glass-works.

Now he had returned to the jute mills where he had first begun with winding bobbins. But promotion was waiting for him. He was a good worker. He would next go on the starcher, and later he would go into the loom room. There was nothing after that except increased efficiency.

The machinery ran faster than when he had first gone to work, and his mind ran slower. He no longer dreamed at all, though his earlier years had been full of dreaming. Once he had been in love. It was when he first began guiding the cloth over the hot roller, and it was with the daughter of the superintendent. She was much older than he, a young woman, and he had seen her at a distance only a paltry half-dozen times. But that made no difference. On the surface of the cloth stream that poured past him, he pictured radiant futures wherein he performed prodigies of toil, invented miraculous machines, won to the mastership of the mills, and in the end took her in his arms and kissed her soberly on the brow.

But that was all in the long ago, before he had grown too old and tired to love. Also, she had married and gone away, and his mind had gone to sleep. Yet it had been a wonderful experience, and he used often to look back upon it as other men and women look back upon the time they believed in fairies. He had never believed in fairies nor Santa Claus; but he had believed implicitly in the smiling future his imagination had wrought into the steaming cloth stream.

He had become a man very early in life. At seven, when he drew his first wages, began his adolescence. A certain feeling of independence crept up in him, and the relationship between him and his mother changed. Somehow, as an earner and breadwinner, doing his own work in the world, he was more like an equal with her. Manhood, full-blown manhood, had come when he was eleven, at which time he had gone to work on the night shift for six months. No child works on the night shift and remains a child.

There had been several great events in his life. One of these had been when his mother bought some California prunes. Two others had been the two times when she cooked custard. Those had been events. He remembered them kindly. And at that time his mother had told him of a blissful dish she would sometime make—"floating island," she had called it, "better than custard." For years he had looked forward to the day when he would sit down to the table with floating island before him, until at last he had relegated the idea of it to the limbo of unattainable ideals.

Once he found a silver quarter lying on the sidewalk. That, also, was a great event in his life, withal a tragic one. He knew his duty on the instant the silver flashed on his eyes, before even he had picked it up. At home, as usual, there was not enough to eat, and home he should have taken it as he did his wages every Saturday night. Right conduct in this case was obvious; but he never had any spending of his money, and he was suffering from candy hunger. He was ravenous for the sweets that only on red-letter days he had ever tasted in his life.

He did not attempt to deceive himself. He knew it was sin, and deliberately he sinned when he went on a fifteen-cent candy debauch. Ten cents he saved for a future orgy; but not being accustomed to the carrying of money, he lost the ten cents. This occurred at the time when he was suffering all the torments of conscience, and it was to him an act of divine retribution. He had a frightened sense of the closeness of an awful and wrathful God. God had seen, and God had been swift to punish, denying him even the full wages of sin.

In memory he always looked back upon that as the one great criminal deed of his life, and at the recollection his conscience always awoke and gave him another twinge. It was the one skeleton in his closet. Also, being so made, and circumstanced, he looked back upon the deed with regret. He was dissatisfied with the manner in which he had spent the quarter. He could have invested it better, and, out of his later knowledge of the quickness of God, he would have beaten God out by spending the whole quarter at one fell swoop. In retrospect he spent the quarter a thousand times, and each time to better advantage.

There was one other memory of the past, dim and faded, but stamped into his soul everlasting by the savage feet of his father. It was more like a nightmare than a remembered vision of a concrete thing—more like the race-memory of man that makes him fall in his sleep and that goes back to his arboreal ancestry.

This particular memory never came to Johnny in broad daylight when he was wide awake. It came at night, in bed, at the moment that his consciousness was sinking down and losing itself in sleep. It always aroused him to frightened wakefulness, and for the moment, in the first sickening start, it seemed to him that he lay crosswise on the foot of the bed. In the bed were the vague forms of his father and mother. He never saw what his father looked like. He had but one impression of his father, and that was that he had savage and pitiless feet.

His earlier memories lingered with him, but he had no late memories. All days were alike. Yesterday or last year were the same as a thousand years— or a minute. Nothing ever happened. There were no events to mark the march of time. Time did not march. It stood always still. It was only the whirling machines that moved, and they moved nowhere—in spite of the fact that they moved faster.

When he was fourteen, he went to work on the starcher. It was a colossal event. Something had at last happened that could be remembered beyond a night's sleep or a week's pay-day. It marked an era. It was a machine Olympiad, a thing to date from. "When I went to work on the starcher," or, "after," or "before I went to work on the starcher," were sentences often on his lips.

He celebrated his sixteenth birthday by going into the loom room and taking a loom. Here was an incentive again, for it was piece-work. And he excelled, because the clay of him had been moulded by the mills into the perfect machine. At the end of three months he was running two looms, and, later, three and four.

At the end of his second year at the looms he was turning out more yards than any other weaver, and more than twice as much as some of the less skilful ones. And at home things began to prosper as he approached the full stature of his earning power. Not, however, that his increased earnings were in excess of need. The children were growing up. They ate more. And they were going to school, and school-books cost money. And somehow, the faster he worked, the faster climbed the prices of things. Even the rent went up, though the house had fallen from bad to worse disrepair.

He had grown taller; but with his increased height he seemed leaner than ever. Also, he was more nervous. With the nervousness increased his peevishness and irritability. The children had learned by many bitter lessons to fight shy of him. His mother respected him for his earning power, but somehow her respect was tinctured with fear.

There was no joyousness in life for him. The procession of the days he never saw. The nights he slept away in twitching unconsciousness. The rest of the time he worked, and his consciousness was machine consciousness. Outside this his mind was a blank. He had no ideals, and but one illusion; namely, that he drank excellent coffee. He was a work-beast. He had no mental life whatever; yet deep down in the crypts of his mind, unknown to him, were being weighed and sifted every hour of his toil, every movement of his hands, every twitch of his muscles, and preparations were making for a future course of action that would amaze him and all his little world.

It was in the late spring that he came home from work one night aware of unusual tiredness. There was a keen expectancy in the air as he sat down to the table, but he did not notice. He went through the meal in moody silence, mechanically eating what was before him. The children um'd and ah'd and made smacking noises with their mouths. But he was deaf to them.

"D'ye know what you're eatin'?" his mother demanded at last, desperately.

He looked vacantly at the dish before him, and vacantly at her.

"Floatin' island," she announced triumphantly.

"Oh," he said.

"Floating island!" the children chorussed loudly.

"Oh," he said. And after two or three mouthfuls, he added, "I guess I ain't hungry to-night."

He dropped the spoon, shoved back his chair, and arose wearily from the table.

"An' I guess I'll go to bed."

His feet dragged more heavily than usual as he crossed the kitchen floor. Undressing was a Titan's task, a monstrous futility, and he wept weakly as he crawled into bed, one shoe still on. He was aware of a rising, swelling something inside his head that made his brain thick and fuzzy. His lean fingers felt as big as his wrist, while in the ends of them was a remoteness of sensation vague and fuzzy like his brain. The small of his back ached intolerably. All his bones ached. He ached everywhere. And in his head began the shrieking, pounding, crashing, roaring of a million looms. All space was filled with flying shuttles. They darted in and out, intricately, amongst the stars. He worked a thousand looms himself, and ever they speeded up, faster and faster, and his brain unwound, faster and faster, and became the thread that fed the thousand flying shuttles.

He did not go to work next morning. He was too busy weaving colossally on the thousand looms that ran inside his head. His mother went to work, but first she sent for the doctor. It was a severe attack of la grippe, he said. Jennie served as nurse and carried out his instructions.

It was a very severe attack, and it was a week before Johnny dressed and tottered feebly across the floor. Another week, the doctor said, and he would be fit to return to work. The foreman of the loom room visited him on

Sunday afternoon, the first day of his convalescence. The best weaver in the room, the foreman told his mother. His job would be held for him. He could come back to work a week from Monday.

"Why don't you thank 'im, Johnny?" his mother asked anxiously.

"He's ben that sick he ain't himself yet," she explained apologetically to the visitor.

Johnny sat hunched up and gazing steadfastly at the floor. He sat in the same position long after the foreman had gone. It was warm outdoors, and he sat on the stoop in the afternoon. Sometimes his lips moved. He seemed lost in endless calculations.

Next morning, after the day grew warm, he took his seat on the stoop. He had pencil and paper this time with which to continue his calculations, and he calculated painfully and amazingly.

"What comes after millions?" he asked at noon, when Will came home from school. "An' how d'ye work 'em?"

That afternoon finished his task. Each day, but without paper and pencil, he returned to the stoop. He was greatly absorbed in the one tree that grew across the street. He studied it for hours at a time, and was unusually intereste when the wind swayed its branches and fluttered its leaves. Throughout week he seemed lost in a great communion with himself. On Sunday, s on the stoop, he laughed aloud, several times, to the perturbation mother, who had not heard him laugh for years.

Next morning, in the early darkness, she came to his bed to rc He had had his fill of sleep all the week, and awoke easily. He struggle, nor did he attempt to hold on to the bedding when she from him. He lay quietly, and spoke quietly.

"It ain't no use, ma."

"You'll be late," she said, under the impression that he with sleep.

"I'm awake, ma, an' I tell you it ain't no use. You might as well lemme alone. I ain't goin' to git up."

"But you'll lose your job!" she cried.

"I ain't goin' to git up," he repeated in a strange, passionless voice.

She did not go to work herself that morning. This was sickness beyond any sickness she had ever known. Fever and delirium she could understand; but this was insanity. She pulled the bedding up over him and sent Jennie for the doctor.

When that person arrived, Johnny was sleeping gently, and gently he awoke and allowed his pulse to be taken.

"Nothing the matter with him," the doctor reported. "Badly debilitated, that's all. Not much meat on his bones."

"He's always been that way," his mother volunteered.

"Now go 'way, ma, an' let me finish my snooze."

Johnny spoke sweetly and placidly, and sweetly and placidly he rolled over on his side and went to sleep.

At ten o'clock he awoke and dressed himself. He walked out into the kitchen, where he found his mother with a frightened expression on her face.

"I'm goin' away, ma," he announced, "an' I jes' want to say good-bye."

She threw her apron over her head and sat down suddenly and wept. He waited patiently.

"I might a-known it," she was sobbing.

"Where?" she finally asked, removing the apron from her head and looking up at him with a stricken face in which there was little curiosity.

"I don't know—anywhere."

As he spoke, the tree across the street appeared with dazzling brightness on his inner vision. It seemed to lurk just under his eyelids, and he could see it whenever he wished.

"An' your job?" she quavered.

"I ain't never goin' to work again."

"My God, Johnny!" she wailed, "don't say that!"

What he had said was blasphemy to her. As a mother who hears her child deny God, was Johnny's mother shocked by his words.

"What's got into you, anyway?" she demanded, with a lame attempt at imperativeness.

"Figures," he answered. "Jes' figures. I've ben doin' a lot of figurin' this week, an' it's most surprisin'."

"I don't see what that's got to do with it," she sniffled.

Johnny smiled patiently, and his mother was aware of a distinct shock at the persistent absence of his peevishness and irritability.

"I'll show you," he said. "I'm plum' tired out. What makes me tired? Moves. I've ben movin' ever since I was born. I'm tired of movin', an' I ain't goin' to move any more. Remember when I worked in the glass-house? I used to do three hundred dozen a day. Now I reckon I made about ten different moves to each bottle. That's thirty-six thousan' moves a day. Ten days, three hundred an' sixty thousan' moves. One month, one million an' eighty thousan' moves. Chuck out the eighty thousan'"—he spoke with the complacent beneficence of a philanthropist—"chuck out the eighty thousan', that leaves a million moves a month—twelve million moves a year.

"At the looms I'm movin' twic'st as much. That makes twenty-five million moves a year, an' it seems to me I've ben a movin' that way 'most a million years.

"Now this week I ain't moved at all. I ain't made one move in hours an' hours. I tell you it was swell, jes' settin' there, hours an' hours, an' doin' nothin'. I ain't never ben happy before. I never had any time. I've ben movin' all the time. That ain't no way to be happy. An' I ain't going to do it any more. I'm jes' goin' to set, an' set, an' rest, an' rest, and then rest some more."

209

"But what's goin' to come of Will an' the children?" she asked despairingly.

"That's it, 'Will an' the children,'" he repeated.

But there was no bitterness in his voice. He had long known his mother's ambition for the younger boy, but the thought of it no longer rankled. Nothing mattered any more. Not even that.

"I know, ma, what you've ben plannin' for Will—keepin' him in school to make a book-keeper out of him. But it ain't no use, I've quit. He's got to go to work."

"An' after I have brung you up the way I have," she wept, starting to cover her head with the apron and changing her mind.

"You never brung me up," he answered with sad kindliness. "I brung myself up, ma, an' I brung up Will. He's bigger'n me, an' heavier, an' taller. When I was a kid, I reckon I didn't git enough to eat. When he come along an' was a kid, I was workin' an' earnin' grub for him too. But that's done with. Will can go to work, same as me, or he can go to hell, I don't care which. I'm tired. I'm goin' now. Ain't you goin' to say goodbye?"

She made no reply. The apron had gone over her head again, and she was crying. He paused a moment in the doorway.

"I'm sure I done the best I knew how," she was sobbing.

He passed out of the house and down the street. A wan delight came into his face at the sight of the lone tree. "Jes' ain't goin' to do nothin'," he said to himself, half aloud, in a crooning tone. He glanced wistfully up at the sky, but the bright sun dazzled and blinded him.

It was a long walk he took, and he did not walk fast. It took him past the jute-mill. The muffled roar of the loom room came to his ears, and he smiled. It was a gentle, placid smile. He hated no one, not even the pounding, shrieking machines. There was no bitterness in him, nothing but an inordinate hunger for rest.

The houses and factories thinned out and the open spaces increased as he approached the country. At last the city was behind him, and he was walking down a leafy lane beside the railroad track. He did not walk like a man. He did not look like a man. He was a travesty of the human. It was a twisted and stunted and nameless piece of life that shambled like a sickly ape, arms loose-hanging, stoop-shouldered, narrow-chested, grotesque and terrible.

He passed by a small railroad station and lay down in the grass under a tree. All afternoon he lay there. Sometimes he dozed, with muscles that twitched in his sleep. When awake, he lay without movement, watching the birds or looking up at the sky through the branches of the tree above him. Once or twice he laughed aloud, but without relevance to anything he had seen or felt.

After twilight had gone, in the first darkness of the night, a freight train rumbled into the station. When the engine was switching cars on to the side-track, Johnny crept along the side of the train. He pulled open the side-door of an empty box-car and awkwardly and laboriously climbed in. He closed the door. The engine whistled. Johnny was lying down, and in the darkness he smiled.

A WICKED WOMAN

It was because she had broken with Billy that Loretta had come visiting to Santa Clara. Billy could not understand. His sister had reported that he had walked the floor and cried all night. Loretta had not slept all night either, while she had wept most of the night. Daisy knew this, because it was in her arms that the weeping had been done. And Daisy's husband, Captain Kitt, knew, too. The tears of Loretta, and the comforting by Daisy, had lost him some sleep.

Now Captain Kitt did not like to lose sleep. Neither did he want Loretta to marry Billy—nor anybody else. It was Captain Kitt's belief that Daisy needed the help of her younger sister in the household. But he did not say this aloud. Instead, he always insisted that Loretta was too young to think of marriage. So it was Captain Kitt's idea that Loretta should be packed off on a visit to Mrs. Hemingway. There wouldn't be any Billy there.

Before Loretta had been at Santa Clara a week, she was convinced that Captain Kitt's idea was a good one. In the first place, though Billy wouldn't believe it, she did not want to marry Billy. And in the second place, though Captain Kitt wouldn't believe it, she did not want to leave Daisy. By the time Loretta had been at Santa Clara two weeks, she was absolutely certain that she did not want to marry Billy. But she was not so sure about not wanting to leave Daisy. Not that she loved Daisy less, but that she—had doubts.

The day of Loretta's arrival, a nebulous plan began shaping itself in Mrs. Hemingway's brain. The second day she remarked to Jack Hemingway, her husband, that Loretta was so innocent a young thing that were it not for her sweet guilelessness she would be positively stupid. In proof of which, Mrs. Hemingway told her husband several things that made him chuckle. By the third day Mrs. Hemingway's plan had taken recognizable form. Then it was that she composed a letter. On the envelope she wrote: "Mr. Edward Bashford, Athenian Club, San Francisco."

"Dear Ned," the letter began. She had once been violently loved by him for three weeks in her pre-marital days. But she had covenanted herself to Jack Hemingway, who had prior claims, and her heart as well; and Ned Bashford had philosophically not broken his heart over it. He merely added the experience to a large fund of similarly collected data out of which he manufactured philosophy. Artistically and temperamentally he was a Greek—a tired Greek. He was fond of quoting from Nietzsche, in token that he, too, had passed through the long sickness that follows upon the ardent search for truth; that he too had emerged, too experienced, too shrewd, too profound, ever again to be afflicted by the madness of youths in their love of truth. "'To worship appearance,'" he often quoted; "'to believe in forms, in tones, in words, in the whole Olympus of appearance!'" This particular excerpt he always concluded with, "'Those Greeks were superficial—OUT OF PROFUNDITY!'"

He was a fairly young Greek, jaded and worn. Women were faithless and unveracious, he held—at such times that he had relapses and descended to pessimism from his wonted high philosophical calm. He did not believe in the truth of women; but, faithful to his German master, he did not strip from them the airy gauzes that veiled their untruth. He was content to accept them as appearances and to make the best of it. He was superficial—OUT OF PROFUNDITY.

"Jack says to be sure to say to you, 'good swimming,'" Mrs. Hemingway wrote in her letter; "and also 'to bring your fishing duds along.'" Mrs. Hemingway wrote other things in the letter. She told him that at last she was prepared to exhibit to him an absolutely true, unsullied, and innocent woman. "A more guileless, immaculate bud of womanhood never blushed on the planet," was one of the several ways in which she phrased the inducement. And to her husband she said triumphantly, "If I don't marry Ned off this time—" leaving unstated the terrible alternative that she lacked either vocabulary to express or imagination to conceive.

Contrary to all her forebodings, Loretta found that she was not unhappy at Santa Clara. Truly, Billy wrote to her every day, but his letters were less distressing than his presence. Also, the ordeal of being away from Daisy was

213

not so severe as she had expected. For the first time in her life she was not lost in eclipse in the blaze of Daisy's brilliant and mature personality. Under such favourable circumstances Loretta came rapidly to the front, while Mrs. Hemingway modestly and shamelessly retreated into the background.

Loretta began to discover that she was not a pale orb shining by reflection. Quite unconsciously she became a small centre of things. When she was at the piano, there was some one to turn the pages for her and to express preferences for certain songs. When she dropped her handkerchief, there was some one to pick it up. And there was some one to accompany her in ramblings and flower gatherings. Also, she learned to cast flies in still pools and below savage riffles, and how not to entangle silk lines and gut-leaders with the shrubbery.

Jack Hemingway did not care to teach beginners, and fished much by himself, or not at all, thus giving Ned Bashford ample time in which to consider Loretta as an appearance. As such, she was all that his philosophy demanded. Her blue eyes had the direct gaze of a boy, and out of his profundity he delighted in them and forbore to shudder at the duplicity his philosophy bade him to believe lurked in their depths. She had the grace of a slender flower, the fragility of colour and line of fine china, in all of which he pleasured greatly, without thought of the Life Force palpitating beneath and in spite of Bernard Shaw—in whom he believed.

Loretta burgeoned. She swiftly developed personality. She discovered a will of her own and wishes of her own that were not everlastingly entwined with the will and the wishes of Daisy. She was petted by Jack Hemingway, spoiled by Alice Hemingway, and devotedly attended by Ned Bashford. They encouraged her whims and laughed at her follies, while she developed the pretty little tyrannies that are latent in all pretty and delicate women. Her environment acted as a soporific upon her ancient desire always to live with Daisy. This desire no longer prodded her as in the days of her companionship with Billy. The more she saw of Billy, the more certain she had been that she could not live away from Daisy. The more she saw of Ned Bashford, the more she forgot her pressing need of Daisy.

Ned Bashford likewise did some forgetting. He confused superficiality with profundity, and entangled appearance with reality until he accounted them one. Loretta was different from other women. There was no masquerade about her. She was real. He said as much to Mrs. Hemingway, and more, who agreed with him and at the same time caught her husband's eyelid drooping down for the moment in an unmistakable wink.

It was at this time that Loretta received a letter from Billy that was somewhat different from his others. In the main, like all his letters, it was pathological. It was a long recital of symptoms and sufferings, his nervousness, his sleeplessness, and the state of his heart. Then followed reproaches, such as he had never made before. They were sharp enough to make her weep, and true enough to put tragedy into her face. This tragedy she carried down to the breakfast table. It made Jack and Mrs. Hemingway speculative, and it worried Ned. They glanced to him for explanation, but he shook his head.

"I'll find out to-night," Mrs. Hemingway said to her husband.

But Ned caught Loretta in the afternoon in the big living-room. She tried to turn away. He caught her hands, and she faced him with wet lashes and trembling lips. He looked at her, silently and kindly. The lashes grew wetter.

"There, there, don't cry, little one," he said soothingly.

He put his arm protectingly around her shoulder. And to his shoulder, like a tired child, she turned her face. He thrilled in ways unusual for a Greek who has recovered from the long sickness.

"Oh, Ned," she sobbed on his shoulder, "if you only knew how wicked I am!"

He smiled indulgently, and breathed in a great breath freighted with the fragrance of her hair. He thought of his world-experience of women, and drew another long breath. There seemed to emanate from her the perfect sweetness of a child—"the aura of a white soul," was the way he phrased it to himself.

Then he noticed that her sobs were increasing.

"What's the matter, little one?" he asked pettingly and almost paternally. "Has Jack been bullying you? Or has your dearly beloved sister failed to write?"

She did not answer, and he felt that he really must kiss her hair, that he could not be responsible if the situation continued much longer.

"Tell me," he said gently, "and we'll see what I can do."

"I can't. You will despise me.—Oh, Ned, I am so ashamed!"

He laughed incredulously, and lightly touched her hair with his lips—so lightly that she did not know.

"Dear little one, let us forget all about it, whatever it is. I want to tell you how I love—"

She uttered a sharp cry that was all delight, and then moaned—

"Too late!"

"Too late?" he echoed in surprise.

"Oh, why did I? Why did I?" she was moaning.

He was aware of a swift chill at his heart.

"What?" he asked.

"Oh, I... he... Billy.

"I am such a wicked woman, Ned. I know you will never speak to me again."

"This—er—this Billy," he began haltingly. "He is your brother?"

"No... he... I didn't know. I was so young. I could not help it. Oh, I shall go mad! I shall go mad!"

It was then that Loretta felt his shoulder and the encircling arm become limp. He drew away from her gently, and gently he deposited her in a big chair, where she buried her face and sobbed afresh. He twisted his moustache fiercely, then drew up another chair and sat down.

216

"I—I do not understand," he said.

"I am so unhappy," she wailed.

"Why unhappy?"

"Because... he... he wants me to marry him."

His face cleared on the instant, and he placed a hand soothingly on hers.

"That should not make any girl unhappy," he remarked sagely. "Because you don't love him is no reason—of course, you don't love him?"

Loretta shook her head and shoulders in a vigorous negative.

"What?"

Bashford wanted to make sure.

"No," she asserted explosively. "I don't love Billy! I don't want to love Billy!"

"Because you don't love him," Bashford resumed with confidence, "is no reason that you should be unhappy just because he has proposed to you."

She sobbed again, and from the midst of her sobs she cried—

"That's the trouble. I wish I did love him. Oh, I wish I were dead!"

"Now, my dear child, you are worrying yourself over trifles." His other hand crossed over after its mate and rested on hers. "Women do it every day. Because you have changed your mind or did not know your mind, because you have—to use an unnecessarily harsh word—jilted a man—"

"Jilted!" She had raised her head and was looking at him with tear-dimmed eyes. "Oh, Ned, if that were all!"

"All?" he asked in a hollow voice, while his hands slowly retreated from hers. He was about to speak further, then remained silent.

"But I don't want to marry him," Loretta broke forth protestingly.

"Then I shouldn't," he counselled.

"But I ought to marry him."

"OUGHT to marry him?"

She nodded.

"That is a strong word."

"I know it is," she acquiesced, while she strove to control her trembling lips. Then she spoke more calmly. "I am a wicked woman, a terribly wicked woman. No one knows how wicked I am—except Billy."

There was a pause. Ned Bashford's face was grave, and he looked queerly at Loretta.

"He—Billy knows?" he asked finally.

A reluctant nod and flaming cheeks was the reply.

He debated with himself for a while, seeming, like a diver, to be preparing himself for the plunge.

"Tell me about it." He spoke very firmly. "You must tell me all of it."

"And will you—ever—forgive me?" she asked in a faint, small voice.

He hesitated, drew a long breath, and made the plunge.

"Yes," he said desperately. "I'll forgive you. Go ahead."

"There was no one to tell me," she began. "We were with each other so much. I did not know anything of the world—then."

She paused to meditate. Bashford was biting his lip impatiently.

"If I had only known—"

She paused again.

"Yes, go on," he urged.

"We were together almost every evening."

"Billy?" he demanded, with a savageness that startled her.

218

"Yes, of course, Billy. We were with each other so much... If I had only known... There was no one to tell me... I was so young—"

Her lips parted as though to speak further, and she regarded him anxiously.

"The scoundrel!"

With the explosion Ned Bashford was on his feet, no longer a tired Greek, but a violently angry young man.

"Billy is not a scoundrel; he is a good man," Loretta defended, with a firmness that surprised Bashford.

"I suppose you'll be telling me next that it was all your fault," he said sarcastically.

She nodded.

"What?" he shouted.

"It was all my fault," she said steadily. "I should never have let him. I was to blame."

Bashford ceased from his pacing up and down, and when he spoke, his voice was resigned.

"All right," he said. "I don't blame you in the least, Loretta. And you have been very honest. But Billy is right, and you are wrong. You must get married."

"To Billy?" she asked, in a dim, far-away voice.

"Yes, to Billy. I'll see to it. Where does he live? I'll make him."

"But I don't want to marry Billy!" she cried out in alarm. "Oh, Ned, you won't do that?"

"I shall," he answered sternly. "You must. And Billy must. Do you understand?"

Loretta buried her face in the cushioned chair back, and broke into a passionate storm of sobs.

All that Bashford could make out at first, as he listened, was: "But I don't want to leave Daisy! I don't want to leave Daisy!"

He paced grimly back and forth, then stopped curiously to listen.

"How was I to know?—Boo—hoo," Loretta was crying. "He didn't tell me. Nobody else ever kissed me. I never dreamed a kiss could be so terrible... until, boo-hoo... until he wrote to me. I only got the letter this morning."

His face brightened. It seemed as though light was dawning on him.

"Is that what you're crying about?"

"N—no."

His heart sank.

"Then what are you crying about?" he asked in a hopeless voice.

"Because you said I had to marry Billy. And I don't want to marry Billy. I don't want to leave Daisy. I don't know what I want. I wish I were dead."

He nerved himself for another effort.

"Now look here, Loretta, be sensible. What is this about kisses. You haven't told me everything?"

"I—I don't want to tell you everything."

She looked at him beseechingly in the silence that fell.

"Must I?" she quavered finally.

"You must," he said imperatively. "You must tell me everything."

"Well, then... must I?"

"You must."

"He... I... we..." she began flounderingly. Then blurted out, "I let him, and he kissed me."

"Go on," Bashford commanded desperately.

"That's all," she answered.

"All?" There was a vast incredulity in his voice.

"All?" In her voice was an interrogation no less vast.

"I mean—er—nothing worse?" He was overwhelmingly aware of his own awkwardness.

"Worse?" She was frankly puzzled. "As though there could be! Billy said—"

"When did he say it?" Bashford demanded abruptly.

"In his letter I got this morning. Billy said that my... our... our kisses were terrible if we didn't get married."

Bashford's head was swimming.

"What else did Billy say?" he asked.

"He said that when a woman allowed a man to kiss her, she always married him—that it was terrible if she didn't. It was the custom, he said; and I say it is a bad, wicked custom, and I don't like it. I know I'm terrible," she added defiantly, "but I can't help it."

Bashford absent-mindedly brought out a cigarette.

"Do you mind if I smoke?" he asked, as he struck a match.

Then he came to himself.

"I beg your pardon," he cried, flinging away match and cigarette. "I don't want to smoke. I didn't mean that at all. What I mean is—"

He bent over Loretta, caught her hands in his, then sat on the arm of the chair and softly put one arm around her.

"Loretta, I am a fool. I mean it. And I mean something more. I want you to be my wife."

He waited anxiously in the pause that followed.

"You might answer me," he urged.

"I will... if—"

"Yes, go on. If what?"

"If I don't have to marry Billy."

"You can't marry both of us," he almost shouted.

"And it isn't the custom... what... what Billy said?"

"No, it isn't the custom. Now, Loretta, will you marry me?"

"Don't be angry with me," she pouted demurely.

He gathered her into his arms and kissed her.

"I wish it were the custom," she said in a faint voice, from the midst of the embrace, "because then I'd have to marry you, Ned dear... wouldn't I?"

JUST MEAT

He strolled to the corner and glanced up and down the intersecting street, but saw nothing save the oases of light shed by the street lamps at the successive crossings. Then he strolled back the way he had come. He was a shadow of a man, sliding noiselessly and without undue movement through the semi-darkness. Also he was very alert, like a wild animal in the jungle, keenly perceptive and receptive. The movement of another in the darkness about him would need to have been more shadowy than he to have escaped him.

In addition to the running advertisement of the state of affairs carried to him by his senses, he had a subtler perception, a FEEL, of the atmosphere around him. He knew that the house in front of which he paused for a moment, contained children. Yet by no willed effort of perception did he have this knowledge. For that matter, he was not even aware that he knew, so occult was the impression. Yet, did a moment arise in which action, in relation to that house, were imperative, he would have acted on the assumption that it contained children. He was not aware of all that he knew about the neighbourhood.

In the same way, he knew not how, he knew that no danger threatened in the footfalls that came up the cross street. Before he saw the walker, he knew him for a belated pedestrian hurrying home. The walker came into view at the crossing and disappeared on up the street. The man that watched, noted a light that flared up in the window of a house on the corner, and as it died down he knew it for an expiring match. This was conscious identification of familiar phenomena, and through his mind flitted the thought, "Wanted to know what time." In another house one room was lighted. The light burned dimly and steadily, and he had the feel that it was a sick-room.

He was especially interested in a house across the street in the middle of the block. To this house he paid most attention. No matter what way he looked, nor what way he walked, his looks and his steps always returned to it. Except for an open window above the porch, there was nothing unusual about the house. Nothing came in nor out. Nothing happened. There were no lighted windows, nor had lights appeared and disappeared in any of the windows. Yet it was the central point of his consideration. He rallied to it each time after a divination of the state of the neighbourhood.

Despite his feel of things, he was not confident. He was supremely conscious of the precariousness of his situation. Though unperturbed by the footfalls of the chance pedestrian, he was as keyed up and sensitive and ready to be startled as any timorous deer. He was aware of the possibility of other intelligences prowling about in the darkness—intelligences similar to his own in movement, perception, and divination.

Far down the street he caught a glimpse of something that moved. And he knew it was no late home-goer, but menace and danger. He whistled twice to the house across the street, then faded away shadow-like to the corner and around the corner. Here he paused and looked about him carefully. Reassured, he peered back around the corner and studied the object that moved and that was coming nearer. He had divined aright. It was a policeman.

The man went down the cross street to the next corner, from the shelter of which he watched the corner he had just left. He saw the policeman pass by, going straight on up the street. He paralleled the policeman's course, and from the next corner again watched him go by; then he returned the way he had come. He whistled once to the house across the street, and after a time whistled once again. There was reassurance in the whistle, just as there had been warning in the previous double whistle.

He saw a dark bulk outline itself on the roof of the porch and slowly descend a pillar. Then it came down the steps, passed through the small iron gate, and went down the sidewalk, taking on the form of a man. He that watched kept on his own side of the street and moved on abreast to the corner, where he crossed over and joined the other. He was quite small alongside the man he accosted.

"How'd you make out, Matt?" he asked.

The other grunted indistinctly, and walked on in silence a few steps.

"I reckon I landed the goods," he said.

Jim chuckled in the darkness, and waited for further information. The blocks passed by under their feet, and he grew impatient.

"Well, how about them goods?" he asked. "What kind of a haul did you make, anyway?"

"I was too busy to figger it out, but it's fat. I can tell you that much, Jim, it's fat. I don't dast to think how fat it is. Wait till we get to the room."

Jim looked at him keenly under the street lamp of the next crossing, and saw that his face was a trifle grim and that he carried his left arm peculiarly.

"What's the matter with your arm?" he demanded.

"The little cuss bit me. Hope I don't get hydrophoby. Folks gets hydrophoby from manbite sometimes, don't they?"

"Gave you fight, eh?" Jim asked encouragingly.

The other grunted.

"You're harder'n hell to get information from," Jim burst out irritably. "Tell us about it. You ain't goin' to lose money just a-tellin' a guy."

"I guess I choked him some," came the answer. Then, by way of explanation, "He woke up on me."

"You did it neat. I never heard a sound."

"Jim," the other said with seriousness, "it's a hangin' matter. I fixed 'm. I had to. He woke up on me. You an' me's got to do some layin' low for a spell."

Jim gave a low whistle of comprehension.

"Did you hear me whistle?" he asked suddenly.

"Sure. I was all done. I was just comin' out."

225

"It was a bull. But he wasn't on a little bit. Went right by an' kept a-paddin' the hoof out a sight. Then I come back an' gave you the whistle. What made you take so long after that?"

"I was waitin' to make sure," Matt explained. "I was mighty glad when I heard you whistle again. It's hard work waitin'. I just sat there an' thought an' thought... oh, all kinds of things. It's remarkable what a fellow'll think about. And then there was a darn cat that kept movin' around the house all' botherin' me with its noises."

"An' it's fat!" Jim exclaimed irrelevantly and with joy.

"I'm sure tellin' you, Jim, it's fat. I'm plum' anxious for another look at 'em."

Unconsciously the two men quickened their pace. Yet they did not relax from their caution. Twice they changed their course in order to avoid policemen, and they made very sure that they were not observed when they dived into the dark hallway of a cheap rooming house down town.

Not until they had gained their own room on the top floor, did they scratch a match. While Jim lighted a lamp, Matt locked the door and threw the bolts into place. As he turned, he noticed that his partner was waiting expectantly. Matt smiled to himself at the other's eagerness.

"Them search-lights is all right," he said, drawing forth a small pocket electric lamp and examining it. "But we got to get a new battery. It's runnin' pretty weak. I thought once or twice it'd leave me in the dark. Funny arrangements in that house. I near got lost. His room was on the left, an' that fooled me some."

"I told you it was on the left," Jim interrupted.

"You told me it was on the right," Matt went on. "I guess I know what you told me, an' there's the map you drew."

Fumbling in his vest pocket, he drew out a folded slip of paper. As he unfolded it, Jim bent over and looked.

"I did make a mistake," he confessed.

"You sure did. It got me guessin' some for a while."

"But it don't matter now," Jim cried. "Let's see what you got."

"It does matter," Matt retorted. "It matters a lot... to me. I've got to run all the risk. I put my head in the trap while you stay on the street. You got to get on to yourself an' be more careful. All right, I'll show you."

He dipped loosely into his trousers pocket and brought out a handful of small diamonds. He spilled them out in a blazing stream on the greasy table. Jim let out a great oath.

"That's nothing," Matt said with triumphant complacence. "I ain't begun yet."

From one pocket after another he continued bringing forth the spoil. There were many diamonds wrapped in chamois skin that were larger than those in the first handful. From one pocket he brought out a handful of very small cut gems.

"Sun dust," he remarked, as he spilled them on the table in a space by themselves.

Jim examined them.

"Just the same, they retail for a couple of dollars each," he said. "Is that all?"

"Ain't it enough?" the other demanded in an aggrieved tone.

"Sure it is," Jim answered with unqualified approval. "Better'n I expected. I wouldn't take a cent less than ten thousan' for the bunch."

"Ten thousan'," Matt sneered. "They're worth twic't that, an' I don't know anything about joolery, either. Look at that big boy!"

He picked it out from the sparkling heap and held it near to the lamp with the air of an expert, weighing and judging.

"Worth a thousan' all by its lonely," was Jim's quicker judgment.

"A thousan' your grandmother," was Matt's scornful rejoinder. "You couldn't buy it for three."

"Wake me up! I'm dreamin'!" The sparkle of the gems was in Jim's eyes, and he began sorting out the larger diamonds and examining them. "We're rich men, Matt—we'll be regular swells."

"It'll take years to get rid of 'em," was Matt's more practical thought.

"But think how we'll live! Nothin' to do but spend the money an' go on gettin' rid of em."

Matt's eyes were beginning to sparkle, though sombrely, as his phlegmatic nature woke up.

"I told you I didn't dast think how fat it was," he murmured in a low voice.

"What a killin'! What a killin'!" was the other's more ecstatic utterance.

"I almost forgot," Matt said, thrusting his hand into his inside coat pocket.

A string of large pearls emerged from wrappings of tissue paper and chamois skin. Jim scarcely glanced at them.

"They're worth money," he said, and returned to the diamonds.

A silence fell on the two men. Jim played with the gems, running them through his fingers, sorting them into piles, and spreading them out flat and wide. He was a slender, weazened man, nervous, irritable, high-strung, and anaemic—a typical child of the gutter, with unbeautiful twisted features, small-eyed, with face and mouth perpetually and feverishly hungry, brutish in a cat-like way, stamped to the core with degeneracy.

Matt did not finger the diamonds. He sat with chin on hands and elbows on table, blinking heavily at the blazing array. He was in every way a contrast to the other. No city had bred him. He was heavy-muscled and hairy, gorilla-like in strength and aspect. For him there was no unseen world. His eyes were full and wide apart, and there seemed in them a certain bold brotherliness. They inspired confidence. But a closer inspection would have shown that his eyes were just a trifle too full, just a shade too wide apart. He exceeded, spilled over the limits of normality, and his features told lies about the man beneath.

"The bunch is worth fifty thousan'," Jim remarked suddenly.

"A hundred thousan'," Matt said.

The silence returned and endured a long time, to be broken again by Jim.

"What in hell was he doin' with 'em all at the house?—that's what I want to know. I'd a-thought he'd kept 'em in the safe down at the store."

Matt had just been considering the vision of the throttled man as he had last looked upon him in the dim light of the electric lantern; but he did not start at the mention of him.

"There's no tellin'," he answered. "He might a-ben gettin' ready to chuck his pardner. He might a-pulled out in the mornin' for parts unknown, if we hadn't happened along. I guess there's just as many thieves among honest men as there is among thieves. You read about such things in the papers, Jim. Pardners is always knifin' each other."

A queer, nervous look came into the other's eyes. Matt did not betray that he noted it, though he said—

"What was you thinkin' about, Jim?"

Jim was a trifle awkward for the moment.

"Nothin'," he answered. "Only I was thinkin' just how funny it was—all them jools at his house. What made you ask?"

"Nothin'. I was just wonderin', that was all."

The silence settled down, broken by an occasional low and nervous giggle on the part of Jim. He was overcome by the spread of gems. It was not that he felt their beauty. He was unaware that they were beautiful in themselves. But in them his swift imagination visioned the joys of life they would buy, and all the desires and appetites of his diseased mind and sickly flesh were tickled by the promise they extended. He builded wondrous, orgy-haunted castles out of their brilliant fires, and was appalled at what he builded. Then it was that he giggled. It was all too impossible to be real. And yet there they blazed on the table before him, fanning the flame of the lust of him, and he giggled again.

"I guess we might as well count 'em," Matt said suddenly, tearing himself away from his own visions. "You watch me an' see that it's square, because you an' me has got to be on the square, Jim. Understand?"

Jim did not like this, and betrayed it in his eyes, while Matt did not like what he saw in his partner's eyes.

"Understand?" Matt repeated, almost menacingly.

"Ain't we always ben square?" the other replied, on the defensive because of the treachery already whispering in him.

"It don't cost nothin', bein' square in hard times," Matt retorted. "It's bein' square in prosperity that counts. When we ain't got nothin', we can't help bein' square. We're prosperous now, an' we've got to be business men—honest business men. Understand?"

"That's the talk for me," Jim approved, but deep down in the meagre soul of him,—and in spite of him,—wanton and lawless thoughts were stirring like chained beasts.

Matt stepped to the food shelf behind the two-burner kerosene cooking stove. He emptied the tea from a paper bag, and from a second bag emptied some red peppers. Returning to the table with the bags, he put into them the two sizes of small diamonds. Then he counted the large gems and wrapped them in their tissue paper and chamois skin.

"Hundred an' forty-seven good-sized ones," was his inventory; "twenty real big ones; two big boys and one whopper; an' a couple of fistfuls of teeny ones an' dust."

He looked at Jim.

"Correct," was the response.

He wrote the count out on a slip of memorandum paper, and made a copy of it, giving one slip to his partner and retaining the other.

"Just for reference," he said.

Again he had recourse to the food shelf, where he emptied the sugar from a large paper bag. Into this he thrust the diamonds, large and small, wrapped it up in a bandanna handkerchief, and stowed it away under his pillow. Then he sat down on the edge of the bed and took off his shoes.

"An' you think they're worth a hundred thousan'?" Jim asked, pausing and looking up from the unlacing of his shoe.

"Sure," was the answer. "I seen a dance-house girl down in Arizona once, with some big sparklers on her. They wasn't real. She said if they was she wouldn't be dancin'. Said they'd be worth all of fifty thousan', an' she didn't have a dozen of 'em all told."

"Who'd work for a livin'?" Jim triumphantly demanded. "Pick an' shovel work!" he sneered. "Work like a dog all my life, an' save all my wages, an' I wouldn't have half as much as we got tonight."

"Dish washin's about your measure, an' you couldn't get more'n twenty a month an' board. Your figgers is 'way off, but your point is well taken. Let them that likes it, work. I rode range for thirty a month when I was young an' foolish. Well, I'm older, an' I ain't ridin' range."

He got into bed on one side. Jim put out the light and followed him in on the other side.

"How's your arm feel?" Jim queried amiably.

Such concern was unusual, and Matt noted it, and replied—

"I guess there's no danger of hydrophoby. What made you ask?"

Jim felt in himself a guilty stir, and under his breath he cursed the other's way of asking disagreeable questions; but aloud he answered—

231

"Nothin', only you seemed scared of it at first. What are you goin' to do with your share, Matt?"

"Buy a cattle ranch in Arizona an' set down an' pay other men to ride range for me. There's some several I'd like to see askin' a job from me, damn them! An' now you shut your face, Jim. It'll be some time before I buy that ranch. Just now I'm goin' to sleep."

But Jim lay long awake, nervous and twitching, rolling about restlessly and rolling himself wide awake every time he dozed. The diamonds still blazed under his eyelids, and the fire of them hurt. Matt, in spite of his heavy nature, slept lightly, like a wild animal alert in its sleep; and Jim noticed, every time he moved, that his partner's body moved sufficiently to show that it had received the impression and that it was trembling on the verge of awakening. For that matter, Jim did not know whether or not, frequently, the other was awake. Once, quietly, betokening complete consciousness, Matt said to him: "Aw, go to sleep, Jim. Don't worry about them jools. They'll keep." And Jim had thought that at that particular moment Matt had been surely asleep.

In the late morning Matt was awake with Jim's first movement, and thereafter he awoke and dozed with him until midday, when they got up together and began dressing.

"I'm goin' out to get a paper an' some bread," Matt said. "You boil the coffee."

As Jim listened, unconsciously his gaze left Matt's face and roved to the pillow, beneath which was the bundle wrapped in the bandanna handkerchief. On the instant Matt's face became like a wild beast's.

"Look here, Jim," he snarled. "You've got to play square. If you do me dirt, I'll fix you. Understand? I'd eat you, Jim. You know that. I'd bite right into your throat an' eat you like that much beefsteak."

His sunburned skin was black with the surge of blood in it, and his tobacco-stained teeth were exposed by the snarling lips. Jim shivered and involuntarily cowered. There was death in the man he looked at. Only the night before that black-faced man had killed another with his hands, and it had not hurt his sleep. And in his own heart Jim was aware of a sneaking guilt, of a train of thought that merited all that was threatened.

Matt passed out, leaving him still shivering. Then a hatred twisted his own face, and he softly hurled savage curses at the door. He remembered the jewels, and hastened to the bed, feeling under the pillow for the bandanna bundle. He crushed it with his fingers to make certain that it still contained the diamonds. Assured that Matt had not carried them away, he looked toward the kerosene stove with a guilty start. Then he hurriedly lighted it, filled the coffee-pot at the sink, and put it over the flame.

The coffee was boiling when Matt returned, and while the latter cut the bread and put a slice of butter on the table, Jim poured out the coffee. It was not until he sat down and had taken a few sips of the coffee, that Matt pulled out the morning paper from his pocket.

"We was way off," he said. "I told you I didn't dast figger out how fat it was. Look at that."

He pointed to the head-lines on the first page.

"SWIFT NEMESIS ON BUJANNOFF'S TRACK," they read. "MURDERED IN HIS SLEEP AFTER ROBBING HIS PARTNER."

"There you have it!" Matt cried. "He robbed his partner—robbed him like a dirty thief."

"Half a million of jewels missin'," Jim read aloud. He put the paper down and stared at Matt.

"That's what I told you," the latter said. "What in hell do we know about jools? Half a million!—an' the best I could figger it was a hundred thousan'. Go on an' read the rest of it."

They read on silently, their heads side by side, the untouched coffee growing cold; and ever and anon one or the other burst forth with some salient printed fact.

"I'd like to seen Metzner's face when he opened the safe at the store this mornin'," Jim gloated.

"He hit the high places right away for Bujannoff's house," Matt explained. "Go on an' read."

"Was to have sailed last night at ten on the Sajoda for the South Seas—steamship delayed by extra freight—"

"That's why we caught 'm in bed," Matt interrupted. "It was just luck—like pickin' a fifty-to-one winner."

"Sajoda sailed at six this mornin'—"

"He didn't catch her," Matt said. "I saw his alarm-clock was set at five. That'd given 'm plenty of time... only I come along an' put the kibosh on his time. Go on."

"Adolph Metzner in despair—the famous Haythorne pearl necklace—magnificently assorted pearls—valued by experts at from fifty to seventy thousan' dollars."

Jim broke off to swear vilely and solemnly, concluding with, "Those damn oyster-eggs worth all that money!"

He licked his lips and added, "They was beauties an' no mistake."

"Big Brazilian gem," he read on. "Eighty thousan' dollars—many valuable gems of the first water—several thousan' small diamonds well worth forty thousan'."

"What you don't know about jools is worth knowin'," Matt smiled good-humouredly.

"Theory of the sleuths," Jim read. "Thieves must have known—cleverly kept watch on Bujannoff's actions—must have learned his plan and trailed him to his house with the fruits of his robbery—"

"Clever—hell!" Matt broke out. "That's the way reputations is made... in the noospapers. How'd we know he was robbin' his pardner?"

"Anyway, we've got the goods," Jim grinned. "Let's look at 'em again."

He assured himself that the door was locked and bolted, while Matt brought out the bundle in the bandanna and opened it on the table.

234

"Ain't they beauties, though!" Jim exclaimed at sight of the pearls; and for a time he had eyes only for them. "Accordin' to the experts, worth from fifty to seventy thousan' dollars."

"An' women like them things," Matt commented. "An' they'll do everything to get 'em—sell themselves, commit murder, anything."

"Just like you an' me."

"Not on your life," Matt retorted. "I'll commit murder for 'em, but not for their own sakes, but for sake of what they'll get me. That's the difference. Women want the jools for themselves, an' I want the jools for the women an' such things they'll get me."

"Lucky that men an' women don't want the same things," Jim remarked.

"That's what makes commerce," Matt agreed; "people wantin' different things."

In the middle of the afternoon Jim went out to buy food. While he was gone, Matt cleared the table of the jewels, wrapping them up as before and putting them under the pillow. Then he lighted the kerosene stove and started to boil water for coffee. A few minutes later, Jim returned.

"Most surprising," he remarked. "Streets, an' stores, an' people just like they always was. Nothin' changed. An' me walking along through it all a millionaire. Nobody looked at me an' guessed it."

Matt grunted unsympathetically. He had little comprehension of the lighter whims and fancies of his partner's imagination.

"Did you get a porterhouse?" he demanded.

"Sure, an' an inch thick. It's a peach. Look at it."

He unwrapped the steak and held it up for the other's inspection. Then he made the coffee and set the table, while Matt fried the steak.

"Don't put on too much of them red peppers," Jim warned. "I ain't used to your Mexican cookin'. You always season too hot."

Matt grunted a laugh and went on with his cooking. Jim poured out the coffee, but first, into the nicked china cup, he emptied a powder he had carried in his vest pocket wrapped in a rice-paper. He had turned his back for the moment on his partner, but he did not dare to glance around at him. Matt placed a newspaper on the table, and on the newspaper set the hot frying-pan. He cut the steak in half, and served Jim and himself.

"Eat her while she's hot," he counselled, and with knife and fork set the example.

"She's a dandy," was Jim's judgment, after his first mouthful. "But I tell you one thing straight. I'm never goin' to visit you on that Arizona ranch, so you needn't ask me."

"What's the matter now?" Matt asked.

"Hell's the matter," was the answer. "The Mexican cookin' on your ranch'd be too much for me. If I've got hell a-comin' in the next life, I'm not goin' to torment my insides in this one. Damned peppers!"

He smiled, expelled his breath forcibly to cool his burning mouth, drank some coffee, and went on eating the steak.

"What do you think about the next life anyway, Matt?" he asked a little later, while secretly he wondered why the other had not yet touched his coffee.

"Ain't no next life," Matt answered, pausing from the steak to take his first sip of coffee. "Nor heaven nor hell, nor nothin'. You get all that's comin' right here in this life."

"An' afterward?" Jim queried out of his morbid curiosity, for he knew that he looked upon a man that was soon to die. "An' afterward?" he repeated.

"Did you ever see a man two weeks dead?" the other asked.

Jim shook his head.

"Well, I have. He was like this beefsteak you an' me is eatin'. It was once steer cavortin' over the landscape. But now it's just meat. That's all, just meat. An' that's what you an' me an' all people come to—meat."

Matt gulped down the whole cup of coffee, and refilled the cup.

"Are you scared to die?" he asked.

Jim shook his head. "What's the use? I don't die anyway. I pass on an' live again—"

"To go stealin', an' lyin' an' snivellin' through another life, an' go on that way forever an' ever an' ever?" Matt sneered.

"Maybe I'll improve," Jim suggested hopefully. "Maybe stealin' won't be necessary in the life to come."

He ceased abruptly, and stared straight before him, a frightened expression on his face.

"What's the matter!" Matt demanded.

"Nothin'. I was just wonderin'"—Jim returned to himself with an effort—"about this dyin', that was all."

But he could not shake off the fright that had startled him. It was as if an unseen thing of gloom had passed him by, casting upon him the intangible shadow of its presence. He was aware of a feeling of foreboding. Something ominous was about to happen. Calamity hovered in the air. He gazed fixedly across the table at the other man. He could not understand. Was it that he had blundered and poisoned himself? No, Matt had the nicked cup, and he had certainly put the poison in the nicked cup.

It was all his own imagination, was his next thought. It had played him tricks before. Fool! Of course it was. Of course something was about to happen, but it was about to happen to Matt. Had not Matt drunk the whole cup of coffee?

Jim brightened up and finished his steak, sopping bread in the gravy when the meat was gone.

"When I was a kid—" he began, but broke off abruptly.

Again the unseen thing of gloom had fluttered, and his being was vibrant with premonition of impending misfortune. He felt a disruptive influence at work in the flesh of him, and in all his muscles there was a seeming that they were about to begin to twitch. He sat back suddenly, and as suddenly leaned forward with his elbows on the table. A tremor ran dimly through the muscles of his body. It was like the first rustling of leaves before the oncoming of wind. He clenched his teeth. It came again, a spasmodic tensing of his muscles. He knew panic at the revolt within his being. His muscles no longer recognized his mastery over them. Again they spasmodically tensed, despite the will of him, for he had willed that they should not tense. This was revolution within himself, this was anarchy; and the terror of impotence rushed up in him as his flesh gripped and seemed to seize him in a clutch, chills running up and down his back and sweat starting on his brow. He glanced about the room, and all the details of it smote him with a strange sense of familiarity. It was as though he had just returned from a long journey. He looked across the table at his partner. Matt was watching him and smiling. An expression of horror spread over Jim's face.

"My God, Matt!" he screamed. "You ain't doped me?"

Matt smiled and continued to watch him. In the paroxysm that followed, Jim did not become unconscious. His muscles tensed and twitched and knotted, hurting him and crushing him in their savage grip. And in the midst of it all, it came to him that Matt was acting queerly. He was travelling the same road. The smile had gone from his face, and there was on it an intent expression, as if he were listening to some inner tale of himself and trying to divine the message. Matt got up and walked across the room and back again, then sat down.

"You did this, Jim," he said quietly.

"But I didn't think you'd try to fix ME," Jim answered reproachfully.

"Oh, I fixed you all right," Matt said, with teeth close together and shivering body. "What did you give me?"

"Strychnine."

"Same as I gave you," Matt volunteered. "It's a hell of a mess, ain't it?"

"You're lyin', Matt," Jim pleaded. "You ain't doped me, have you?"

"I sure did, Jim; an' I didn't overdose you, neither. I cooked it in as neat as you please in your half the porterhouse.—Hold on! Where're you goin'?"

Jim had made a dash for the door, and was throwing back the bolts. Matt sprang in between and shoved him away.

"Drug store," Jim panted. "Drug store."

"No you don't. You'll stay right here. There ain't goin' to be any runnin' out an' makin' a poison play on the street—not with all them jools reposin' under the pillow. Savve? Even if you didn't die, you'd be in the hands of the police with a whole lot of explanations comin'. Emetics is the stuff for poison. I'm just as bad bit as you, an' I'm goin' to take a emetic. That's all they'd give you at a drug store, anyway."

He thrust Jim back into the middle of the room and shot the bolts into place. As he went across the floor to the food shelf, he passed one hand over his brow and flung off the beaded sweat. It spattered audibly on the floor. Jim watched agonizedly as Matt got the mustard-can and a cup and ran for the sink. He stirred a cupful of mustard and water and drank it down. Jim had followed him and was reaching with trembling hands for the empty cup. Again Matt shoved him away. As he mixed a second cupful, he demanded—

"D'you think one cup'll do for me? You can wait till I'm done."

Jim started to totter toward the door, but Matt checked him.

"If you monkey with that door, I'll twist your neck. Savve? You can take yours when I'm done. An' if it saves you, I'll twist your neck, anyway. You ain't got no chance, nohow. I told you many times what you'd get if you did me dirt."

"But you did me dirt, too," Jim articulated with an effort.

Matt was drinking the second cupful, and did not answer. The sweat had got into Jim's eyes, and he could scarcely see his way to the table, where he got a cup for himself. But Matt was mixing a third cupful, and, as before, thrust him away.

"I told you to wait till I was done," Matt growled. "Get outa my way."

And Jim supported his twitching body by holding on to the sink, the while he yearned toward the yellowish concoction that stood for life. It was by sheer will that he stood and clung to the sink. His flesh strove to double him up and bring him to the floor. Matt drank the third cupful, and with difficulty managed to get to a chair and sit down. His first paroxysm was passing. The spasms that afflicted him were dying away. This good effect he ascribed to the mustard and water. He was safe, at any rate. He wiped the sweat from his face, and, in the interval of calm, found room for curiosity. He looked at his partner.

A spasm had shaken the mustard can out of Jim's hands, and the contents were spilled upon the floor. He stooped to scoop some of the mustard into the cup, and the succeeding spasm doubled him upon the floor. Matt smiled.

"Stay with it," he encouraged. "It's the stuff all right. It's fixed me up."

Jim heard him and turned toward him a stricken face, twisted with suffering and pleading. Spasm now followed spasm till he was in convulsions, rolling on the floor and yellowing his face and hair in the mustard.

Matt laughed hoarsely at the sight, but the laugh broke midway. A tremor had run through his body. A new paroxysm was beginning. He arose and staggered across to the sink, where, with probing forefinger, he vainly strove to assist the action of the emetic. In the end, he clung to the sink as Jim had clung, filled with the horror of going down to the floor.

The other's paroxysm had passed, and he sat up, weak and fainting, too weak to rise, his forehead dripping, his lips flecked with a foam made yellow by the mustard in which he had rolled. He rubbed his eyes with his knuckles, and groans that were like whines came from his throat.

"What are you snifflin' about?" Matt demanded out of his agony. "All you got to do is die. An' when you die you're dead."

"I... ain't... snifflin'... it's... the... mustard... stingin'... my... eyes," Jim panted with desperate slowness.

It was his last successful attempt at speech. Thereafter he babbled incoherently, pawing the air with shaking arms till a fresh convulsion stretched him on the floor.

Matt struggled back to the chair, and, doubled up on it, with his arms clasped about his knees, he fought with his disintegrating flesh. He came out of the convulsion cool and weak. He looked to see how it went with the other, and saw him lying motionless.

He tried to soliloquize, to be facetious, to have his last grim laugh at life, but his lips made only incoherent sounds. The thought came to him that the emetic had failed, and that nothing remained but the drug store. He looked toward the door and drew himself to his feet. There he saved himself from falling by clutching the chair. Another paroxysm had begun. And in the midst of the paroxysm, with his body and all the parts of it flying apart and writhing and twisting back again into knots, he clung to the chair and shoved it before him across the floor. The last shreds of his will were leaving him when he gained the door. He turned the key and shot back one bolt. He fumbled for the second bolt, but failed. Then he leaned his weight against the door and slid down gently to the floor.

CREATED HE THEM

She met him at the door.

"I did not think you would be so early."

"It is half past eight." He looked at his watch. "The train leaves at 9.12."

He was very businesslike, until he saw her lips tremble as she abruptly turned and led the way.

"It'll be all right, little woman," he said soothingly. "Doctor Bodineau's the man. He'll pull him through, you'll see."

They entered the living-room. His glance quested apprehensively about, then turned to her.

"Where's Al?"

She did not answer, but with a sudden impulse came close to him and stood motionless. She was a slender, dark-eyed woman, in whose face was stamped the strain and stress of living. But the fine lines and the haunted look in the eyes were not the handiwork of mere worry. He knew whose handiwork it was as he looked upon it, and she knew when she consulted her mirror.

"It's no use, Mary," he said. He put his hand on her shoulder. "We've tried everything. It's a wretched business, I know, but what else can we do? You've failed. Doctor Bodineau's all that's left."

"If I had another chance..." she began falteringly.

"We've threshed that all out," he answered harshly. "You've got to buck up, now. You know what conclusion we arrived at. You know you haven't the ghost of a hope in another chance."

She shook her head. "I know it. But it is terrible, the thought of his going away to fight it out alone."

"He won't be alone. There's Doctor Bodineau. And besides, it's a beautiful place."

She remained silent.

"It is the only thing," he said.

"It is the only thing," she repeated mechanically.

He looked at his watch. "Where's Al?"

"I'll send him."

When the door had closed behind her, he walked over to the window and looked out, drumming absently with his knuckles on the pane.

"Hello."

He turned and responded to the greeting of the man who had just entered. There was a perceptible drag to the man's feet as he walked across toward the window and paused irresolutely halfway.

"I've changed my mind, George," he announced hurriedly and nervously. "I'm not going."

He plucked at his sleeve, shuffled with his feet, dropped his eyes, and with a strong effort raised them again to confront the other.

George regarded him silently, his nostrils distending and his lean fingers unconsciously crooking like an eagle's talons about to clutch.

In line and feature, there was much of resemblance between the two men; and yet, in the strongest resemblances there was a radical difference. Theirs were the same black eyes, but those of the man at the window were sharp and straight looking, while those of the man in the middle of the room were cloudy and furtive. He could not face the other's gaze, and continually and vainly struggled with himself to do so. The high cheek bones with the hollows beneath were the same, yet the texture of the hollows seemed different. The thin-lipped mouths were from the same mould, but George's lips were firm and muscular, while Al's were soft and loose—the lips of an

243

ascetic turned voluptuary. There was also a sag at the corners. His flesh hinted of grossness, especially so in the eagle-like aquiline nose that must once have been like the other's, but that had lost the austerity the other's still retained.

Al fought for steadiness in the middle of the floor. The silence bothered him. He had a feeling that he was about to begin swaying back and forth. He moistened his lips with his tongue.

"I'm going to stay," he said desperately.

He dropped his eyes and plucked again at his sleeve.

"And you are only twenty-six years old," George said at last. "You poor, feeble old man."

"Don't be so sure of that," Al retorted, with a flash of belligerence.

"Do you remember when we swam that mile and a half across the channel?"

"Well, and what of it?" A sullen expression was creeping across Al's face.

"And do you remember when we boxed in the barn after school?"

"I could take all you gave me."

"All I gave you!" George's voice rose momentarily to a higher pitch. "You licked me four afternoons out of five. You were twice as strong as I—three times as strong. And now I'd be afraid to land on you with a sofa cushion; you'd crumple up like a last year's leaf. You'd die, you poor, miserable old man."

"You needn't abuse me just because I've changed my mind," the other protested, the hint of a whine in his voice.

His wife entered, and he looked appealingly to her; but the man at the window strode suddenly up to him and burst out—

"You don't know your own mind for two successive minutes! You haven't any mind, you spineless, crawling worm!"

"You can't make me angry." Al smiled with cunning, and glanced triumphantly at his wife. "You can't make me angry," he repeated, as though the idea were thoroughly gratifying to him. "I know your game. It's my stomach, I tell you. I can't help it. Before God, I can't! Isn't it my stomach, Mary?"

She glanced at George and spoke composedly, though she hid a trembling hand in a fold of her skirt.

"Isn't it time?" she asked softly.

Her husband turned upon her savagely. "I'm not going to go!" he cried. "That's just what I've been telling... him. And I tell you again, all of you, I'm not going. You can't bully me."

"Why, Al, dear, you said—" she began.

"Never mind what I said!" he broke out. "I've said something else right now, and you've heard it, and that settles it."

He walked across the room and threw himself with emphasis into a Morris chair. But the other man was swiftly upon him. The talon-like fingers gripped his shoulders, jerked him to his feet, and held him there.

"You've reached the limit, Al, and I want you to understand it. I've tried to treat you like... like my brother, but hereafter I shall treat you like the thing that you are. Do you understand?"

The anger in his voice was cold. The blaze in his eyes was cold. It was vastly more effective than any outburst, and Al cringed under it and under the clutching hand that was bruising his shoulder muscles.

"It is only because of me that you have this house, that you have the food you eat. Your position? Any other man would have been shown the door a year ago—two years ago. I have held you in it. Your salary has been charity. It has been paid out of my pocket. Mary... her dresses... that gown she has on is made over; she wears the discarded dresses of her sisters, of my wife. Charity—do you understand? Your children—they are wearing the discarded clothes of my children, of the children of my neighbours who think the clothes went to some orphan asylum. And it is an orphan asylum... or it soon will be."

He emphasized each point with an unconscious tightening of his grip on the shoulder. Al was squirming with the pain of it. The sweat was starting out on his forehead.

"Now listen well to me," his brother went on. "In three minutes you will tell me that you are going with me. If you don't, Mary and the children will be taken away from you—to-day. You needn't ever come to the office. This house will be closed to you. And in six months I shall have the pleasure of burying you. You have three minutes to make up your mind."

Al made a strangling movement, and reached up with weak fingers to the clutching hand.

"My heart... let me go... you'll be the death of me," he gasped.

The hand thrust him down forcibly into the Morris chair and released him.

The clock on the mantle ticked loudly. George glanced at it, and at Mary. She was leaning against the table, unable to conceal her trembling. He became unpleasantly aware of the feeling of his brother's fingers on his hand. Quite unconsciously he wiped the back of the hand upon his coat. The clock ticked on in the silence. It seemed to George that the room reverberated with his voice. He could hear himself still speaking.

"I'll go," came from the Morris chair.

It was a weak and shaken voice, and it was a weak and shaken man that pulled himself out of the Morris chair. He started toward the door.

"Where are you going?" George demanded.

"Suit case," came the response. "Mary'll send the trunk later. I'll be back in a minute."

The door closed after him. A moment later, struck with sudden suspicion, George was opening the door. He glanced in. His brother stood at a sideboard, in one hand a decanter, in the other hand, bottom up and to his lips, a whisky glass.

Across the glass Al saw that he was observed. It threw him into a panic. Hastily he tried to refill the glass and get it to his lips; but glass and decanter were sent smashing to the floor. He snarled. It was like the sound of a wild beast. But the grip on his shoulder subdued and frightened him. He was being propelled toward the door.

"The suit case," he gasped. "It's there in that room. Let me get it."

"Where's the key?" his brother asked, when he had brought it.

"It isn't locked."

The next moment the suit case was spread open, and George's hand was searching the contents. From one side it brought out a bottle of whisky, from the other side a flask. He snapped the case to.

"Come on," he said. "If we miss one car, we miss that train."

He went out into the hallway, leaving Al with his wife. It was like a funeral, George thought, as he waited.

His brother's overcoat caught on the knob of the front door and delayed its closing long enough for Mary's first sob to come to their ears. George's lips were very thin and compressed as he went down the steps. In one hand he carried the suit case. With the other hand he held his brother's arm.

As they neared the corner, he heard the electric car a block away, and urged his brother on. Al was breathing hard. His feet dragged and shuffled, and he held back.

"A hell of a brother YOU are," he panted.

For reply, he received a vicious jerk on his arm. It reminded him of his childhood when he was hurried along by some angry grown-up. And like a child, he had to be helped up the car step. He sank down on an outside seat, panting, sweating, overcome by the exertion. He followed George's eyes as the latter looked him up and down.

247

"A hell of a brother YOU are," was George's comment when he had finished the inspection.

Moisture welled into Al's eyes.

"It's my stomach," he said with self-pity.

"I don't wonder," was the retort. "Burnt out like the crater of a volcano. Fervent heat isn't a circumstance."

Thereafter they did not speak. When they arrived at the transfer point, George came to himself with a start. He smiled. With fixed gaze that did not see the houses that streamed across his field of vision, he had himself been sunk deep in self-pity. He helped his brother from the car, and looked up the intersecting street. The car they were to take was not in sight.

Al's eyes chanced upon the corner grocery and saloon across the way. At once he became restless. His hands passed beyond his control, and he yearned hungrily across the street to the door that swung open even as he looked and let in a happy pilgrim. And in that instant he saw the white-jacketed bartender against an array of glittering glass. Quite unconsciously he started to cross the street.

"Hold on." George's hand was on his arm.

"I want some whisky," he answered.

"You've already had some."

"That was hours ago. Go on, George, let me have some. It's the last day. Don't shut off on me until we get there—God knows it will be soon enough."

George glanced desperately up the street. The car was in sight.

"There isn't time for a drink," he said.

"I don't want a drink. I want a bottle." Al's voice became wheedling. "Go on, George. It's the last, the very last."

"No." The denial was as final as George's thin lips could make it.

Al glanced at the approaching car. He sat down suddenly on the curbstone.

"What's the matter?" his brother asked, with momentary alarm.

"Nothing. I want some whisky. It's my stomach."

"Come on now, get up."

George reached for him, but was anticipated, for his brother sprawled flat on the pavement, oblivious to the dirt and to the curious glances of the passers-by. The car was clanging its gong at the crossing, a block away.

"You'll miss it," Al grinned from the pavement. "And it will be your fault."

George's fists clenched tightly.

"For two cents I'd give you a thrashing."

"And miss the car," was the triumphant comment from the pavement.

George looked at the car. It was halfway down the block. He looked at his watch. He debated a second longer.

"All right," he said. "I'll get it. But you get on that car. If you miss it, I'll break the bottle over your head."

He dashed across the street and into the saloon. The car came in and stopped. There were no passengers to get off. Al dragged himself up the steps and sat down. He smiled as the conductor rang the bell and the car started. The swinging door of the saloon burst open. Clutching in his hand the suit case and a pint bottle of whisky, George started in pursuit. The conductor, his hand on the bell cord, waited to see if it would be necessary to stop. It was not. George swung lightly aboard, sat down beside his brother, and passed him the bottle.

"You might have got a quart," Al said reproachfully.

He extracted the cork with a pocket corkscrew, and elevated the bottle.

"I'm sick... my stomach," he explained in apologetic tones to the passenger who sat next to him.

In the train they sat in the smoking-car. George felt that it was imperative. Also, having successfully caught the train, his heart softened. He felt more kindly toward his brother, and accused himself of unnecessary harshness. He strove to atone by talking about their mother, and sisters, and the little affairs and interests of the family. But Al was morose, and devoted himself to the bottle. As the time passed, his mouth hung looser and looser, while the rings under his eyes seemed to puff out and all his facial muscles to relax.

"It's my stomach," he said, once, when he finished the bottle and dropped it under the seat; but the swift hardening of his brother's face did not encourage further explanations.

The conveyance that met them at the station had all the dignity and luxuriousness of a private carriage. George's eyes were keen for the ear marks of the institution to which they were going, but his apprehensions were allayed from moment to moment. As they entered the wide gateway and rolled on through the spacious grounds, he felt sure that the institutional side of the place would not jar upon his brother. It was more like a summer hotel, or, better yet, a country club. And as they swept on through the spring sunshine, the songs of birds in his ears, and in his nostrils the breath of flowers, George sighed for a week of rest in such a place, and before his eyes loomed the arid vista of summer in town and at the office. There was not room in his income for his brother and himself.

"Let us take a walk in the grounds," he suggested, after they had met Doctor Bodineau and inspected the quarters assigned to Al. "The carriage leaves for the station in half an hour, and we'll just have time."

"It's beautiful," he remarked a moment later. Under his feet was the velvet grass, the trees arched overhead, and he stood in mottled sunshine. "I wish I could stay for a month."

"I'll trade places with you," Al said quickly.

George laughed it off, but he felt a sinking of the heart.

"Look at that oak!" he cried. "And that woodpecker! Isn't he a beauty!"

"I don't like it here," he heard his brother mutter.

George's lips tightened in preparation for the struggle, but he said—

"I'm going to send Mary and the children off to the mountains. She needs it, and so do they. And when you're in shape, I'll send you right on to join them. Then you can take your summer vacation before you come back to the office."

"I'm not going to stay in this damned hole, for all you talk about it," Al announced abruptly.

"Yes you are, and you're going to get your health and strength back again, so that the look of you will put the colour in Mary's cheeks where it used to be."

"I'm going back with you." Al's voice was firm. "I'm going to take the same train back. It's about time for that carriage, I guess."

"I haven't told you all my plans," George tried to go on, but Al cut him off.

"You might as well quit that. I don't want any of your soapy talking. You treat me like a child. I'm not a child. My mind's made up, and I'll show you how long it can stay made up. You needn't talk to me. I don't care a rap for what you're going to say."

A baleful light was in his eyes, and to his brother he seemed for all the world like a cornered rat, desperate and ready to fight. As George looked at him he remembered back to their childhood, and it came to him that at last was aroused in Al the same old stubborn strain that had enabled him, as a child, to stand against all force and persuasion.

George abandoned hope. He had lost. This creature was not human. The last fine instinct of the human had fled. It was a brute, sluggish and stolid, impossible to move—just the raw stuff of life, combative, rebellious, and indomitable. And as he contemplated his brother he felt in himself the rising up of a similar brute. He became suddenly aware that his fingers were tensing and crooking like a thug's, and he knew the desire to kill. And his reason, turned traitor at last, counselled that he should kill, that it was the only thing left for him to do.

He was aroused by a servant calling to him through the trees that the carriage was waiting. He answered. Then, looking straight before him, he discovered his brother. He had forgotten it was his brother. It had been only a thing the moment before. He began to talk, and as he talked the way became clear to him. His reason had not turned traitor. The brute in him had merely orientated his reason.

"You are no earthly good, Al," he said. "You know that. You've made Mary's life a hell. You are a curse to your children. And you have not made life exactly a paradise for the rest of us."

"There's no use your talking," Al interjected. "I'm not going to stay here."

"That's what I'm coming to," George continued. "You don't have to stay here." (Al's face brightened, and he involuntarily made a movement, as though about to start toward the carriage.) "On the other hand, it is not necessary that you should return with me. There is another way."

George's hand went to his hip pocket and appeared with a revolver. It lay along his palm, the butt toward Al, and toward Al he extended it. At the same time, with his head, he indicated the near-by thicket.

"You can't bluff me," Al snarled.

"It is not a bluff, Al. Look at me. I mean it. And if you don't do it for yourself, I shall have to do it for you."

They faced each other, the proffered revolver still extended. Al debated for a moment, then his eyes blazed. With a quick movement he seized the revolver.

"My God! I'll do it," he said. "I'll show you what I've got in me."

George felt suddenly sick. He turned away. He did not see his brother enter the thicket, but he heard the passage of his body through the leaves and branches.

"Good-bye, Al," he called.

"Good-bye," came from the thicket.

George felt the sweat upon his forehead. He began mopping his face with his handkerchief. He heard, as from a remote distance, the voice of the servant again calling to him that the carriage was waiting. The woodpecker dropped down through the mottled sunshine and lighted on the trunk of a tree a dozen feet away. George felt that it was all a dream, and yet through it all he felt supreme justification. It was the right thing to do. It was the only thing.

His whole body gave a spasmodic start, as though the revolver had been fired. It was the voice of Al, close at his back.

"Here's your gun," Al said. "I'll stay."

The servant appeared among the trees, approaching rapidly and calling anxiously. George put the weapon in his pocket and caught both his brother's hands in his own.

"God bless you, old man," he murmured; "and"—with a final squeeze of the hands—"good luck!"

"I'm coming," he called to the servant, and turned and ran through the trees toward the carriage.

THE CHINAGO

"The coral waxes, the palm grows, but man departs."

—*Tahitian proverb.*

Ah Cho did not understand French. He sat in the crowded court room, very weary and bored, listening to the unceasing, explosive French that now one official and now another uttered. It was just so much gabble to Ah Cho, and he marvelled at the stupidity of the Frenchmen who took so long to find out the murderer of Chung Ga, and who did not find him at all. The five hundred coolies on the plantation knew that Ah San had done the killing, and here was Ah San not even arrested. It was true that all the coolies had agreed secretly not to testify against one another; but then, it was so simple, the Frenchmen should have been able to discover that Ah San was the man. They were very stupid, these Frenchmen.

Ah Cho had done nothing of which to be afraid. He had had no hand in the killing. It was true he had been present at it, and Schemmer, the overseer on the plantation, had rushed into the barracks immediately afterward and caught him there, along with four or five others; but what of that? Chung Ga had been stabbed only twice. It stood to reason that five or six men could not inflict two stab wounds. At the most, if a man had struck but once, only two men could have done it.

So it was that Ah Cho reasoned, when he, along with his four companions, had lied and blocked and obfuscated in their statements to the court concerning what had taken place. They had heard the sounds of the killing, and, like Schemmer, they had run to the spot. They had got there before Schemmer—that was all. True, Schemmer had testified that, attracted by the sound of quarrelling as he chanced to pass by, he had stood for at least five minutes outside; that then, when he entered, he found the prisoners already inside; and that they had not entered just before, because he had been standing by the one door to the barracks. But what of that? Ah Cho and his four fellow-prisoners had testified that Schemmer was mistaken. In the end they would be let go. They were all confident of that. Five men could not have their heads cut off for two stab wounds. Besides, no foreign devil had seen the killing. But these Frenchmen were so stupid. In China, as Ah Cho well knew, the magistrate would order all of them to the torture and learn the truth. The truth was very easy to learn under torture. But these Frenchmen did not torture—bigger fools they! Therefore they would never find out who killed Chung Ga.

But Ah Cho did not understand everything. The English Company that owned the plantation had imported into Tahiti, at great expense, the five hundred coolies. The stockholders were clamouring for dividends, and the Company had not yet paid any; wherefore the Company did not want its costly contract labourers to start the practice of killing one another. Also, there were the French, eager and willing to impose upon the Chinagos the virtues and excellences of French law. There was nothing like setting an example once in a while; and, besides, of what use was New Caledonia except to send men to live out their days in misery and pain in payment of the penalty for being frail and human?

Ah Cho did not understand all this. He sat in the court room and waited for the baffled judgment that would set him and his comrades free to go back to the plantation and work out the terms of their contracts. This judgment would soon be rendered. Proceedings were drawing to a close. He could see that. There was no more testifying, no more gabble of tongues. The French devils were tired, too, and evidently waiting for the judgment. And as he waited he remembered back in his life to the time when he had signed the contract and set sail in the ship for Tahiti. Times had been hard in his sea-coast village, and when he indentured himself to labour for five years in the South Seas at fifty cents Mexican a day, he had thought himself fortunate. There were men in his village who toiled a whole year for ten dollars Mexican, and there were women who made nets all the year round for five dollars, while in the houses of shopkeepers there were maidservants who received four dollars for a year of service. And here he was to receive fifty cents a day; for one day, only one day, he was to receive that princely sum! What if the work were hard? At the end of the five years he would return home—that was in the contract—and he would never have to work again. He would be a rich man for life, with a house of his own, a wife, and children growing up to venerate him. Yes, and back of the house he would have a small garden, a place of meditation and repose, with goldfish in a tiny lakelet, and wind bells tinkling in the several trees, and there would be a high wall all around so that his meditation and repose should be undisturbed.

Well, he had worked out three of those five years. He was already a wealthy man (in his own country) through his earnings, and only two years more intervened between the cotton plantation on Tahiti and the meditation and repose that awaited him. But just now he was losing money because of the unfortunate accident of being present at the killing of Chung Ga. He had lain three weeks in prison, and for each day of those three weeks he had lost fifty cents. But now judgment would soon be given, and he would go back to work.

Ah Cho was twenty-two years old. He was happy and good-natured, and it was easy for him to smile. While his body was slim in the Asiatic way, his face was rotund. It was round, like the moon, and it irradiated a gentle complacence and a sweet kindliness of spirit that was unusual among his countrymen. Nor did his looks belie him. He never caused trouble, never took part in wrangling. He did not gamble. His soul was not harsh enough for the soul that must belong to a gambler. He was content with little things and simple pleasures. The hush and quiet in the cool of the day after the blazing toil in the cotton field was to him an infinite satisfaction. He could sit for hours gazing at a solitary flower and philosophizing about the mysteries and riddles of being. A blue heron on a tiny crescent of sandy beach, a silvery splatter of flying fish, or a sunset of pearl and rose across the lagoon, could entrance him to all forgetfulness of the procession of wearisome days and of the heavy lash of Schemmer.

Schemmer, Karl Schemmer, was a brute, a brutish brute. But he earned his salary. He got the last particle of strength out of the five hundred slaves;

for slaves they were until their term of years was up. Schemmer worked hard to extract the strength from those five hundred sweating bodies and to transmute it into bales of fluffy cotton ready for export. His dominant, iron-clad, primeval brutishness was what enabled him to effect the transmutation. Also, he was assisted by a thick leather belt, three inches wide and a yard in length, with which he always rode and which, on occasion, could come down on the naked back of a stooping coolie with a report like a pistol-shot. These reports were frequent when Schemmer rode down the furrowed field.

Once, at the beginning of the first year of contract labour, he had killed a coolie with a single blow of his fist. He had not exactly crushed the man's head like an egg-shell, but the blow had been sufficient to addle what was inside, and, after being sick for a week, the man had died. But the Chinese had not complained to the French devils that ruled over Tahiti. It was their own look out. Schemmer was their problem. They must avoid his wrath as they avoided the venom of the centipedes that lurked in the grass or crept into the sleeping quarters on rainy nights. The Chinagos—such they were called by the indolent, brown-skinned island folk—saw to it that they did not displease Schemmer too greatly. This was equivalent to rendering up to him a full measure of efficient toil. That blow of Schemmer's fist had been worth thousands of dollars to the Company, and no trouble ever came of it to Schemmer.

The French, with no instinct for colonization, futile in their childish playgame of developing the resources of the island, were only too glad to see the English Company succeed. What matter of Schemmer and his redoubtable fist? The Chinago that died? Well, he was only a Chinago. Besides, he died of sunstroke, as the doctor's certificate attested. True, in all the history of Tahiti no one had ever died of sunstroke. But it was that, precisely that, which made the death of this Chinago unique. The doctor said as much in his report. He was very candid. Dividends must be paid, or else one more failure would be added to the long history of failure in Tahiti.

There was no understanding these white devils. Ah Cho pondered their inscrutableness as he sat in the court room waiting the judgment. There was no telling what went on at the back of their minds. He had seen a few of the white devils. They were all alike—the officers and sailors on the ship, the French officials, the several white men on the plantation, including Schemmer. Their minds all moved in mysterious ways there was no getting at. They grew angry without apparent cause, and their anger was always dangerous. They were like wild beasts at such times. They worried about little things, and on occasion could out-toil even a Chinago. They were not temperate as Chinagos were temperate; they were gluttons, eating prodigiously and drinking more prodigiously. A Chinago never knew when an act would please them or arouse a storm of wrath. A Chinago could never tell. What pleased one time, the very next time might provoke an outburst of anger. There was a curtain behind the eyes of the white devils that screened the backs of their minds from the Chinago's gaze. And then, on top of it all, was that terrible efficiency of the white devils, that ability to do things, to make things go, to work results, to bend to their wills all creeping, crawling things, and the powers of the very elements themselves. Yes, the white men were strange and wonderful, and they were devils. Look at Schemmer.

Ah Cho wondered why the judgment was so long in forming. Not a man on trial had laid hand on Chung Ga. Ah San alone had killed him. Ah San had done it, bending Chung Ga's head back with one hand by a grip of his queue, and with the other hand, from behind, reaching over and driving the knife into his body. Twice had he driven it in. There in the court room, with closed eyes, Ah Cho saw the killing acted over again—the squabble, the vile words bandied back and forth, the filth and insult flung upon venerable ancestors, the curses laid upon unbegotten generations, the leap of Ah San, the grip on the queue of Chung Ga, the knife that sank twice into his flesh, the bursting open of the door, the irruption of Schemmer, the dash for the door, the escape of Ah San, the flying belt of Schemmer that drove the rest into the corner, and the firing of the revolver as a signal that brought help to Schemmer. Ah Cho shivered as he lived it over. One blow of the belt had bruised his cheek, taking off some of the skin. Schemmer had pointed to the bruises when, on the witness-stand, he had identified Ah Cho. It was only just now that the marks had become no longer visible. That had been a blow. Half an inch nearer the centre and it would have taken out his eye. Then Ah Cho forgot the whole happening in a vision he caught of the garden of meditation and repose that would be his when he returned to his own land.

He sat with impassive face, while the magistrate rendered the judgment. Likewise were the faces of his four companions impassive. And they remained impassive when the interpreter explained that the five of them had been found guilty of the murder of Chung Ga, and that Ah Chow should have his head cut off, Ah Cho serve twenty years in prison in New Caledonia, Wong Li twelve years, and Ah Tong ten years. There was no use in getting excited about it. Even Ah Chow remained expressionless as a mummy, though it was his head that was to be cut off. The magistrate added a few words, and the interpreter explained that Ah Chow's face having been most severely bruised by Schemmer's strap had made his identification so positive that, since one man must die, he might as well be that man. Also, the fact that Ah Cho's face likewise had been severely bruised, conclusively proving his presence at the murder and his undoubted participation, had merited him the twenty years of penal servitude. And down to the ten years of Ah Tong, the proportioned reason for each sentence was explained. Let the Chinagos take the lesson to heart, the Court said finally, for they must learn that the law would be fulfilled in Tahiti though the heavens fell.

The five Chinagos were taken back to jail. They were not shocked nor grieved. The sentences being unexpected was quite what they were accustomed to in their dealings with the white devils. From them a Chinago rarely expected more than the unexpected. The heavy punishment for a crime they had not committed was no stranger than the countless strange things that white devils did. In the weeks that followed, Ah Cho often contemplated Ah Chow with mild curiosity. His head was to be cut off by the guillotine that was being erected on the plantation. For him there would be no declining years, no gardens of tranquillity. Ah Cho philosophized and speculated about life and death. As for himself, he was not perturbed. Twenty years were merely twenty years. By that much was his garden removed from him—that was all. He was young, and the patience of Asia was in his bones. He could wait those twenty years, and by that time the heats of his blood would be assuaged and he would be better fitted for that garden of calm delight. He thought of a name for it; he would call it The Garden of the Morning Calm. He was made happy all day by the thought, and he was inspired to devise a moral maxim on the virtue of patience, which maxim proved a great comfort, especially to Wong Li and Ah Tong. Ah Chow, however, did not care for the maxim. His head was to be separated from his body in so short a time that he had no need for patience to wait for that event. He smoked well, ate well, slept well, and did not worry about the slow passage of time.

Cruchot was a gendarme. He had seen twenty years of service in the colonies, from Nigeria and Senegal to the South Seas, and those twenty years had not perceptibly brightened his dull mind. He was as slow-witted and stupid as in his peasant days in the south of France. He knew discipline and fear of authority, and from God down to the sergeant of gendarmes the only difference to him was the measure of slavish obedience which he rendered. In point of fact, the sergeant bulked bigger in his mind than God, except on Sundays when God's mouthpieces had their say. God was usually very remote, while the sergeant was ordinarily very close at hand.

Cruchot it was who received the order from the Chief Justice to the jailer commanding that functionary to deliver over to Cruchot the person of Ah Chow. Now, it happened that the Chief Justice had given a dinner the night before to the captain and officers of the French man-of-war. His hand was shaking when he wrote out the order, and his eyes were aching so dreadfully that he did not read over the order. It was only a Chinago's life he was signing away, anyway. So he did not notice that he had omitted the final letter in Ah Chow's name. The order read "Ah Cho," and, when Cruchot presented the order, the jailer turned over to him the person of Ah Cho. Cruchot took that person beside him on the seat of a wagon, behind two mules, and drove away.

Ah Cho was glad to be out in the sunshine. He sat beside the gendarme and beamed. He beamed more ardently than ever when he noted the mules headed south toward Atimaono. Undoubtedly Schemmer had sent for him to be brought back. Schemmer wanted him to work. Very well, he would work well. Schemmer would never have cause to complain. It was a hot day. There had been a stoppage of the trades. The mules sweated, Cruchot sweated, and Ah Cho sweated. But it was Ah Cho that bore the heat with the least concern. He had toiled three years under that sun on the plantation. He beamed and beamed with such genial good nature that even Cruchot's heavy mind was stirred to wonderment.

"You are very funny," he said at last.

Ah Cho nodded and beamed more ardently. Unlike the magistrate, Cruchot spoke to him in the Kanaka tongue, and this, like all Chinagos and all foreign devils, Ah Cho understood.

"You laugh too much," Cruchot chided. "One's heart should be full of tears on a day like this."

"I am glad to get out of the jail."

"Is that all?" The gendarme shrugged his shoulders.

"Is it not enough?" was the retort.

"Then you are not glad to have your head cut off?"

Ah Cho looked at him in abrupt perplexity, and said—

"Why, I am going back to Atimaono to work on the plantation for Schemmer. Are you not taking me to Atimaono?"

Cruchot stroked his long moustaches reflectively. "Well, well," he said finally, with a flick of the whip at the off mule, "so you don't know?"

"Know what?" Ah Cho was beginning to feel a vague alarm. "Won't Schemmer let me work for him any more?"

"Not after to-day." Cruchot laughed heartily. It was a good joke. "You see, you won't be able to work after to-day. A man with his head off can't work, eh?" He poked the Chinago in the ribs, and chuckled.

Ah Cho maintained silence while the mules trotted a hot mile. Then he spoke: "Is Schemmer going to cut off my head?"

Cruchot grinned as he nodded.

"It is a mistake," said Ah Cho, gravely. "I am not the Chinago that is to have his head cut off. I am Ah Cho. The honourable judge has determined that I am to stop twenty years in New Caledonia."

The gendarme laughed. It was a good joke, this funny Chinago trying to cheat the guillotine. The mules trotted through a coconut grove and for half a mile beside the sparkling sea before Ah Cho spoke again.

"I tell you I am not Ah Chow. The honourable judge did not say that my head was to go off."

"Don't be afraid," said Cruchot, with the philanthropic intention of making it easier for his prisoner. "It is not difficult to die that way." He snapped his fingers. "It is quick—like that. It is not like hanging on the end of a rope and kicking and making faces for five minutes. It is like killing a chicken with a hatchet. You cut its head off, that is all. And it is the same with a man. Pouf!—it is over. It doesn't hurt. You don't even think it hurts. You don't think. Your head is gone, so you cannot think. It is very good. That is the way I want to die—quick, ah, quick. You are lucky to die that way. You might get the leprosy and fall to pieces slowly, a finger at a time, and now and again a thumb, also the toes. I knew a man who was burned by hot water. It took him two days to die. You could hear him yelling a kilometre away. But you? Ah! so easy! Chck!—the knife cuts your neck like that. It is finished. The knife may even tickle. Who can say? Nobody who died that way ever came back to say."

He considered this last an excruciating joke, and permitted himself to be convulsed with laughter for half a minute. Part of his mirth was assumed, but he considered it his humane duty to cheer up the Chinago.

"But I tell you I am Ah Cho," the other persisted. "I don't want my head cut off."

Cruchot scowled. The Chinago was carrying the foolishness too far.

"I am not Ah Chow—" Ah Cho began.

"That will do," the gendarme interrupted. He puffed up his cheeks and strove to appear fierce.

"I tell you I am not—" Ah Cho began again.

"Shut up!" bawled Cruchot.

After that they rode along in silence. It was twenty miles from Papeete to Atimaono, and over half the distance was covered by the time the Chinago again ventured into speech.

"I saw you in the court room, when the honourable judge sought after our guilt," he began. "Very good. And do you remember that Ah Chow, whose head is to be cut off—do you remember that he—Ah Chow—was a tall man? Look at me."

He stood up suddenly, and Cruchot saw that he was a short man. And just as suddenly Cruchot caught a glimpse of a memory picture of Ah Chow, and in that picture Ah Chow was tall. To the gendarme all Chinagos looked alike. One face was like another. But between tallness and shortness he could differentiate, and he knew that he had the wrong man beside him on the seat. He pulled up the mules abruptly, so that the pole shot ahead of them, elevating their collars.

"You see, it was a mistake," said Ah Cho, smiling pleasantly.

But Cruchot was thinking. Already he regretted that he had stopped the wagon. He was unaware of the error of the Chief Justice, and he had no way of working it out; but he did know that he had been given this Chinago to take to Atimaono and that it was his duty to take him to Atimaono. What if he was the wrong man and they cut his head off? It was only a Chinago when all was said, and what was a Chinago, anyway? Besides, it might not be a mistake. He did not know what went on in the minds of his superiors. They knew their business best. Who was he to do their thinking for them? Once, in the long ago, he had attempted to think for them, and the sergeant had said: "Cruchot, you are a fool! The quicker you know that, the better you will get on. You are not to think; you are to obey and leave thinking to your betters." He smarted under the recollection. Also, if he turned back to Papeete, he would delay the execution at Atimaono, and if he were wrong in turning back, he would get a reprimand from the sergeant who was waiting for the prisoner. And, furthermore, he would get a reprimand at Papeete as well.

He touched the mules with the whip and drove on. He looked at his watch. He would be half an hour late as it was, and the sergeant was bound to be angry. He put the mules into a faster trot. The more Ah Cho persisted in explaining the mistake, the more stubborn Cruchot became. The knowledge that he had the wrong man did not make his temper better. The knowledge that it was through no mistake of his confirmed him in the belief that the wrong he was doing was the right. And, rather than incur the displeasure of the sergeant, he would willingly have assisted a dozen wrong Chinagos to their doom.

As for Ah Cho, after the gendarme had struck him over the head with the butt of the whip and commanded him in a loud voice to shut up, there remained nothing for him to do but to shut up. The long ride continued in silence. Ah Cho pondered the strange ways of the foreign devils. There was no explaining them. What they were doing with him was of a piece with everything they did. First they found guilty five innocent men, and next they cut off the head of the man that even they, in their benighted ignorance, had deemed meritorious of no more than twenty years' imprisonment. And there was nothing he could do. He could only sit idly and take what these lords of life measured out to him. Once, he got in a panic, and the sweat upon his body turned cold; but he fought his way out of it. He endeavoured to resign himself to his fate by remembering and repeating certain passages from the "Yin Chih Wen" ("The Tract of the Quiet Way"); but, instead, he kept seeing his dream-garden of meditation and repose. This bothered him, until he abandoned himself to the dream and sat in his garden listening to the tinkling of the windbells in the several trees. And lo! sitting thus, in the dream, he was able to remember and repeat the passages from "The Tract of the Quiet Way."

So the time passed nicely until Atimaono was reached and the mules trotted up to the foot of the scaffold, in the shade of which stood the impatient sergeant. Ah Cho was hurried up the ladder of the scaffold. Beneath him on one side he saw assembled all the coolies of the plantation. Schemmer had decided that the event would be a good object-lesson, and so he called in the coolies from the fields and compelled them to be present. As they caught sight of Ah Cho they gabbled among themselves in low voices. They saw the mistake; but they kept it to themselves. The inexplicable white devils had doubtlessly changed their minds. Instead of taking the life of one innocent man, they were taking the life of another innocent man. Ah Chow or Ah Cho—what did it matter which? They could never understand the white dogs any more than could the white dogs understand them. Ah Cho was going to have his head cut off, but they, when their two remaining years of servitude were up, were going back to China.

Schemmer had made the guillotine himself. He was a handy man, and though he had never seen a guillotine, the French officials had explained the principle to him. It was on his suggestion that they had ordered the execution to take place at Atimaono instead of at Papeete. The scene of the crime, Schemmer had argued, was the best possible place for the punishment, and, in addition, it would have a salutary influence upon the half-thousand Chinagos on the plantation. Schemmer had also volunteered to act as executioner, and in that capacity he was now on the scaffold, experimenting with the instrument he had made. A banana tree, of the size and consistency of a man's neck, lay under the guillotine. Ah Cho watched with fascinated eyes. The German, turning a small crank, hoisted the blade to the top of the little derrick he had rigged. A jerk on a stout piece of cord loosed the blade and it dropped with a flash, neatly severing the banana trunk.

"How does it work?" The sergeant, coming out on top the scaffold, had asked the question.

"Beautifully," was Schemmer's exultant answer. "Let me show you."

Again he turned the crank that hoisted the blade, jerked the cord, and sent the blade crashing down on the soft tree. But this time it went no more than two-thirds of the way through.

The sergeant scowled. "That will not serve," he said.

Schemmer wiped the sweat from his forehead. "What it needs is more weight," he announced. Walking up to the edge of the scaffold, he called his orders to the blacksmith for a twenty-five-pound piece of iron. As he stooped over to attach the iron to the broad top of the blade, Ah Cho glanced at the sergeant and saw his opportunity.

"The honourable judge said that Ah Chow was to have his head cut off," he began.

The sergeant nodded impatiently. He was thinking of the fifteen-mile ride before him that afternoon, to the windward side of the island, and of Berthe, the pretty half-caste daughter of Lafiere, the pearl-trader, who was waiting for him at the end of it.

"Well, I am not Ah Chow. I am Ah Cho. The honourable jailer has made a mistake. Ah Chow is a tall man, and you see I am short."

The sergeant looked at him hastily and saw the mistake. "Schemmer!" he called, imperatively. "Come here."

The German grunted, but remained bent over his task till the chunk of iron was lashed to his satisfaction. "Is your Chinago ready?" he demanded.

"Look at him," was the answer. "Is he the Chinago?"

Schemmer was surprised. He swore tersely for a few seconds, and looked regretfully across at the thing he had made with his own hands and which he was eager to see work. "Look here," he said finally, "we can't postpone this affair. I've lost three hours' work already out of those five hundred Chinagos. I can't afford to lose it all over again for the right man. Let's put the performance through just the same. It is only a Chinago."

The sergeant remembered the long ride before him, and the pearl-trader's daughter, and debated with himself.

"They will blame it on Cruchot—if it is discovered," the German urged. "But there's little chance of its being discovered. Ah Chow won't give it away, at any rate."

"The blame won't lie with Cruchot, anyway," the sergeant said. "It must have been the jailer's mistake."

"Then let's go on with it. They can't blame us. Who can tell one Chinago from another? We can say that we merely carried out instructions with the Chinago that was turned over to us. Besides, I really can't take all those coolies a second time away from their labour."

They spoke in French, and Ah Cho, who did not understand a word of it, nevertheless knew that they were determining his destiny. He knew, also, that the decision rested with the sergeant, and he hung upon that official's lips.

"All right," announced the sergeant. "Go ahead with it. He is only a Chinago."

"I'm going to try it once more, just to make sure." Schemmer moved the banana trunk forward under the knife, which he had hoisted to the top of the derrick.

Ah Cho tried to remember maxims from "The Tract of the Quiet Way." "Live in concord," came to him; but it was not applicable. He was not going to live. He was about to die. No, that would not do. "Forgive malice"—yes, but there was no malice to forgive. Schemmer and the rest were doing this thing without malice. It was to them merely a piece of work that had to be done, just as clearing the jungle, ditching the water, and planting cotton were pieces of work that had to be done. Schemmer jerked the cord, and Ah Cho forgot "The Tract of the Quiet Way." The knife shot down with a thud, making a clean slice of the tree.

"Beautiful!" exclaimed the sergeant, pausing in the act of lighting a cigarette. "Beautiful, my friend."

Schemmer was pleased at the praise.

"Come on, Ah Chow," he said, in the Tahitian tongue.

"But I am not Ah Chow—" Ah Cho began.

"Shut up!" was the answer. "If you open your mouth again, I'll break your head."

The overseer threatened him with a clenched fist, and he remained silent. What was the good of protesting? Those foreign devils always had their way. He allowed himself to be lashed to the vertical board that was the size of his body. Schemmer drew the buckles tight—so tight that the straps cut into his flesh and hurt. But he did not complain. The hurt would not last long. He

267

felt the board tilting over in the air toward the horizontal, and closed his eyes. And in that moment he caught a last glimpse of his garden of meditation and repose. It seemed to him that he sat in the garden. A cool wind was blowing, and the bells in the several trees were tinkling softly. Also, birds were making sleepy noises, and from beyond the high wall came the subdued sound of village life.

Then he was aware that the board had come to rest, and from muscular pressures and tensions he knew that he was lying on his back. He opened his eyes. Straight above him he saw the suspended knife blazing in the sunshine. He saw the weight which had been added, and noted that one of Schemmer's knots had slipped. Then he heard the sergeant's voice in sharp command. Ah Cho closed his eyes hastily. He did not want to see that knife descend. But he felt it—for one great fleeting instant. And in that instant he remembered Cruchot and what Cruchot had said. But Cruchot was wrong. The knife did not tickle. That much he knew before he ceased to know.

MAKE WESTING

Whatever you do, make westing! make westing!
—Sailing directions for Cape Horn.

For seven weeks the Mary Rogers had been between 50 degrees south in the Atlantic and 50 degrees south in the Pacific, which meant that for seven weeks she had been struggling to round Cape Horn. For seven weeks she had been either in dirt, or close to dirt, save once, and then, following upon six days of excessive dirt, which she had ridden out under the shelter of the redoubtable Terra del Fuego coast, she had almost gone ashore during a heavy swell in the dead calm that had suddenly fallen. For seven weeks she had wrestled with the Cape Horn graybeards, and in return been buffeted and smashed by them. She was a wooden ship, and her ceaseless straining had opened her seams, so that twice a day the watch took its turn at the pumps.

The Mary Rogers was strained, the crew was strained, and big Dan Cullen, master, was likewise strained. Perhaps he was strained most of all, for upon him rested the responsibility of that titanic struggle. He slept most of the time in his clothes, though he rarely slept. He haunted the deck at night, a great, burly, robust ghost, black with the sunburn of thirty years of sea and hairy as an orang-outang. He, in turn, was haunted by one thought of action, a sailing direction for the Horn: Whatever you do, make westing! make westing! It was an obsession. He thought of nothing else, except, at times, to blaspheme God for sending such bitter weather.

Make westing! He hugged the Horn, and a dozen times lay hove to with the iron Cape bearing east-by-north, or north-north-east, a score of miles away. And each time the eternal west wind smote him back and he made easting. He fought gale after gale, south to 64 degrees, inside the antarctic drift-ice, and pledged his immortal soul to the Powers of Darkness for a bit of westing, for a slant to take him around. And he made easting. In despair, he had tried to make the passage through the Straits of Le Maire. Halfway through, the wind hauled to the north'ard of north-west, the glass dropped to 28.88, and he turned and ran before a gale of cyclonic fury, missing, by a hair's-breadth, piling up the Mary Rogers on the black-toothed rocks. Twice he had made west to the Diego Ramirez Rocks, one of the times saved between two snow-squalls by sighting the gravestones of ships a quarter of a mile dead ahead.

Blow! Captain Dan Cullen instanced all his thirty years at sea to prove that never had it blown so before. The Mary Rogers was hove to at the time he gave the evidence, and, to clinch it, inside half an hour the Mary Rogers was hove down to the hatches. Her new maintopsail and brand new spencer were blown away like tissue paper; and five sails, furled and fast under double gaskets, were blown loose and stripped from the yards. And before morning the Mary Rogers was hove down twice again, and holes were knocked in her bulwarks to ease her decks from the weight of ocean that pressed her down.

On an average of once a week Captain Dan Cullen caught glimpses of the sun. Once, for ten minutes, the sun shone at midday, and ten minutes afterward a new gale was piping up, both watches were shortening sail, and all was buried in the obscurity of a driving snow-squall. For a fortnight, once, Captain Dan Cullen was without a meridian or a chronometer sight. Rarely did he know his position within half of a degree, except when in sight of land; for sun and stars remained hidden behind the sky, and it was so gloomy that even at the best the horizons were poor for accurate observations. A gray gloom shrouded the world. The clouds were gray; the great driving seas were leaden gray; the smoking crests were a gray churning; even the occasional albatrosses were gray, while the snow-flurries were not white, but gray, under the sombre pall of the heavens.

Life on board the Mary Rogers was gray—gray and gloomy. The faces of the sailors were blue-gray; they were afflicted with sea-cuts and sea-boils, and suffered exquisitely. They were shadows of men. For seven weeks, in the forecastle or on deck, they had not known what it was to be dry. They had forgotten what it was to sleep out a watch, and all watches it was, "All hands on deck!" They caught snatches of agonized sleep, and they slept in their oilskins ready for the everlasting call. So weak and worn were they that it took both watches to do the work of one. That was why both watches were on deck so much of the time. And no shadow of a man could shirk duty. Nothing less than a broken leg could enable a man to knock off work; and there were two such, who had been mauled and pulped by the seas that broke aboard.

One other man who was the shadow of a man was George Dorety. He was the only passenger on board, a friend of the firm, and he had elected to make the voyage for his health. But seven weeks of Cape Horn had not bettered his health. He gasped and panted in his bunk through the long, heaving nights; and when on deck he was so bundled up for warmth that he resembled a peripatetic old-clothes shop. At midday, eating at the cabin table in a gloom so deep that the swinging sea-lamps burned always, he looked as blue-gray as the sickest, saddest man for'ard. Nor did gazing across the table at Captain Dan Cullen have any cheering effect upon him. Captain Cullen chewed and scowled and kept silent. The scowls were for God, and with every chew he reiterated the sole thought of his existence, which was make westing. He was a big, hairy brute, and the sight of him was not stimulating to the other's appetite. He looked upon George Dorety as a Jonah, and told him so, once each meal, savagely transferring the scowl from God to the passenger and back again.

Nor did the mate prove a first aid to a languid appetite. Joshua Higgins by name, a seaman by profession and pull, but a pot-wolloper by capacity, he was a loose-jointed, sniffling creature, heartless and selfish and cowardly, without a soul, in fear of his life of Dan Cullen, and a bully over the sailors, who knew that behind the mate was Captain Cullen, the law-giver and compeller, the driver and the destroyer, the incarnation of a dozen bucko mates. In that wild weather at the southern end of the earth, Joshua Higgins ceased washing. His grimy face usually robbed George Dorety of what little appetite he managed to accumulate. Ordinarily this lavatorial dereliction would have caught Captain Cullen's eye and vocabulary, but in the present his mind was filled with making westing, to the exclusion of all other things not contributory thereto. Whether the mate's face was clean or dirty had no bearing upon westing. Later on, when 50 degrees south in the Pacific had been reached, Joshua Higgins would wash his face very abruptly. In the meantime, at the cabin table, where gray twilight alternated with lamplight while the lamps were being filled, George Dorety sat between the two men, one a tiger and the other a hyena, and wondered why God had made them. The second mate, Matthew Turner, was a true sailor and a man, but George Dorety did not have the solace of his company, for he ate by himself, solitary, when they had finished.

On Saturday morning, July 24, George Dorety awoke to a feeling of life and headlong movement. On deck he found the Mary Rogers running off before a howling south-easter. Nothing was set but the lower topsails and the foresail. It was all she could stand, yet she was making fourteen knots, as Mr. Turner shouted in Dorety's ear when he came on deck. And it was all westing. She was going around the Horn at last... if the wind held. Mr. Turner looked happy. The end of the struggle was in sight. But Captain Cullen did not look happy. He scowled at Dorety in passing. Captain Cullen did not want God to know that he was pleased with that wind. He had a conception of a malicious God, and believed in his secret soul that if God knew it was a desirable wind, God would promptly efface it and send a snorter from the west. So he walked softly before God, smothering his joy down under scowls and muttered curses, and, so, fooling God, for God was the only thing in the universe of which Dan Cullen was afraid.

All Saturday and Saturday night the Mary Rogers raced her westing. Persistently she logged her fourteen knots, so that by Sunday morning she had covered three hundred and fifty miles. If the wind held, she would make around. If it failed, and the snorter came from anywhere between south-west and north, back the Mary Rogers would be hurled and be no better off than she had been seven weeks before. And on Sunday morning the wind was failing. The big sea was going down and running smooth. Both watches were on deck setting sail after sail as fast as the ship could stand it. And now Captain Cullen went around brazenly before God, smoking a big cigar, smiling jubilantly, as if the failing wind delighted him, while down underneath he was raging against God for taking the life out of the blessed wind. Make westing! So he would, if God would only leave him alone. Secretly, he pledged himself anew to the Powers of Darkness, if they would let him make westing. He pledged himself so easily because he did not believe in the Powers of Darkness. He really believed only in God, though he did not know it. And in his inverted theology God was really the Prince of Darkness. Captain Cullen was a devil-worshipper, but he called the devil by another name, that was all.

At midday, after calling eight bells, Captain Cullen ordered the royals on. The men went aloft faster than they had gone in weeks. Not alone were they nimble because of the westing, but a benignant sun was shining down and limbering their stiff bodies. George Dorety stood aft, near Captain Cullen, less bundled in clothes than usual, soaking in the grateful warmth as he watched the scene. Swiftly and abruptly the incident occurred. There was a cry from the foreroyal-yard of "Man overboard!" Somebody threw a life-buoy over the side, and at the same instant the second mate's voice came aft, ringing and peremptory—

"Hard down your helm!"

The man at the wheel never moved a spoke. He knew better, for Captain Dan Cullen was standing alongside of him. He wanted to move a spoke, to move all the spokes, to grind the wheel down, hard down, for his comrade drowning in the sea. He glanced at Captain Dan Cullen, and Captain Dan Cullen gave no sign.

"Down! Hard down!" the second mate roared, as he sprang aft.

But he ceased springing and commanding, and stood still, when he saw Dan Cullen by the wheel. And big Dan Cullen puffed at his cigar and said nothing. Astern, and going astern fast, could be seen the sailor. He had caught the life-buoy and was clinging to it. Nobody spoke. Nobody moved. The men aloft clung to the royal yards and watched with terror-stricken faces. And the Mary Rogers raced on, making her westing. A long, silent minute passed.

"Who was it?" Captain Cullen demanded.

"Mops, sir," eagerly answered the sailor at the wheel.

Mops topped a wave astern and disappeared temporarily in the trough. It was a large wave, but it was no graybeard. A small boat could live easily in such a sea, and in such a sea the Mary Rogers could easily come to. But she could not come to and make westing at the same time.

For the first time in all his years, George Dorety was seeing a real drama of life and death—a sordid little drama in which the scales balanced an unknown sailor named Mops against a few miles of longitude. At first he had watched the man astern, but now he watched big Dan Cullen, hairy and black, vested with power of life and death, smoking a cigar.

Captain Dan Cullen smoked another long, silent minute. Then he removed the cigar from his mouth. He glanced aloft at the spars of the Mary Rogers, and overside at the sea.

"Sheet home the royals!" he cried.

Fifteen minutes later they sat at table, in the cabin, with food served before them. On one side of George Dorety sat Dan Cullen, the tiger, on the other side, Joshua Higgins, the hyena. Nobody spoke. On deck the men were sheeting home the skysails. George Dorety could hear their cries, while a persistent vision haunted him of a man called Mops, alive and well, clinging to a life-buoy miles astern in that lonely ocean. He glanced at Captain Cullen, and experienced a feeling of nausea, for the man was eating his food with relish, almost bolting it.

"Captain Cullen," Dorety said, "you are in command of this ship, and it is not proper for me to comment now upon what you do. But I wish to say one thing. There is a hereafter, and yours will be a hot one."

Captain Cullen did not even scowl. In his voice was regret as he said—

"It was blowing a living gale. It was impossible to save the man."

"He fell from the royal-yard," Dorety cried hotly. "You were setting the royals at the time. Fifteen minutes afterward you were setting the skysails."

"It was a living gale, wasn't it, Mr. Higgins?" Captain Cullen said, turning to the mate.

"If you'd brought her to, it'd have taken the sticks out of her," was the mate's answer. "You did the proper thing, Captain Cullen. The man hadn't a ghost of a show."

George Dorety made no answer, and to the meal's end no one spoke. After that, Dorety had his meals served in his state-room. Captain Cullen scowled at him no longer, though no speech was exchanged between them, while the Mary Rogers sped north toward warmer latitudes. At the end of the week, Dan Cullen cornered Dorety on deck.

"What are you going to do when we get to 'Frisco?" he demanded bluntly.

"I am going to swear out a warrant for your arrest," Dorety answered quietly. "I am going to charge you with murder, and I am going to see you hanged for it."

"You're almighty sure of yourself," Captain Cullen sneered, turning on his heel.

A second week passed, and one morning found George Dorety standing in the coach-house companionway at the for'ard end of the long poop, taking his first gaze around the deck. The Mary Rogers was reaching full-and-by, in a stiff breeze. Every sail was set and drawing, including the staysails. Captain Cullen strolled for'ard along the poop. He strolled carelessly, glancing at the passenger out of the corner of his eye. Dorety was looking the other way, standing with head and shoulders outside the companionway, and only the back of his head was to be seen. Captain Cullen, with swift eye, embraced the mainstaysail-block and the head and estimated the distance. He glanced about him. Nobody was looking. Aft, Joshua Higgins, pacing up and down, had just turned his back and was going the other way. Captain Cullen bent over suddenly and cast the staysail-sheet off from its pin. The heavy block hurtled through the air, smashing Dorety's head like an egg-shell and hurtling on and back and forth as the staysail whipped and slatted in the wind. Joshua Higgins turned around to see what had carried away, and met the full blast of the vilest portion of Captain Cullen's profanity.

"I made the sheet fast myself," whimpered the mate in the first lull, "with an extra turn to make sure. I remember it distinctly."

"Made fast?" the Captain snarled back, for the benefit of the watch as it struggled to capture the flying sail before it tore to ribbons. "You couldn't make your grandmother fast, you useless hell's scullion. If you made that sheet fast with an extra turn, why in hell didn't it stay fast? That's what I want to know. Why in hell didn't it stay fast?"

The mate whined inarticulately.

"Oh, shut up!" was the final word of Captain Cullen.

Half an hour later he was as surprised as any when the body of George Dorety was found inside the companionway on the floor. In the afternoon, alone in his room, he doctored up the log.

"Ordinary seaman, Karl Brun," he wrote, "lost overboard from foreroyal-yard in a gale of wind. Was running at the time, and for the safety of the ship did not dare come up to the wind. Nor could a boat have lived in the sea that was running."

On another page, he wrote

"Had often warned Mr. Dorety about the danger he ran because of his carelessness on deck. I told him, once, that some day he would get his head knocked off by a block. A carelessly fastened mainstaysail sheet was the cause of the accident, which was deeply to be regretted because Mr. Dorety was a favourite with all of us."

Captain Dan Cullen read over his literary effort with admiration, blotted the page, and closed the log. He lighted a cigar and stared before him. He felt the Mary Rogers lift, and heel, and surge along, and knew that she was making nine knots. A smile of satisfaction slowly dawned on his black and hairy face. Well, anyway, he had made his westing and fooled God.

SEMPER IDEM

Doctor Bicknell was in a remarkably gracious mood. Through a minor accident, a slight bit of carelessness, that was all, a man who might have pulled through had died the preceding night. Though it had been only a sailorman, one of the innumerable unwashed, the steward of the receiving hospital had been on the anxious seat all the morning. It was not that the man had died that gave him discomfort, he knew the Doctor too well for that, but his distress lay in the fact that the operation had been done so well. One of the most delicate in surgery, it had been as successful as it was clever and audacious. All had then depended upon the treatment, the nurses, the steward. And the man had died. Nothing much, a bit of carelessness, yet enough to bring the professional wrath of Doctor Bicknell about his ears and to perturb the working of the staff and nurses for twenty-four hours to come.

But, as already stated, the Doctor was in a remarkably gracious mood. When informed by the steward, in fear and trembling, of the man's unexpected take-off, his lips did not so much as form one syllable of censure; nay, they were so pursed that snatches of rag-time floated softly from them, to be broken only by a pleasant query after the health of the other's eldest-born. The steward, deeming it impossible that he could have caught the gist of the case, repeated it.

"Yes, yes," Doctor Bicknell said impatiently; "I understand. But how about Semper Idem? Is he ready to leave?"

"Yes. They're helping him dress now," the steward answered, passing on to the round of his duties, content that peace still reigned within the iodine-saturated walls.

It was Semper Idem's recovery which had so fully compensated Doctor Bicknell for the loss of the sailorman. Lives were to him as nothing, the unpleasant but inevitable incidents of the profession, but cases, ah, cases were everything. People who knew him were prone to brand him a butcher, but his colleagues were at one in the belief that a bolder and yet a more capable man never stood over the table. He was not an imaginative man. He did not possess, and hence had no tolerance for, emotion. His nature was accurate, precise, scientific. Men were to him no more than pawns, without individuality or personal value. But as cases it was different. The more broken a man was, the more precarious his grip on life, the greater his significance in the eyes of Doctor Bicknell. He would as readily forsake a poet laureate suffering from a common accident for a nameless, mangled vagrant who defied every law of life by refusing to die, as would a child forsake a Punch and Judy for a circus.

So it had been in the case of Semper Idem. The mystery of the man had not appealed to him, nor had his silence and the veiled romance which the yellow reporters had so sensationally and so fruitlessly exploited in divers Sunday editions. But Semper Idem's throat had been cut. That was the point. That was where his interest had centred. Cut from ear to ear, and not one surgeon in a thousand to give a snap of the fingers for his chance of recovery. But, thanks to the swift municipal ambulance service and to Doctor Bicknell, he had been dragged back into the world he had sought to leave. The Doctor's co-workers had shaken their heads when the case was brought in. Impossible, they said. Throat, windpipe, jugular, all but actually severed, and the loss of blood frightful. As it was such a foregone conclusion, Doctor Bicknell had employed methods and done things which made them, even in their professional capacities, shudder. And lo! the man had recovered.

So, on this morning that Semper Idem was to leave the hospital, hale and hearty, Doctor Bicknell's geniality was in nowise disturbed by the steward's report, and he proceeded cheerfully to bring order out of the chaos of a child's body which had been ground and crunched beneath the wheels of an electric car.

As many will remember, the case of Semper Idem aroused a vast deal of unseemly yet highly natural curiosity. He had been found in a slum lodging, with throat cut as aforementioned, and blood dripping down upon the inmates of the room below and disturbing their festivities. He had evidently done the deed standing, with head bowed forward that he might gaze his last upon a photograph which stood on the table propped against a candlestick. It was this attitude which had made it possible for Doctor Bicknell to save him. So terrific had been the sweep of the razor that had he had his head thrown back, as he should have done to have accomplished the act properly, with his neck stretched and the elastic vascular walls distended, he would have of a certainty well-nigh decapitated himself.

At the hospital, during all the time he travelled the repugnant road back to life, not a word had left his lips. Nor could anything be learned of him by the sleuths detailed by the chief of police. Nobody knew him, nor had ever seen or heard of him before. He was strictly, uniquely, of the present. His clothes and surroundings were those of the lowest labourer, his hands the hands of a gentleman. But not a shred of writing was discovered, nothing, save in one particular, which would serve to indicate his past or his position in life.

And that one particular was the photograph. If it were at all a likeness, the woman who gazed frankly out upon the onlooker from the card-mount must have been a striking creature indeed. It was an amateur production, for the detectives were baffled in that no professional photographer's signature or studio was appended. Across a corner of the mount, in delicate feminine tracery, was written: "Semper idem; semper fidelis." And she looked it. As many recollect, it was a face one could never forget. Clever half-tones, remarkably like, were published in all the leading papers at the time; but such procedure gave rise to nothing but the uncontrollable public curiosity and interminable copy to the space-writers.

For want of a better name, the rescued suicide was known to the hospital attendants, and to the world, as Semper Idem. And Semper Idem he remained. Reporters, detectives, and nurses gave him up in despair. Not one word could he be persuaded to utter; yet the flitting conscious light of his eyes showed that his ears heard and his brain grasped every question put to him.

But this mystery and romance played no part in Doctor Bicknell's interest when he paused in the office to have a parting word with his patient. He, the Doctor, had performed a prodigy in the matter of this man, done what was virtually unprecedented in the annals of surgery. He did not care who or what the man was, and it was highly improbable that he should ever see him again; but, like the artist gazing upon a finished creation, he wished to look for the last time upon the work of his hand and brain.

Semper Idem still remained mute. He seemed anxious to be gone. Not a word could the Doctor extract from him, and little the Doctor cared. He examined the throat of the convalescent carefully, idling over the hideous scar with the lingering, half-caressing fondness of a parent. It was not a particularly pleasing sight. An angry line circled the throat—for all the world as though the man had just escaped the hangman's noose—and, disappearing below the ear on either side, had the appearance of completing the fiery periphery at the nape of the neck.

Maintaining his dogged silence, yielding to the other's examination in much the manner of a leashed lion, Semper Idem betrayed only his desire to drop from out of the public eye.

"Well, I'll not keep you," Doctor Bicknell finally said, laying a hand on the man's shoulder and stealing a last glance at his own handiwork. "But let me give you a bit of advice. Next time you try it on, hold your chin up, so. Don't snuggle it down and butcher yourself like a cow. Neatness and despatch, you know. Neatness and despatch."

Semper Idem's eyes flashed in token that he heard, and a moment later the hospital door swung to on his heel.

It was a busy day for Doctor Bicknell, and the afternoon was well along when he lighted a cigar preparatory to leaving the table upon which it seemed the sufferers almost clamoured to be laid. But the last one, an old rag-picker with a broken shoulder-blade, had been disposed of, and the first fragrant smoke wreaths had begun to curl about his head, when the gong of a hurrying ambulance came through the open window from the street, followed by the inevitable entry of the stretcher with its ghastly freight.

"Lay it on the table," the Doctor directed, turning for a moment to place his cigar in safety. "What is it?"

"Suicide—throat cut," responded one of the stretcher bearers. "Down on Morgan Alley. Little hope, I think, sir. He's 'most gone."

"Eh? Well, I'll give him a look, anyway." He leaned over the man at the moment when the quick made its last faint flutter and succumbed.

"It's Semper Idem come back again," the steward said.

"Ay," replied Doctor Bicknell, "and gone again. No bungling this time. Properly done, upon my life, sir, properly done. Took my advice to the letter. I'm not required here. Take it along to the morgue."

Doctor Bicknell secured his cigar and relighted it. "That," he said between the puffs, looking at the steward, "that evens up for the one you lost last night. We're quits now."

A NOSE FOR THE KING

In the morning calm of Korea, when its peace and tranquillity truly merited its ancient name, "Cho-sen," there lived a politician by name Yi Chin Ho. He was a man of parts, and—who shall say?—perhaps in no wise worse than politicians the world over. But, unlike his brethren in other lands, Yi Chin Ho was in jail. Not that he had inadvertently diverted to himself public moneys, but that he had inadvertently diverted too much. Excess is to be deplored in all things, even in grafting, and Yi Chin Ho's excess had brought him to most deplorable straits.

Ten thousand strings of cash he owed the Government, and he lay in prison under sentence of death. There was one advantage to the situation—he had plenty of time in which to think. And he thought well. Then called he the jailer to him.

"Most worthy man, you see before you one most wretched," he began. "Yet all will be well with me if you will but let me go free for one short hour this night. And all will be well with you, for I shall see to your advancement through the years, and you shall come at length to the directorship of all the prisons of Cho-sen."

"How now?" demanded the jailer. "What foolishness is this? One short hour, and you but waiting for your head to be chopped off! And I, with an aged and much-to-be-respected mother, not to say anything of a wife and several children of tender years! Out upon you for the scoundrel that you are!"

"From the Sacred City to the ends of all the Eight Coasts there is no place for me to hide," Yi Chin Ho made reply. "I am a man of wisdom, but of what worth my wisdom here in prison? Were I free, well I know I could seek out and obtain the money wherewith to repay the Government. I know of a nose that will save me from all my difficulties."

"A nose!" cried the jailer.

"A nose," said Yi Chin Ho. "A remarkable nose, if I may say so, a most remarkable nose."

The jailer threw up his hands despairingly. "Ah, what a wag you are, what a wag," he laughed. "To think that that very admirable wit of yours must go the way of the chopping-block!"

And so saying, he turned and went away. But in the end, being a man soft of head and heart, when the night was well along he permitted Yi Chin Ho to go.

Straight he went to the Governor, catching him alone and arousing him from his sleep.

"Yi Chin Ho, or I'm no Governor!" cried the Governor. "What do you here who should be in prison waiting on the chopping-block?"

"I pray Your Excellency to listen to me," said Yi Chin Ho, squatting on his hams by the bedside and lighting his pipe from the fire-box. "A dead man is without value. It is true, I am as a dead man, without value to the Government, to Your Excellency, or to myself. But if, so to say, Your Excellency were to give me my freedom—"

"Impossible!" cried the Governor. "Beside, you are condemned to death."

"Your Excellency well knows that if I can repay the ten thousand strings of cash, the Government will pardon me," Yi Chin Ho went on. "So, as I say, if Your Excellency were to give me my freedom for a few days, being a man of understanding, I should then repay the Government and be in position to be of service to Your Excellency. I should be in position to be of very great service to Your Excellency."

"Have you a plan whereby you hope to obtain this money?" asked the Governor.

"I have," said Yi Chin Ho.

"Then come with it to me to-morrow night; I would now sleep," said the Governor, taking up his snore where it had been interrupted.

On the following night, having again obtained leave of absence from the jailer, Yi Chin Ho presented himself at the Governor's bedside.

"Is it you, Yi Chin Ho?" asked the Governor. "And have you the plan?"

"It is I, Your Excellency," answered Yi Chin Ho, "and the plan is here."

"Speak," commanded the Governor.

"The plan is here," repeated Yi Chin Ho, "here in my hand."

The Governor sat up and opened his eyes. Yi Chin Ho proffered in his hand a sheet of paper. The Governor held it to the light.

"Nothing but a nose," said he.

"A bit pinched, so, and so, Your Excellency," said Yi Chin Ho.

"Yes, a bit pinched here and there, as you say," said the Governor.

"Withal it is an exceeding corpulent nose, thus, and so, all in one place, at the end," proceeded Yi Chin Ho. "Your Excellency would seek far and wide and many a day for that nose and find it not!"

"An unusual nose," admitted the Governor.

"There is a wart upon it," said Yi Chin Ho.

"A most unusual nose," said the Governor. "Never have I seen the like. But what do you with this nose, Yi Chin Ho?"

"I seek it whereby to repay the money to the Government," said Yi Chin Ho. "I seek it to be of service to Your Excellency, and I seek it to save my own worthless head. Further, I seek Your Excellency's seal upon this picture of the nose."

And the Governor laughed and affixed the seal of State, and Yi Chin Ho departed. For a month and a day he travelled the King's Road which leads to the shore of the Eastern Sea; and there, one night, at the gate of the largest mansion of a wealthy city he knocked loudly for admittance.

"None other than the master of the house will I see," said he fiercely to the frightened servants. "I travel upon the King's business."

Straightway was he led to an inner room, where the master of the house was roused from his sleep and brought blinking before him.

"You are Pak Chung Chang, head man of this city," said Yi Chin Ho in tones that were all-accusing. "I am upon the King's business."

Pak Chung Chang trembled. Well he knew the King's business was ever a terrible business. His knees smote together, and he near fell to the floor.

"The hour is late," he quavered. "Were it not well to—"

"The King's business never waits!" thundered Yi Chin Ho. "Come apart with me, and swiftly. I have an affair of moment to discuss with you.

"It is the King's affair," he added with even greater fierceness; so that Pak Chung Chang's silver pipe dropped from his nerveless fingers and clattered on the floor.

"Know then," said Yi Chin Ho, when they had gone apart, "that the King is troubled with an affliction, a very terrible affliction. In that he failed to cure, the Court physician has had nothing else than his head chopped off. From all the Eight Provinces have the physicians come to wait upon the King. Wise consultation have they held, and they have decided that for a remedy for the King's affliction nothing else is required than a nose, a certain kind of nose, a very peculiar certain kind of nose.

"Then by none other was I summoned than His Excellency the Prime Minister himself. He put a paper into my hand. Upon this paper was the very peculiar kind of nose drawn by the physicians of the Eight Provinces, with the seal of State upon it.

"'Go,' said His Excellency the Prime Minister. 'Seek out this nose, for the King's affliction is sore. And wheresoever you find this nose upon the face of a man, strike it off forthright and bring it in all haste to the Court, for the King must be cured. Go, and come not back until your search is rewarded.'

"And so I departed upon my quest," said Yi Chin Ho. "I have sought out the remotest corners of the kingdom; I have travelled the Eight Highways, searched the Eight Provinces, and sailed the seas of the Eight Coasts. And here I am."

With a great flourish he drew a paper from his girdle, unrolled it with many snappings and cracklings, and thrust it before the face of Pak Chung Chang. Upon the paper was the picture of the nose.

Pak Chung Chang stared upon it with bulging eyes.

"Never have I beheld such a nose," he began.

"There is a wart upon it," said Yi Chin Ho.

"Never have I beheld—" Pak Chung Chang began again.

"Bring your father before me," Yi Chin Ho interrupted sternly.

"My ancient and very-much-to-be-respected ancestor sleeps," said Pak Chung Chang.

"Why dissemble?" demanded Yi Chin Ho. "You know it is your father's nose. Bring him before me that I may strike it off and be gone. Hurry, lest I make bad report of you."

"Mercy!" cried Pak Chung Chang, falling on his knees. "It is impossible! It is impossible! You cannot strike off my father's nose. He cannot go down without his nose to the grave. He will become a laughter and a byword, and all my days and nights will be filled with woe. O reflect! Report that you have seen no such nose in your travels. You, too, have a father."

Pak Chung Chang clasped Yi Chin Ho's knees and fell to weeping on his sandals.

"My heart softens strangely at your tears," said Yi Chin Ho. "I, too, know filial piety and regard. But—" He hesitated, then added, as though thinking aloud, "It is as much as my head is worth."

"How much is your head worth?" asked Pak Chung Chang in a thin, small voice.

"A not remarkable head," said Yi Chin Ho. "An absurdly unremarkable head; but, such is my great foolishness, I value it at nothing less than one hundred thousand strings of cash."

"So be it," said Pak Chung Chang, rising to his feet.

"I shall need horses to carry the treasure," said Yi Chin Ho, "and men to guard it well as I journey through the mountains. There are robbers abroad in the land."

"There are robbers abroad in the land," said Pak Chung Chang, sadly. "But it shall be as you wish, so long as my ancient and very-much-to-be-respected ancestor's nose abide in its appointed place."

"Say nothing to any man of this occurrence," said Yi Chin Ho, "else will other and more loyal servants than I be sent to strike off your father's nose."

And so Yi Chin Ho departed on his way through the mountains, blithe of heart and gay of song as he listened to the jingling bells of his treasure-laden ponies.

There is little more to tell. Yi Chin Ho prospered through the years. By his efforts the jailer attained at length to the directorship of all the prisons of Cho-sen; the Governor ultimately betook himself to the Sacred City to be Prime Minister to the King, while Yi Chin Ho became the King's boon companion and sat at table with him to the end of a round, fat life. But Pak Chung Chang fell into a melancholy, and ever after he shook his head sadly, with tears in his eyes, whenever he regarded the expensive nose of his ancient and very-much-to-be-respected ancestor.

THE "FRANCIS SPAIGHT"
(A TRUE TALE RETOLD)

The Francis Spaight was running before it solely under a mizzentopsail, when the thing happened. It was not due to carelessness so much as to the lack of discipline of the crew and to the fact that they were indifferent seamen at best. The man at the wheel in particular, a Limerick man, had had no experience with salt water beyond that of rafting timber on the Shannon between the Quebec vessels and the shore. He was afraid of the huge seas that rose out of the murk astern and bore down upon him, and he was more given to cowering away from their threatened impact than he was to meeting their blows with the wheel and checking the ship's rush to broach to.

It was three in the morning when his unseamanlike conduct precipitated the catastrophe. At sight of a sea far larger than its fellows, he crouched down, releasing his hands from the spokes. The Francis Spaight sheered as her stern lifted on the sea, receiving the full fling of the cap on her quarter. The next instant she was in the trough, her lee-rail buried till the ocean was level with her hatch-coamings, sea after sea breaking over her weather rail and sweeping what remained exposed of the deck with icy deluges.

The men were out of hand, helpless and hopeless, stupid in their bewilderment and fear, and resolute only in that they would not obey orders. Some wailed, others clung silently in the weather shrouds, and still others muttered prayers or shrieked vile imprecations; and neither captain nor mate could get them to bear a hand at the pumps or at setting patches of sails to bring the vessel up to the wind and sea. Inside the hour the ship was over on her beam ends, the lubberly cowards climbing up her side and hanging on in the rigging. When she went over, the mate was caught and drowned in the after-cabin, as were two sailors who had sought refuge in the forecastle.

The mate had been the ablest man on board, and the captain was now scarcely less helpless than his men. Beyond cursing them for their worthlessness, he did nothing; and it remained for a man named Mahoney, a Belfast man, and a boy, O'Brien, of Limerick, to cut away the fore and main masts. This they did at great risk on the perpendicular wall of the wreck, sending the mizzentopmast overside along in the general crash. The Francis Spaight righted, and it was well that she was lumber laden, else she would have sunk, for she was already water-logged. The mainmast, still fast by the shrouds, beat like a thunderous sledge-hammer against the ship's side, every stroke bringing groans from the men.

Day dawned on the savage ocean, and in the cold gray light all that could be seen of the Francis Spaight emerging from the sea were the poop, the shattered mizzenmast, and a ragged line of bulwarks. It was midwinter in the North Atlantic, and the wretched men were half-dead from cold. But there was no place where they could find rest. Every sea breached clean over the wreck, washing away the salt incrustations from their bodies and depositing fresh incrustations. The cabin under the poop was awash to the knees, but here at least was shelter from the chill wind, and here the survivors congregated, standing upright, holding on by the cabin furnishings, and leaning against one another for support.

In vain Mahoney strove to get the men to take turns in watching aloft from the mizzenmast for any chance vessel. The icy gale was too much for them, and they preferred the shelter of the cabin. O'Brien, the boy, who was only fifteen, took turns with Mahoney on the freezing perch. It was the boy, at three in the afternoon, who called down that he had sighted a sail. This did bring them from the cabin, and they crowded the poop rail and weather mizzen shrouds as they watched the strange ship. But its course did not lie near, and when it disappeared below the skyline, they returned shivering to the cabin, not one offering to relieve the watch at the mast head.

By the end of the second day, Mahoney and O'Brien gave up their attempt, and thereafter the vessel drifted in the gale uncared for and without a lookout. There were thirteen alive, and for seventy-two hours they stood knee-deep in the sloshing water on the cabin floor, half-frozen, without food, and with but three bottles of wine shared among them. All food and fresh water were below, and there was no getting at such supplies in the water-logged condition of the wreck. As the days went by, no food whatever passed their lips. Fresh water, in small quantities, they were able to obtain by holding a cover of a tureen under the saddle of the mizzenmast. But the rain fell infrequently, and they were hard put. When it rained, they also soaked their handkerchiefs, squeezing them out into their mouths or into their shoes. As the wind and sea went down, they were even able to mop the exposed portions of the deck that were free from brine and so add to their water supply. But food they had none, and no way of getting it, though sea-birds flew repeatedly overhead.

In the calm weather that followed the gale, after having remained on their feet for ninety-six hours, they were able to find dry planks in the cabin on which to lie. But the long hours of standing in the salt water had caused sores to form on their legs. These sores were extremely painful. The slightest contact or scrape caused severe anguish, and in their weak condition and crowded situation they were continually hurting one another in this manner. Not a man could move about without being followed by volleys of abuse, curses, and groans. So great was their misery that the strong oppressed the weak, shoving them aside from the dry planks to shift for themselves in the cold and wet. The boy, O'Brien, was specially maltreated. Though there were three other boys, it was O'Brien who came in for most of the abuse. There was no explaining it, except on the ground that his was a stronger and more dominant spirit than those of the other boys, and that he stood up more for his rights, resenting the petty injustices that were meted out to all the boys by the men. Whenever O'Brien came near the men in search of a dry place to sleep, or merely moved about, he was kicked and cuffed away. In return, he cursed them for their selfish brutishness, and blows and kicks and curses were rained upon him. Miserable as were all of them, he was thus made far more miserable; and it was only the flame of life, unusually strong in him, that enabled him to endure.

As the days went by and they grew weaker, their peevishness and ill-temper increased, which, in turn, increased the ill-treatment and sufferings of O'Brien. By the sixteenth day all hands were far gone with hunger, and they stood together in small groups, talking in undertones and occasionally glancing at O'Brien. It was at high noon that the conference came to a head. The captain was the spokesman. All were collected on the poop.

"Men," the captain began, "we have been a long time without food— two weeks and two days it is, though it seems more like two years and two months. We can't hang out much longer. It is beyond human nature to go on hanging out with nothing in our stomachs. There is a serious question to consider: whether it is better for all to die, or for one to die. We are standing with our feet in our graves. If one of us dies, the rest may live until a ship is sighted. What say you?"

Michael Behane, the man who had been at the wheel when the Francis Spaight broached to, called out that it was well. The others joined in the cry.

"Let it be one of the b'ys!" cried Sullivan, a Tarbert man, glancing at the same time significantly at O'Brien.

"It is my opinion," the captain went on, "that it will be a good deed for one of us to die for the rest."

"A good deed! A good deed!" the men interjected.

"And it is my opinion that 'tis best for one of the boys to die. They have no families to support, nor would they be considered so great a loss to their friends as those who have wives and children."

"'Tis right." "Very right." "Very fit it should be done," the men muttered one to another.

But the four boys cried out against the injustice of it.

"Our lives is just as dear to us as the rest iv yez," O'Brien protested. "An' our famblies, too. As for wives an' childer, who is there savin' meself to care for me old mother that's a widow, as you know well, Michael Behane, that comes from Limerick? 'Tis not fair. Let the lots be drawn between all of us, men an' b'ys."

Mahoney was the only man who spoke in favour of the boys, declaring that it was the fair thing for all to share alike. Sullivan and the captain insisted

291

on the drawing of lots being confined to the boys. There were high words, in the midst of which Sullivan turned upon O'Brien, snarling—

"'Twould be a good deed to put you out of the way. You deserve it. 'Twould be the right way to serve you, an' serve you we will."

He started toward O'Brien, with intent to lay hands on him and proceed at once with the killing, while several others likewise shuffled toward him and reached for him. He stumbled backwards to escape them, at the same time crying that he would submit to the drawing of the lots among the boys.

The captain prepared four sticks of different lengths and handed them to Sullivan.

"You're thinkin' the drawin'll not be fair," the latter sneered to O'Brien. "So it's yerself'll do the drawin'."

To this O'Brien agreed. A handkerchief was tied over his eyes, blindfolding him, and he knelt down on the deck with his back to Sullivan.

"Whoever you name for the shortest stick'll die," the captain said.

Sullivan held up one of the sticks. The rest were concealed in his hand so that no one could see whether it was the short stick or not.

"An' whose stick will it be?" Sullivan demanded.

"For little Johnny Sheehan," O'Brien answered.

Sullivan laid the stick aside. Those who looked could not tell if it were the fatal one. Sullivan held up another stick.

"Whose will it be?"

"For George Burns," was the reply.

The stick was laid with the first one, and a third held up.

"An' whose is this wan?"

"For myself," said O'Brien.

With a quick movement, Sullivan threw the four sticks together. No one had seen.

"'Tis for yourself ye've drawn it," Sullivan announced.

"A good deed," several of the men muttered.

O'Brien was very quiet. He arose to his feet, took the bandage off, and looked around.

"Where is ut?" he demanded. "The short stick? The wan for me?"

The captain pointed to the four sticks lying on the deck.

"How do you know the stick was mine?" O'Brien questioned. "Did you see ut, Johnny Sheehan?"

Johnny Sheehan, who was the youngest of the boys, did not answer.

"Did you see ut?" O'Brien next asked Mahoney.

"No, I didn't see ut."

The men were muttering and growling.

"'Twas a fair drawin'," Sullivan said. "Ye had yer chanct an' ye lost, that's all iv ut."

"A fair drawin'," the captain added. "Didn't I behold it myself? The stick was yours, O'Brien, an' ye may as well get ready. Where's the cook? Gorman, come here. Fetch the tureen cover, some of ye. Gorman, do your duty like a man."

"But how'll I do it," the cook demanded. He was a weak-eyed, weak-chinned, indecisive man.

"'Tis a damned murder!" O'Brien cried out.

"I'll have none of ut," Mahoney announced. "Not a bite shall pass me lips."

"Then 'tis yer share for better men than yerself," Sullivan sneered. "Go on with yer duty, cook."

"'Tis not me duty, the killin' of b'ys," Gorman protested irresolutely.

"If yez don't make mate for us, we'll be makin' mate of yerself," Behane threatened. "Somebody must die, an' as well you as another."

Johnny Sheehan began to cry. O'Brien listened anxiously. His face was pale. His lips trembled, and at times his whole body shook.

"I signed on as cook," Gorman enounced. "An' cook I wud if galley there was. But I'll not lay me hand to murder. 'Tis not in the articles. I'm the cook—"

"An' cook ye'll be for wan minute more only," Sullivan said grimly, at the same moment gripping the cook's head from behind and bending it back till the windpipe and jugular were stretched taut. "Where's yer knife, Mike? Pass it along."

At the touch of the steel, Gorman whimpered.

"I'll do ut, if yez'll hold the b'y."

The pitiable condition of the cook seemed in some fashion to nerve up O'Brien.

"It's all right, Gorman," he said. "Go on with ut. 'Tis meself knows yer not wantin' to do ut. It's all right, sir"—this to the captain, who had laid a hand heavily on his arm. "Ye won't have to hold me, sir. I'll stand still."

"Stop yer blitherin', an' go an' get the tureen cover," Behane commanded Johnny Sheehan, at the same time dealing him a heavy cuff alongside the head.

The boy, who was scarcely more than a child, fetched the cover. He crawled and tottered along the deck, so weak was he from hunger. The tears still ran down his cheeks. Behane took the cover from him, at the same time administering another cuff.

O'Brien took off his coat and bared his right arm. His under lip still trembled, but he held a tight grip on himself. The captain's penknife was opened and passed to Gorman.

"Mahoney, tell me mother what happened to me, if ever ye get back," O'Brien requested.

Mahoney nodded.

"'Tis black murder, black an' damned," he said. "The b'y's flesh'll do none iv yez anny good. Mark me words. Ye'll not profit by it, none iv yez."

"Get ready," the captain ordered. "You, Sullivan, hold the cover—that's it—close up. Spill nothing. It's precious stuff."

Gorman made an effort. The knife was dull. He was weak. Besides, his hand was shaking so violently that he nearly dropped the knife. The three boys were crouched apart, in a huddle, crying and sobbing. With the exception of Mahoney, the men were gathered about the victim, craning their necks to see.

"Be a man, Gorman," the captain cautioned.

The wretched cook was seized with a spasm of resolution, sawing back and forth with the blade on O'Brien's wrist. The veins were severed. Sullivan held the tureen cover close underneath. The cut veins gaped wide, but no ruddy flood gushed forth. There was no blood at all. The veins were dry and empty. No one spoke. The grim and silent figures swayed in unison with each heave of the ship. Every eye was turned fixedly upon that inconceivable and monstrous thing, the dry veins of a creature that was alive.

"'Tis a warnin'," Mahoney cried. "Lave the b'y alone. Mark me words. His death'll do none iv yez anny good."

"Try at the elbow—the left elbow, 'tis nearer the heart," the captain said finally, in a dim and husky voice that was unlike his own.

"Give me the knife," O'Brien said roughly, taking it out of the cook's hand. "I can't be lookin' at ye puttin' me to hurt."

Quite coolly he cut the vein at the left elbow, but, like the cook, he failed to bring blood.

"This is all iv no use," Sullivan said. "'Tis better to put him out iv his misery by bleedin' him at the throat."

295

The strain had been too much for the lad.

"Don't be doin' ut," he cried. "There'll be no blood in me throat. Give me a little time. 'Tis cold an' weak I am. Be lettin' me lay down an' slape a bit. Then I'll be warm an' the blood'll flow."

"'Tis no use," Sullivan objected. "As if ye cud be slapin' at a time like this. Ye'll not slape, and ye'll not warm up. Look at ye now. You've an ague."

"I was sick at Limerick wan night," O'Brien hurried on, "an' the dochtor cudn't bleed me. But after slapin' a few hours an' gettin' warm in bed the blood came freely. It's God's truth I'm tellin' yez. Don't be murderin' me!"

"His veins are open now," the captain said. "'Tis no use leavin' him in his pain. Do it now an' be done with it."

They started to reach for O'Brien, but he backed away.

"I'll be the death iv yez!" he screamed. "Take yer hands off iv me, Sullivan! I'll come back! I'll haunt yez! Wakin' or slapin', I'll haunt yez till you die!"

"'Tis disgraceful!" yelled Behane. "If the short stick'd ben mine, I'd a-let me mates cut the head off iv me an' died happy."

Sullivan leaped in and caught the unhappy lad by the hair. The rest of the men followed, O'Brien kicked and struggled, snarling and snapping at the hands that clutched him from every side. Little Johnny Sheehan broke out into wild screaming, but the men took no notice of him. O'Brien was bent backward to the deck, the tureen cover under his neck. Gorman was shoved forward. Some one had thrust a large sheath-knife into his hand.

"Do yer duty! Do yer duty!" the men cried.

The cook bent over, but he caught the boy's eyes and faltered.

"If ye don't, I'll kill ye with me own hands," Behane shouted.

From every side a torrent of abuse and threats poured in upon the cook. Still he hung back.

"Maybe there'll be more blood in his veins than O'Brien's," Sullivan suggested significantly.

Behane caught Gorman by the hair and twisted his head back, while Sullivan attempted to take possession of the sheath-knife. But Gorman clung to it desperately.

"Lave go, an' I'll do ut!" he screamed frantically. "Don't be cuttin' me throat! I'll do the deed! I'll do the deed!"

"See that you do it, then," the captain threatened him.

Gorman allowed himself to be shoved forward. He looked at the boy, closed his eyes, and muttered a prayer. Then, without opening his eyes, he did the deed that had been appointed him. O'Brien emitted a shriek that sank swiftly to a gurgling sob. The men held him till his struggles ceased, when he was laid upon the deck. They were eager and impatient, and with oaths and threats they urged Gorman to hurry with the preparation of the meal.

"Lave ut, you bloody butchers," Mahoney said quietly. "Lave ut, I tell yez. Ye'll not be needin' anny iv ut now. 'Tis as I said: ye'll not be profitin' by the lad's blood. Empty ut overside, Behane. Empty ut overside."

Behane, still holding the tureen cover in both his hands, glanced to windward. He walked to the rail and threw the cover and contents into the sea. A full-rigged ship was bearing down upon them a short mile away. So occupied had they been with the deed just committed, that none had had eyes for a lookout. All hands watched her coming on—the brightly coppered forefoot parting the water like a golden knife, the headsails flapping lazily and emptily at each downward surge, and the towering canvas tiers dipping and curtsying with each stately swing of the sea. No man spoke.

As she hove to, a cable length away, the captain of the Francis Spaight bestirred himself and ordered a tarpaulin to be thrown over O'Brien's corpse. A boat was lowered from the stranger's side and began to pull toward them. John Gorman laughed. He laughed softly at first, but he accompanied each stroke of the oars with spasmodically increasing glee. It was this maniacal laughter that greeted the rescue boat as it hauled alongside and the first officer clambered on board.

A CURIOUS FRAGMENT

[The capitalist, or industrial oligarch, Roger Vanderwater, mentioned in the narrative, has been identified as the ninth in the line of the Vanderwaters that controlled for hundreds of years the cotton factories of the South. This Roger Vanderwater flourished in the last decades of the twenty-sixth century after Christ, which was the fifth century of the terrible industrial oligarchy that was reared upon the ruins of the early Republic.

From internal evidences we are convinced that the narrative which follows was not reduced to writing till the twenty-ninth century. Not only was it unlawful to write or print such matter during that period, but the working-class was so illiterate that only in rare instances were its members able to read and write. This was the dark reign of the overman, in whose speech the great mass of the people were characterized as the "herd animals." All literacy was frowned upon and stamped out. From the statute-books of the times may be instanced that black law that made it a capital offence for any man, no matter of what class, to teach even the alphabet to a member of the working-class. Such stringent limitation of education to the ruling class was necessary if that class was to continue to rule.

One result of the foregoing was the development of the professional story-tellers. These story-tellers were paid by the oligarchy, and the tales they told were legendary, mythical, romantic, and harmless. But the spirit of freedom never quite died out, and agitators, under the guise of story-tellers, preached revolt to the slave class. That the following tale was banned by the oligarchs we have proof from the records of the criminal police court of Ashbury, wherein, on January 27, 2734, one John Tourney, found guilty of telling the tale in a boozing-ken of labourers, was sentenced to five years' penal servitude in the borax mines of the Arizona Desert.—EDITOR'S NOTE.]

Listen, my brothers, and I will tell you a tale of an arm. It was the arm of Tom Dixon, and Tom Dixon was a weaver of the first class in a factory of that hell-hound and master, Roger Vanderwater. This factory was called "Hell's Bottom"... by the slaves who toiled in it, and I guess they ought to know; and it was situated in Kingsbury, at the other end of the town from Vanderwater's summer palace. You do not know where Kingsbury is? There are many things, my brothers, that you do not know, and it is sad. It is because you do not know that you are slaves. When I have told you this tale, I should like to form a class among you for the learning of written and printed speech. Our masters read and write and possess many books, and it is because of that that they are our masters, and live in palaces, and do not work. When the toilers learn to read and write—all of them—they will grow strong; then they will use their strength to break their bonds, and there will be no more masters and no more slaves.

Kingsbury, my brothers, is in the old State of Alabama. For three hundred years the Vanderwaters have owned Kingsbury and its slave pens and factories, and slave pens and factories in many other places and States. You have heard of the Vanderwaters—who has not?—but let me tell you things you do not know about them. The first Vanderwater was a slave, even as you and I. Have you got that? He was a slave, and that was over three hundred years ago. His father was a machinist in the slave pen of Alexander Burrell, and his mother was a washerwoman in the same slave pen. There is no doubt about this. I am telling you truth. It is history. It is printed, every word of it, in the history books of our masters, which you cannot read because your masters will not permit you to learn to read. You can understand why they will not permit you to learn to read, when there are such things in the books. They know, and they are very wise. If you did read such things, you might be wanting in respect to your masters, which would be a dangerous thing... to your masters. But I know, for I can read, and I am telling you what I have read with my own eyes in the history books of our masters.

The first Vanderwater's name was not Vanderwater; it was Vange—Bill Vange, the son of Yergis Vange, the machinist, and Laura Carnly, the washerwoman. Young Bill Vange was strong. He might have remained with the slaves and led them to freedom; instead, however, he served the masters and was well rewarded. He began his service, when yet a small child, as a spy in his home slave pen. He is known to have informed on his own father for seditious utterance. This is fact. I have read it with my own eyes in the records. He was too good a slave for the slave pen. Alexander Burrell took him out, while yet a child, and he was taught to read and write. He was taught many things, and he was entered in the secret service of the Government. Of course, he no longer wore the slave dress, except for disguise at such times when he sought to penetrate the secrets and plots of the slaves. It was he, when but eighteen years of age, who brought that great hero and comrade, Ralph Jacobus, to trial and execution in the electric chair. Of course, you have all heard the sacred name of Ralph Jacobus, but it is news to you that he was brought to his death by the first Vanderwater, whose name was Vange. I know. I have read it in the books. There are many interesting things like that in the books.

And after Ralph Jacobus died his shameful death, Bill Vange's name began the many changes it was to undergo. He was known as "Sly Vange" far and wide. He rose high in the secret service, and he was rewarded in grand ways, but still he was not a member of the master class. The men were willing that he should become so; it was the women of the master class who refused to have Sly Vange one of them. Sly Vange gave good service to the masters. He had been a slave himself, and he knew the ways of the slaves. There was no fooling him. In those days the slaves were braver than now, and they were always trying for their freedom. And Sly Vange was everywhere, in all their schemes and plans, bringing their schemes and plans to naught and their leaders to the electric chair. It was in 2255 that his name was next changed for him. It was in that year that the Great Mutiny took place. In that region west of the Rocky Mountains, seventeen millions of slaves strove bravely to overthrow their masters. Who knows, if Sly Vange had not lived, but that they would have succeeded? But Sly Vange was very much alive. The masters gave him supreme command of the situation. In eight months of fighting, one million and three hundred and fifty thousand slaves were killed. Vange, Bill Vange, Sly Vange, killed them, and he broke the Great Mutiny. And he was greatly rewarded, and so red were his hands with the blood of the slaves that thereafter he was called "Bloody Vange." You see, my brothers, what interesting things are to be found in the books when one can read them. And, take my word for it, there are many other things, even more interesting, in the books. And if you will but study with me, in a year's time you can read those books for yourselves—ay, in six months some of you will be able to read those books for yourselves.

Bloody Vange lived to a ripe old age, and always, to the last, was he received in the councils of the masters; but never was he made a master himself. He had first opened his eyes, you see, in a slave pen. But oh, he was well rewarded! He had a dozen palaces in which to live. He, who was no master, owned thousands of slaves. He had a great pleasure yacht upon the sea that was a floating palace, and he owned a whole island in the sea where toiled ten thousand slaves on his coffee plantations. But in his old age he was lonely, for he lived apart, hated by his brothers, the slaves, and looked down upon by those he had served and who refused to be his brothers. The masters looked down upon him because he had been born a slave. Enormously wealthy he died; but he died horribly, tormented by his conscience, regretting all he had done and the red stain on his name.

But with his children it was different. They had not been born in the slave pen, and by the special ruling of the Chief Oligarch of that time, John Morrison, they were elevated to the master class. And it was then that the name of Vange disappears from the page of history. It becomes Vanderwater, and Jason Vange, the son of Bloody Vange, becomes Jason Vanderwater, the founder of the Vanderwater line. But that was three hundred years ago, and the Vanderwaters of to-day forget their beginnings and imagine that somehow the clay of their bodies is different stuff from the clay in your body and mine and in the bodies of all slaves. And I ask you, Why should a slave become the master of another slave? And why should the son of a slave become the master of many slaves? I leave these questions for you to answer for yourselves, but do not forget that in the beginning the Vanderwaters were slaves.

And now, my brothers, I come back to the beginning of my tale to tell you of Tom Dixon's arm. Roger Vanderwater's factory in Kingsbury was rightly named "Hell's Bottom," but the men who toiled in it were men, as you shall see. Women toiled there, too, and children, little children. All that toiled there had the regular slave rights under the law, but only under the law, for they were deprived of many of their rights by the two overseers of Hell's Bottom, Joseph Clancy and Adolph Munster.

It is a long story, but I shall not tell all of it to you. I shall tell only about the arm. It happened that, according to the law, a portion of the starvation wage of the slaves was held back each month and put into a fund. This fund was for the purpose of helping such unfortunate fellow-workmen as happened to be injured by accidents or to be overtaken by sickness. As you know with yourselves, these funds are controlled by the overseers. It is the law, and so it was that the fund at Hell's Bottom was controlled by the two overseers of accursed memory.

Now, Clancy and Munster took this fund for their own use. When accidents happened to the workmen, their fellows, as was the custom, made grants from the fund; but the overseers refused to pay over the grants. What could the slaves do? They had their rights under the law, but they had no access to the law. Those that complained to the overseers were punished. You know yourselves what form such punishment takes—the fines for faulty work that is not faulty; the overcharging of accounts in the Company's store; the vile treatment of one's women and children; and the allotment to bad machines whereon, work as one will, he starves.

Once, the slaves of Hell's Bottom protested to Vanderwater. It was the time of the year when he spent several months in Kingsbury. One of the slaves could write; it chanced that his mother could write, and she had secretly taught him as her mother had secretly taught her. So this slave wrote a round robin, wherein was contained their grievances, and all the slaves signed by mark. And, with proper stamps upon the envelope, the round robin was mailed to Roger Vanderwater. And Roger Vanderwater did nothing, save to turn the round robin over to the two overseers. Clancy and Munster were angered. They turned the guards loose at night on the slave pen. The guards were armed with pick handles. It is said that next day only half of the slaves were able to work in Hell's Bottom. They were well beaten. The slave who could write was so badly beaten that he lived only three months. But before he died, he wrote once more, to what purpose you shall hear.

Four or five weeks afterward, Tom Dixon, a slave, had his arm torn off by a belt in Hell's Bottom. His fellow-workmen, as usual, made a grant to him from the fund, and Clancy and Munster, as usual, refused to pay it over from the fund. The slave who could write, and who even then was dying, wrote anew a recital of their grievances. And this document was thrust into the hand of the arm that had been torn from Tom Dixon's body.

Now it chanced that Roger Vanderwater was lying ill in his palace at the other end of Kingsbury—not the dire illness that strikes down you and me, brothers; just a bit of biliousness, mayhap, or no more than a bad headache because he had eaten too heartily or drunk too deeply. But it was enough for him, being tender and soft from careful rearing. Such men, packed in cotton wool all their lives, are exceeding tender and soft. Believe me, brothers, Roger Vanderwater felt as badly with his aching head, or THOUGHT he felt as badly, as Tom Dixon really felt with his arm torn out by the roots.

It happened that Roger Vanderwater was fond of scientific farming, and that on his farm, three miles outside of Kingsbury, he had managed to grow a new kind of strawberry. He was very proud of that new strawberry of his, and he would have been out to see and pick the first ripe ones, had it not been for his illness. Because of his illness he had ordered the old farm slave to bring in personally the first box of the berries. All this was learned from the gossip of a palace scullion, who slept each night in the slave pen. The overseer of the plantation should have brought in the berries, but he was on his back with a broken leg from trying to break a colt. The scullion brought the word in the night, and it was known that next day the berries would come in. And the men in the slave pen of Hell's Bottom, being men and not cowards, held a council.

The slave who could write, and who was sick and dying from the pick-handle beating, said he would carry Tom Dixon's arm; also, he said he must die anyway, and that it mattered nothing if he died a little sooner. So five slaves stole from the slave pen that night after the guards had made their last rounds. One of the slaves was the man who could write. They lay in the brush by the roadside until late in the morning, when the old farm slave came driving to town with the precious fruit for the master. What of the farm slave being old and rheumatic, and of the slave who could write being stiff and injured from his beating, they moved their bodies about when they walked, very much in the same fashion. The slave who could write put on the other's clothes, pulled the broad-brimmed hat over his eyes, climbed upon the seat of the wagon, and drove on to town. The old farm slave was kept tied all day in the bushes until evening, when the others loosed him and went back to the slave pen to take their punishment for having broken bounds.

In the meantime, Roger Vanderwater lay waiting for the berries in his wonderful bedroom—such wonders and such comforts were there that they would have blinded the eyes of you and me who have never seen such things. The slave who could write said afterward that it was like a glimpse of Paradise! And why not? The labour and the lives of ten thousand slaves had gone to the making of that bedchamber, while they themselves slept in vile lairs like wild beasts. The slave who could write brought in the berries on a silver tray or platter—you see, Roger Vanderwater wanted to speak with him in person about the berries.

The slave who could write tottered his dying body across the wonderful room and knelt by the couch of Vanderwater, holding out before him the tray. Large green leaves covered the top of the tray, and these the body-servant alongside whisked away so that Vanderwater could see. And Roger Vanderwater, propped upon his elbow, saw. He saw the fresh, wonderful fruit lying there like precious jewels, and in the midst of it the arm of Tom Dixon as it had been torn from his body, well washed, of course, my brothers, and very white against the blood-red fruit. And also he saw, clutched in the stiff, dead fingers, the petition of his slaves who toiled in Hell's Bottom.

"Take and read," said the slave who could write. And even as the master took the petition, the body-servant, who till then had been motionless with surprise, struck with his fist the kneeling slave upon the mouth. The slave was dying anyway, and was very weak, and did not mind. He made no sound, and, having fallen over on his side, he lay there quietly, bleeding from the blow on the mouth. The physician, who had run for the palace guards, came back with them, and the slave was dragged upright upon his feet. But as they dragged him up, his hand clutched Tom Dixon's arm from where it had fallen on the floor.

"He shall be flung alive to the hounds!" the body-servant was crying in great wrath. "He shall be flung alive to the hounds!"

But Roger Vanderwater, forgetting his headache, still leaning on his elbow, commanded silence, and went on reading the petition. And while he read, there was silence, all standing upright, the wrathful body-servant, the physician, the palace guards, and in their midst the slave, bleeding at the mouth and still holding Tom Dixon's arm. And when Roger Vanderwater had done, he turned upon the slave, saying—

"If in this paper there be one lie, you shall be sorry that you were ever born."

And the slave said, "I have been sorry all my life that I was born."

Roger Vanderwater looked at him closely, and the slave said—

"You have done your worst to me. I am dying now. In a week I shall be dead, so it does not matter if you kill me now."

"What do you with that?" the master asked, pointing to the arm; and the slave made answer—

"I take it back to the pen to give it burial. Tom Dixon was my friend. We worked beside each other at our looms."

There is little more to my tale, brothers. The slave and the arm were sent back in a cart to the pen. Nor were any of the slaves punished for what they had done. Indeed, Roger Vanderwater made investigation and punished the two overseers, Joseph Clancy and Adolph Munster. Their freeholds were taken from them. They were branded, each upon the forehead, their right hands were cut off, and they were turned loose upon the highway to wander and beg until they died. And the fund was managed rightfully thereafter for a time—for a time only, my brothers; for after Roger Vanderwater came his son, Albert, who was a cruel master and half mad.

Brothers, that slave who carried the arm into the presence of the master was my father. He was a brave man. And even as his mother secretly taught him to read, so did he teach me. Because he died shortly after from the pick-handle beating, Roger Vanderwater took me out of the slave pen and tried to make various better things out of me. I might have become an overseer in Hell's Bottom, but I chose to become a story-teller, wandering over the land and getting close to my brothers, the slaves, everywhere. And I tell you stories like this, secretly, knowing that you will not betray me; for if you did, you know as well as I that my tongue will be torn out and that I shall tell stories no more. And my message is, brothers, that there is a good time coming, when all will be well in the world and there will be neither masters nor slaves. But first you must prepare for that good time by learning to read. There is power in the printed word. And here am I to teach you to read, and as well there are others to see that you get the books when I am gone along upon my way—the history books wherein you will learn about your masters, and learn to become strong even as they.

[EDITOR'S NOTE.—From "Historical Fragments and Sketches," first published in fifty volumes in 4427, and now, after two hundred years, because of its accuracy and value, edited and republished by the National Committee on Historical Research.]

A PIECE OF STEAK

With the last morsel of bread Tom King wiped his plate clean of the last particle of flour gravy and chewed the resulting mouthful in a slow and meditative way. When he arose from the table, he was oppressed by the feeling that he was distinctly hungry. Yet he alone had eaten. The two children in the other room had been sent early to bed in order that in sleep they might forget they had gone supperless. His wife had touched nothing, and had sat silently and watched him with solicitous eyes. She was a thin, worn woman of the working-class, though signs of an earlier prettiness were not wanting in her face. The flour for the gravy she had borrowed from the neighbour across the hall. The last two ha'pennies had gone to buy the bread.

He sat down by the window on a rickety chair that protested under his weight, and quite mechanically he put his pipe in his mouth and dipped into the side pocket of his coat. The absence of any tobacco made him aware of his action, and, with a scowl for his forgetfulness, he put the pipe away. His movements were slow, almost hulking, as though he were burdened by the heavy weight of his muscles. He was a solid-bodied, stolid-looking man, and his appearance did not suffer from being overprepossessing. His rough clothes were old and slouchy. The uppers of his shoes were too weak to carry the heavy re-soling that was itself of no recent date. And his cotton shirt, a cheap, two shilling affair, showed a frayed collar and ineradicable paint stains.

But it was Tom King's face that advertised him unmistakably for what he was. It was the face of a typical prize-fighter; of one who had put in long years of service in the squared ring and, by that means, developed and emphasized all the marks of the fighting beast. It was distinctly a lowering countenance, and, that no feature of it might escape notice, it was clean-shaven. The lips were shapeless and constituted a mouth harsh to excess, that was like a gash in his face. The jaw was aggressive, brutal, heavy. The eyes, slow of movement and heavy-lidded, were almost expressionless under the shaggy, indrawn brows. Sheer animal that he was, the eyes were the most animal-like feature about him. They were sleepy, lion-like—the eyes of a fighting animal. The forehead slanted quickly back to the hair, which, clipped close, showed every bump of a villainous-looking head. A nose twice broken and moulded variously by countless blows, and a cauliflower ear, permanently swollen and distorted to twice its size, completed his adornment, while the beard, fresh-shaven as it was, sprouted in the skin and gave the face a blue-black stain.

Altogether, it was the face of a man to be afraid of in a dark alley or lonely place. And yet Tom King was not a criminal, nor had he ever done anything criminal. Outside of brawls, common to his walk in life, he had harmed no one. Nor had he ever been known to pick a quarrel. He was a professional, and all the fighting brutishness of him was reserved for his professional appearances. Outside the ring he was slow-going, easy-natured, and, in his younger days, when money was flush, too open-handed for his own good. He bore no grudges and had few enemies. Fighting was a business with him. In the ring he struck to hurt, struck to maim, struck to destroy; but there was no animus in it. It was a plain business proposition. Audiences assembled and paid for the spectacle of men knocking each other out. The winner took the big end of the purse. When Tom King faced the Woolloomoolloo Gouger, twenty years before, he knew that the Gouger's jaw was only four months healed after having been broken in a Newcastle bout. And he had played for that jaw and broken it again in the ninth round, not because he bore the Gouger any ill-will, but because that was the surest way to put the Gouger out and win the big end of the purse. Nor had the Gouger borne him any ill-will for it. It was the game, and both knew the game and played it.

Tom King had never been a talker, and he sat by the window, morosely silent, staring at his hands. The veins stood out on the backs of the hands, large and swollen; and the knuckles, smashed and battered and malformed, testified to the use to which they had been put. He had never heard that a man's life was the life of his arteries, but well he knew the meaning of those big upstanding veins. His heart had pumped too much blood through them at top pressure. They no longer did the work. He had stretched the elasticity out of them, and with their distension had passed his endurance. He tired easily now. No longer could he do a fast twenty rounds, hammer and tongs, fight, fight, fight, from gong to gong, with fierce rally on top of fierce rally, beaten to the ropes and in turn beating his opponent to the ropes, and rallying fiercest and fastest of all in that last, twentieth round, with the house on its feet and yelling, himself rushing, striking, ducking, raining showers of blows upon showers of blows and receiving showers of blows in return, and all the time the heart faithfully pumping the surging blood through the adequate veins. The veins, swollen at the time, had always shrunk down again, though each time, imperceptibly at first, not quite—remaining just a trifle larger than before. He stared at them and at his battered knuckles, and, for the moment, caught a vision of the youthful excellence of those hands before the first knuckle had been smashed on the head of Benny Jones, otherwise known as the Welsh Terror.

The impression of his hunger came back on him.

"Blimey, but couldn't I go a piece of steak!" he muttered aloud, clenching his huge fists and spitting out a smothered oath.

"I tried both Burke's an' Sawley's," his wife said half apologetically.

"An' they wouldn't?" he demanded.

"Not a ha'penny. Burke said—" She faltered.

"G'wan! Wot'd he say?"

"As how 'e was thinkin' Sandel ud do ye to-night, an' as how yer score was comfortable big as it was."

Tom King grunted, but did not reply. He was busy thinking of the bull terrier he had kept in his younger days to which he had fed steaks without end. Burke would have given him credit for a thousand steaks—then. But times had changed. Tom King was getting old; and old men, fighting before second-rate clubs, couldn't expect to run bills of any size with the tradesmen.

He had got up in the morning with a longing for a piece of steak, and the longing had not abated. He had not had a fair training for this fight. It was a drought year in Australia, times were hard, and even the most irregular work was difficult to find. He had had no sparring partner, and his food had not been of the best nor always sufficient. He had done a few days' navvy work when he could get it, and he had run around the Domain in the early mornings to get his legs in shape. But it was hard, training without a partner and with a wife and two kiddies that must be fed. Credit with the tradesmen had undergone very slight expansion when he was matched with Sandel. The secretary of the Gayety Club had advanced him three pounds—the loser's end of the purse—and beyond that had refused to go. Now and again he had managed to borrow a few shillings from old pals, who would have lent more only that it was a drought year and they were hard put themselves. No—and there was no use in disguising the fact—his training had not been satisfactory. He should have had better food and no worries. Besides, when a man is forty, it is harder to get into condition than when he is twenty.

"What time is it, Lizzie?" he asked.

His wife went across the hall to inquire, and came back.

"Quarter before eight."

"They'll be startin' the first bout in a few minutes," he said. "Only a try-out. Then there's a four-round spar 'tween Dealer Wells an' Gridley, an' a ten-round go 'tween Starlight an' some sailor bloke. I don't come on for over an hour."

At the end of another silent ten minutes, he rose to his feet.

"Truth is, Lizzie, I ain't had proper trainin'."

He reached for his hat and started for the door. He did not offer to kiss her—he never did on going out—but on this night she dared to kiss him, throwing her arms around him and compelling him to bend down to her face. She looked quite small against the massive bulk of the man.

"Good luck, Tom," she said. "You gotter do 'im."

"Ay, I gotter do 'im," he repeated. "That's all there is to it. I jus' gotter do 'im."

He laughed with an attempt at heartiness, while she pressed more closely against him. Across her shoulders he looked around the bare room. It was all he had in the world, with the rent overdue, and her and the kiddies. And he was leaving it to go out into the night to get meat for his mate and cubs—not like a modern working-man going to his machine grind, but in the old, primitive, royal, animal way, by fighting for it.

"I gotter do 'im," he repeated, this time a hint of desperation in his voice. "If it's a win, it's thirty quid—an' I can pay all that's owin', with a lump o' money left over. If it's a lose, I get naught—not even a penny for me to ride home on the tram. The secretary's give all that's comin' from a loser's end. Good-bye, old woman. I'll come straight home if it's a win."

"An' I'll be waitin' up," she called to him along the hall.

It was full two miles to the Gayety, and as he walked along he remembered how in his palmy days—he had once been the heavyweight champion of New South Wales—he would have ridden in a cab to the fight, and how, most likely, some heavy backer would have paid for the cab and ridden with him. There were Tommy Burns and that Yankee nigger, Jack Johnson—they rode about in motor-cars. And he walked! And, as any man knew, a hard two miles was not the best preliminary to a fight. He was an old un, and the world did not wag well with old uns. He was good for nothing now except navvy work, and his broken nose and swollen ear were against him even in that. He found himself wishing that he had learned a trade. It would have been better in the long run. But no one had told him, and he knew, deep down in his heart, that he would not have listened if they had. It had been so easy. Big money—sharp, glorious fights—periods of rest and loafing in between—a following of eager flatterers, the slaps on the back, the shakes of the hand, the toffs glad to buy him a drink for the privilege of five minutes' talk—and the glory of it, the yelling houses, the whirlwind finish, the referee's "King wins!" and his name in the sporting columns next day.

Those had been times! But he realized now, in his slow, ruminating way, that it was the old uns he had been putting away. He was Youth, rising; and they were Age, sinking. No wonder it had been easy—they with their swollen veins and battered knuckles and weary in the bones of them from the long battles they had already fought. He remembered the time he put out old Stowsher Bill, at Rush-Cutters Bay, in the eighteenth round, and how old Bill had cried afterward in the dressing-room like a baby. Perhaps old Bill's rent had been overdue. Perhaps he'd had at home a missus an' a couple of kiddies. And perhaps Bill, that very day of the fight, had had a hungering for a piece of steak. Bill had fought game and taken incredible punishment. He could see now, after he had gone through the mill himself, that Stowsher Bill had fought for a bigger stake, that night twenty years ago, than had young Tom King, who had fought for glory and easy money. No wonder Stowsher Bill had cried afterward in the dressing-room.

Well, a man had only so many fights in him, to begin with. It was the iron law of the game. One man might have a hundred hard fights in him, another man only twenty; each, according to the make of him and the quality of his fibre, had a definite number, and, when he had fought them, he was done. Yes, he had had more fights in him than most of them, and he had had far more than his share of the hard, gruelling fights—the kind that worked the heart and lungs to bursting, that took the elastic out of the arteries and made hard knots of muscle out of Youth's sleek suppleness, that wore out nerve and stamina and made brain and bones weary from excess of effort and endurance overwrought. Yes, he had done better than all of them. There were none of his old fighting partners left. He was the last of the old guard. He had seen them all finished, and he had had a hand in finishing some of them.

They had tried him out against the old uns, and one after another he had put them away—laughing when, like old Stowsher Bill, they cried in the dressing-room. And now he was an old un, and they tried out the youngsters on him. There was that bloke, Sandel. He had come over from New Zealand with a record behind him. But nobody in Australia knew anything about him, so they put him up against old Tom King. If Sandel made a showing, he would be given better men to fight, with bigger purses to win; so it was to be depended upon that he would put up a fierce battle. He had everything to win by it—money and glory and career; and Tom King was the grizzled old chopping-block that guarded the highway to fame and fortune. And he had nothing to win except thirty quid, to pay to the landlord and the tradesmen. And, as Tom King thus ruminated, there came to his stolid vision the form of Youth, glorious Youth, rising exultant and invincible, supple of muscle and silken of skin, with heart and lungs that had never been tired and torn and that laughed at limitation of effort. Yes, Youth was the Nemesis. It destroyed the old uns and recked not that, in so doing, it destroyed itself. It enlarged its arteries and smashed its knuckles, and was in turn destroyed by Youth. For Youth was ever youthful. It was only Age that grew old.

At Castlereagh Street he turned to the left, and three blocks along came to the Gayety. A crowd of young larrikins hanging outside the door made respectful way for him, and he heard one say to another: "That's 'im! That's Tom King!"

Inside, on the way to his dressing-room, he encountered the secretary, a keen-eyed, shrewd-faced young man, who shook his hand.

"How are you feelin', Tom?" he asked.

"Fit as a fiddle," King answered, though he knew that he lied, and that if he had a quid, he would give it right there for a good piece of steak.

When he emerged from the dressing-room, his seconds behind him, and came down the aisle to the squared ring in the centre of the hall, a burst of greeting and applause went up from the waiting crowd. He acknowledged salutations right and left, though few of the faces did he know. Most of them were the faces of kiddies unborn when he was winning his first laurels in the squared ring. He leaped lightly to the raised platform and ducked through the ropes to his corner, where he sat down on a folding stool. Jack Ball, the referee, came over and shook his hand. Ball was a broken-down pugilist who for over ten years had not entered the ring as a principal. King was glad that he had him for referee. They were both old uns. If he should rough it with Sandel a bit beyond the rules, he knew Ball could be depended upon to pass it by.

Aspiring young heavyweights, one after another, were climbing into the ring and being presented to the audience by the referee. Also, he issued their challenges for them.

"Young Pronto," Bill announced, "from North Sydney, challenges the winner for fifty pounds side bet."

The audience applauded, and applauded again as Sandel himself sprang through the ropes and sat down in his corner. Tom King looked across the ring at him curiously, for in a few minutes they would be locked together in merciless combat, each trying with all the force of him to knock the other into unconsciousness. But little could he see, for Sandel, like himself, had trousers and sweater on over his ring costume. His face was strongly handsome, crowned with a curly mop of yellow hair, while his thick, muscular neck hinted at bodily magnificence.

Young Pronto went to one corner and then the other, shaking hands with the principals and dropping down out of the ring. The challenges went on. Ever Youth climbed through the ropes—Youth unknown, but insatiable—crying out to mankind that with strength and skill it would match issues with the winner. A few years before, in his own heyday of invincibleness, Tom King would have been amused and bored by these preliminaries. But now he sat fascinated, unable to shake the vision of Youth from his eyes. Always were these youngsters rising up in the boxing game, springing through the ropes and shouting their defiance; and always were the old uns going down before them. They climbed to success over the bodies of the old uns. And ever they came, more and more youngsters—Youth unquenchable and irresistible—and ever they put the old uns away, themselves becoming old uns and travelling the same downward path, while behind them, ever pressing on them, was Youth eternal—the new babies, grown lusty and dragging their elders down, with behind them more babies to the end of time—Youth that must have its will and that will never die.

King glanced over to the press box and nodded to Morgan, of the Sportsman, and Corbett, of the Referee. Then he held out his hands, while Sid Sullivan and Charley Bates, his seconds, slipped on his gloves and laced them tight, closely watched by one of Sandel's seconds, who first examined critically the tapes on King's knuckles. A second of his own was in Sandel's corner, performing a like office. Sandel's trousers were pulled off, and, as he stood up, his sweater was skinned off over his head. And Tom King, looking, saw Youth incarnate, deep-chested, heavy-thewed, with muscles that slipped and slid like live things under the white satin skin. The whole body was a-crawl with life, and Tom King knew that it was a life that had never oozed its freshness out through the aching pores during the long fights wherein Youth paid its toll and departed not quite so young as when it entered.

The two men advanced to meet each other, and, as the gong sounded and the seconds clattered out of the ring with the folding stools, they shook hands and instantly took their fighting attitudes. And instantly, like a mechanism of steel and springs balanced on a hair trigger, Sandel was in and out and in again, landing a left to the eyes, a right to the ribs, ducking a counter, dancing lightly away and dancing menacingly back again. He was swift and clever. It was a dazzling exhibition. The house yelled its approbation. But King was not dazzled. He had fought too many fights and too many youngsters. He knew the blows for what they were—too quick and too deft to be dangerous. Evidently Sandel was going to rush things from the start. It was to be expected. It was the way of Youth, expending its splendour and excellence in wild insurgence and furious onslaught, overwhelming opposition with its own unlimited glory of strength and desire.

Sandel was in and out, here, there, and everywhere, light-footed and eager-hearted, a living wonder of white flesh and stinging muscle that wove itself into a dazzling fabric of attack, slipping and leaping like a flying shuttle from action to action through a thousand actions, all of them centred upon the destruction of Tom King, who stood between him and fortune. And Tom King patiently endured. He knew his business, and he knew Youth now that Youth was no longer his. There was nothing to do till the other lost some of his steam, was his thought, and he grinned to himself as he deliberately ducked so as to receive a heavy blow on the top of his head. It was a wicked thing to do, yet eminently fair according to the rules of the boxing game. A man was supposed to take care of his own knuckles, and, if he insisted on hitting an opponent on the top of the head, he did so at his own peril. King could have ducked lower and let the blow whiz harmlessly past, but he remembered his own early fights and how he smashed his first knuckle on the head of the Welsh Terror. He was but playing the game. That duck had accounted for one of Sandel's knuckles. Not that Sandel would mind it now. He would go on, superbly regardless, hitting as hard as ever throughout the fight. But later on, when the long ring battles had begun to tell, he would regret that knuckle and look back and remember how he smashed it on Tom King's head.

The first round was all Sandel's, and he had the house yelling with the rapidity of his whirlwind rushes. He overwhelmed King with avalanches of punches, and King did nothing. He never struck once, contenting himself with covering up, blocking and ducking and clinching to avoid punishment. He occasionally feinted, shook his head when the weight of a punch landed, and moved stolidly about, never leaping or springing or wasting an ounce of strength. Sandel must foam the froth of Youth away before discreet Age could dare to retaliate. All King's movements were slow and methodical, and his heavy-lidded, slow-moving eyes gave him the appearance of being half asleep or dazed. Yet they were eyes that saw everything, that had been trained to see everything through all his twenty years and odd in the ring. They were eyes that did not blink or waver before an impending blow, but that coolly saw and measured distance.

Seated in his corner for the minute's rest at the end of the round, he lay back with outstretched legs, his arms resting on the right angle of the ropes, his chest and abdomen heaving frankly and deeply as he gulped down the air driven by the towels of his seconds. He listened with closed eyes to the voices of the house, "Why don't yeh fight, Tom?" many were crying. "Yeh ain't afraid of 'im, are yeh?"

"Muscle-bound," he heard a man on a front seat comment. "He can't move quicker. Two to one on Sandel, in quids."

The gong struck and the two men advanced from their corners. Sandel came forward fully three-quarters of the distance, eager to begin again; but King was content to advance the shorter distance. It was in line with his policy of economy. He had not been well trained, and he had not had enough to eat, and every step counted. Besides, he had already walked two miles to the ringside. It was a repetition of the first round, with Sandel attacking like a whirlwind and with the audience indignantly demanding why King did not fight. Beyond feinting and several slowly delivered and ineffectual blows he did nothing save block and stall and clinch. Sandel wanted to make the pace fast, while King, out of his wisdom, refused to accommodate him. He grinned with a certain wistful pathos in his ring-battered countenance, and went on cherishing his strength with the jealousy of which only Age is capable. Sandel was Youth, and he threw his strength away with the munificent abandon of Youth. To King belonged the ring generalship, the wisdom bred of long, aching fights. He watched with cool eyes and head, moving slowly and waiting for Sandel's froth to foam away. To the majority of the onlookers it seemed as though King was hopelessly outclassed, and they voiced their opinion in offers of three to one on Sandel. But there were wise ones, a few, who knew King of old time, and who covered what they considered easy money.

The third round began as usual, one-sided, with Sandel doing all the leading, and delivering all the punishment. A half-minute had passed when Sandel, over-confident, left an opening. King's eyes and right arm flashed in the same instant. It was his first real blow—a hook, with the twisted arch of the arm to make it rigid, and with all the weight of the half-pivoted body behind it. It was like a sleepy-seeming lion suddenly thrusting out a lightning paw. Sandel, caught on the side of the jaw, was felled like a bullock. The audience gasped and murmured awe-stricken applause. The man was not muscle-bound, after all, and he could drive a blow like a trip-hammer.

Sandel was shaken. He rolled over and attempted to rise, but the sharp yells from his seconds to take the count restrained him. He knelt on one knee, ready to rise, and waited, while the referee stood over him, counting the seconds loudly in his ear. At the ninth he rose in fighting attitude, and Tom King, facing him, knew regret that the blow had not been an inch nearer the point of the jaw. That would have been a knock-out, and he could have carried the thirty quid home to the missus and the kiddies.

The round continued to the end of its three minutes, Sandel for the first time respectful of his opponent and King slow of movement and sleepy-eyed as ever. As the round neared its close, King, warned of the fact by sight of the seconds crouching outside ready for the spring in through the ropes, worked the fight around to his own corner. And when the gong struck, he sat down immediately on the waiting stool, while Sandel had to walk all the way across the diagonal of the square to his own corner. It was a little thing, but it was the sum of little things that counted. Sandel was compelled to walk that many more steps, to give up that much energy, and to lose a part of the precious minute of rest. At the beginning of every round King loafed slowly out from his corner, forcing his opponent to advance the greater distance. The end of every round found the fight manoeuvred by King into his own corner so that he could immediately sit down.

Two more rounds went by, in which King was parsimonious of effort and Sandel prodigal. The latter's attempt to force a fast pace made King uncomfortable, for a fair percentage of the multitudinous blows showered upon him went home. Yet King persisted in his dogged slowness, despite the crying of the young hot-heads for him to go in and fight. Again, in the sixth round, Sandel was careless, again Tom King's fearful right flashed out to the jaw, and again Sandel took the nine seconds count.

By the seventh round Sandel's pink of condition was gone, and he settled down to what he knew was to be the hardest fight in his experience. Tom King was an old un, but a better old un than he had ever encountered—an old un who never lost his head, who was remarkably able at defence, whose blows had the impact of a knotted club, and who had a knockout in either hand. Nevertheless, Tom King dared not hit often. He never forgot his battered knuckles, and knew that every hit must count if the knuckles were to last out the fight. As he sat in his corner, glancing across at his opponent, the thought came to him that the sum of his wisdom and Sandel's youth would constitute a world's champion heavyweight. But that was the trouble. Sandel would never become a world champion. He lacked the wisdom, and the only way for him to get it was to buy it with Youth; and when wisdom was his, Youth would have been spent in buying it.

King took every advantage he knew. He never missed an opportunity to clinch, and in effecting most of the clinches his shoulder drove stiffly into the other's ribs. In the philosophy of the ring a shoulder was as good as a punch so far as damage was concerned, and a great deal better so far as concerned expenditure of effort. Also, in the clinches King rested his weight on his opponent, and was loath to let go. This compelled the interference of the referee, who tore them apart, always assisted by Sandel, who had not yet learned to rest. He could not refrain from using those glorious flying arms and writhing muscles of his, and when the other rushed into a clinch, striking shoulder against ribs, and with head resting under Sandel's left arm, Sandel almost invariably swung his right behind his own back and into the projecting face. It was a clever stroke, much admired by the audience, but it was not dangerous, and was, therefore, just that much wasted strength. But Sandel was tireless and unaware of limitations, and King grinned and doggedly endured.

Sandel developed a fierce right to the body, which made it appear that King was taking an enormous amount of punishment, and it was only the old ringsters who appreciated the deft touch of King's left glove to the other's biceps just before the impact of the blow. It was true, the blow landed each time; but each time it was robbed of its power by that touch on the biceps. In the ninth round, three times inside a minute, King's right hooked its twisted arch to the jaw; and three times Sandel's body, heavy as it was, was levelled to the mat. Each time he took the nine seconds allowed him and rose to his feet, shaken and jarred, but still strong. He had lost much of his speed, and he wasted less effort. He was fighting grimly; but he continued to draw upon his chief asset, which was Youth. King's chief asset was experience. As his vitality had dimmed and his vigour abated, he had replaced them with cunning, with wisdom born of the long fights and with a careful shepherding of strength. Not alone had he learned never to make a superfluous movement, but he had learned how to seduce an opponent into throwing his strength away. Again and again, by feint of foot and hand and body he continued to inveigle Sandel into leaping back, ducking, or countering. King rested, but he never permitted Sandel to rest. It was the strategy of Age.

Early in the tenth round King began stopping the other's rushes with straight lefts to the face, and Sandel, grown wary, responded by drawing the left, then by ducking it and delivering his right in a swinging hook to the side of the head. It was too high up to be vitally effective; but when first it landed, King knew the old, familiar descent of the black veil of unconsciousness across his mind. For the instant, or for the slighest fraction of an instant, rather, he ceased. In the one moment he saw his opponent ducking out of his field of vision and the background of white, watching faces; in the next moment he again saw his opponent and the background of faces. It was as if he had slept for a time and just opened his eyes again, and yet the interval of unconsciousness was so microscopically short that there had been no time for him to fall. The audience saw him totter and his knees give, and then saw him recover and tuck his chin deeper into the shelter of his left shoulder.

Several times Sandel repeated the blow, keeping King partially dazed, and then the latter worked out his defence, which was also a counter. Feinting with his left he took a half-step backward, at the same time upper cutting with the whole strength of his right. So accurately was it timed that it landed squarely on Sandel's face in the full, downward sweep of the duck, and Sandel lifted in the air and curled backward, striking the mat on his head and shoulders. Twice King achieved this, then turned loose and hammered his opponent to the ropes. He gave Sandel no chance to rest or to set himself, but smashed blow in upon blow till the house rose to its feet and the air was filled with an unbroken roar of applause. But Sandel's strength and endurance were superb, and he continued to stay on his feet. A knock-out seemed certain, and a captain of police, appalled at the dreadful punishment, arose by the ringside to stop the fight. The gong struck for the end of the round and Sandel staggered to his corner, protesting to the captain that he was sound and strong. To prove it, he threw two back-air-springs, and the police captain gave in.

Tom King, leaning back in his corner and breathing hard, was disappointed. If the fight had been stopped, the referee, perforce, would have rendered him the decision and the purse would have been his. Unlike Sandel, he was not fighting for glory or career, but for thirty quid. And now Sandel would recuperate in the minute of rest.

Youth will be served—this saying flashed into King's mind, and he remembered the first time he had heard it, the night when he had put away Stowsher Bill. The toff who had bought him a drink after the fight and patted him on the shoulder had used those words. Youth will be served! The toff was right. And on that night in the long ago he had been Youth. To-night Youth sat in the opposite corner. As for himself, he had been fighting for half an hour now, and he was an old man. Had he fought like Sandel, he would not have lasted fifteen minutes. But the point was that he did not recuperate. Those upstanding arteries and that sorely tried heart would not enable him to gather strength in the intervals between the rounds. And he had not had sufficient strength in him to begin with. His legs were heavy under him and beginning to cramp. He should not have walked those two miles to the fight. And there was the steak which he had got up longing for that morning. A great and terrible hatred rose up in him for the butchers who had refused him credit. It was hard for an old man to go into a fight without enough to eat. And a piece of steak was such a little thing, a few pennies at best; yet it meant thirty quid to him.

With the gong that opened the eleventh round, Sandel rushed, making a show of freshness which he did not really possess. King knew it for what it was—a bluff as old as the game itself. He clinched to save himself, then, going free, allowed Sandel to get set. This was what King desired. He feinted with his left, drew the answering duck and swinging upward hook, then made the half-step backward, delivered the upper cut full to the face and crumpled Sandel over to the mat. After that he never let him rest, receiving punishment himself, but inflicting far more, smashing Sandel to the ropes, hooking and driving all manner of blows into him, tearing away from his clinches or punching him out of attempted clinches, and ever when Sandel would have fallen, catching him with one uplifting hand and with the other immediately smashing him into the ropes where he could not fall.

The house by this time had gone mad, and it was his house, nearly every voice yelling: "Go it, Tom!" "Get 'im! Get 'im!" "You've got 'im, Tom! You've got 'im!" It was to be a whirlwind finish, and that was what a ringside audience paid to see.

And Tom King, who for half an hour had conserved his strength, now expended it prodigally in the one great effort he knew he had in him. It was his one chance—now or not at all. His strength was waning fast, and his hope was that before the last of it ebbed out of him he would have beaten his opponent down for the count. And as he continued to strike and force, coolly estimating the weight of his blows and the quality of the damage wrought, he realized how hard a man Sandel was to knock out. Stamina and endurance were his to an extreme degree, and they were the virgin stamina and endurance of Youth. Sandel was certainly a coming man. He had it in him. Only out of such rugged fibre were successful fighters fashioned.

Sandel was reeling and staggering, but Tom King's legs were cramping and his knuckles going back on him. Yet he steeled himself to strike the fierce blows, every one of which brought anguish to his tortured hands. Though now he was receiving practically no punishment, he was weakening as rapidly as the other. His blows went home, but there was no longer the weight behind them, and each blow was the result of a severe effort of will. His legs were like lead, and they dragged visibly under him; while Sandel's backers, cheered by this symptom, began calling encouragement to their man.

King was spurred to a burst of effort. He delivered two blows in succession—a left, a trifle too high, to the solar plexus, and a right cross to the jaw. They were not heavy blows, yet so weak and dazed was Sandel that he went down and lay quivering. The referee stood over him, shouting the count of the fatal seconds in his ear. If before the tenth second was called, he did not rise, the fight was lost. The house stood in hushed silence. King rested on trembling legs. A mortal dizziness was upon him, and before his eyes the sea of faces sagged and swayed, while to his ears, as from a remote distance, came the count of the referee. Yet he looked upon the fight as his. It was impossible that a man so punished could rise.

Only Youth could rise, and Sandel rose. At the fourth second he rolled over on his face and groped blindly for the ropes. By the seventh second he had dragged himself to his knee, where he rested, his head rolling groggily on his shoulders. As the referee cried "Nine!" Sandel stood upright, in proper stalling position, his left arm wrapped about his face, his right wrapped about his stomach. Thus were his vital points guarded, while he lurched forward toward King in the hope of effecting a clinch and gaining more time.

At the instant Sandel arose, King was at him, but the two blows he delivered were muffled on the stalled arms. The next moment Sandel was in the clinch and holding on desperately while the referee strove to drag the two men apart. King helped to force himself free. He knew the rapidity with which Youth recovered, and he knew that Sandel was his if he could prevent that recovery. One stiff punch would do it. Sandel was his, indubitably his. He had out-generalled him, out-fought him, out-pointed him. Sandel reeled out of the clinch, balanced on the hair line between defeat or survival. One good blow would topple him over and down and out. And Tom King, in a flash of bitterness, remembered the piece of steak and wished that he had it then behind that necessary punch he must deliver. He nerved himself for the blow, but it was not heavy enough nor swift enough. Sandel swayed, but did not fall, staggering back to the ropes and holding on. King staggered after him, and, with a pang like that of dissolution, delivered another blow. But his body had deserted him. All that was left of him was a fighting intelligence that was dimmed and clouded from exhaustion. The blow that was aimed for the jaw struck no higher than the shoulder. He had willed the blow higher, but the tired muscles had not been able to obey. And, from the impact of the blow, Tom King himself reeled back and nearly fell. Once again he strove. This time his punch missed altogether, and, from absolute weakness, he fell against Sandel and clinched, holding on to him to save himself from sinking to the floor.

King did not attempt to free himself. He had shot his bolt. He was gone. And Youth had been served. Even in the clinch he could feel Sandel growing stronger against him. When the referee thrust them apart, there, before his eyes, he saw Youth recuperate. From instant to instant Sandel grew stronger. His punches, weak and futile at first, became stiff and accurate. Tom King's bleared eyes saw the gloved fist driving at his jaw, and he willed to guard it by interposing his arm. He saw the danger, willed the act; but the arm was too heavy. It seemed burdened with a hundredweight of lead. It would not lift itself, and he strove to lift it with his soul. Then the gloved fist landed home. He experienced a sharp snap that was like an electric spark, and, simultaneously, the veil of blackness enveloped him.

When he opened his eyes again he was in his corner, and he heard the yelling of the audience like the roar of the surf at Bondi Beach. A wet sponge was being pressed against the base of his brain, and Sid Sullivan was blowing cold water in a refreshing spray over his face and chest. His gloves had already been removed, and Sandel, bending over him, was shaking his hand. He bore no ill-will toward the man who had put him out and he returned the grip with a heartiness that made his battered knuckles protest. Then Sandel stepped to the centre of the ring and the audience hushed its pandemonium to hear him accept young Pronto's challenge and offer to increase the side bet to one hundred pounds. King looked on apathetically while his seconds mopped the streaming water from him, dried his face, and prepared him to leave the ring. He felt hungry. It was not the ordinary, gnawing kind, but a great faintness, a palpitation at the pit of the stomach that communicated itself to all his body. He remembered back into the fight to the moment when he had Sandel swaying and tottering on the hair-line balance of defeat. Ah, that piece of steak would have done it! He had lacked just that for the decisive blow, and he had lost. It was all because of the piece of steak.

His seconds were half-supporting him as they helped him through the ropes. He tore free from them, ducked through the ropes unaided, and leaped heavily to the floor, following on their heels as they forced a passage for him down the crowded centre aisle. Leaving the dressing-room for the street, in the entrance to the hall, some young fellow spoke to him.

"W'y didn't yuh go in an' get 'im when yuh 'ad 'im?" the young fellow asked.

"Aw, go to hell!" said Tom King, and passed down the steps to the sidewalk.

The doors of the public-house at the corner were swinging wide, and he saw the lights and the smiling barmaids, heard the many voices discussing the fight and the prosperous chink of money on the bar. Somebody called to him to have a drink. He hesitated perceptibly, then refused and went on his way.

He had not a copper in his pocket, and the two-mile walk home seemed very long. He was certainly getting old. Crossing the Domain, he sat down suddenly on a bench, unnerved by the thought of the missus sitting up for him, waiting to learn the outcome of the fight. That was harder than any knockout, and it seemed almost impossible to face.

He felt weak and sore, and the pain of his smashed knuckles warned him that, even if he could find a job at navvy work, it would be a week before he could grip a pick handle or a shovel. The hunger palpitation at the pit of the stomach was sickening. His wretchedness overwhelmed him, and into his eyes came an unwonted moisture. He covered his face with his hands, and, as he cried, he remembered Stowsher Bill and how he had served him that night in the long ago. Poor old Stowsher Bill! He could understand now why Bill had cried in the dressing-room.

WHITE FANG

PART I

CHAPTER I—THE TRAIL OF THE MEAT

Dark spruce forest frowned on either side the frozen waterway. The trees had been stripped by a recent wind of their white covering of frost, and they seemed to lean towards each other, black and ominous, in the fading light. A vast silence reigned over the land. The land itself was a desolation, lifeless, without movement, so lone and cold that the spirit of it was not even that of sadness. There was a hint in it of laughter, but of a laughter more terrible than any sadness—a laughter that was mirthless as the smile of the sphinx, a laughter cold as the frost and partaking of the grimness of infallibility. It was the masterful and incommunicable wisdom of eternity laughing at the futility of life and the effort of life. It was the Wild, the savage, frozen-hearted Northland Wild.

But there *was* life, abroad in the land and defiant. Down the frozen waterway toiled a string of wolfish dogs. Their bristly fur was rimed with frost. Their breath froze in the air as it left their mouths, spouting forth in spumes of vapour that settled upon the hair of their bodies and formed into crystals of frost. Leather harness was on the dogs, and leather traces attached them to a sled which dragged along behind. The sled was without runners. It was made of stout birch-bark, and its full surface rested on the snow. The front end of the sled was turned up, like a scroll, in order to force down and under the bore of soft snow that surged like a wave before it. On the sled, securely lashed, was a long and narrow oblong box. There were other things on the sled—blankets, an axe, and a coffee-pot and frying-pan; but prominent, occupying most of the space, was the long and narrow oblong box.

In advance of the dogs, on wide snowshoes, toiled a man. At the rear of the sled toiled a second man. On the sled, in the box, lay a third man whose toil was over,—a man whom the Wild had conquered and beaten down until he would never move nor struggle again. It is not the way of the Wild to like movement. Life is an offence to it, for life is movement; and the Wild aims always to destroy movement. It freezes the water to prevent it running to the sea; it drives the sap out of the trees till they are frozen to their mighty hearts; and most ferociously and terribly of all does the Wild harry and crush into submission man—man who is the most restless of life, ever in revolt against the dictum that all movement must in the end come to the cessation of movement.

But at front and rear, unawed and indomitable, toiled the two men who were not yet dead. Their bodies were covered with fur and soft-tanned leather. Eyelashes and cheeks and lips were so coated with the crystals from their frozen breath that their faces were not discernible. This gave them the seeming of ghostly masques, undertakers in a spectral world at the funeral of some ghost. But under it all they were men, penetrating the land of desolation and mockery and silence, puny adventurers bent on colossal adventure, pitting themselves against the might of a world as remote and alien and pulseless as the abysses of space.

They travelled on without speech, saving their breath for the work of their bodies. On every side was the silence, pressing upon them with a tangible presence. It affected their minds as the many atmospheres of deep water affect the body of the diver. It crushed them with the weight of unending vastness and unalterable decree. It crushed them into the remotest recesses of their own minds, pressing out of them, like juices from the grape, all the false ardours and exaltations and undue self-values of the human soul, until they perceived themselves finite and small, specks and motes, moving with weak cunning and little wisdom amidst the play and inter-play of the great blind elements and forces.

An hour went by, and a second hour. The pale light of the short sunless day was beginning to fade, when a faint far cry arose on the still air. It soared upward with a swift rush, till it reached its topmost note, where it persisted, palpitant and tense, and then slowly died away. It might have been a lost soul wailing, had it not been invested with a certain sad fierceness and hungry eagerness. The front man turned his head until his eyes met the eyes of the man behind. And then, across the narrow oblong box, each nodded to the other.

A second cry arose, piercing the silence with needle-like shrillness. Both men located the sound. It was to the rear, somewhere in the snow expanse they had just traversed. A third and answering cry arose, also to the rear and to the left of the second cry.

"They're after us, Bill," said the man at the front.

His voice sounded hoarse and unreal, and he had spoken with apparent effort.

"Meat is scarce," answered his comrade. "I ain't seen a rabbit sign for days."

Thereafter they spoke no more, though their ears were keen for the hunting-cries that continued to rise behind them.

At the fall of darkness they swung the dogs into a cluster of spruce trees on the edge of the waterway and made a camp. The coffin, at the side of the fire, served for seat and table. The wolf-dogs, clustered on the far side of the fire, snarled and bickered among themselves, but evinced no inclination to stray off into the darkness.

"Seems to me, Henry, they're stayin' remarkable close to camp," Bill commented.

Henry, squatting over the fire and settling the pot of coffee with a piece of ice, nodded. Nor did he speak till he had taken his seat on the coffin and begun to eat.

"They know where their hides is safe," he said. "They'd sooner eat grub than be grub. They're pretty wise, them dogs."

Bill shook his head. "Oh, I don't know."

His comrade looked at him curiously. "First time I ever heard you say anything about their not bein' wise."

"Henry," said the other, munching with deliberation the beans he was eating, "did you happen to notice the way them dogs kicked up when I was a-feedin' 'em?"

"They did cut up more'n usual," Henry acknowledged.

"How many dogs 've we got, Henry?"

"Six."

"Well, Henry . . . " Bill stopped for a moment, in order that his words might gain greater significance. "As I was sayin', Henry, we've got six dogs. I took six fish out of the bag. I gave one fish to each dog, an', Henry, I was one fish short."

"You counted wrong."

"We've got six dogs," the other reiterated dispassionately. "I took out six fish. One Ear didn't get no fish. I came back to the bag afterward an' got 'm his fish."

"We've only got six dogs," Henry said.

"Henry," Bill went on. "I won't say they was all dogs, but there was seven of 'm that got fish."

Henry stopped eating to glance across the fire and count the dogs.

"There's only six now," he said.

"I saw the other one run off across the snow," Bill announced with cool positiveness. "I saw seven."

Henry looked at him commiseratingly, and said, "I'll be almighty glad when this trip's over."

"What d'ye mean by that?" Bill demanded.

"I mean that this load of ourn is gettin' on your nerves, an' that you're beginnin' to see things."

"I thought of that," Bill answered gravely. "An' so, when I saw it run off across the snow, I looked in the snow an' saw its tracks. Then I counted the dogs an' there was still six of 'em. The tracks is there in the snow now. D'ye want to look at 'em? I'll show 'em to you."

Henry did not reply, but munched on in silence, until, the meal finished, he topped it with a final cup of coffee. He wiped his mouth with the back of his hand and said:

"Then you're thinkin' as it was—"

A long wailing cry, fiercely sad, from somewhere in the darkness, had interrupted him. He stopped to listen to it, then he finished his sentence with a wave of his hand toward the sound of the cry, "—one of them?"

Bill nodded. "I'd a blame sight sooner think that than anything else. You noticed yourself the row the dogs made."

Cry after cry, and answering cries, were turning the silence into a bedlam. From every side the cries arose, and the dogs betrayed their fear by huddling together and so close to the fire that their hair was scorched by the heat. Bill threw on more wood, before lighting his pipe.

"I'm thinking you're down in the mouth some," Henry said.

"Henry . . . " He sucked meditatively at his pipe for some time before he went on. "Henry, I was a-thinkin' what a blame sight luckier he is than you an' me'll ever be."

He indicated the third person by a downward thrust of the thumb to the box on which they sat.

"You an' me, Henry, when we die, we'll be lucky if we get enough stones over our carcases to keep the dogs off of us."

"But we ain't got people an' money an' all the rest, like him," Henry rejoined. "Long-distance funerals is somethin' you an' me can't exactly afford."

"What gets me, Henry, is what a chap like this, that's a lord or something in his own country, and that's never had to bother about grub nor blankets; why he comes a-buttin' round the Godforsaken ends of the earth—that's what I can't exactly see."

335

"He might have lived to a ripe old age if he'd stayed at home," Henry agreed.

Bill opened his mouth to speak, but changed his mind. Instead, he pointed towards the wall of darkness that pressed about them from every side. There was no suggestion of form in the utter blackness; only could be seen a pair of eyes gleaming like live coals. Henry indicated with his head a second pair, and a third. A circle of the gleaming eyes had drawn about their camp. Now and again a pair of eyes moved, or disappeared to appear again a moment later.

The unrest of the dogs had been increasing, and they stampeded, in a surge of sudden fear, to the near side of the fire, cringing and crawling about the legs of the men. In the scramble one of the dogs had been overturned on the edge of the fire, and it had yelped with pain and fright as the smell of its singed coat possessed the air. The commotion caused the circle of eyes to shift restlessly for a moment and even to withdraw a bit, but it settled down again as the dogs became quiet.

"Henry, it's a blame misfortune to be out of ammunition."

Bill had finished his pipe and was helping his companion to spread the bed of fur and blanket upon the spruce boughs which he had laid over the snow before supper. Henry grunted, and began unlacing his moccasins.

"How many cartridges did you say you had left?" he asked.

"Three," came the answer. "An' I wisht 'twas three hundred. Then I'd show 'em what for, damn 'em!"

He shook his fist angrily at the gleaming eyes, and began securely to prop his moccasins before the fire.

"An' I wisht this cold snap'd break," he went on. "It's ben fifty below for two weeks now. An' I wisht I'd never started on this trip, Henry. I don't like the looks of it. I don't feel right, somehow. An' while I'm wishin', I wisht the trip was over an' done with, an' you an' me a-sittin' by the fire in Fort McGurry just about now an' playing cribbage—that's what I wisht."

Henry grunted and crawled into bed. As he dozed off he was aroused by his comrade's voice.

"Say, Henry, that other one that come in an' got a fish—why didn't the dogs pitch into it? That's what's botherin' me."

"You're botherin' too much, Bill," came the sleepy response. "You was never like this before. You jes' shut up now, an' go to sleep, an' you'll be all hunkydory in the mornin'. Your stomach's sour, that's what's botherin' you."

The men slept, breathing heavily, side by side, under the one covering. The fire died down, and the gleaming eyes drew closer the circle they had flung about the camp. The dogs clustered together in fear, now and again snarling menacingly as a pair of eyes drew close. Once their uproar became so loud that Bill woke up. He got out of bed carefully, so as not to disturb the sleep of his comrade, and threw more wood on the fire. As it began to flame up, the circle of eyes drew farther back. He glanced casually at the huddling dogs. He rubbed his eyes and looked at them more sharply. Then he crawled back into the blankets.

"Henry," he said. "Oh, Henry."

Henry groaned as he passed from sleep to waking, and demanded, "What's wrong now?"

"Nothin'," came the answer; "only there's seven of 'em again. I just counted."

Henry acknowledged receipt of the information with a grunt that slid into a snore as he drifted back into sleep.

In the morning it was Henry who awoke first and routed his companion out of bed. Daylight was yet three hours away, though it was already six o'clock; and in the darkness Henry went about preparing breakfast, while Bill rolled the blankets and made the sled ready for lashing.

"Say, Henry," he asked suddenly, "how many dogs did you say we had?"

"Six."

"Wrong," Bill proclaimed triumphantly.

"Seven again?" Henry queried.

"No, five; one's gone."

"The hell!" Henry cried in wrath, leaving the cooking to come and count the dogs.

"You're right, Bill," he concluded. "Fatty's gone."

"An' he went like greased lightnin' once he got started. Couldn't 've seen 'm for smoke."

"No chance at all," Henry concluded. "They jes' swallowed 'm alive. I bet he was yelpin' as he went down their throats, damn 'em!"

"He always was a fool dog," said Bill.

"But no fool dog ought to be fool enough to go off an' commit suicide that way." He looked over the remainder of the team with a speculative eye that summed up instantly the salient traits of each animal. "I bet none of the others would do it."

"Couldn't drive 'em away from the fire with a club," Bill agreed. "I always did think there was somethin' wrong with Fatty anyway."

And this was the epitaph of a dead dog on the Northland trail—less scant than the epitaph of many another dog, of many a man.

CHAPTER II—THE SHE-WOLF

Breakfast eaten and the slim camp-outfit lashed to the sled, the men turned their backs on the cheery fire and launched out into the darkness. At once began to rise the cries that were fiercely sad—cries that called through the darkness and cold to one another and answered back. Conversation ceased. Daylight came at nine o'clock. At midday the sky to the south warmed to rose-colour, and marked where the bulge of the earth intervened between the meridian sun and the northern world. But the rose-colour swiftly faded. The grey light of day that remained lasted until three o'clock, when it, too, faded, and the pall of the Arctic night descended upon the lone and silent land.

As darkness came on, the hunting-cries to right and left and rear drew closer—so close that more than once they sent surges of fear through the toiling dogs, throwing them into short-lived panics.

At the conclusion of one such panic, when he and Henry had got the dogs back in the traces, Bill said:

"I wisht they'd strike game somewheres, an' go away an' leave us alone."

"They do get on the nerves horrible," Henry sympathised.

They spoke no more until camp was made.

Henry was bending over and adding ice to the babbling pot of beans when he was startled by the sound of a blow, an exclamation from Bill, and a sharp snarling cry of pain from among the dogs. He straightened up in time to see a dim form disappearing across the snow into the shelter of the dark. Then he saw Bill, standing amid the dogs, half triumphant, half crestfallen, in one hand a stout club, in the other the tail and part of the body of a sun-cured salmon.

"It got half of it," he announced; "but I got a whack at it jes' the same. D'ye hear it squeal?"

"What'd it look like?" Henry asked.

"Couldn't see. But it had four legs an' a mouth an' hair an' looked like any dog."

"Must be a tame wolf, I reckon."

"It's damned tame, whatever it is, comin' in here at feedin' time an' gettin' its whack of fish."

That night, when supper was finished and they sat on the oblong box and pulled at their pipes, the circle of gleaming eyes drew in even closer than before.

"I wisht they'd spring up a bunch of moose or something, an' go away an' leave us alone," Bill said.

Henry grunted with an intonation that was not all sympathy, and for a quarter of an hour they sat on in silence, Henry staring at the fire, and Bill at the circle of eyes that burned in the darkness just beyond the firelight.

"I wisht we was pullin' into McGurry right now," he began again.

"Shut up your wishin' and your croakin'," Henry burst out angrily. "Your stomach's sour. That's what's ailin' you. Swallow a spoonful of sody, an' you'll sweeten up wonderful an' be more pleasant company."

In the morning Henry was aroused by fervid blasphemy that proceeded from the mouth of Bill. Henry propped himself up on an elbow and looked to see his comrade standing among the dogs beside the replenished fire, his arms raised in objurgation, his face distorted with passion.

"Hello!" Henry called. "What's up now?"

"Frog's gone," came the answer.

"No."

"I tell you yes."

Henry leaped out of the blankets and to the dogs. He counted them with care, and then joined his partner in cursing the power of the Wild that had robbed them of another dog.

"Frog was the strongest dog of the bunch," Bill pronounced finally.

"An' he was no fool dog neither," Henry added.

And so was recorded the second epitaph in two days.

A gloomy breakfast was eaten, and the four remaining dogs were harnessed to the sled. The day was a repetition of the days that had gone before. The men toiled without speech across the face of the frozen world. The silence was unbroken save by the cries of their pursuers, that, unseen, hung upon their rear. With the coming of night in the mid-afternoon, the cries sounded closer as the pursuers drew in according to their custom; and the dogs grew excited and frightened, and were guilty of panics that tangled the traces and further depressed the two men.

"There, that'll fix you fool critters," Bill said with satisfaction that night, standing erect at completion of his task.

Henry left the cooking to come and see. Not only had his partner tied the dogs up, but he had tied them, after the Indian fashion, with sticks. About the neck of each dog he had fastened a leather thong. To this, and so close to the neck that the dog could not get his teeth to it, he had tied a stout stick four or five feet in length. The other end of the stick, in turn, was made fast to a stake in the ground by means of a leather thong. The dog was unable to gnaw through the leather at his own end of the stick. The stick prevented him from getting at the leather that fastened the other end.

Henry nodded his head approvingly.

"It's the only contraption that'll ever hold One Ear," he said. "He can gnaw through leather as clean as a knife an' jes' about half as quick. They all'll be here in the mornin' hunkydory."

"You jes' bet they will," Bill affirmed. "If one of em' turns up missin', I'll go without my coffee."

"They jes' know we ain't loaded to kill," Henry remarked at bed-time, indicating the gleaming circle that hemmed them in. "If we could put a couple of shots into 'em, they'd be more respectful. They come closer every night. Get the firelight out of your eyes an' look hard—there! Did you see that one?"

For some time the two men amused themselves with watching the movement of vague forms on the edge of the firelight. By looking closely and steadily at where a pair of eyes burned in the darkness, the form of the animal would slowly take shape. They could even see these forms move at times.

A sound among the dogs attracted the men's attention. One Ear was uttering quick, eager whines, lunging at the length of his stick toward the darkness, and desisting now and again in order to make frantic attacks on the stick with his teeth.

"Look at that, Bill," Henry whispered.

Full into the firelight, with a stealthy, sidelong movement, glided a doglike animal. It moved with commingled mistrust and daring, cautiously observing the men, its attention fixed on the dogs. One Ear strained the full length of the stick toward the intruder and whined with eagerness.

"That fool One Ear don't seem scairt much," Bill said in a low tone.

"It's a she-wolf," Henry whispered back, "an' that accounts for Fatty an' Frog. She's the decoy for the pack. She draws out the dog an' then all the rest pitches in an' eats 'm up."

The fire crackled. A log fell apart with a loud spluttering noise. At the sound of it the strange animal leaped back into the darkness.

"Henry, I'm a-thinkin'," Bill announced.

"Thinkin' what?"

"I'm a-thinkin' that was the one I lambasted with the club."

"Ain't the slightest doubt in the world," was Henry's response.

"An' right here I want to remark," Bill went on, "that that animal's familyarity with campfires is suspicious an' immoral."

342

"It knows for certain more'n a self-respectin' wolf ought to know," Henry agreed. "A wolf that knows enough to come in with the dogs at feedin' time has had experiences."

"Ol' Villan had a dog once that run away with the wolves," Bill cogitates aloud. "I ought to know. I shot it out of the pack in a moose pasture over 'on Little Stick. An' Ol' Villan cried like a baby. Hadn't seen it for three years, he said. Ben with the wolves all that time."

"I reckon you've called the turn, Bill. That wolf's a dog, an' it's eaten fish many's the time from the hand of man."

"An if I get a chance at it, that wolf that's a dog'll be jes' meat," Bill declared. "We can't afford to lose no more animals."

"But you've only got three cartridges," Henry objected.

"I'll wait for a dead sure shot," was the reply.

In the morning Henry renewed the fire and cooked breakfast to the accompaniment of his partner's snoring.

"You was sleepin' jes' too comfortable for anything," Henry told him, as he routed him out for breakfast. "I hadn't the heart to rouse you."

Bill began to eat sleepily. He noticed that his cup was empty and started to reach for the pot. But the pot was beyond arm's length and beside Henry.

"Say, Henry," he chided gently, "ain't you forgot somethin'?"

Henry looked about with great carefulness and shook his head. Bill held up the empty cup.

"You don't get no coffee," Henry announced.

"Ain't run out?" Bill asked anxiously.

"Nope."

"Ain't thinkin' it'll hurt my digestion?"

"Nope."

A flush of angry blood pervaded Bill's face.

"Then it's jes' warm an' anxious I am to be hearin' you explain yourself," he said.

"Spanker's gone," Henry answered.

Without haste, with the air of one resigned to misfortune Bill turned his head, and from where he sat counted the dogs.

"How'd it happen?" he asked apathetically.

Henry shrugged his shoulders. "Don't know. Unless One Ear gnawed 'm loose. He couldn't a-done it himself, that's sure."

"The darned cuss." Bill spoke gravely and slowly, with no hint of the anger that was raging within. "Jes' because he couldn't chew himself loose, he chews Spanker loose."

"Well, Spanker's troubles is over anyway; I guess he's digested by this time an' cavortin' over the landscape in the bellies of twenty different wolves," was Henry's epitaph on this, the latest lost dog. "Have some coffee, Bill."

But Bill shook his head.

"Go on," Henry pleaded, elevating the pot.

Bill shoved his cup aside. "I'll be ding-dong-danged if I do. I said I wouldn't if ary dog turned up missin', an' I won't."

"It's darn good coffee," Henry said enticingly.

But Bill was stubborn, and he ate a dry breakfast washed down with mumbled curses at One Ear for the trick he had played.

"I'll tie 'em up out of reach of each other to-night," Bill said, as they took the trail.

They had travelled little more than a hundred yards, when Henry, who was in front, bent down and picked up something with which his snowshoe

344

had collided. It was dark, and he could not see it, but he recognised it by the touch. He flung it back, so that it struck the sled and bounced along until it fetched up on Bill's snowshoes.

"Mebbe you'll need that in your business," Henry said.

Bill uttered an exclamation. It was all that was left of Spanker—the stick with which he had been tied.

"They ate 'm hide an' all," Bill announced. "The stick's as clean as a whistle. They've ate the leather offen both ends. They're damn hungry, Henry, an' they'll have you an' me guessin' before this trip's over."

Henry laughed defiantly. "I ain't been trailed this way by wolves before, but I've gone through a whole lot worse an' kept my health. Takes more'n a handful of them pesky critters to do for yours truly, Bill, my son."

"I don't know, I don't know," Bill muttered ominously.

"Well, you'll know all right when we pull into McGurry."

"I ain't feelin' special enthusiastic," Bill persisted.

"You're off colour, that's what's the matter with you," Henry dogmatised. "What you need is quinine, an' I'm goin' to dose you up stiff as soon as we make McGurry."

Bill grunted his disagreement with the diagnosis, and lapsed into silence. The day was like all the days. Light came at nine o'clock. At twelve o'clock the southern horizon was warmed by the unseen sun; and then began the cold grey of afternoon that would merge, three hours later, into night.

It was just after the sun's futile effort to appear, that Bill slipped the rifle from under the sled-lashings and said:

"You keep right on, Henry, I'm goin' to see what I can see."

"You'd better stick by the sled," his partner protested. "You've only got three cartridges, an' there's no tellin' what might happen."

"Who's croaking now?" Bill demanded triumphantly.

Henry made no reply, and plodded on alone, though often he cast anxious glances back into the grey solitude where his partner had disappeared. An hour later, taking advantage of the cut-offs around which the sled had to go, Bill arrived.

"They're scattered an' rangin' along wide," he said: "keeping up with us an' lookin' for game at the same time. You see, they're sure of us, only they know they've got to wait to get us. In the meantime they're willin' to pick up anything eatable that comes handy."

"You mean they *think* they're sure of us," Henry objected pointedly.

But Bill ignored him. "I seen some of them. They're pretty thin. They ain't had a bite in weeks I reckon, outside of Fatty an' Frog an' Spanker; an' there's so many of 'em that that didn't go far. They're remarkable thin. Their ribs is like wash-boards, an' their stomachs is right up against their backbones. They're pretty desperate, I can tell you. They'll be goin' mad, yet, an' then watch out."

A few minutes later, Henry, who was now travelling behind the sled, emitted a low, warning whistle. Bill turned and looked, then quietly stopped the dogs. To the rear, from around the last bend and plainly into view, on the very trail they had just covered, trotted a furry, slinking form. Its nose was to the trail, and it trotted with a peculiar, sliding, effortless gait. When they halted, it halted, throwing up its head and regarding them steadily with nostrils that twitched as it caught and studied the scent of them.

"It's the she-wolf," Bill answered.

The dogs had lain down in the snow, and he walked past them to join his partner in the sled. Together they watched the strange animal that had pursued them for days and that had already accomplished the destruction of half their dog-team.

After a searching scrutiny, the animal trotted forward a few steps. This it repeated several times, till it was a short hundred yards away. It paused, head up, close by a clump of spruce trees, and with sight and scent studied the outfit of the watching men. It looked at them in a strangely wistful way, after the manner of a dog; but in its wistfulness there was none of the dog affection. It was a wistfulness bred of hunger, as cruel as its own fangs, as merciless as the frost itself.

It was large for a wolf, its gaunt frame advertising the lines of an animal that was among the largest of its kind.

"Stands pretty close to two feet an' a half at the shoulders," Henry commented. "An' I'll bet it ain't far from five feet long."

"Kind of strange colour for a wolf," was Bill's criticism. "I never seen a red wolf before. Looks almost cinnamon to me."

The animal was certainly not cinnamon-coloured. Its coat was the true wolf-coat. The dominant colour was grey, and yet there was to it a faint reddish hue—a hue that was baffling, that appeared and disappeared, that was more like an illusion of the vision, now grey, distinctly grey, and again giving hints and glints of a vague redness of colour not classifiable in terms of ordinary experience.

"Looks for all the world like a big husky sled-dog," Bill said. "I wouldn't be s'prised to see it wag its tail."

"Hello, you husky!" he called. "Come here, you whatever-your-name-is."

"Ain't a bit scairt of you," Henry laughed.

Bill waved his hand at it threateningly and shouted loudly; but the animal betrayed no fear. The only change in it that they could notice was an accession of alertness. It still regarded them with the merciless wistfulness of hunger. They were meat, and it was hungry; and it would like to go in and eat them if it dared.

"Look here, Henry," Bill said, unconsciously lowering his voice to a whisper because of what he imitated. "We've got three cartridges. But it's a dead shot. Couldn't miss it. It's got away with three of our dogs, an' we oughter put a stop to it. What d'ye say?"

Henry nodded his consent. Bill cautiously slipped the gun from under the sled-lashing. The gun was on the way to his shoulder, but it never got there. For in that instant the she-wolf leaped sidewise from the trail into the clump of spruce trees and disappeared.

The two men looked at each other. Henry whistled long and comprehendingly.

"I might have knowed it," Bill chided himself aloud as he replaced the gun. "Of course a wolf that knows enough to come in with the dogs at feedin' time, 'd know all about shooting-irons. I tell you right now, Henry, that critter's the cause of all our trouble. We'd have six dogs at the present time, 'stead of three, if it wasn't for her. An' I tell you right now, Henry, I'm goin' to get her. She's too smart to be shot in the open. But I'm goin' to lay for her. I'll bushwhack her as sure as my name is Bill."

"You needn't stray off too far in doin' it," his partner admonished. "If that pack ever starts to jump you, them three cartridges'd be wuth no more'n three whoops in hell. Them animals is damn hungry, an' once they start in, they'll sure get you, Bill."

They camped early that night. Three dogs could not drag the sled so fast nor for so long hours as could six, and they were showing unmistakable signs of playing out. And the men went early to bed, Bill first seeing to it that the dogs were tied out of gnawing-reach of one another.

But the wolves were growing bolder, and the men were aroused more than once from their sleep. So near did the wolves approach, that the dogs became frantic with terror, and it was necessary to replenish the fire from time to time in order to keep the adventurous marauders at safer distance.

"I've hearn sailors talk of sharks followin' a ship," Bill remarked, as he crawled back into the blankets after one such replenishing of the fire. "Well, them wolves is land sharks. They know their business better'n we do, an' they ain't a-holdin' our trail this way for their health. They're goin' to get us. They're sure goin' to get us, Henry."

"They've half got you a'ready, a-talkin' like that," Henry retorted sharply. "A man's half licked when he says he is. An' you're half eaten from the way you're goin' on about it."

"They've got away with better men than you an' me," Bill answered.

"Oh, shet up your croakin'. You make me all-fired tired."

Henry rolled over angrily on his side, but was surprised that Bill made no similar display of temper. This was not Bill's way, for he was easily angered by sharp words. Henry thought long over it before he went to sleep, and as his eyelids fluttered down and he dozed off, the thought in his mind was: "There's no mistakin' it, Bill's almighty blue. I'll have to cheer him up tomorrow."

CHAPTER III—THE HUNGER CRY

The day began auspiciously. They had lost no dogs during the night, and they swung out upon the trail and into the silence, the darkness, and the cold with spirits that were fairly light. Bill seemed to have forgotten his forebodings of the previous night, and even waxed facetious with the dogs when, at midday, they overturned the sled on a bad piece of trail.

It was an awkward mix-up. The sled was upside down and jammed between a tree-trunk and a huge rock, and they were forced to unharness the dogs in order to straighten out the tangle. The two men were bent over the sled and trying to right it, when Henry observed One Ear sidling away.

"Here, you, One Ear!" he cried, straightening up and turning around on the dog.

But One Ear broke into a run across the snow, his traces trailing behind him. And there, out in the snow of their back track, was the she-wolf waiting for him. As he neared her, he became suddenly cautious. He slowed down to an alert and mincing walk and then stopped. He regarded her carefully and dubiously, yet desirefully. She seemed to smile at him, showing her teeth in an ingratiating rather than a menacing way. She moved toward him a few steps, playfully, and then halted. One Ear drew near to her, still alert and cautious, his tail and ears in the air, his head held high.

He tried to sniff noses with her, but she retreated playfully and coyly. Every advance on his part was accompanied by a corresponding retreat on her part. Step by step she was luring him away from the security of his human companionship. Once, as though a warning had in vague ways flitted through his intelligence, he turned his head and looked back at the overturned sled, at his team-mates, and at the two men who were calling to him.

But whatever idea was forming in his mind, was dissipated by the she-wolf, who advanced upon him, sniffed noses with him for a fleeting instant, and then resumed her coy retreat before his renewed advances.

In the meantime, Bill had bethought himself of the rifle. But it was jammed beneath the overturned sled, and by the time Henry had helped him to right the load, One Ear and the she-wolf were too close together and the distance too great to risk a shot.

Too late One Ear learned his mistake. Before they saw the cause, the two men saw him turn and start to run back toward them. Then, approaching at right angles to the trail and cutting off his retreat they saw a dozen wolves, lean and grey, bounding across the snow. On the instant, the she-wolf's coyness and playfulness disappeared. With a snarl she sprang upon One Ear. He thrust her off with his shoulder, and, his retreat cut off and still intent on regaining the sled, he altered his course in an attempt to circle around to it. More wolves were appearing every moment and joining in the chase. The she-wolf was one leap behind One Ear and holding her own.

"Where are you goin'?" Henry suddenly demanded, laying his hand on his partner's arm.

Bill shook it off. "I won't stand it," he said. "They ain't a-goin' to get any more of our dogs if I can help it."

Gun in hand, he plunged into the underbrush that lined the side of the trail. His intention was apparent enough. Taking the sled as the centre of the circle that One Ear was making, Bill planned to tap that circle at a point in advance of the pursuit. With his rifle, in the broad daylight, it might be possible for him to awe the wolves and save the dog.

"Say, Bill!" Henry called after him. "Be careful! Don't take no chances!"

Henry sat down on the sled and watched. There was nothing else for him to do. Bill had already gone from sight; but now and again, appearing and disappearing amongst the underbrush and the scattered clumps of spruce, could be seen One Ear. Henry judged his case to be hopeless. The dog was thoroughly alive to its danger, but it was running on the outer circle while the wolf-pack was running on the inner and shorter circle. It was vain to think of One Ear so outdistancing his pursuers as to be able to cut across their circle in advance of them and to regain the sled.

351

The different lines were rapidly approaching a point. Somewhere out there in the snow, screened from his sight by trees and thickets, Henry knew that the wolf-pack, One Ear, and Bill were coming together. All too quickly, far more quickly than he had expected, it happened. He heard a shot, then two shots, in rapid succession, and he *knew* that Bill's ammunition was gone. Then he heard a great outcry of snarls and yelps. He recognised One Ear's yell of pain and terror, and he heard a wolf-cry that bespoke a stricken animal. And that was all. The snarls ceased. The yelping died away. Silence settled down again over the lonely land.

He sat for a long while upon the sled. There was no need for him to go and see what had happened. He knew it as though it had taken place before his eyes. Once, he roused with a start and hastily got the axe out from underneath the lashings. But for some time longer he sat and brooded, the two remaining dogs crouching and trembling at his feet.

At last he arose in a weary manner, as though all the resilience had gone out of his body, and proceeded to fasten the dogs to the sled. He passed a rope over his shoulder, a man-trace, and pulled with the dogs. He did not go far. At the first hint of darkness he hastened to make a camp, and he saw to it that he had a generous supply of firewood. He fed the dogs, cooked and ate his supper, and made his bed close to the fire.

But he was not destined to enjoy that bed. Before his eyes closed the wolves had drawn too near for safety. It no longer required an effort of the vision to see them. They were all about him and the fire, in a narrow circle, and he could see them plainly in the firelight lying down, sitting up, crawling forward on their bellies, or slinking back and forth. They even slept. Here and there he could see one curled up in the snow like a dog, taking the sleep that was now denied himself.

He kept the fire brightly blazing, for he knew that it alone intervened between the flesh of his body and their hungry fangs. His two dogs stayed close by him, one on either side, leaning against him for protection, crying and whimpering, and at times snarling desperately when a wolf approached a little closer than usual. At such moments, when his dogs snarled, the whole circle would be agitated, the wolves coming to their feet and pressing tentatively forward, a chorus of snarls and eager yelps rising about him. Then the circle would lie down again, and here and there a wolf would resume its broken nap.

But this circle had a continuous tendency to draw in upon him. Bit by bit, an inch at a time, with here a wolf bellying forward, and there a wolf bellying forward, the circle would narrow until the brutes were almost within springing distance. Then he would seize brands from the fire and hurl them into the pack. A hasty drawing back always resulted, accompanied by angry yelps and frightened snarls when a well-aimed brand struck and scorched a too daring animal.

Morning found the man haggard and worn, wide-eyed from want of sleep. He cooked breakfast in the darkness, and at nine o'clock, when, with the coming of daylight, the wolf-pack drew back, he set about the task he had planned through the long hours of the night. Chopping down young saplings, he made them cross-bars of a scaffold by lashing them high up to the trunks of standing trees. Using the sled-lashing for a heaving rope, and with the aid of the dogs, he hoisted the coffin to the top of the scaffold.

"They got Bill, an' they may get me, but they'll sure never get you, young man," he said, addressing the dead body in its tree-sepulchre.

Then he took the trail, the lightened sled bounding along behind the willing dogs; for they, too, knew that safety lay open in the gaining of Fort McGurry. The wolves were now more open in their pursuit, trotting sedately behind and ranging along on either side, their red tongues lolling out, their lean sides showing the undulating ribs with every movement. They were very lean, mere skin-bags stretched over bony frames, with strings for muscles—so lean that Henry found it in his mind to marvel that they still kept their feet and did not collapse forthright in the snow.

He did not dare travel until dark. At midday, not only did the sun warm the southern horizon, but it even thrust its upper rim, pale and golden, above the sky-line. He received it as a sign. The days were growing longer. The sun was returning. But scarcely had the cheer of its light departed, than he went into camp. There were still several hours of grey daylight and sombre twilight, and he utilised them in chopping an enormous supply of fire-wood.

With night came horror. Not only were the starving wolves growing bolder, but lack of sleep was telling upon Henry. He dozed despite himself, crouching by the fire, the blankets about his shoulders, the axe between his knees, and on either side a dog pressing close against him. He awoke once and saw in front of him, not a dozen feet away, a big grey wolf, one of the largest of the pack. And even as he looked, the brute deliberately stretched himself after the manner of a lazy dog, yawning full in his face and looking upon him with a possessive eye, as if, in truth, he were merely a delayed meal that was soon to be eaten.

This certitude was shown by the whole pack. Fully a score he could count, staring hungrily at him or calmly sleeping in the snow. They reminded him of children gathered about a spread table and awaiting permission to begin to eat. And he was the food they were to eat! He wondered how and when the meal would begin.

As he piled wood on the fire he discovered an appreciation of his own body which he had never felt before. He watched his moving muscles and was interested in the cunning mechanism of his fingers. By the light of the fire he crooked his fingers slowly and repeatedly now one at a time, now all together, spreading them wide or making quick gripping movements. He studied the nail-formation, and prodded the finger-tips, now sharply, and again softly, gauging the while the nerve-sensations produced. It fascinated him, and he grew suddenly fond of this subtle flesh of his that worked so beautifully and smoothly and delicately. Then he would cast a glance of fear at the wolf-circle drawn expectantly about him, and like a blow the realisation would strike him that this wonderful body of his, this living flesh, was no more than so much meat, a quest of ravenous animals, to be torn and slashed by their hungry fangs, to be sustenance to them as the moose and the rabbit had often been sustenance to him.

He came out of a doze that was half nightmare, to see the red-hued she-wolf before him. She was not more than half a dozen feet away sitting in the snow and wistfully regarding him. The two dogs were whimpering and snarling at his feet, but she took no notice of them. She was looking at the man, and for some time he returned her look. There was nothing threatening about her. She looked at him merely with a great wistfulness, but he knew it to be the wistfulness of an equally great hunger. He was the food, and the sight of him excited in her the gustatory sensations. Her mouth opened, the saliva drooled forth, and she licked her chops with the pleasure of anticipation.

A spasm of fear went through him. He reached hastily for a brand to throw at her. But even as he reached, and before his fingers had closed on the missile, she sprang back into safety; and he knew that she was used to having things thrown at her. She had snarled as she sprang away, baring her white fangs to their roots, all her wistfulness vanishing, being replaced by a carnivorous malignity that made him shudder. He glanced at the hand that held the brand, noticing the cunning delicacy of the fingers that gripped it, how they adjusted themselves to all the inequalities of the surface, curling over and under and about the rough wood, and one little finger, too close to the burning portion of the brand, sensitively and automatically writhing back from the hurtful heat to a cooler gripping-place; and in the same instant he seemed to see a vision of those same sensitive and delicate fingers being crushed and torn by the white teeth of the she-wolf. Never had he been so fond of this body of his as now when his tenure of it was so precarious.

All night, with burning brands, he fought off the hungry pack. When he dozed despite himself, the whimpering and snarling of the dogs aroused him. Morning came, but for the first time the light of day failed to scatter the wolves. The man waited in vain for them to go. They remained in a circle about him and his fire, displaying an arrogance of possession that shook his courage born of the morning light.

He made one desperate attempt to pull out on the trail. But the moment he left the protection of the fire, the boldest wolf leaped for him, but leaped short. He saved himself by springing back, the jaws snapping together a scant six inches from his thigh. The rest of the pack was now up and surging upon him, and a throwing of firebrands right and left was necessary to drive them back to a respectful distance.

Even in the daylight he did not dare leave the fire to chop fresh wood. Twenty feet away towered a huge dead spruce. He spent half the day extending his campfire to the tree, at any moment a half dozen burning faggots ready at hand to fling at his enemies. Once at the tree, he studied the surrounding forest in order to fell the tree in the direction of the most firewood.

The night was a repetition of the night before, save that the need for sleep was becoming overpowering. The snarling of his dogs was losing its efficacy. Besides, they were snarling all the time, and his benumbed and drowsy senses no longer took note of changing pitch and intensity. He awoke with a start. The she-wolf was less than a yard from him. Mechanically, at short range, without letting go of it, he thrust a brand full into her open and snarling mouth. She sprang away, yelling with pain, and while he took delight in the smell of burning flesh and hair, he watched her shaking her head and growling wrathfully a score of feet away.

But this time, before he dozed again, he tied a burning pine-knot to his right hand. His eyes were closed but few minutes when the burn of the flame on his flesh awakened him. For several hours he adhered to this programme. Every time he was thus awakened he drove back the wolves with flying brands, replenished the fire, and rearranged the pine-knot on his hand. All worked well, but there came a time when he fastened the pine-knot insecurely. As his eyes closed it fell away from his hand.

He dreamed. It seemed to him that he was in Fort McGurry. It was warm and comfortable, and he was playing cribbage with the Factor. Also, it seemed to him that the fort was besieged by wolves. They were howling at the very gates, and sometimes he and the Factor paused from the game to listen and laugh at the futile efforts of the wolves to get in. And then, so strange was the dream, there was a crash. The door was burst open. He could see the wolves flooding into the big living-room of the fort. They were leaping straight for him and the Factor. With the bursting open of the door, the noise of their howling had increased tremendously. This howling now bothered him. His dream was merging into something else—he knew not what; but through it all, following him, persisted the howling.

And then he awoke to find the howling real. There was a great snarling and yelping. The wolves were rushing him. They were all about him and upon him. The teeth of one had closed upon his arm. Instinctively he leaped into the fire, and as he leaped, he felt the sharp slash of teeth that tore through the flesh of his leg. Then began a fire fight. His stout mittens temporarily protected his hands, and he scooped live coals into the air in all directions, until the campfire took on the semblance of a volcano.

But it could not last long. His face was blistering in the heat, his eyebrows and lashes were singed off, and the heat was becoming unbearable to his feet. With a flaming brand in each hand, he sprang to the edge of the fire. The wolves had been driven back. On every side, wherever the live coals had fallen, the snow was sizzling, and every little while a retiring wolf, with wild leap and snort and snarl, announced that one such live coal had been stepped upon.

Flinging his brands at the nearest of his enemies, the man thrust his smouldering mittens into the snow and stamped about to cool his feet. His two dogs were missing, and he well knew that they had served as a course in the protracted meal which had begun days before with Fatty, the last course of which would likely be himself in the days to follow.

"You ain't got me yet!" he cried, savagely shaking his fist at the hungry beasts; and at the sound of his voice the whole circle was agitated, there was a general snarl, and the she-wolf slid up close to him across the snow and watched him with hungry wistfulness.

He set to work to carry out a new idea that had come to him. He extended the fire into a large circle. Inside this circle he crouched, his sleeping outfit under him as a protection against the melting snow. When he had thus disappeared within his shelter of flame, the whole pack came curiously to the rim of the fire to see what had become of him. Hitherto they had been denied access to the fire, and they now settled down in a close-drawn circle, like so many dogs, blinking and yawning and stretching their lean bodies in the unaccustomed warmth. Then the she-wolf sat down, pointed her nose at a star, and began to howl. One by one the wolves joined her, till the whole pack, on haunches, with noses pointed skyward, was howling its hunger cry.

Dawn came, and daylight. The fire was burning low. The fuel had run out, and there was need to get more. The man attempted to step out of his circle of flame, but the wolves surged to meet him. Burning brands made them spring aside, but they no longer sprang back. In vain he strove to drive them back. As he gave up and stumbled inside his circle, a wolf leaped for him, missed, and landed with all four feet in the coals. It cried out with terror, at the same time snarling, and scrambled back to cool its paws in the snow.

The man sat down on his blankets in a crouching position. His body leaned forward from the hips. His shoulders, relaxed and drooping, and his head on his knees advertised that he had given up the struggle. Now and again he raised his head to note the dying down of the fire. The circle of flame and coals was breaking into segments with openings in between. These openings grew in size, the segments diminished.

"I guess you can come an' get me any time," he mumbled. "Anyway, I'm goin' to sleep."

Once he awakened, and in an opening in the circle, directly in front of him, he saw the she-wolf gazing at him.

Again he awakened, a little later, though it seemed hours to him. A mysterious change had taken place—so mysterious a change that he was shocked wider awake. Something had happened. He could not understand at first. Then he discovered it. The wolves were gone. Remained only the trampled snow to show how closely they had pressed him. Sleep was welling up and gripping him again, his head was sinking down upon his knees, when he roused with a sudden start.

There were cries of men, and churn of sleds, the creaking of harnesses, and the eager whimpering of straining dogs. Four sleds pulled in from the river bed to the camp among the trees. Half a dozen men were about the man who crouched in the centre of the dying fire. They were shaking and prodding him into consciousness. He looked at them like a drunken man and maundered in strange, sleepy speech.

"Red she-wolf. . . . Come in with the dogs at feedin' time. . . . First she ate the dog-food. . . . Then she ate the dogs. . . . An' after that she ate Bill. . . . "

"Where's Lord Alfred?" one of the men bellowed in his ear, shaking him roughly.

He shook his head slowly. "No, she didn't eat him. . . . He's roostin' in a tree at the last camp."

"Dead?" the man shouted.

"An' in a box," Henry answered. He jerked his shoulder petulantly away from the grip of his questioner. "Say, you lemme alone. . . . I'm jes' plump tuckered out. . . . Goo' night, everybody."

His eyes fluttered and went shut. His chin fell forward on his chest. And even as they eased him down upon the blankets his snores were rising on the frosty air.

But there was another sound. Far and faint it was, in the remote distance, the cry of the hungry wolf-pack as it took the trail of other meat than the man it had just missed.

PART II

CHAPTER I—THE BATTLE OF THE FANGS

It was the she-wolf who had first caught the sound of men's voices and the whining of the sled-dogs; and it was the she-wolf who was first to spring away from the cornered man in his circle of dying flame. The pack had been loath to forego the kill it had hunted down, and it lingered for several minutes, making sure of the sounds, and then it, too, sprang away on the trail made by the she-wolf.

Running at the forefront of the pack was a large grey wolf—one of its several leaders. It was he who directed the pack's course on the heels of the she-wolf. It was he who snarled warningly at the younger members of the pack or slashed at them with his fangs when they ambitiously tried to pass him. And it was he who increased the pace when he sighted the she-wolf, now trotting slowly across the snow.

She dropped in alongside by him, as though it were her appointed position, and took the pace of the pack. He did not snarl at her, nor show his teeth, when any leap of hers chanced to put her in advance of him. On the contrary, he seemed kindly disposed toward her—too kindly to suit her, for he was prone to run near to her, and when he ran too near it was she who snarled and showed her teeth. Nor was she above slashing his shoulder sharply on occasion. At such times he betrayed no anger. He merely sprang to the side and ran stiffly ahead for several awkward leaps, in carriage and conduct resembling an abashed country swain.

This was his one trouble in the running of the pack; but she had other troubles. On her other side ran a gaunt old wolf, grizzled and marked with the scars of many battles. He ran always on her right side. The fact that he had but one eye, and that the left eye, might account for this. He, also, was addicted to crowding her, to veering toward her till his scarred muzzle touched her body, or shoulder, or neck. As with the running mate on the left, she repelled these attentions with her teeth; but when both bestowed their attentions at the same time she was roughly jostled, being compelled, with quick snaps to either side, to drive both lovers away and at the same time to maintain her forward leap with the pack and see the way of her feet before her. At such times her running mates flashed their teeth and growled threateningly across at each other. They might have fought, but even wooing and its rivalry waited upon the more pressing hunger-need of the pack.

After each repulse, when the old wolf sheered abruptly away from the sharp-toothed object of his desire, he shouldered against a young three-year-old that ran on his blind right side. This young wolf had attained his full size; and, considering the weak and famished condition of the pack, he possessed more than the average vigour and spirit. Nevertheless, he ran with his head even with the shoulder of his one-eyed elder. When he ventured to run abreast of the older wolf (which was seldom), a snarl and a snap sent him back even with the shoulder again. Sometimes, however, he dropped cautiously and slowly behind and edged in between the old leader and the she-wolf. This was doubly resented, even triply resented. When she snarled her displeasure, the old leader would whirl on the three-year-old. Sometimes she whirled with him. And sometimes the young leader on the left whirled, too.

At such times, confronted by three sets of savage teeth, the young wolf stopped precipitately, throwing himself back on his haunches, with fore-legs stiff, mouth menacing, and mane bristling. This confusion in the front of the moving pack always caused confusion in the rear. The wolves behind collided with the young wolf and expressed their displeasure by administering sharp nips on his hind-legs and flanks. He was laying up trouble for himself, for lack of food and short tempers went together; but with the boundless faith of youth he persisted in repeating the manoeuvre every little while, though it never succeeded in gaining anything for him but discomfiture.

Had there been food, love-making and fighting would have gone on apace, and the pack-formation would have been broken up. But the situation of the pack was desperate. It was lean with long-standing hunger. It ran below its ordinary speed. At the rear limped the weak members, the very young and the very old. At the front were the strongest. Yet all were more like skeletons than full-bodied wolves. Nevertheless, with the exception of the ones that limped, the movements of the animals were effortless and tireless. Their stringy muscles seemed founts of inexhaustible energy. Behind every steel-like contraction of a muscle, lay another steel-like contraction, and another, and another, apparently without end.

They ran many miles that day. They ran through the night. And the next day found them still running. They were running over the surface of a world frozen and dead. No life stirred. They alone moved through the vast inertness. They alone were alive, and they sought for other things that were alive in order that they might devour them and continue to live.

They crossed low divides and ranged a dozen small streams in a lower-lying country before their quest was rewarded. Then they came upon moose. It was a big bull they first found. Here was meat and life, and it was guarded by no mysterious fires nor flying missiles of flame. Splay hoofs and palmated antlers they knew, and they flung their customary patience and caution to the wind. It was a brief fight and fierce. The big bull was beset on every side. He ripped them open or split their skulls with shrewdly driven blows of his great hoofs. He crushed them and broke them on his large horns. He stamped them into the snow under him in the wallowing struggle. But he was foredoomed, and he went down with the she-wolf tearing savagely at his throat, and with other teeth fixed everywhere upon him, devouring him alive, before ever his last struggles ceased or his last damage had been wrought.

There was food in plenty. The bull weighed over eight hundred pounds—fully twenty pounds of meat per mouth for the forty-odd wolves of the pack. But if they could fast prodigiously, they could feed prodigiously, and soon a few scattered bones were all that remained of the splendid live brute that had faced the pack a few hours before.

There was now much resting and sleeping. With full stomachs, bickering and quarrelling began among the younger males, and this continued through the few days that followed before the breaking-up of the pack. The famine was over. The wolves were now in the country of game, and though they still hunted in pack, they hunted more cautiously, cutting out heavy cows or crippled old bulls from the small moose-herds they ran across.

There came a day, in this land of plenty, when the wolf-pack split in half and went in different directions. The she-wolf, the young leader on her left, and the one-eyed elder on her right, led their half of the pack down to the Mackenzie River and across into the lake country to the east. Each day this remnant of the pack dwindled. Two by two, male and female, the wolves were deserting. Occasionally a solitary male was driven out by the sharp teeth of his rivals. In the end there remained only four: the she-wolf, the young leader, the one-eyed one, and the ambitious three-year-old.

The she-wolf had by now developed a ferocious temper. Her three suitors all bore the marks of her teeth. Yet they never replied in kind, never defended themselves against her. They turned their shoulders to her most savage slashes, and with wagging tails and mincing steps strove to placate her wrath. But if they were all mildness toward her, they were all fierceness toward one another. The three-year-old grew too ambitious in his fierceness. He caught the one-eyed elder on his blind side and ripped his ear into ribbons. Though the grizzled old fellow could see only on one side, against the youth and vigour of the other he brought into play the wisdom of long years of experience. His lost eye and his scarred muzzle bore evidence to the nature of his experience. He had survived too many battles to be in doubt for a moment about what to do.

The battle began fairly, but it did not end fairly. There was no telling what the outcome would have been, for the third wolf joined the elder, and together, old leader and young leader, they attacked the ambitious three-year-old and proceeded to destroy him. He was beset on either side by the merciless fangs of his erstwhile comrades. Forgotten were the days they had hunted together, the game they had pulled down, the famine they had suffered. That business was a thing of the past. The business of love was at hand—ever a sterner and crueller business than that of food-getting.

And in the meanwhile, the she-wolf, the cause of it all, sat down contentedly on her haunches and watched. She was even pleased. This was her day—and it came not often—when manes bristled, and fang smote fang or ripped and tore the yielding flesh, all for the possession of her.

And in the business of love the three-year-old, who had made this his first adventure upon it, yielded up his life. On either side of his body stood his two rivals. They were gazing at the she-wolf, who sat smiling in the snow. But the elder leader was wise, very wise, in love even as in battle. The younger leader turned his head to lick a wound on his shoulder. The curve of his neck was turned toward his rival. With his one eye the elder saw the opportunity. He darted in low and closed with his fangs. It was a long, ripping slash, and deep as well. His teeth, in passing, burst the wall of the great vein of the throat. Then he leaped clear.

The young leader snarled terribly, but his snarl broke midmost into a tickling cough. Bleeding and coughing, already stricken, he sprang at the elder and fought while life faded from him, his legs going weak beneath him, the light of day dulling on his eyes, his blows and springs falling shorter and shorter.

And all the while the she-wolf sat on her haunches and smiled. She was made glad in vague ways by the battle, for this was the love-making of the Wild, the sex-tragedy of the natural world that was tragedy only to those that died. To those that survived it was not tragedy, but realisation and achievement.

When the young leader lay in the snow and moved no more, One Eye stalked over to the she-wolf. His carriage was one of mingled triumph and caution. He was plainly expectant of a rebuff, and he was just as plainly surprised when her teeth did not flash out at him in anger. For the first time she met him with a kindly manner. She sniffed noses with him, and even condescended to leap about and frisk and play with him in quite puppyish fashion. And he, for all his grey years and sage experience, behaved quite as puppyishly and even a little more foolishly.

Forgotten already were the vanquished rivals and the love-tale red-written on the snow. Forgotten, save once, when old One Eye stopped for a moment to lick his stiffening wounds. Then it was that his lips half writhed into a snarl, and the hair of his neck and shoulders involuntarily bristled, while he half crouched for a spring, his claws spasmodically clutching into the snow-surface for firmer footing. But it was all forgotten the next moment, as he sprang after the she-wolf, who was coyly leading him a chase through the woods.

After that they ran side by side, like good friends who have come to an understanding. The days passed by, and they kept together, hunting their meat and killing and eating it in common. After a time the she-wolf began to grow restless. She seemed to be searching for something that she could not find. The hollows under fallen trees seemed to attract her, and she spent much time nosing about among the larger snow-piled crevices in the rocks and in the caves of overhanging banks. Old One Eye was not interested at all, but he followed her good-naturedly in her quest, and when her investigations in particular places were unusually protracted, he would lie down and wait until she was ready to go on.

They did not remain in one place, but travelled across country until they regained the Mackenzie River, down which they slowly went, leaving it often to hunt game along the small streams that entered it, but always returning to it again. Sometimes they chanced upon other wolves, usually in pairs; but there was no friendliness of intercourse displayed on either side, no gladness at meeting, no desire to return to the pack-formation. Several times they encountered solitary wolves. These were always males, and they were pressingly insistent on joining with One Eye and his mate. This he resented, and when she stood shoulder to shoulder with him, bristling and showing her teeth, the aspiring solitary ones would back off, turn-tail, and continue on their lonely way.

One moonlight night, running through the quiet forest, One Eye suddenly halted. His muzzle went up, his tail stiffened, and his nostrils dilated as he scented the air. One foot also he held up, after the manner of a dog. He was not satisfied, and he continued to smell the air, striving to understand the message borne upon it to him. One careless sniff had satisfied his mate, and she trotted on to reassure him. Though he followed her, he was still dubious, and he could not forbear an occasional halt in order more carefully to study the warning.

She crept out cautiously on the edge of a large open space in the midst of the trees. For some time she stood alone. Then One Eye, creeping and crawling, every sense on the alert, every hair radiating infinite suspicion, joined her. They stood side by side, watching and listening and smelling.

To their ears came the sounds of dogs wrangling and scuffling, the guttural cries of men, the sharper voices of scolding women, and once the shrill and plaintive cry of a child. With the exception of the huge bulks of the skin-lodges, little could be seen save the flames of the fire, broken by the movements of intervening bodies, and the smoke rising slowly on the quiet air. But to their nostrils came the myriad smells of an Indian camp, carrying a story that was largely incomprehensible to One Eye, but every detail of which the she-wolf knew.

She was strangely stirred, and sniffed and sniffed with an increasing delight. But old One Eye was doubtful. He betrayed his apprehension, and started tentatively to go. She turned and touched his neck with her muzzle in a reassuring way, then regarded the camp again. A new wistfulness was in her face, but it was not the wistfulness of hunger. She was thrilling to a desire that urged her to go forward, to be in closer to that fire, to be squabbling with the dogs, and to be avoiding and dodging the stumbling feet of men.

One Eye moved impatiently beside her; her unrest came back upon her, and she knew again her pressing need to find the thing for which she searched. She turned and trotted back into the forest, to the great relief of One Eye, who trotted a little to the fore until they were well within the shelter of the trees.

As they slid along, noiseless as shadows, in the moonlight, they came upon a run-way. Both noses went down to the footprints in the snow. These footprints were very fresh. One Eye ran ahead cautiously, his mate at his heels. The broad pads of their feet were spread wide and in contact with the snow were like velvet. One Eye caught sight of a dim movement of white in the midst of the white. His sliding gait had been deceptively swift, but it was as nothing to the speed at which he now ran. Before him was bounding the faint patch of white he had discovered.

They were running along a narrow alley flanked on either side by a growth of young spruce. Through the trees the mouth of the alley could be seen, opening out on a moonlit glade. Old One Eye was rapidly overhauling the fleeing shape of white. Bound by bound he gained. Now he was upon it. One leap more and his teeth would be sinking into it. But that leap was never made. High in the air, and straight up, soared the shape of white, now a struggling snowshoe rabbit that leaped and bounded, executing a fantastic dance there above him in the air and never once returning to earth.

One Eye sprang back with a snort of sudden fright, then shrank down to the snow and crouched, snarling threats at this thing of fear he did not understand. But the she-wolf coolly thrust past him. She poised for a moment, then sprang for the dancing rabbit. She, too, soared high, but not so high as the quarry, and her teeth clipped emptily together with a metallic snap. She made another leap, and another.

Her mate had slowly relaxed from his crouch and was watching her. He now evinced displeasure at her repeated failures, and himself made a mighty spring upward. His teeth closed upon the rabbit, and he bore it back to earth with him. But at the same time there was a suspicious crackling movement beside him, and his astonished eye saw a young spruce sapling bending down above him to strike him. His jaws let go their grip, and he leaped backward to escape this strange danger, his lips drawn back from his fangs, his throat snarling, every hair bristling with rage and fright. And in that moment the sapling reared its slender length upright and the rabbit soared dancing in the air again.

The she-wolf was angry. She sank her fangs into her mate's shoulder in reproof; and he, frightened, unaware of what constituted this new onslaught, struck back ferociously and in still greater fright, ripping down the side of the she-wolf's muzzle. For him to resent such reproof was equally unexpected to her, and she sprang upon him in snarling indignation. Then he discovered his mistake and tried to placate her. But she proceeded to punish him roundly, until he gave over all attempts at placation, and whirled in a circle, his head away from her, his shoulders receiving the punishment of her teeth.

In the meantime the rabbit danced above them in the air. The she-wolf sat down in the snow, and old One Eye, now more in fear of his mate than of the mysterious sapling, again sprang for the rabbit. As he sank back with it between his teeth, he kept his eye on the sapling. As before, it followed him back to earth. He crouched down under the impending blow, his hair bristling, but his teeth still keeping tight hold of the rabbit. But the blow did not fall. The sapling remained bent above him. When he moved it moved, and he growled at it through his clenched jaws; when he remained still, it remained still, and he concluded it was safer to continue remaining still. Yet the warm blood of the rabbit tasted good in his mouth.

It was his mate who relieved him from the quandary in which he found himself. She took the rabbit from him, and while the sapling swayed and teetered threateningly above her she calmly gnawed off the rabbit's head. At once the sapling shot up, and after that gave no more trouble, remaining in the decorous and perpendicular position in which nature had intended it to grow. Then, between them, the she-wolf and One Eye devoured the game which the mysterious sapling had caught for them.

There were other run-ways and alleys where rabbits were hanging in the air, and the wolf-pair prospected them all, the she-wolf leading the way, old One Eye following and observant, learning the method of robbing snares—a knowledge destined to stand him in good stead in the days to come.

CHAPTER II—THE LAIR

For two days the she-wolf and One Eye hung about the Indian camp. He was worried and apprehensive, yet the camp lured his mate and she was loath to depart. But when, one morning, the air was rent with the report of a rifle close at hand, and a bullet smashed against a tree trunk several inches from One Eye's head, they hesitated no more, but went off on a long, swinging lope that put quick miles between them and the danger.

They did not go far—a couple of days' journey. The she-wolf's need to find the thing for which she searched had now become imperative. She was getting very heavy, and could run but slowly. Once, in the pursuit of a rabbit, which she ordinarily would have caught with ease, she gave over and lay down and rested. One Eye came to her; but when he touched her neck gently with his muzzle she snapped at him with such quick fierceness that he tumbled over backward and cut a ridiculous figure in his effort to escape her teeth. Her temper was now shorter than ever; but he had become more patient than ever and more solicitous.

And then she found the thing for which she sought. It was a few miles up a small stream that in the summer time flowed into the Mackenzie, but that then was frozen over and frozen down to its rocky bottom—a dead stream of solid white from source to mouth. The she-wolf was trotting wearily along, her mate well in advance, when she came upon the overhanging, high clay-bank. She turned aside and trotted over to it. The wear and tear of spring storms and melting snows had underwashed the bank and in one place had made a small cave out of a narrow fissure.

She paused at the mouth of the cave and looked the wall over carefully. Then, on one side and the other, she ran along the base of the wall to where its abrupt bulk merged from the softer-lined landscape. Returning to the cave, she entered its narrow mouth. For a short three feet she was compelled to crouch, then the walls widened and rose higher in a little round chamber nearly six feet in diameter. The roof barely cleared her head. It was dry and cosey. She inspected it with painstaking care, while One Eye, who had returned, stood in the entrance and patiently watched her. She dropped her head, with her nose to the ground and directed toward a point near to her closely bunched feet, and around this point she circled several times; then, with a tired sigh that was almost a grunt, she curled her body in, relaxed her legs, and dropped down, her head toward the entrance. One Eye, with pointed, interested ears, laughed at her, and beyond, outlined against the white light, she could see the brush of his tail waving good-naturedly. Her own ears, with a snuggling movement, laid their sharp points backward and down against the head for a moment, while her mouth opened and her tongue lolled peaceably out, and in this way she expressed that she was pleased and satisfied.

One Eye was hungry. Though he lay down in the entrance and slept, his sleep was fitful. He kept awaking and cocking his ears at the bright world without, where the April sun was blazing across the snow. When he dozed, upon his ears would steal the faint whispers of hidden trickles of running water, and he would rouse and listen intently. The sun had come back, and all the awakening Northland world was calling to him. Life was stirring. The feel of spring was in the air, the feel of growing life under the snow, of sap ascending in the trees, of buds bursting the shackles of the frost.

He cast anxious glances at his mate, but she showed no desire to get up. He looked outside, and half a dozen snow-birds fluttered across his field of vision. He started to get up, then looked back to his mate again, and settled down and dozed. A shrill and minute singing stole upon his hearing. Once, and twice, he sleepily brushed his nose with his paw. Then he woke up. There, buzzing in the air at the tip of his nose, was a lone mosquito. It was a full-grown mosquito, one that had lain frozen in a dry log all winter and that had now been thawed out by the sun. He could resist the call of the world no longer. Besides, he was hungry.

He crawled over to his mate and tried to persuade her to get up. But she only snarled at him, and he walked out alone into the bright sunshine to find the snow-surface soft under foot and the travelling difficult. He went up the frozen bed of the stream, where the snow, shaded by the trees, was yet hard and crystalline. He was gone eight hours, and he came back through the darkness hungrier than when he had started. He had found game, but he had not caught it. He had broken through the melting snow crust, and wallowed, while the snowshoe rabbits had skimmed along on top lightly as ever.

He paused at the mouth of the cave with a sudden shock of suspicion. Faint, strange sounds came from within. They were sounds not made by his mate, and yet they were remotely familiar. He bellied cautiously inside and was met by a warning snarl from the she-wolf. This he received without perturbation, though he obeyed it by keeping his distance; but he remained interested in the other sounds—faint, muffled sobbings and slubberings.

His mate warned him irritably away, and he curled up and slept in the entrance. When morning came and a dim light pervaded the lair, he again sought after the source of the remotely familiar sounds. There was a new note in his mate's warning snarl. It was a jealous note, and he was very careful in keeping a respectful distance. Nevertheless, he made out, sheltering between her legs against the length of her body, five strange little bundles of life, very feeble, very helpless, making tiny whimpering noises, with eyes that did not open to the light. He was surprised. It was not the first time in his long and successful life that this thing had happened. It had happened many times, yet each time it was as fresh a surprise as ever to him.

His mate looked at him anxiously. Every little while she emitted a low growl, and at times, when it seemed to her he approached too near, the growl shot up in her throat to a sharp snarl. Of her own experience she had no memory of the thing happening; but in her instinct, which was the experience of all the mothers of wolves, there lurked a memory of fathers that had eaten their new-born and helpless progeny. It manifested itself as a fear strong within her, that made her prevent One Eye from more closely inspecting the cubs he had fathered.

But there was no danger. Old One Eye was feeling the urge of an impulse, that was, in turn, an instinct that had come down to him from all the fathers of wolves. He did not question it, nor puzzle over it. It was there, in the fibre of his being; and it was the most natural thing in the world that he should obey it by turning his back on his new-born family and by trotting out and away on the meat-trail whereby he lived.

Five or six miles from the lair, the stream divided, its forks going off among the mountains at a right angle. Here, leading up the left fork, he came upon a fresh track. He smelled it and found it so recent that he crouched swiftly, and looked in the direction in which it disappeared. Then he turned deliberately and took the right fork. The footprint was much larger than the one his own feet made, and he knew that in the wake of such a trail there was little meat for him.

Half a mile up the right fork, his quick ears caught the sound of gnawing teeth. He stalked the quarry and found it to be a porcupine, standing upright against a tree and trying his teeth on the bark. One Eye approached carefully but hopelessly. He knew the breed, though he had never met it so far north before; and never in his long life had porcupine served him for a meal. But he had long since learned that there was such a thing as Chance, or Opportunity, and he continued to draw near. There was never any telling what might happen, for with live things events were somehow always happening differently.

The porcupine rolled itself into a ball, radiating long, sharp needles in all directions that defied attack. In his youth One Eye had once sniffed too near a similar, apparently inert ball of quills, and had the tail flick out suddenly in his face. One quill he had carried away in his muzzle, where it had remained for weeks, a rankling flame, until it finally worked out. So he lay down, in a comfortable crouching position, his nose fully a foot away, and out of the line of the tail. Thus he waited, keeping perfectly quiet. There was no telling. Something might happen. The porcupine might unroll. There might be opportunity for a deft and ripping thrust of paw into the tender, unguarded belly.

But at the end of half an hour he arose, growled wrathfully at the motionless ball, and trotted on. He had waited too often and futilely in the past for porcupines to unroll, to waste any more time. He continued up the right fork. The day wore along, and nothing rewarded his hunt.

The urge of his awakened instinct of fatherhood was strong upon him. He must find meat. In the afternoon he blundered upon a ptarmigan. He came out of a thicket and found himself face to face with the slow-witted bird. It was sitting on a log, not a foot beyond the end of his nose. Each saw the other. The bird made a startled rise, but he struck it with his paw, and smashed it down to earth, then pounced upon it, and caught it in his teeth as it scuttled across the snow trying to rise in the air again. As his teeth crunched through the tender flesh and fragile bones, he began naturally to eat. Then he remembered, and, turning on the back-track, started for home, carrying the ptarmigan in his mouth.

A mile above the forks, running velvet-footed as was his custom, a gliding shadow that cautiously prospected each new vista of the trail, he came upon later imprints of the large tracks he had discovered in the early morning. As the track led his way, he followed, prepared to meet the maker of it at every turn of the stream.

He slid his head around a corner of rock, where began an unusually large bend in the stream, and his quick eyes made out something that sent him crouching swiftly down. It was the maker of the track, a large female lynx. She was crouching as he had crouched once that day, in front of her the tight-rolled ball of quills. If he had been a gliding shadow before, he now became the ghost of such a shadow, as he crept and circled around, and came up well to leeward of the silent, motionless pair.

He lay down in the snow, depositing the ptarmigan beside him, and with eyes peering through the needles of a low-growing spruce he watched the play of life before him—the waiting lynx and the waiting porcupine, each intent on life; and, such was the curiousness of the game, the way of life for one lay in the eating of the other, and the way of life for the other lay in being not eaten. While old One Eye, the wolf crouching in the covert, played his part, too, in the game, waiting for some strange freak of Chance, that might help him on the meat-trail which was his way of life.

Half an hour passed, an hour; and nothing happened. The ball of quills might have been a stone for all it moved; the lynx might have been frozen to marble; and old One Eye might have been dead. Yet all three animals were keyed to a tenseness of living that was almost painful, and scarcely ever would it come to them to be more alive than they were then in their seeming petrifaction.

One Eye moved slightly and peered forth with increased eagerness. Something was happening. The porcupine had at last decided that its enemy had gone away. Slowly, cautiously, it was unrolling its ball of impregnable armour. It was agitated by no tremor of anticipation. Slowly, slowly, the bristling ball straightened out and lengthened. One Eye watching, felt a sudden moistness in his mouth and a drooling of saliva, involuntary, excited by the living meat that was spreading itself like a repast before him.

Not quite entirely had the porcupine unrolled when it discovered its enemy. In that instant the lynx struck. The blow was like a flash of light. The paw, with rigid claws curving like talons, shot under the tender belly and came back with a swift ripping movement. Had the porcupine been entirely unrolled, or had it not discovered its enemy a fraction of a second before the blow was struck, the paw would have escaped unscathed; but a side-flick of the tail sank sharp quills into it as it was withdrawn.

Everything had happened at once—the blow, the counter-blow, the squeal of agony from the porcupine, the big cat's squall of sudden hurt and astonishment. One Eye half arose in his excitement, his ears up, his tail straight out and quivering behind him. The lynx's bad temper got the best of her. She sprang savagely at the thing that had hurt her. But the porcupine, squealing and grunting, with disrupted anatomy trying feebly to roll up into its ball-protection, flicked out its tail again, and again the big cat squalled with hurt and astonishment. Then she fell to backing away and sneezing, her nose bristling with quills like a monstrous pin-cushion. She brushed her nose with her paws, trying to dislodge the fiery darts, thrust it into the snow, and rubbed it against twigs and branches, and all the time leaping about, ahead, sidewise, up and down, in a frenzy of pain and fright.

She sneezed continually, and her stub of a tail was doing its best toward lashing about by giving quick, violent jerks. She quit her antics, and quieted down for a long minute. One Eye watched. And even he could not repress a start and an involuntary bristling of hair along his back when she suddenly leaped, without warning, straight up in the air, at the same time emitting a long and most terrible squall. Then she sprang away, up the trail, squalling with every leap she made.

It was not until her racket had faded away in the distance and died out that One Eye ventured forth. He walked as delicately as though all the snow were carpeted with porcupine quills, erect and ready to pierce the soft pads of his feet. The porcupine met his approach with a furious squealing and a clashing of its long teeth. It had managed to roll up in a ball again, but it was not quite the old compact ball; its muscles were too much torn for that. It had been ripped almost in half, and was still bleeding profusely.

One Eye scooped out mouthfuls of the blood-soaked snow, and chewed and tasted and swallowed. This served as a relish, and his hunger increased mightily; but he was too old in the world to forget his caution. He waited. He lay down and waited, while the porcupine grated its teeth and uttered grunts and sobs and occasional sharp little squeals. In a little while, One Eye noticed that the quills were drooping and that a great quivering had set up. The quivering came to an end suddenly. There was a final defiant clash of the long teeth. Then all the quills drooped quite down, and the body relaxed and moved no more.

With a nervous, shrinking paw, One Eye stretched out the porcupine to its full length and turned it over on its back. Nothing had happened. It was surely dead. He studied it intently for a moment, then took a careful grip with his teeth and started off down the stream, partly carrying, partly dragging the porcupine, with head turned to the side so as to avoid stepping on the prickly mass. He recollected something, dropped the burden, and trotted back to where he had left the ptarmigan. He did not hesitate a moment. He knew clearly what was to be done, and this he did by promptly eating the ptarmigan. Then he returned and took up his burden.

When he dragged the result of his day's hunt into the cave, the she-wolf inspected it, turned her muzzle to him, and lightly licked him on the neck.

But the next instant she was warning him away from the cubs with a snarl that was less harsh than usual and that was more apologetic than menacing. Her instinctive fear of the father of her progeny was toning down. He was behaving as a wolf-father should, and manifesting no unholy desire to devour the young lives she had brought into the world.

CHAPTER III—THE GREY CUB

He was different from his brothers and sisters. Their hair already betrayed the reddish hue inherited from their mother, the she-wolf; while he alone, in this particular, took after his father. He was the one little grey cub of the litter. He had bred true to the straight wolf-stock—in fact, he had bred true to old One Eye himself, physically, with but a single exception, and that was he had two eyes to his father's one.

The grey cub's eyes had not been open long, yet already he could see with steady clearness. And while his eyes were still closed, he had felt, tasted, and smelled. He knew his two brothers and his two sisters very well. He had begun to romp with them in a feeble, awkward way, and even to squabble, his little throat vibrating with a queer rasping noise (the forerunner of the growl), as he worked himself into a passion. And long before his eyes had opened he had learned by touch, taste, and smell to know his mother—a fount of warmth and liquid food and tenderness. She possessed a gentle, caressing tongue that soothed him when it passed over his soft little body, and that impelled him to snuggle close against her and to doze off to sleep.

Most of the first month of his life had been passed thus in sleeping; but now he could see quite well, and he stayed awake for longer periods of time, and he was coming to learn his world quite well. His world was gloomy; but he did not know that, for he knew no other world. It was dim-lighted; but his eyes had never had to adjust themselves to any other light. His world was very small. Its limits were the walls of the lair; but as he had no knowledge of the wide world outside, he was never oppressed by the narrow confines of his existence.

But he had early discovered that one wall of his world was different from the rest. This was the mouth of the cave and the source of light. He had discovered that it was different from the other walls long before he had any thoughts of his own, any conscious volitions. It had been an irresistible attraction before ever his eyes opened and looked upon it. The light from it had beat upon his sealed lids, and the eyes and the optic nerves had pulsated to little, sparklike flashes, warm-coloured and strangely pleasing. The life of his body, and of every fibre of his body, the life that was the very substance of his body and that was apart from his own personal life, had yearned toward this light and urged his body toward it in the same way that the cunning chemistry of a plant urges it toward the sun.

Always, in the beginning, before his conscious life dawned, he had crawled toward the mouth of the cave. And in this his brothers and sisters were one with him. Never, in that period, did any of them crawl toward the dark corners of the back-wall. The light drew them as if they were plants; the chemistry of the life that composed them demanded the light as a necessity of being; and their little puppet-bodies crawled blindly and chemically, like the tendrils of a vine. Later on, when each developed individuality and became personally conscious of impulsions and desires, the attraction of the light increased. They were always crawling and sprawling toward it, and being driven back from it by their mother.

It was in this way that the grey cub learned other attributes of his mother than the soft, soothing, tongue. In his insistent crawling toward the light, he discovered in her a nose that with a sharp nudge administered rebuke, and later, a paw, that crushed him down and rolled him over and over with swift, calculating stroke. Thus he learned hurt; and on top of it he learned to avoid hurt, first, by not incurring the risk of it; and second, when he had incurred the risk, by dodging and by retreating. These were conscious actions, and were the results of his first generalisations upon the world. Before that he had recoiled automatically from hurt, as he had crawled automatically toward the light. After that he recoiled from hurt because he knew that it was hurt.

He was a fierce little cub. So were his brothers and sisters. It was to be expected. He was a carnivorous animal. He came of a breed of meat-killers and meat-eaters. His father and mother lived wholly upon meat. The milk he had sucked with his first flickering life, was milk transformed directly from meat, and now, at a month old, when his eyes had been open for but a week, he was beginning himself to eat meat—meat half-digested by the she-wolf and disgorged for the five growing cubs that already made too great demand upon her breast.

But he was, further, the fiercest of the litter. He could make a louder rasping growl than any of them. His tiny rages were much more terrible than theirs. It was he that first learned the trick of rolling a fellow-cub over with a cunning paw-stroke. And it was he that first gripped another cub by the ear and pulled and tugged and growled through jaws tight-clenched. And certainly it was he that caused the mother the most trouble in keeping her litter from the mouth of the cave.

The fascination of the light for the grey cub increased from day to day. He was perpetually departing on yard-long adventures toward the cave's entrance, and as perpetually being driven back. Only he did not know it for an entrance. He did not know anything about entrances—passages whereby one goes from one place to another place. He did not know any other place, much less of a way to get there. So to him the entrance of the cave was a wall—a wall of light. As the sun was to the outside dweller, this wall was to him the sun of his world. It attracted him as a candle attracts a moth. He was always striving to attain it. The life that was so swiftly expanding within him, urged him continually toward the wall of light. The life that was within him knew that it was the one way out, the way he was predestined to tread. But he himself did not know anything about it. He did not know there was any outside at all.

There was one strange thing about this wall of light. His father (he had already come to recognise his father as the one other dweller in the world, a creature like his mother, who slept near the light and was a bringer of meat)— his father had a way of walking right into the white far wall and disappearing. The grey cub could not understand this. Though never permitted by his mother to approach that wall, he had approached the other walls, and encountered hard obstruction on the end of his tender nose. This hurt. And after several such adventures, he left the walls alone. Without thinking about it, he accepted this disappearing into the wall as a peculiarity of his father, as milk and half-digested meat were peculiarities of his mother.

In fact, the grey cub was not given to thinking—at least, to the kind of thinking customary of men. His brain worked in dim ways. Yet his conclusions were as sharp and distinct as those achieved by men. He had a method of accepting things, without questioning the why and wherefore. In reality, this was the act of classification. He was never disturbed over why a thing happened. How it happened was sufficient for him. Thus, when he had bumped his nose on the back-wall a few times, he accepted that he would not disappear into walls. In the same way he accepted that his father could disappear into walls. But he was not in the least disturbed by desire to find out the reason for the difference between his father and himself. Logic and physics were no part of his mental make-up.

Like most creatures of the Wild, he early experienced famine. There came a time when not only did the meat-supply cease, but the milk no longer came from his mother's breast. At first, the cubs whimpered and cried, but for the most part they slept. It was not long before they were reduced to a coma of hunger. There were no more spats and squabbles, no more tiny rages nor attempts at growling; while the adventures toward the far white wall ceased altogether. The cubs slept, while the life that was in them flickered and died down.

One Eye was desperate. He ranged far and wide, and slept but little in the lair that had now become cheerless and miserable. The she-wolf, too, left her litter and went out in search of meat. In the first days after the birth of the cubs, One Eye had journeyed several times back to the Indian camp and robbed the rabbit snares; but, with the melting of the snow and the opening of the streams, the Indian camp had moved away, and that source of supply was closed to him.

When the grey cub came back to life and again took interest in the far white wall, he found that the population of his world had been reduced. Only one sister remained to him. The rest were gone. As he grew stronger, he found himself compelled to play alone, for the sister no longer lifted her head nor moved about. His little body rounded out with the meat he now ate; but the food had come too late for her. She slept continuously, a tiny skeleton flung round with skin in which the flame flickered lower and lower and at last went out.

Then there came a time when the grey cub no longer saw his father appearing and disappearing in the wall nor lying down asleep in the entrance. This had happened at the end of a second and less severe famine. The she-wolf knew why One Eye never came back, but there was no way by which she could tell what she had seen to the grey cub. Hunting herself for meat, up the left fork of the stream where lived the lynx, she had followed a day-old trail of One Eye. And she had found him, or what remained of him, at the end of the trail. There were many signs of the battle that had been fought, and of the lynx's withdrawal to her lair after having won the victory. Before she went away, the she-wolf had found this lair, but the signs told her that the lynx was inside, and she had not dared to venture in.

After that, the she-wolf in her hunting avoided the left fork. For she knew that in the lynx's lair was a litter of kittens, and she knew the lynx for a fierce, bad-tempered creature and a terrible fighter. It was all very well for half a dozen wolves to drive a lynx, spitting and bristling, up a tree; but it was quite a different matter for a lone wolf to encounter a lynx—especially when the lynx was known to have a litter of hungry kittens at her back.

But the Wild is the Wild, and motherhood is motherhood, at all times fiercely protective whether in the Wild or out of it; and the time was to come when the she-wolf, for her grey cub's sake, would venture the left fork, and the lair in the rocks, and the lynx's wrath.

381

CHAPTER IV—THE WALL OF THE WORLD

By the time his mother began leaving the cave on hunting expeditions, the cub had learned well the law that forbade his approaching the entrance. Not only had this law been forcibly and many times impressed on him by his mother's nose and paw, but in him the instinct of fear was developing. Never, in his brief cave-life, had he encountered anything of which to be afraid. Yet fear was in him. It had come down to him from a remote ancestry through a thousand thousand lives. It was a heritage he had received directly from One Eye and the she-wolf; but to them, in turn, it had been passed down through all the generations of wolves that had gone before. Fear!—that legacy of the Wild which no animal may escape nor exchange for pottage.

So the grey cub knew fear, though he knew not the stuff of which fear was made. Possibly he accepted it as one of the restrictions of life. For he had already learned that there were such restrictions. Hunger he had known; and when he could not appease his hunger he had felt restriction. The hard obstruction of the cave-wall, the sharp nudge of his mother's nose, the smashing stroke of her paw, the hunger unappeased of several famines, had borne in upon him that all was not freedom in the world, that to life there was limitations and restraints. These limitations and restraints were laws. To be obedient to them was to escape hurt and make for happiness.

He did not reason the question out in this man fashion. He merely classified the things that hurt and the things that did not hurt. And after such classification he avoided the things that hurt, the restrictions and restraints, in order to enjoy the satisfactions and the remunerations of life.

Thus it was that in obedience to the law laid down by his mother, and in obedience to the law of that unknown and nameless thing, fear, he kept away from the mouth of the cave. It remained to him a white wall of light. When his mother was absent, he slept most of the time, while during the intervals that he was awake he kept very quiet, suppressing the whimpering cries that tickled in his throat and strove for noise.

Once, lying awake, he heard a strange sound in the white wall. He did not know that it was a wolverine, standing outside, all a-trembling with its own daring, and cautiously scenting out the contents of the cave. The cub knew only that the sniff was strange, a something unclassified, therefore unknown and terrible—for the unknown was one of the chief elements that went into the making of fear.

The hair bristled upon the grey cub's back, but it bristled silently. How was he to know that this thing that sniffed was a thing at which to bristle? It was not born of any knowledge of his, yet it was the visible expression of the fear that was in him, and for which, in his own life, there was no accounting. But fear was accompanied by another instinct—that of concealment. The cub was in a frenzy of terror, yet he lay without movement or sound, frozen, petrified into immobility, to all appearances dead. His mother, coming home, growled as she smelt the wolverine's track, and bounded into the cave and licked and nozzled him with undue vehemence of affection. And the cub felt that somehow he had escaped a great hurt.

But there were other forces at work in the cub, the greatest of which was growth. Instinct and law demanded of him obedience. But growth demanded disobedience. His mother and fear impelled him to keep away from the white wall. Growth is life, and life is for ever destined to make for light. So there was no damming up the tide of life that was rising within him—rising with every mouthful of meat he swallowed, with every breath he drew. In the end, one day, fear and obedience were swept away by the rush of life, and the cub straddled and sprawled toward the entrance.

Unlike any other wall with which he had had experience, this wall seemed to recede from him as he approached. No hard surface collided with the tender little nose he thrust out tentatively before him. The substance of the wall seemed as permeable and yielding as light. And as condition, in his eyes, had the seeming of form, so he entered into what had been wall to him and bathed in the substance that composed it.

It was bewildering. He was sprawling through solidity. And ever the light grew brighter. Fear urged him to go back, but growth drove him on. Suddenly he found himself at the mouth of the cave. The wall, inside which he had thought himself, as suddenly leaped back before him to an immeasurable distance. The light had become painfully bright. He was dazzled by it. Likewise he was made dizzy by this abrupt and tremendous extension of space. Automatically, his eyes were adjusting themselves to the brightness, focusing themselves to meet the increased distance of objects. At first, the wall had leaped beyond his vision. He now saw it again; but it had taken upon itself a remarkable remoteness. Also, its appearance had changed. It was now a variegated wall, composed of the trees that fringed the stream, the opposing mountain that towered above the trees, and the sky that out-towered the mountain.

A great fear came upon him. This was more of the terrible unknown. He crouched down on the lip of the cave and gazed out on the world. He was very much afraid. Because it was unknown, it was hostile to him. Therefore the hair stood up on end along his back and his lips wrinkled weakly in an attempt at a ferocious and intimidating snarl. Out of his puniness and fright he challenged and menaced the whole wide world.

Nothing happened. He continued to gaze, and in his interest he forgot to snarl. Also, he forgot to be afraid. For the time, fear had been routed by growth, while growth had assumed the guise of curiosity. He began to notice near objects—an open portion of the stream that flashed in the sun, the blasted pine-tree that stood at the base of the slope, and the slope itself, that ran right up to him and ceased two feet beneath the lip of the cave on which he crouched.

Now the grey cub had lived all his days on a level floor. He had never experienced the hurt of a fall. He did not know what a fall was. So he stepped boldly out upon the air. His hind-legs still rested on the cave-lip, so he fell forward head downward. The earth struck him a harsh blow on the nose that made him yelp. Then he began rolling down the slope, over and over. He was in a panic of terror. The unknown had caught him at last. It had gripped savagely hold of him and was about to wreak upon him some terrific hurt. Growth was now routed by fear, and he ki-yi'd like any frightened puppy.

The unknown bore him on he knew not to what frightful hurt, and he yelped and ki-yi'd unceasingly. This was a different proposition from crouching in frozen fear while the unknown lurked just alongside. Now the unknown had caught tight hold of him. Silence would do no good. Besides, it was not fear, but terror, that convulsed him.

But the slope grew more gradual, and its base was grass-covered. Here the cub lost momentum. When at last he came to a stop, he gave one last agonised yell and then a long, whimpering wail. Also, and quite as a matter of course, as though in his life he had already made a thousand toilets, he proceeded to lick away the dry clay that soiled him.

After that he sat up and gazed about him, as might the first man of the earth who landed upon Mars. The cub had broken through the wall of the world, the unknown had let go its hold of him, and here he was without hurt. But the first man on Mars would have experienced less unfamiliarity than did he. Without any antecedent knowledge, without any warning whatever that such existed, he found himself an explorer in a totally new world.

Now that the terrible unknown had let go of him, he forgot that the unknown had any terrors. He was aware only of curiosity in all the things about him. He inspected the grass beneath him, the moss-berry plant just beyond, and the dead trunk of the blasted pine that stood on the edge of an open space among the trees. A squirrel, running around the base of the trunk, came full upon him, and gave him a great fright. He cowered down and snarled. But the squirrel was as badly scared. It ran up the tree, and from a point of safety chattered back savagely.

This helped the cub's courage, and though the woodpecker he next encountered gave him a start, he proceeded confidently on his way. Such was his confidence, that when a moose-bird impudently hopped up to him, he reached out at it with a playful paw. The result was a sharp peck on the end of his nose that made him cower down and ki-yi. The noise he made was too much for the moose-bird, who sought safety in flight.

But the cub was learning. His misty little mind had already made an unconscious classification. There were live things and things not alive. Also,

385

he must watch out for the live things. The things not alive remained always in one place, but the live things moved about, and there was no telling what they might do. The thing to expect of them was the unexpected, and for this he must be prepared.

He travelled very clumsily. He ran into sticks and things. A twig that he thought a long way off, would the next instant hit him on the nose or rake along his ribs. There were inequalities of surface. Sometimes he overstepped and stubbed his nose. Quite as often he understepped and stubbed his feet. Then there were the pebbles and stones that turned under him when he trod upon them; and from them he came to know that the things not alive were not all in the same state of stable equilibrium as was his cave—also, that small things not alive were more liable than large things to fall down or turn over. But with every mishap he was learning. The longer he walked, the better he walked. He was adjusting himself. He was learning to calculate his own muscular movements, to know his physical limitations, to measure distances between objects, and between objects and himself.

His was the luck of the beginner. Born to be a hunter of meat (though he did not know it), he blundered upon meat just outside his own cave-door on his first foray into the world. It was by sheer blundering that he chanced upon the shrewdly hidden ptarmigan nest. He fell into it. He had essayed to walk along the trunk of a fallen pine. The rotten bark gave way under his feet, and with a despairing yelp he pitched down the rounded crescent, smashed through the leafage and stalks of a small bush, and in the heart of the bush, on the ground, fetched up in the midst of seven ptarmigan chicks.

They made noises, and at first he was frightened at them. Then he perceived that they were very little, and he became bolder. They moved. He placed his paw on one, and its movements were accelerated. This was a source of enjoyment to him. He smelled it. He picked it up in his mouth. It struggled and tickled his tongue. At the same time he was made aware of a sensation of hunger. His jaws closed together. There was a crunching of fragile bones, and warm blood ran in his mouth. The taste of it was good. This was meat, the same as his mother gave him, only it was alive between his teeth and therefore better. So he ate the ptarmigan. Nor did he stop till he had devoured the whole brood. Then he licked his chops in quite the same way his mother did, and began to crawl out of the bush.

He encountered a feathered whirlwind. He was confused and blinded by the rush of it and the beat of angry wings. He hid his head between his paws and yelped. The blows increased. The mother ptarmigan was in a fury. Then he became angry. He rose up, snarling, striking out with his paws. He sank his tiny teeth into one of the wings and pulled and tugged sturdily. The ptarmigan struggled against him, showering blows upon him with her free wing. It was his first battle. He was elated. He forgot all about the unknown. He no longer was afraid of anything. He was fighting, tearing at a live thing that was striking at him. Also, this live thing was meat. The lust to kill was on him. He had just destroyed little live things. He would now destroy a big live thing. He was too busy and happy to know that he was happy. He was thrilling and exulting in ways new to him and greater to him than any he had known before.

He held on to the wing and growled between his tight-clenched teeth. The ptarmigan dragged him out of the bush. When she turned and tried to drag him back into the bush's shelter, he pulled her away from it and on into the open. And all the time she was making outcry and striking with her free wing, while feathers were flying like a snow-fall. The pitch to which he was aroused was tremendous. All the fighting blood of his breed was up in him and surging through him. This was living, though he did not know it. He was realising his own meaning in the world; he was doing that for which he was made—killing meat and battling to kill it. He was justifying his existence, than which life can do no greater; for life achieves its summit when it does to the uttermost that which it was equipped to do.

After a time, the ptarmigan ceased her struggling. He still held her by the wing, and they lay on the ground and looked at each other. He tried to growl threateningly, ferociously. She pecked on his nose, which by now, what of previous adventures was sore. He winced but held on. She pecked him again and again. From wincing he went to whimpering. He tried to back away from her, oblivious to the fact that by his hold on her he dragged her after him. A rain of pecks fell on his ill-used nose. The flood of fight ebbed

387

down in him, and, releasing his prey, he turned tail and scampered on across the open in inglorious retreat.

He lay down to rest on the other side of the open, near the edge of the bushes, his tongue lolling out, his chest heaving and panting, his nose still hurting him and causing him to continue his whimper. But as he lay there, suddenly there came to him a feeling as of something terrible impending. The unknown with all its terrors rushed upon him, and he shrank back instinctively into the shelter of the bush. As he did so, a draught of air fanned him, and a large, winged body swept ominously and silently past. A hawk, driving down out of the blue, had barely missed him.

While he lay in the bush, recovering from his fright and peering fearfully out, the mother-ptarmigan on the other side of the open space fluttered out of the ravaged nest. It was because of her loss that she paid no attention to the winged bolt of the sky. But the cub saw, and it was a warning and a lesson to him—the swift downward swoop of the hawk, the short skim of its body just above the ground, the strike of its talons in the body of the ptarmigan, the ptarmigan's squawk of agony and fright, and the hawk's rush upward into the blue, carrying the ptarmigan away with it.

It was a long time before the cub left its shelter. He had learned much. Live things were meat. They were good to eat. Also, live things when they were large enough, could give hurt. It was better to eat small live things like ptarmigan chicks, and to let alone large live things like ptarmigan hens. Nevertheless he felt a little prick of ambition, a sneaking desire to have another battle with that ptarmigan hen—only the hawk had carried her away. May be there were other ptarmigan hens. He would go and see.

He came down a shelving bank to the stream. He had never seen water before. The footing looked good. There were no inequalities of surface. He stepped boldly out on it; and went down, crying with fear, into the embrace of the unknown. It was cold, and he gasped, breathing quickly. The water rushed into his lungs instead of the air that had always accompanied his act of breathing. The suffocation he experienced was like the pang of death. To him it signified death. He had no conscious knowledge of death, but like every animal of the Wild, he possessed the instinct of death. To him it stood as the greatest of hurts. It was the very essence of the unknown; it was the sum of the terrors of the unknown, the one culminating and unthinkable catastrophe that could happen to him, about which he knew nothing and about which he feared everything.

He came to the surface, and the sweet air rushed into his open mouth. He did not go down again. Quite as though it had been a long-established custom of his he struck out with all his legs and began to swim. The near bank was a yard away; but he had come up with his back to it, and the first thing his eyes rested upon was the opposite bank, toward which he immediately began to swim. The stream was a small one, but in the pool it widened out to a score of feet.

Midway in the passage, the current picked up the cub and swept him downstream. He was caught in the miniature rapid at the bottom of the pool. Here was little chance for swimming. The quiet water had become suddenly angry. Sometimes he was under, sometimes on top. At all times he was in violent motion, now being turned over or around, and again, being smashed against a rock. And with every rock he struck, he yelped. His progress was a series of yelps, from which might have been adduced the number of rocks he encountered.

Below the rapid was a second pool, and here, captured by the eddy, he was gently borne to the bank, and as gently deposited on a bed of gravel. He crawled frantically clear of the water and lay down. He had learned some more about the world. Water was not alive. Yet it moved. Also, it looked as solid as the earth, but was without any solidity at all. His conclusion was that things were not always what they appeared to be. The cub's fear of the unknown was an inherited distrust, and it had now been strengthened by experience. Thenceforth, in the nature of things, he would possess an abiding distrust of appearances. He would have to learn the reality of a thing before he could put his faith into it.

One other adventure was destined for him that day. He had recollected that there was such a thing in the world as his mother. And then there came to him a feeling that he wanted her more than all the rest of the things in the world. Not only was his body tired with the adventures it had undergone, but his little brain was equally tired. In all the days he had lived it had not worked so hard as on this one day. Furthermore, he was sleepy. So he started out to look for the cave and his mother, feeling at the same time an overwhelming rush of loneliness and helplessness.

He was sprawling along between some bushes, when he heard a sharp intimidating cry. There was a flash of yellow before his eyes. He saw a weasel leaping swiftly away from him. It was a small live thing, and he had no fear. Then, before him, at his feet, he saw an extremely small live thing, only several inches long, a young weasel, that, like himself, had disobediently gone out adventuring. It tried to retreat before him. He turned it over with his paw. It made a queer, grating noise. The next moment the flash of yellow reappeared before his eyes. He heard again the intimidating cry, and at the same instant received a sharp blow on the side of the neck and felt the sharp teeth of the mother-weasel cut into his flesh.

While he yelped and ki-yi'd and scrambled backward, he saw the mother-weasel leap upon her young one and disappear with it into the neighbouring thicket. The cut of her teeth in his neck still hurt, but his feelings were hurt more grievously, and he sat down and weakly whimpered. This mother-weasel was so small and so savage. He was yet to learn that for size and weight the weasel was the most ferocious, vindictive, and terrible of all the killers of the Wild. But a portion of this knowledge was quickly to be his.

He was still whimpering when the mother-weasel reappeared. She did not rush him, now that her young one was safe. She approached more cautiously, and the cub had full opportunity to observe her lean, snakelike body, and her head, erect, eager, and snake-like itself. Her sharp, menacing cry sent the hair bristling along his back, and he snarled warningly at her. She came closer and closer. There was a leap, swifter than his unpractised sight, and the lean, yellow body disappeared for a moment out of the field of his vision. The next moment she was at his throat, her teeth buried in his hair and flesh.

At first he snarled and tried to fight; but he was very young, and this was only his first day in the world, and his snarl became a whimper, his fight a struggle to escape. The weasel never relaxed her hold. She hung on, striving to press down with her teeth to the great vein where his life-blood bubbled. The weasel was a drinker of blood, and it was ever her preference to drink from the throat of life itself.

The grey cub would have died, and there would have been no story to write about him, had not the she-wolf come bounding through the bushes. The weasel let go the cub and flashed at the she-wolf's throat, missing, but getting a hold on the jaw instead. The she-wolf flirted her head like the snap of a whip, breaking the weasel's hold and flinging it high in the air. And, still in the air, the she-wolf's jaws closed on the lean, yellow body, and the weasel knew death between the crunching teeth.

The cub experienced another access of affection on the part of his mother. Her joy at finding him seemed even greater than his joy at being found. She nozzled him and caressed him and licked the cuts made in him by the weasel's teeth. Then, between them, mother and cub, they ate the blood-drinker, and after that went back to the cave and slept.

CHAPTER V—THE LAW OF MEAT

The cub's development was rapid. He rested for two days, and then ventured forth from the cave again. It was on this adventure that he found the young weasel whose mother he had helped eat, and he saw to it that the young weasel went the way of its mother. But on this trip he did not get lost. When he grew tired, he found his way back to the cave and slept. And every day thereafter found him out and ranging a wider area.

He began to get accurate measurement of his strength and his weakness, and to know when to be bold and when to be cautious. He found it expedient to be cautious all the time, except for the rare moments, when, assured of his own intrepidity, he abandoned himself to petty rages and lusts.

He was always a little demon of fury when he chanced upon a stray ptarmigan. Never did he fail to respond savagely to the chatter of the squirrel he had first met on the blasted pine. While the sight of a moose-bird almost invariably put him into the wildest of rages; for he never forgot the peck on the nose he had received from the first of that ilk he encountered.

But there were times when even a moose-bird failed to affect him, and those were times when he felt himself to be in danger from some other prowling meat hunter. He never forgot the hawk, and its moving shadow always sent him crouching into the nearest thicket. He no longer sprawled and straddled, and already he was developing the gait of his mother, slinking and furtive, apparently without exertion, yet sliding along with a swiftness that was as deceptive as it was imperceptible.

In the matter of meat, his luck had been all in the beginning. The seven ptarmigan chicks and the baby weasel represented the sum of his killings. His desire to kill strengthened with the days, and he cherished hungry ambitions for the squirrel that chattered so volubly and always informed all wild creatures that the wolf-cub was approaching. But as birds flew in the air, squirrels could climb trees, and the cub could only try to crawl unobserved upon the squirrel when it was on the ground.

The cub entertained a great respect for his mother. She could get meat, and she never failed to bring him his share. Further, she was unafraid of things. It did not occur to him that this fearlessness was founded upon experience and knowledge. Its effect on him was that of an impression of power. His mother represented power; and as he grew older he felt this power in the sharper admonishment of her paw; while the reproving nudge of her nose gave place to the slash of her fangs. For this, likewise, he respected his mother. She compelled obedience from him, and the older he grew the shorter grew her temper.

Famine came again, and the cub with clearer consciousness knew once more the bite of hunger. The she-wolf ran herself thin in the quest for meat. She rarely slept any more in the cave, spending most of her time on the meat-trail, and spending it vainly. This famine was not a long one, but it was severe while it lasted. The cub found no more milk in his mother's breast, nor did he get one mouthful of meat for himself.

Before, he had hunted in play, for the sheer joyousness of it; now he hunted in deadly earnestness, and found nothing. Yet the failure of it accelerated his development. He studied the habits of the squirrel with greater carefulness, and strove with greater craft to steal upon it and surprise it. He studied the wood-mice and tried to dig them out of their burrows; and he learned much about the ways of moose-birds and woodpeckers. And there came a day when the hawk's shadow did not drive him crouching into the bushes. He had grown stronger and wiser, and more confident. Also, he was desperate. So he sat on his haunches, conspicuously in an open space, and challenged the hawk down out of the sky. For he knew that there, floating in the blue above him, was meat, the meat his stomach yearned after so insistently. But the hawk refused to come down and give battle, and the cub crawled away into a thicket and whimpered his disappointment and hunger.

The famine broke. The she-wolf brought home meat. It was strange meat, different from any she had ever brought before. It was a lynx kitten, partly grown, like the cub, but not so large. And it was all for him. His mother had satisfied her hunger elsewhere; though he did not know that it was the rest of the lynx litter that had gone to satisfy her. Nor did he know the desperateness of her deed. He knew only that the velvet-furred kitten was meat, and he ate and waxed happier with every mouthful.

A full stomach conduces to inaction, and the cub lay in the cave, sleeping against his mother's side. He was aroused by her snarling. Never had he heard her snarl so terribly. Possibly in her whole life it was the most terrible snarl she ever gave. There was reason for it, and none knew it better than she. A lynx's lair is not despoiled with impunity. In the full glare of the afternoon light, crouching in the entrance of the cave, the cub saw the lynx-mother. The hair rippled up along his back at the sight. Here was fear, and it did not require his instinct to tell him of it. And if sight alone were not sufficient, the cry of rage the intruder gave, beginning with a snarl and rushing abruptly upward into a hoarse screech, was convincing enough in itself.

The cub felt the prod of the life that was in him, and stood up and snarled valiantly by his mother's side. But she thrust him ignominiously away and behind her. Because of the low-roofed entrance the lynx could not leap in, and when she made a crawling rush of it the she-wolf sprang upon her and pinned her down. The cub saw little of the battle. There was a tremendous snarling and spitting and screeching. The two animals threshed about, the lynx ripping and tearing with her claws and using her teeth as well, while the she-wolf used her teeth alone.

Once, the cub sprang in and sank his teeth into the hind leg of the lynx. He clung on, growling savagely. Though he did not know it, by the weight of his body he clogged the action of the leg and thereby saved his mother much damage. A change in the battle crushed him under both their bodies and wrenched loose his hold. The next moment the two mothers separated, and, before they rushed together again, the lynx lashed out at the cub with a huge fore-paw that ripped his shoulder open to the bone and sent him hurtling sidewise against the wall. Then was added to the uproar the cub's shrill yelp of pain and fright. But the fight lasted so long that he had time to cry himself out and to experience a second burst of courage; and the end of the battle found him again clinging to a hind-leg and furiously growling between his teeth.

The lynx was dead. But the she-wolf was very weak and sick. At first she caressed the cub and licked his wounded shoulder; but the blood she had lost had taken with it her strength, and for all of a day and a night she lay by her dead foe's side, without movement, scarcely breathing. For a week she never left the cave, except for water, and then her movements were slow and painful. At the end of that time the lynx was devoured, while the she-wolf's wounds had healed sufficiently to permit her to take the meat-trail again.

The cub's shoulder was stiff and sore, and for some time he limped from the terrible slash he had received. But the world now seemed changed. He went about in it with greater confidence, with a feeling of prowess that had not been his in the days before the battle with the lynx. He had looked upon life in a more ferocious aspect; he had fought; he had buried his teeth in the flesh of a foe; and he had survived. And because of all this, he carried himself more boldly, with a touch of defiance that was new in him. He was no longer afraid of minor things, and much of his timidity had vanished, though the unknown never ceased to press upon him with its mysteries and terrors, intangible and ever-menacing.

He began to accompany his mother on the meat-trail, and he saw much of the killing of meat and began to play his part in it. And in his own dim way he learned the law of meat. There were two kinds of life—his own kind and the other kind. His own kind included his mother and himself. The other kind included all live things that moved. But the other kind was divided. One portion was what his own kind killed and ate. This portion was composed of the non-killers and the small killers. The other portion killed and ate his own kind, or was killed and eaten by his own kind. And out of this classification arose the law. The aim of life was meat. Life itself was meat. Life lived on life. There were the eaters and the eaten. The law was: EAT OR BE EATEN. He did not formulate the law in clear, set terms and moralise about it. He did not even think the law; he merely lived the law without thinking about it at all.

He saw the law operating around him on every side. He had eaten the ptarmigan chicks. The hawk had eaten the ptarmigan-mother. The hawk would also have eaten him. Later, when he had grown more formidable, he wanted to eat the hawk. He had eaten the lynx kitten. The lynx-mother would have eaten him had she not herself been killed and eaten. And so it went. The law was being lived about him by all live things, and he himself was part and parcel of the law. He was a killer. His only food was meat, live meat, that ran away swiftly before him, or flew into the air, or climbed trees, or hid in the ground, or faced him and fought with him, or turned the tables and ran after him.

Had the cub thought in man-fashion, he might have epitomised life as a voracious appetite and the world as a place wherein ranged a multitude of appetites, pursuing and being pursued, hunting and being hunted, eating and being eaten, all in blindness and confusion, with violence and disorder, a chaos of gluttony and slaughter, ruled over by chance, merciless, planless, endless.

But the cub did not think in man-fashion. He did not look at things with wide vision. He was single-purposed, and entertained but one thought or desire at a time. Besides the law of meat, there were a myriad other and lesser laws for him to learn and obey. The world was filled with surprise. The stir of the life that was in him, the play of his muscles, was an unending happiness. To run down meat was to experience thrills and elations. His rages and battles were pleasures. Terror itself, and the mystery of the unknown, led to his living.

And there were easements and satisfactions. To have a full stomach, to doze lazily in the sunshine—such things were remuneration in full for his ardours and toils, while his ardours and tolls were in themselves self-remunerative. They were expressions of life, and life is always happy when it is expressing itself. So the cub had no quarrel with his hostile environment. He was very much alive, very happy, and very proud of himself.

PART III

CHAPTER I—THE MAKERS OF FIRE

The cub came upon it suddenly. It was his own fault. He had been careless. He had left the cave and run down to the stream to drink. It might have been that he took no notice because he was heavy with sleep. (He had been out all night on the meat-trail, and had but just then awakened.) And his carelessness might have been due to the familiarity of the trail to the pool. He had travelled it often, and nothing had ever happened on it.

He went down past the blasted pine, crossed the open space, and trotted in amongst the trees. Then, at the same instant, he saw and smelt. Before him, sitting silently on their haunches, were five live things, the like of which he had never seen before. It was his first glimpse of mankind. But at the sight of him the five men did not spring to their feet, nor show their teeth, nor snarl. They did not move, but sat there, silent and ominous.

Nor did the cub move. Every instinct of his nature would have impelled him to dash wildly away, had there not suddenly and for the first time arisen in him another and counter instinct. A great awe descended upon him. He was beaten down to movelessness by an overwhelming sense of his own weakness and littleness. Here was mastery and power, something far and away beyond him.

The cub had never seen man, yet the instinct concerning man was his. In dim ways he recognised in man the animal that had fought itself to primacy over the other animals of the Wild. Not alone out of his own eyes, but out of the eyes of all his ancestors was the cub now looking upon man— out of eyes that had circled in the darkness around countless winter camp-fires, that had peered from safe distances and from the hearts of thickets at the strange, two-legged animal that was lord over living things. The spell of the cub's heritage was upon him, the fear and the respect born of the centuries of struggle and the accumulated experience of the generations. The heritage was too compelling for a wolf that was only a cub. Had he been full-grown, he would have run away. As it was, he cowered down in a paralysis of fear, already half proffering the submission that his kind had proffered from the first time a wolf came in to sit by man's fire and be made warm.

One of the Indians arose and walked over to him and stooped above him. The cub cowered closer to the ground. It was the unknown, objectified at last, in concrete flesh and blood, bending over him and reaching down to seize hold of him. His hair bristled involuntarily; his lips writhed back and his little fangs were bared. The hand, poised like doom above him, hesitated, and the man spoke laughing, "*Wabam wabisca ip pit tah.*" ("Look! The white fangs!")

The other Indians laughed loudly, and urged the man on to pick up the cub. As the hand descended closer and closer, there raged within the cub a battle of the instincts. He experienced two great impulsions—to yield and to fight. The resulting action was a compromise. He did both. He yielded till the hand almost touched him. Then he fought, his teeth flashing in a snap that sank them into the hand. The next moment he received a clout alongside the head that knocked him over on his side. Then all fight fled out of him. His puppyhood and the instinct of submission took charge of him. He sat up on his haunches and ki-yi'd. But the man whose hand he had bitten was angry. The cub received a clout on the other side of his head. Whereupon he sat up and ki-yi'd louder than ever.

The four Indians laughed more loudly, while even the man who had been bitten began to laugh. They surrounded the cub and laughed at him, while he wailed out his terror and his hurt. In the midst of it, he heard something. The Indians heard it too. But the cub knew what it was, and with a last, long wail that had in it more of triumph than grief, he ceased his noise and waited for the coming of his mother, of his ferocious and indomitable mother who fought and killed all things and was never afraid. She was snarling as she ran. She had heard the cry of her cub and was dashing to save him.

She bounded in amongst them, her anxious and militant motherhood making her anything but a pretty sight. But to the cub the spectacle of her protective rage was pleasing. He uttered a glad little cry and bounded to meet her, while the man-animals went back hastily several steps. The she-wolf stood over against her cub, facing the men, with bristling hair, a snarl rumbling deep in her throat. Her face was distorted and malignant with menace, even the bridge of the nose wrinkling from tip to eyes so prodigious was her snarl.

Then it was that a cry went up from one of the men. "Kiche!" was what he uttered. It was an exclamation of surprise. The cub felt his mother wilting at the sound.

"Kiche!" the man cried again, this time with sharpness and authority.

And then the cub saw his mother, the she-wolf, the fearless one, crouching down till her belly touched the ground, whimpering, wagging her tail, making peace signs. The cub could not understand. He was appalled. The awe of man rushed over him again. His instinct had been true. His mother verified it. She, too, rendered submission to the man-animals.

The man who had spoken came over to her. He put his hand upon her head, and she only crouched closer. She did not snap, nor threaten to snap. The other men came up, and surrounded her, and felt her, and pawed her, which actions she made no attempt to resent. They were greatly excited, and made many noises with their mouths. These noises were not indication of danger, the cub decided, as he crouched near his mother still bristling from time to time but doing his best to submit.

"It is not strange," an Indian was saying. "Her father was a wolf. It is true, her mother was a dog; but did not my brother tie her out in the woods all of three nights in the mating season? Therefore was the father of Kiche a wolf."

"It is a year, Grey Beaver, since she ran away," spoke a second Indian.

"It is not strange, Salmon Tongue," Grey Beaver answered. "It was the time of the famine, and there was no meat for the dogs."

"She has lived with the wolves," said a third Indian.

"So it would seem, Three Eagles," Grey Beaver answered, laying his hand on the cub; "and this be the sign of it."

The cub snarled a little at the touch of the hand, and the hand flew back to administer a clout. Whereupon the cub covered its fangs, and sank down submissively, while the hand, returning, rubbed behind his ears, and up and down his back.

"This be the sign of it," Grey Beaver went on. "It is plain that his mother is Kiche. But his father was a wolf. Wherefore is there in him little dog and much wolf. His fangs be white, and White Fang shall be his name. I have spoken. He is my dog. For was not Kiche my brother's dog? And is not my brother dead?"

The cub, who had thus received a name in the world, lay and watched. For a time the man-animals continued to make their mouth-noises. Then Grey Beaver took a knife from a sheath that hung around his neck, and went into the thicket and cut a stick. White Fang watched him. He notched the stick at each end and in the notches fastened strings of raw-hide. One string he tied around the throat of Kiche. Then he led her to a small pine, around which he tied the other string.

White Fang followed and lay down beside her. Salmon Tongue's hand reached out to him and rolled him over on his back. Kiche looked on anxiously. White Fang felt fear mounting in him again. He could not quite suppress a snarl, but he made no offer to snap. The hand, with fingers crooked and spread apart, rubbed his stomach in a playful way and rolled him from side to side. It was ridiculous and ungainly, lying there on his back with legs sprawling in the air. Besides, it was a position of such utter helplessness that White Fang's whole nature revolted against it. He could do nothing to defend himself. If this man-animal intended harm, White Fang knew that he could not escape it. How could he spring away with his four legs in the air above him? Yet submission made him master his fear, and he only growled softly. This growl he could not suppress; nor did the man-animal resent it by giving him a blow on the head. And furthermore, such was the strangeness of it, White Fang experienced an unaccountable sensation of pleasure as the hand rubbed back and forth. When he was rolled on his side he ceased to growl, when the fingers pressed and prodded at the base of his ears the pleasurable sensation increased; and when, with a final rub and scratch, the man left him alone and went away, all fear had died out of White Fang. He was to know fear many times in his dealing with man; yet it was a token of the fearless companionship with man that was ultimately to be his.

After a time, White Fang heard strange noises approaching. He was quick in his classification, for he knew them at once for man-animal noises. A few minutes later the remainder of the tribe, strung out as it was on the march, trailed in. There were more men and many women and children, forty souls of them, and all heavily burdened with camp equipage and outfit. Also there were many dogs; and these, with the exception of the part-grown puppies, were likewise burdened with camp outfit. On their backs, in bags that fastened tightly around underneath, the dogs carried from twenty to thirty pounds of weight.

White Fang had never seen dogs before, but at sight of them he felt that they were his own kind, only somehow different. But they displayed little difference from the wolf when they discovered the cub and his mother. There was a rush. White Fang bristled and snarled and snapped in the face of the open-mouthed oncoming wave of dogs, and went down and under them, feeling the sharp slash of teeth in his body, himself biting and tearing at the legs and bellies above him. There was a great uproar. He could hear the snarl of Kiche as she fought for him; and he could hear the cries of the man-animals, the sound of clubs striking upon bodies, and the yelps of pain from the dogs so struck.

Only a few seconds elapsed before he was on his feet again. He could now see the man-animals driving back the dogs with clubs and stones, defending him, saving him from the savage teeth of his kind that somehow was not his kind. And though there was no reason in his brain for a clear conception of so abstract a thing as justice, nevertheless, in his own way, he felt the justice of the man-animals, and he knew them for what they were—makers of law and executors of law. Also, he appreciated the power with which they administered the law. Unlike any animals he had ever encountered, they did not bite nor claw. They enforced their live strength with the power of dead things. Dead things did their bidding. Thus, sticks and stones, directed by these strange creatures, leaped through the air like living things, inflicting grievous hurts upon the dogs.

To his mind this was power unusual, power inconceivable and beyond the natural, power that was godlike. White Fang, in the very nature of him, could never know anything about gods; at the best he could know only things that were beyond knowing—but the wonder and awe that he had of these man-animals in ways resembled what would be the wonder and awe of man at sight of some celestial creature, on a mountain top, hurling thunderbolts from either hand at an astonished world.

The last dog had been driven back. The hubbub died down. And White Fang licked his hurts and meditated upon this, his first taste of pack-cruelty and his introduction to the pack. He had never dreamed that his own kind consisted of more than One Eye, his mother, and himself. They had constituted a kind apart, and here, abruptly, he had discovered many more creatures apparently of his own kind. And there was a subconscious resentment that these, his kind, at first sight had pitched upon him and tried to destroy him. In the same way he resented his mother being tied with a stick, even though it was done by the superior man-animals. It savoured of the trap, of bondage. Yet of the trap and of bondage he knew nothing. Freedom to roam and run and lie down at will, had been his heritage; and here it was being infringed upon. His mother's movements were restricted to the length of a stick, and by the length of that same stick was he restricted, for he had not yet got beyond the need of his mother's side.

He did not like it. Nor did he like it when the man-animals arose and went on with their march; for a tiny man-animal took the other end of the stick and led Kiche captive behind him, and behind Kiche followed White Fang, greatly perturbed and worried by this new adventure he had entered upon.

They went down the valley of the stream, far beyond White Fang's widest ranging, until they came to the end of the valley, where the stream ran into the Mackenzie River. Here, where canoes were cached on poles high in the air and where stood fish-racks for the drying of fish, camp was made; and White Fang looked on with wondering eyes. The superiority of these man-animals increased with every moment. There was their mastery over all these sharp-fanged dogs. It breathed of power. But greater than that, to the wolf-cub, was their mastery over things not alive; their capacity to communicate motion to unmoving things; their capacity to change the very face of the world.

It was this last that especially affected him. The elevation of frames of poles caught his eye; yet this in itself was not so remarkable, being done by the same creatures that flung sticks and stones to great distances. But when the frames of poles were made into tepees by being covered with cloth and skins, White Fang was astounded. It was the colossal bulk of them that impressed him. They arose around him, on every side, like some monstrous quick-growing form of life. They occupied nearly the whole circumference of his field of vision. He was afraid of them. They loomed ominously above him; and when the breeze stirred them into huge movements, he cowered down in fear, keeping his eyes warily upon them, and prepared to spring away if they attempted to precipitate themselves upon him.

But in a short while his fear of the tepees passed away. He saw the women and children passing in and out of them without harm, and he saw the dogs trying often to get into them, and being driven away with sharp words and flying stones. After a time, he left Kiche's side and crawled cautiously toward the wall of the nearest tepee. It was the curiosity of growth that urged him on—the necessity of learning and living and doing that brings experience. The last few inches to the wall of the tepee were crawled with painful slowness and precaution. The day's events had prepared him for the unknown to manifest itself in most stupendous and unthinkable ways. At last his nose touched the canvas. He waited. Nothing happened. Then he smelled the strange fabric, saturated with the man-smell. He closed on the canvas with his teeth and gave a gentle tug. Nothing happened, though the adjacent portions of the tepee moved. He tugged harder. There was a greater movement. It was delightful. He tugged still harder, and repeatedly, until the whole tepee was in motion. Then the sharp cry of a squaw inside sent him scampering back to Kiche. But after that he was afraid no more of the looming bulks of the tepees.

A moment later he was straying away again from his mother. Her stick was tied to a peg in the ground and she could not follow him. A part-grown puppy, somewhat larger and older than he, came toward him slowly, with ostentatious and belligerent importance. The puppy's name, as White Fang was afterward to hear him called, was Lip-lip. He had had experience in puppy fights and was already something of a bully.

Lip-lip was White Fang's own kind, and, being only a puppy, did not seem dangerous; so White Fang prepared to meet him in a friendly spirit. But when the strangers walk became stiff-legged and his lips lifted clear of his teeth, White Fang stiffened too, and answered with lifted lips. They half circled about each other, tentatively, snarling and bristling. This lasted several minutes, and White Fang was beginning to enjoy it, as a sort of game. But suddenly, with remarkable swiftness, Lip-lip leaped in, delivering a slashing snap, and leaped away again. The snap had taken effect on the shoulder that had been hurt by the lynx and that was still sore deep down near the bone. The surprise and hurt of it brought a yelp out of White Fang; but the next moment, in a rush of anger, he was upon Lip-lip and snapping viciously.

But Lip-lip had lived his life in camp and had fought many puppy fights. Three times, four times, and half a dozen times, his sharp little teeth scored on the newcomer, until White Fang, yelping shamelessly, fled to the protection of his mother. It was the first of the many fights he was to have with Lip-lip, for they were enemies from the start, born so, with natures destined perpetually to clash.

Kiche licked White Fang soothingly with her tongue, and tried to prevail upon him to remain with her. But his curiosity was rampant, and several minutes later he was venturing forth on a new quest. He came upon one of the man-animals, Grey Beaver, who was squatting on his hams and doing something with sticks and dry moss spread before him on the ground. White Fang came near to him and watched. Grey Beaver made mouth-noises which White Fang interpreted as not hostile, so he came still nearer.

Women and children were carrying more sticks and branches to Grey Beaver. It was evidently an affair of moment. White Fang came in until he touched Grey Beaver's knee, so curious was he, and already forgetful that this was a terrible man-animal. Suddenly he saw a strange thing like mist beginning to arise from the sticks and moss beneath Grey Beaver's hands. Then, amongst the sticks themselves, appeared a live thing, twisting and turning, of a colour like the colour of the sun in the sky. White Fang knew nothing about fire. It drew him as the light, in the mouth of the cave had drawn him in his early puppyhood. He crawled the several steps toward the flame. He heard Grey Beaver chuckle above him, and he knew the sound was not hostile. Then his nose touched the flame, and at the same instant his little tongue went out to it.

For a moment he was paralysed. The unknown, lurking in the midst of the sticks and moss, was savagely clutching him by the nose. He scrambled backward, bursting out in an astonished explosion of ki-yi's. At the sound, Kiche leaped snarling to the end of her stick, and there raged terribly because she could not come to his aid. But Grey Beaver laughed loudly, and slapped his thighs, and told the happening to all the rest of the camp, till everybody was laughing uproariously. But White Fang sat on his haunches and ki-yi'd and ki-yi'd, a forlorn and pitiable little figure in the midst of the man-animals.

It was the worst hurt he had ever known. Both nose and tongue had been scorched by the live thing, sun-coloured, that had grown up under Grey Beaver's hands. He cried and cried interminably, and every fresh wail was greeted by bursts of laughter on the part of the man-animals. He tried to soothe his nose with his tongue, but the tongue was burnt too, and the two hurts coming together produced greater hurt; whereupon he cried more hopelessly and helplessly than ever.

And then shame came to him. He knew laughter and the meaning of it. It is not given us to know how some animals know laughter, and know when they are being laughed at; but it was this same way that White Fang knew it. And he felt shame that the man-animals should be laughing at him. He turned and fled away, not from the hurt of the fire, but from the laughter that sank even deeper, and hurt in the spirit of him. And he fled to Kiche, raging at the end of her stick like an animal gone mad—to Kiche, the one creature in the world who was not laughing at him.

Twilight drew down and night came on, and White Fang lay by his mother's side. His nose and tongue still hurt, but he was perplexed by a greater trouble. He was homesick. He felt a vacancy in him, a need for the hush and quietude of the stream and the cave in the cliff. Life had become too populous. There were so many of the man-animals, men, women, and children, all making noises and irritations. And there were the dogs, ever squabbling and bickering, bursting into uproars and creating confusions. The restful loneliness of the only life he had known was gone. Here the very air was palpitant with life. It hummed and buzzed unceasingly. Continually changing its intensity and abruptly variant in pitch, it impinged on his nerves and senses, made him nervous and restless and worried him with a perpetual imminence of happening.

He watched the man-animals coming and going and moving about the camp. In fashion distantly resembling the way men look upon the gods they create, so looked White Fang upon the man-animals before him. They were superior creatures, of a verity, gods. To his dim comprehension they were as much wonder-workers as gods are to men. They were creatures of mastery, possessing all manner of unknown and impossible potencies, overlords of the alive and the not alive—making obey that which moved, imparting movement to that which did not move, and making life, sun-coloured and biting life, to grow out of dead moss and wood. They were fire-makers! They were gods.

CHAPTER II—THE BONDAGE

The days were thronged with experience for White Fang. During the time that Kiche was tied by the stick, he ran about over all the camp, inquiring, investigating, learning. He quickly came to know much of the ways of the man-animals, but familiarity did not breed contempt. The more he came to know them, the more they vindicated their superiority, the more they displayed their mysterious powers, the greater loomed their god-likeness.

To man has been given the grief, often, of seeing his gods overthrown and his altars crumbling; but to the wolf and the wild dog that have come in to crouch at man's feet, this grief has never come. Unlike man, whose gods are of the unseen and the overguessed, vapours and mists of fancy eluding the garmenture of reality, wandering wraiths of desired goodness and power, intangible out-croppings of self into the realm of spirit—unlike man, the wolf and the wild dog that have come in to the fire find their gods in the living flesh, solid to the touch, occupying earth-space and requiring time for the accomplishment of their ends and their existence. No effort of faith is necessary to believe in such a god; no effort of will can possibly induce disbelief in such a god. There is no getting away from it. There it stands, on its two hind-legs, club in hand, immensely potential, passionate and wrathful and loving, god and mystery and power all wrapped up and around by flesh that bleeds when it is torn and that is good to eat like any flesh.

And so it was with White Fang. The man-animals were gods unmistakable and unescapable. As his mother, Kiche, had rendered her allegiance to them at the first cry of her name, so he was beginning to render his allegiance. He gave them the trail as a privilege indubitably theirs. When they walked, he got out of their way. When they called, he came. When they threatened, he cowered down. When they commanded him to go, he went away hurriedly. For behind any wish of theirs was power to enforce that wish, power that hurt, power that expressed itself in clouts and clubs, in flying stones and stinging lashes of whips.

He belonged to them as all dogs belonged to them. His actions were theirs to command. His body was theirs to maul, to stamp upon, to tolerate. Such was the lesson that was quickly borne in upon him. It came hard, going as it did, counter to much that was strong and dominant in his own nature; and, while he disliked it in the learning of it, unknown to himself he was learning to like it. It was a placing of his destiny in another's hands, a shifting of the responsibilities of existence. This in itself was compensation, for it is always easier to lean upon another than to stand alone.

But it did not all happen in a day, this giving over of himself, body and soul, to the man-animals. He could not immediately forego his wild heritage and his memories of the Wild. There were days when he crept to the edge of the forest and stood and listened to something calling him far and away. And always he returned, restless and uncomfortable, to whimper softly and wistfully at Kiche's side and to lick her face with eager, questioning tongue.

White Fang learned rapidly the ways of the camp. He knew the injustice and greediness of the older dogs when meat or fish was thrown out to be eaten. He came to know that men were more just, children more cruel, and women more kindly and more likely to toss him a bit of meat or bone. And after two or three painful adventures with the mothers of part-grown puppies, he came into the knowledge that it was always good policy to let such mothers alone, to keep away from them as far as possible, and to avoid them when he saw them coming.

But the bane of his life was Lip-lip. Larger, older, and stronger, Lip-lip had selected White Fang for his special object of persecution. White Fang fought willingly enough, but he was outclassed. His enemy was too big. Lip-lip became a nightmare to him. Whenever he ventured away from his mother, the bully was sure to appear, trailing at his heels, snarling at him, picking upon him, and watchful of an opportunity, when no man-animal was near, to spring upon him and force a fight. As Lip-lip invariably won, he enjoyed it hugely. It became his chief delight in life, as it became White Fang's chief torment.

But the effect upon White Fang was not to cow him. Though he suffered most of the damage and was always defeated, his spirit remained unsubdued. Yet a bad effect was produced. He became malignant and morose. His temper had been savage by birth, but it became more savage under this unending persecution. The genial, playful, puppyish side of him found little expression. He never played and gambolled about with the other puppies of the camp. Lip-lip would not permit it. The moment White Fang appeared near them, Lip-lip was upon him, bullying and hectoring him, or fighting with him until he had driven him away.

The effect of all this was to rob White Fang of much of his puppyhood and to make him in his comportment older than his age. Denied the outlet, through play, of his energies, he recoiled upon himself and developed his mental processes. He became cunning; he had idle time in which to devote himself to thoughts of trickery. Prevented from obtaining his share of meat and fish when a general feed was given to the camp-dogs, he became a clever thief. He had to forage for himself, and he foraged well, though he was oft-times a plague to the squaws in consequence. He learned to sneak about camp, to be crafty, to know what was going on everywhere, to see and to hear everything and to reason accordingly, and successfully to devise ways and means of avoiding his implacable persecutor.

It was early in the days of his persecution that he played his first really big crafty game and got there from his first taste of revenge. As Kiche, when with the wolves, had lured out to destruction dogs from the camps of men, so White Fang, in manner somewhat similar, lured Lip-lip into Kiche's avenging jaws. Retreating before Lip-lip, White Fang made an indirect flight that led in and out and around the various tepees of the camp. He was a good runner, swifter than any puppy of his size, and swifter than Lip-lip. But he did not run his best in this chase. He barely held his own, one leap ahead of his pursuer.

Lip-lip, excited by the chase and by the persistent nearness of his victim, forgot caution and locality. When he remembered locality, it was too late. Dashing at top speed around a tepee, he ran full tilt into Kiche lying at the end of her stick. He gave one yelp of consternation, and then her punishing jaws closed upon him. She was tied, but he could not get away from her easily. She rolled him off his legs so that he could not run, while she repeatedly ripped and slashed him with her fangs.

When at last he succeeded in rolling clear of her, he crawled to his feet, badly dishevelled, hurt both in body and in spirit. His hair was standing out all over him in tufts where her teeth had mauled. He stood where he had arisen, opened his mouth, and broke out the long, heart-broken puppy wail. But even this he was not allowed to complete. In the middle of it, White Fang, rushing in, sank his teeth into Lip-lip's hind leg. There was no fight left in Lip-lip, and he ran away shamelessly, his victim hot on his heels and worrying him all the way back to his own tepee. Here the squaws came to his aid, and White Fang, transformed into a raging demon, was finally driven off only by a fusillade of stones.

Came the day when Grey Beaver, deciding that the liability of her running away was past, released Kiche. White Fang was delighted with his mother's freedom. He accompanied her joyfully about the camp; and, so long as he remained close by her side, Lip-lip kept a respectful distance. White-Fang even bristled up to him and walked stiff-legged, but Lip-lip ignored the challenge. He was no fool himself, and whatever vengeance he desired to wreak, he could wait until he caught White Fang alone.

Later on that day, Kiche and White Fang strayed into the edge of the woods next to the camp. He had led his mother there, step by step, and now when she stopped, he tried to inveigle her farther. The stream, the lair, and the quiet woods were calling to him, and he wanted her to come. He ran on a few steps, stopped, and looked back. She had not moved. He whined pleadingly, and scurried playfully in and out of the underbrush. He ran back to her, licked her face, and ran on again. And still she did not move. He stopped and regarded her, all of an intentness and eagerness, physically expressed, that slowly faded out of him as she turned her head and gazed back at the camp.

There was something calling to him out there in the open. His mother heard it too. But she heard also that other and louder call, the call of the fire and of man—the call which has been given alone of all animals to the wolf to answer, to the wolf and the wild-dog, who are brothers.

Kiche turned and slowly trotted back toward camp. Stronger than the physical restraint of the stick was the clutch of the camp upon her. Unseen and occultly, the gods still gripped with their power and would not let her go. White Fang sat down in the shadow of a birch and whimpered softly. There was a strong smell of pine, and subtle wood fragrances filled the air, reminding him of his old life of freedom before the days of his bondage. But he was still only a part-grown puppy, and stronger than the call either of man or of the Wild was the call of his mother. All the hours of his short life he had depended upon her. The time was yet to come for independence. So he arose and trotted forlornly back to camp, pausing once, and twice, to sit down and whimper and to listen to the call that still sounded in the depths of the forest.

In the Wild the time of a mother with her young is short; but under the dominion of man it is sometimes even shorter. Thus it was with White Fang. Grey Beaver was in the debt of Three Eagles. Three Eagles was going away on a trip up the Mackenzie to the Great Slave Lake. A strip of scarlet cloth, a bearskin, twenty cartridges, and Kiche, went to pay the debt. White Fang saw his mother taken aboard Three Eagles' canoe, and tried to follow her. A blow from Three Eagles knocked him backward to the land. The canoe shoved off. He sprang into the water and swam after it, deaf to the sharp cries of Grey Beaver to return. Even a man-animal, a god, White Fang ignored, such was the terror he was in of losing his mother.

But gods are accustomed to being obeyed, and Grey Beaver wrathfully launched a canoe in pursuit. When he overtook White Fang, he reached down and by the nape of the neck lifted him clear of the water. He did not deposit him at once in the bottom of the canoe. Holding him suspended with one hand, with the other hand he proceeded to give him a beating. And it *was* a beating. His hand was heavy. Every blow was shrewd to hurt; and he delivered a multitude of blows.

Impelled by the blows that rained upon him, now from this side, now from that, White Fang swung back and forth like an erratic and jerky pendulum. Varying were the emotions that surged through him. At first, he had known surprise. Then came a momentary fear, when he yelped several times to the impact of the hand. But this was quickly followed by anger. His free nature asserted itself, and he showed his teeth and snarled fearlessly in the face of the wrathful god. This but served to make the god more wrathful. The blows came faster, heavier, more shrewd to hurt.

Grey Beaver continued to beat, White Fang continued to snarl. But this could not last for ever. One or the other must give over, and that one was White Fang. Fear surged through him again. For the first time he was being really man-handled. The occasional blows of sticks and stones he had previously experienced were as caresses compared with this. He broke down and began to cry and yelp. For a time each blow brought a yelp from him; but fear passed into terror, until finally his yelps were voiced in unbroken succession, unconnected with the rhythm of the punishment.

At last Grey Beaver withheld his hand. White Fang, hanging limply, continued to cry. This seemed to satisfy his master, who flung him down roughly in the bottom of the canoe. In the meantime the canoe had drifted down the stream. Grey Beaver picked up the paddle. White Fang was in his way. He spurned him savagely with his foot. In that moment White Fang's free nature flashed forth again, and he sank his teeth into the moccasined foot.

The beating that had gone before was as nothing compared with the beating he now received. Grey Beaver's wrath was terrible; likewise was White Fang's fright. Not only the hand, but the hard wooden paddle was used upon him; and he was bruised and sore in all his small body when he was again flung down in the canoe. Again, and this time with purpose, did Grey Beaver kick him. White Fang did not repeat his attack on the foot. He had learned another lesson of his bondage. Never, no matter what the circumstance, must he dare to bite the god who was lord and master over him; the body of the lord and master was sacred, not to be defiled by the teeth of such as he. That was evidently the crime of crimes, the one offence there was no condoning nor overlooking.

When the canoe touched the shore, White Fang lay whimpering and motionless, waiting the will of Grey Beaver. It was Grey Beaver's will that he should go ashore, for ashore he was flung, striking heavily on his side and hurting his bruises afresh. He crawled tremblingly to his feet and stood whimpering. Lip-lip, who had watched the whole proceeding from the bank, now rushed upon him, knocking him over and sinking his teeth into him. White Fang was too helpless to defend himself, and it would have gone hard with him had not Grey Beaver's foot shot out, lifting Lip-lip into the air with its violence so that he smashed down to earth a dozen feet away. This was the man-animal's justice; and even then, in his own pitiable plight, White Fang experienced a little grateful thrill. At Grey Beaver's heels he limped obediently through the village to the tepee. And so it came that White Fang learned that the right to punish was something the gods reserved for themselves and denied to the lesser creatures under them.

That night, when all was still, White Fang remembered his mother and sorrowed for her. He sorrowed too loudly and woke up Grey Beaver, who beat him. After that he mourned gently when the gods were around. But sometimes, straying off to the edge of the woods by himself, he gave vent to his grief, and cried it out with loud whimperings and wailings.

It was during this period that he might have harkened to the memories of the lair and the stream and run back to the Wild. But the memory of his mother held him. As the hunting man-animals went out and came back, so she would come back to the village some time. So he remained in his bondage waiting for her.

But it was not altogether an unhappy bondage. There was much to interest him. Something was always happening. There was no end to the strange things these gods did, and he was always curious to see. Besides, he was learning how to get along with Grey Beaver. Obedience, rigid, undeviating obedience, was what was exacted of him; and in return he escaped beatings and his existence was tolerated.

Nay, Grey Beaver himself sometimes tossed him a piece of meat, and defended him against the other dogs in the eating of it. And such a piece of meat was of value. It was worth more, in some strange way, then a dozen pieces of meat from the hand of a squaw. Grey Beaver never petted nor caressed. Perhaps it was the weight of his hand, perhaps his justice, perhaps the sheer power of him, and perhaps it was all these things that influenced White Fang; for a certain tie of attachment was forming between him and his surly lord.

Insidiously, and by remote ways, as well as by the power of stick and stone and clout of hand, were the shackles of White Fang's bondage being riveted upon him. The qualities in his kind that in the beginning made it possible for them to come in to the fires of men, were qualities capable of development. They were developing in him, and the camp-life, replete with misery as it was, was secretly endearing itself to him all the time. But White Fang was unaware of it. He knew only grief for the loss of Kiche, hope for her return, and a hungry yearning for the free life that had been his.

CHAPTER III—THE OUTCAST

Lip-lip continued so to darken his days that White Fang became wickeder and more ferocious than it was his natural right to be. Savageness was a part of his make-up, but the savageness thus developed exceeded his make-up. He acquired a reputation for wickedness amongst the man-animals themselves. Wherever there was trouble and uproar in camp, fighting and squabbling or the outcry of a squaw over a bit of stolen meat, they were sure to find White Fang mixed up in it and usually at the bottom of it. They did not bother to look after the causes of his conduct. They saw only the effects, and the effects were bad. He was a sneak and a thief, a mischief-maker, a fomenter of trouble; and irate squaws told him to his face, the while he eyed them alert and ready to dodge any quick-flung missile, that he was a wolf and worthless and bound to come to an evil end.

He found himself an outcast in the midst of the populous camp. All the young dogs followed Lip-lip's lead. There was a difference between White Fang and them. Perhaps they sensed his wild-wood breed, and instinctively felt for him the enmity that the domestic dog feels for the wolf. But be that as it may, they joined with Lip-lip in the persecution. And, once declared against him, they found good reason to continue declared against him. One and all, from time to time, they felt his teeth; and to his credit, he gave more than he received. Many of them he could whip in single fight; but single fight was denied him. The beginning of such a fight was a signal for all the young dogs in camp to come running and pitch upon him.

Out of this pack-persecution he learned two important things: how to take care of himself in a mass-fight against him—and how, on a single dog, to inflict the greatest amount of damage in the briefest space of time. To keep one's feet in the midst of the hostile mass meant life, and this he learnt well. He became cat-like in his ability to stay on his feet. Even grown dogs might hurtle him backward or sideways with the impact of their heavy bodies; and backward or sideways he would go, in the air or sliding on the ground, but always with his legs under him and his feet downward to the mother earth.

When dogs fight, there are usually preliminaries to the actual combat—snarlings and bristlings and stiff-legged struttings. But White Fang learned to omit these preliminaries. Delay meant the coming against him of all the young dogs. He must do his work quickly and get away. So he learnt to give no warning of his intention. He rushed in and snapped and slashed on the instant, without notice, before his foe could prepare to meet him. Thus he learned how to inflict quick and severe damage. Also he learned the value of surprise. A dog, taken off its guard, its shoulder slashed open or its ear ripped in ribbons before it knew what was happening, was a dog half whipped.

Furthermore, it was remarkably easy to overthrow a dog taken by surprise; while a dog, thus overthrown, invariably exposed for a moment the soft underside of its neck—the vulnerable point at which to strike for its life. White Fang knew this point. It was a knowledge bequeathed to him directly from the hunting generation of wolves. So it was that White Fang's method when he took the offensive, was: first to find a young dog alone; second, to surprise it and knock it off its feet; and third, to drive in with his teeth at the soft throat.

Being but partly grown his jaws had not yet become large enough nor strong enough to make his throat-attack deadly; but many a young dog went around camp with a lacerated throat in token of White Fang's intention. And one day, catching one of his enemies alone on the edge of the woods, he managed, by repeatedly overthrowing him and attacking the throat, to cut the great vein and let out the life. There was a great row that night. He had been observed, the news had been carried to the dead dog's master, the squaws remembered all the instances of stolen meat, and Grey Beaver was beset by many angry voices. But he resolutely held the door of his tepee, inside which he had placed the culprit, and refused to permit the vengeance for which his tribespeople clamoured.

White Fang became hated by man and dog. During this period of his development he never knew a moment's security. The tooth of every dog was against him, the hand of every man. He was greeted with snarls by his kind, with curses and stones by his gods. He lived tensely. He was always keyed up, alert for attack, wary of being attacked, with an eye for sudden and unexpected missiles, prepared to act precipitately and coolly, to leap in with a flash of teeth, or to leap away with a menacing snarl.

As for snarling he could snarl more terribly than any dog, young or old, in camp. The intent of the snarl is to warn or frighten, and judgment is required to know when it should be used. White Fang knew how to make it and when to make it. Into his snarl he incorporated all that was vicious, malignant, and horrible. With nose serrulated by continuous spasms, hair bristling in recurrent waves, tongue whipping out like a red snake and whipping back again, ears flattened down, eyes gleaming hatred, lips wrinkled back, and fangs exposed and dripping, he could compel a pause on the part of almost any assailant. A temporary pause, when taken off his guard, gave him the vital moment in which to think and determine his action. But often a pause so gained lengthened out until it evolved into a complete cessation from the attack. And before more than one of the grown dogs White Fang's snarl enabled him to beat an honourable retreat.

An outcast himself from the pack of the part-grown dogs, his sanguinary methods and remarkable efficiency made the pack pay for its persecution of him. Not permitted himself to run with the pack, the curious state of affairs obtained that no member of the pack could run outside the pack. White Fang would not permit it. What of his bushwhacking and waylaying tactics, the young dogs were afraid to run by themselves. With the exception of Lip-lip, they were compelled to hunch together for mutual protection against the terrible enemy they had made. A puppy alone by the river bank meant a puppy dead or a puppy that aroused the camp with its shrill pain and terror as it fled back from the wolf-cub that had waylaid it.

But White Fang's reprisals did not cease, even when the young dogs had learned thoroughly that they must stay together. He attacked them when he caught them alone, and they attacked him when they were bunched. The sight of him was sufficient to start them rushing after him, at which times his swiftness usually carried him into safety. But woe the dog that outran his fellows in such pursuit! White Fang had learned to turn suddenly upon the pursuer that was ahead of the pack and thoroughly to rip him up before the pack could arrive. This occurred with great frequency, for, once in full cry, the dogs were prone to forget themselves in the excitement of the chase, while White Fang never forgot himself. Stealing backward glances as he ran, he was always ready to whirl around and down the overzealous pursuer that outran his fellows.

Young dogs are bound to play, and out of the exigencies of the situation they realised their play in this mimic warfare. Thus it was that the hunt of White Fang became their chief game—a deadly game, withal, and at all times a serious game. He, on the other hand, being the fastest-footed, was unafraid to venture anywhere. During the period that he waited vainly for his mother to come back, he led the pack many a wild chase through the adjacent woods. But the pack invariably lost him. Its noise and outcry warned him of its presence, while he ran alone, velvet-footed, silently, a moving shadow among the trees after the manner of his father and mother before him. Further he was more directly connected with the Wild than they; and he knew more of its secrets and stratagems. A favourite trick of his was to lose his trail in running water and then lie quietly in a near-by thicket while their baffled cries arose around him.

Hated by his kind and by mankind, indomitable, perpetually warred upon and himself waging perpetual war, his development was rapid and one-sided. This was no soil for kindliness and affection to blossom in. Of such things he had not the faintest glimmering. The code he learned was to obey the strong and to oppress the weak. Grey Beaver was a god, and strong. Therefore White Fang obeyed him. But the dog younger or smaller than himself was weak, a thing to be destroyed. His development was in the direction of power. In order to face the constant danger of hurt and even of destruction, his predatory and protective faculties were unduly developed. He became quicker of movement than the other dogs, swifter of foot, craftier, deadlier, more lithe, more lean with ironlike muscle and sinew, more enduring, more cruel, more ferocious, and more intelligent. He had to become all these things, else he would not have held his own nor survive the hostile environment in which he found himself.

CHAPTER IV—THE TRAIL OF THE GODS

In the fall of the year, when the days were shortening and the bite of the frost was coming into the air, White Fang got his chance for liberty. For several days there had been a great hubbub in the village. The summer camp was being dismantled, and the tribe, bag and baggage, was preparing to go off to the fall hunting. White Fang watched it all with eager eyes, and when the tepees began to come down and the canoes were loading at the bank, he understood. Already the canoes were departing, and some had disappeared down the river.

Quite deliberately he determined to stay behind. He waited his opportunity to slink out of camp to the woods. Here, in the running stream where ice was beginning to form, he hid his trail. Then he crawled into the heart of a dense thicket and waited. The time passed by, and he slept intermittently for hours. Then he was aroused by Grey Beaver's voice calling him by name. There were other voices. White Fang could hear Grey Beaver's squaw taking part in the search, and Mit-sah, who was Grey Beaver's son.

White Fang trembled with fear, and though the impulse came to crawl out of his hiding-place, he resisted it. After a time the voices died away, and some time after that he crept out to enjoy the success of his undertaking. Darkness was coming on, and for a while he played about among the trees, pleasuring in his freedom. Then, and quite suddenly, he became aware of loneliness. He sat down to consider, listening to the silence of the forest and perturbed by it. That nothing moved nor sounded, seemed ominous. He felt the lurking of danger, unseen and unguessed. He was suspicious of the looming bulks of the trees and of the dark shadows that might conceal all manner of perilous things.

Then it was cold. Here was no warm side of a tepee against which to snuggle. The frost was in his feet, and he kept lifting first one fore-foot and then the other. He curved his bushy tail around to cover them, and at the same time he saw a vision. There was nothing strange about it. Upon his inward sight was impressed a succession of memory-pictures. He saw the camp again, the tepees, and the blaze of the fires. He heard the shrill voices of the women, the gruff basses of the men, and the snarling of the dogs. He was hungry, and he remembered pieces of meat and fish that had been thrown him. Here was no meat, nothing but a threatening and inedible silence.

His bondage had softened him. Irresponsibility had weakened him. He had forgotten how to shift for himself. The night yawned about him. His senses, accustomed to the hum and bustle of the camp, used to the continuous impact of sights and sounds, were now left idle. There was nothing to do, nothing to see nor hear. They strained to catch some interruption of the silence and immobility of nature. They were appalled by inaction and by the feel of something terrible impending.

He gave a great start of fright. A colossal and formless something was rushing across the field of his vision. It was a tree-shadow flung by the moon, from whose face the clouds had been brushed away. Reassured, he whimpered softly; then he suppressed the whimper for fear that it might attract the attention of the lurking dangers.

A tree, contracting in the cool of the night, made a loud noise. It was directly above him. He yelped in his fright. A panic seized him, and he ran madly toward the village. He knew an overpowering desire for the protection and companionship of man. In his nostrils was the smell of the camp-smoke. In his ears the camp-sounds and cries were ringing loud. He passed out of the forest and into the moonlit open where were no shadows nor darknesses. But no village greeted his eyes. He had forgotten. The village had gone away.

His wild flight ceased abruptly. There was no place to which to flee. He slunk forlornly through the deserted camp, smelling the rubbish-heaps and the discarded rags and tags of the gods. He would have been glad for the rattle of stones about him, flung by an angry squaw, glad for the hand of Grey Beaver descending upon him in wrath; while he would have welcomed with delight Lip-lip and the whole snarling, cowardly pack.

He came to where Grey Beaver's tepee had stood. In the centre of the space it had occupied, he sat down. He pointed his nose at the moon. His throat was afflicted by rigid spasms, his mouth opened, and in a heart-broken cry bubbled up his loneliness and fear, his grief for Kiche, all his past sorrows and miseries as well as his apprehension of sufferings and dangers to come. It was the long wolf-howl, full-throated and mournful, the first howl he had ever uttered.

The coming of daylight dispelled his fears but increased his loneliness. The naked earth, which so shortly before had been so populous; thrust his loneliness more forcibly upon him. It did not take him long to make up his mind. He plunged into the forest and followed the river bank down the stream. All day he ran. He did not rest. He seemed made to run on for ever. His iron-like body ignored fatigue. And even after fatigue came, his heritage of endurance braced him to endless endeavour and enabled him to drive his complaining body onward.

Where the river swung in against precipitous bluffs, he climbed the high mountains behind. Rivers and streams that entered the main river he forded or swam. Often he took to the rim-ice that was beginning to form, and more than once he crashed through and struggled for life in the icy current. Always he was on the lookout for the trail of the gods where it might leave the river and proceed inland.

White Fang was intelligent beyond the average of his kind; yet his mental vision was not wide enough to embrace the other bank of the Mackenzie. What if the trail of the gods led out on that side? It never entered his head. Later on, when he had travelled more and grown older and wiser and come to know more of trails and rivers, it might be that he could grasp and apprehend such a possibility. But that mental power was yet in the future. Just now he ran blindly, his own bank of the Mackenzie alone entering into his calculations.

All night he ran, blundering in the darkness into mishaps and obstacles that delayed but did not daunt. By the middle of the second day he had been running continuously for thirty hours, and the iron of his flesh was giving out. It was the endurance of his mind that kept him going. He had not eaten in forty hours, and he was weak with hunger. The repeated drenchings in the icy water had likewise had their effect on him. His handsome coat was draggled.

The broad pads of his feet were bruised and bleeding. He had begun to limp, and this limp increased with the hours. To make it worse, the light of the sky was obscured and snow began to fall—a raw, moist, melting, clinging snow, slippery under foot, that hid from him the landscape he traversed, and that covered over the inequalities of the ground so that the way of his feet was more difficult and painful.

Grey Beaver had intended camping that night on the far bank of the Mackenzie, for it was in that direction that the hunting lay. But on the near bank, shortly before dark, a moose coming down to drink, had been espied by Kloo-kooch, who was Grey Beaver's squaw. Now, had not the moose come down to drink, had not Mit-sah been steering out of the course because of the snow, had not Kloo-kooch sighted the moose, and had not Grey Beaver killed it with a lucky shot from his rifle, all subsequent things would have happened differently. Grey Beaver would not have camped on the near side of the Mackenzie, and White Fang would have passed by and gone on, either to die or to find his way to his wild brothers and become one of them—a wolf to the end of his days.

Night had fallen. The snow was flying more thickly, and White Fang, whimpering softly to himself as he stumbled and limped along, came upon a fresh trail in the snow. So fresh was it that he knew it immediately for what it was. Whining with eagerness, he followed back from the river bank and in among the trees. The camp-sounds came to his ears. He saw the blaze of the fire, Kloo-kooch cooking, and Grey Beaver squatting on his hams and mumbling a chunk of raw tallow. There was fresh meat in camp!

White Fang expected a beating. He crouched and bristled a little at the thought of it. Then he went forward again. He feared and disliked the beating he knew to be waiting for him. But he knew, further, that the comfort of the fire would be his, the protection of the gods, the companionship of the dogs—the last, a companionship of enmity, but none the less a companionship and satisfying to his gregarious needs.

He came cringing and crawling into the firelight. Grey Beaver saw him, and stopped munching the tallow. White Fang crawled slowly, cringing and grovelling in the abjectness of his abasement and submission. He crawled straight toward Grey Beaver, every inch of his progress becoming slower and more painful. At last he lay at the master's feet, into whose possession he now surrendered himself, voluntarily, body and soul. Of his own choice, he came in to sit by man's fire and to be ruled by him. White Fang trembled, waiting for the punishment to fall upon him. There was a movement of the hand above him. He cringed involuntarily under the expected blow. It did not fall. He stole a glance upward. Grey Beaver was breaking the lump of tallow in half! Grey Beaver was offering him one piece of the tallow! Very gently and somewhat suspiciously, he first smelled the tallow and then proceeded to eat it. Grey Beaver ordered meat to be brought to him, and guarded him from the other dogs while he ate. After that, grateful and content, White Fang lay at Grey Beaver's feet, gazing at the fire that warmed him, blinking and dozing, secure in the knowledge that the morrow would find him, not wandering forlorn through bleak forest-stretches, but in the camp of the man-animals, with the gods to whom he had given himself and upon whom he was now dependent.

CHAPTER V—THE COVENANT

When December was well along, Grey Beaver went on a journey up the Mackenzie. Mit-sah and Kloo-kooch went with him. One sled he drove himself, drawn by dogs he had traded for or borrowed. A second and smaller sled was driven by Mit-sah, and to this was harnessed a team of puppies. It was more of a toy affair than anything else, yet it was the delight of Mit-sah, who felt that he was beginning to do a man's work in the world. Also, he was learning to drive dogs and to train dogs; while the puppies themselves were being broken in to the harness. Furthermore, the sled was of some service, for it carried nearly two hundred pounds of outfit and food.

White Fang had seen the camp-dogs toiling in the harness, so that he did not resent overmuch the first placing of the harness upon himself. About his neck was put a moss-stuffed collar, which was connected by two pulling-traces to a strap that passed around his chest and over his back. It was to this that was fastened the long rope by which he pulled at the sled.

There were seven puppies in the team. The others had been born earlier in the year and were nine and ten months old, while White Fang was only eight months old. Each dog was fastened to the sled by a single rope. No two ropes were of the same length, while the difference in length between any two ropes was at least that of a dog's body. Every rope was brought to a ring at the front end of the sled. The sled itself was without runners, being a birch-bark toboggan, with upturned forward end to keep it from ploughing under the snow. This construction enabled the weight of the sled and load to be distributed over the largest snow-surface; for the snow was crystal-powder and very soft. Observing the same principle of widest distribution of weight, the dogs at the ends of their ropes radiated fan-fashion from the nose of the sled, so that no dog trod in another's footsteps.

There was, furthermore, another virtue in the fan-formation. The ropes of varying length prevented the dogs attacking from the rear those that ran in front of them. For a dog to attack another, it would have to turn upon one at a shorter rope. In which case it would find itself face to face with the dog attacked, and also it would find itself facing the whip of the driver. But the most peculiar virtue of all lay in the fact that the dog that strove to attack one in front of him must pull the sled faster, and that the faster the sled travelled, the faster could the dog attacked run away. Thus, the dog behind could never catch up with the one in front. The faster he ran, the faster ran the one he was after, and the faster ran all the dogs. Incidentally, the sled went faster, and thus, by cunning indirection, did man increase his mastery over the beasts.

Mit-sah resembled his father, much of whose grey wisdom he possessed. In the past he had observed Lip-lip's persecution of White Fang; but at that time Lip-lip was another man's dog, and Mit-sah had never dared more than to shy an occasional stone at him. But now Lip-lip was his dog, and he proceeded to wreak his vengeance on him by putting him at the end of the longest rope. This made Lip-lip the leader, and was apparently an honour! but in reality it took away from him all honour, and instead of being bully and master of the pack, he now found himself hated and persecuted by the pack.

Because he ran at the end of the longest rope, the dogs had always the view of him running away before them. All that they saw of him was his bushy tail and fleeing hind legs—a view far less ferocious and intimidating than his bristling mane and gleaming fangs. Also, dogs being so constituted in their mental ways, the sight of him running away gave desire to run after him and a feeling that he ran away from them.

The moment the sled started, the team took after Lip-lip in a chase that extended throughout the day. At first he had been prone to turn upon his pursuers, jealous of his dignity and wrathful; but at such times Mit-sah would throw the stinging lash of the thirty-foot cariboo-gut whip into his face and compel him to turn tail and run on. Lip-lip might face the pack, but he could not face that whip, and all that was left him to do was to keep his long rope taut and his flanks ahead of the teeth of his mates.

But a still greater cunning lurked in the recesses of the Indian mind. To give point to unending pursuit of the leader, Mit-sah favoured him over the other dogs. These favours aroused in them jealousy and hatred. In their presence Mit-sah would give him meat and would give it to him only. This was maddening to them. They would rage around just outside the throwing-distance of the whip, while Lip-lip devoured the meat and Mit-sah protected him. And when there was no meat to give, Mit-sah would keep the team at a distance and make believe to give meat to Lip-lip.

White Fang took kindly to the work. He had travelled a greater distance than the other dogs in the yielding of himself to the rule of the gods, and he had learned more thoroughly the futility of opposing their will. In addition, the persecution he had suffered from the pack had made the pack less to him in the scheme of things, and man more. He had not learned to be dependent on his kind for companionship. Besides, Kiche was well-nigh forgotten; and the chief outlet of expression that remained to him was in the allegiance he tendered the gods he had accepted as masters. So he worked hard, learned discipline, and was obedient. Faithfulness and willingness characterised his toil. These are essential traits of the wolf and the wild-dog when they have become domesticated, and these traits White Fang possessed in unusual measure.

A companionship did exist between White Fang and the other dogs, but it was one of warfare and enmity. He had never learned to play with them. He knew only how to fight, and fight with them he did, returning to them a hundred-fold the snaps and slashes they had given him in the days when Lip-lip was leader of the pack. But Lip-lip was no longer leader—except when he fled away before his mates at the end of his rope, the sled bounding along behind. In camp he kept close to Mit-sah or Grey Beaver or Kloo-kooch. He did not dare venture away from the gods, for now the fangs of all dogs were against him, and he tasted to the dregs the persecution that had been White Fang's.

With the overthrow of Lip-lip, White Fang could have become leader of the pack. But he was too morose and solitary for that. He merely thrashed his team-mates. Otherwise he ignored them. They got out of his way when he came along; nor did the boldest of them ever dare to rob him of his meat. On the contrary, they devoured their own meat hurriedly, for fear that he would take it away from them. White Fang knew the law well: *to oppress the weak and obey the strong.* He ate his share of meat as rapidly as he could. And then woe the dog that had not yet finished! A snarl and a flash of fangs, and that dog would wail his indignation to the uncomforting stars while White Fang finished his portion for him.

Every little while, however, one dog or another would flame up in revolt and be promptly subdued. Thus White Fang was kept in training. He was jealous of the isolation in which he kept himself in the midst of the pack, and he fought often to maintain it. But such fights were of brief duration. He was too quick for the others. They were slashed open and bleeding before they knew what had happened, were whipped almost before they had begun to fight.

As rigid as the sled-discipline of the gods, was the discipline maintained by White Fang amongst his fellows. He never allowed them any latitude. He compelled them to an unremitting respect for him. They might do as they pleased amongst themselves. That was no concern of his. But it *was* his concern that they leave him alone in his isolation, get out of his way when he elected to walk among them, and at all times acknowledge his mastery over them. A hint of stiff-leggedness on their part, a lifted lip or a bristle of hair, and he would be upon them, merciless and cruel, swiftly convincing them of the error of their way.

He was a monstrous tyrant. His mastery was rigid as steel. He oppressed the weak with a vengeance. Not for nothing had he been exposed to the pitiless struggles for life in the day of his cubhood, when his mother and he, alone and unaided, held their own and survived in the ferocious environment of the Wild. And not for nothing had he learned to walk softly when superior strength went by. He oppressed the weak, but he respected the strong. And in the course of the long journey with Grey Beaver he walked softly indeed amongst the full-grown dogs in the camps of the strange man-animals they encountered.

The months passed by. Still continued the journey of Grey Beaver. White Fang's strength was developed by the long hours on trail and the steady toil at the sled; and it would have seemed that his mental development was well-nigh complete. He had come to know quite thoroughly the world in which he lived. His outlook was bleak and materialistic. The world as he saw it was a fierce and brutal world, a world without warmth, a world in which caresses and affection and the bright sweetnesses of the spirit did not exist.

He had no affection for Grey Beaver. True, he was a god, but a most savage god. White Fang was glad to acknowledge his lordship, but it was a lordship based upon superior intelligence and brute strength. There was something in the fibre of White Fang's being that made his lordship a thing to be desired, else he would not have come back from the Wild when he did to tender his allegiance. There were deeps in his nature which had never been sounded. A kind word, a caressing touch of the hand, on the part of Grey Beaver, might have sounded these deeps; but Grey Beaver did not caress, nor speak kind words. It was not his way. His primacy was savage, and savagely he ruled, administering justice with a club, punishing transgression with the pain of a blow, and rewarding merit, not by kindness, but by withholding a blow.

So White Fang knew nothing of the heaven a man's hand might contain for him. Besides, he did not like the hands of the man-animals. He was suspicious of them. It was true that they sometimes gave meat, but more often they gave hurt. Hands were things to keep away from. They hurled stones, wielded sticks and clubs and whips, administered slaps and clouts, and, when they touched him, were cunning to hurt with pinch and twist and wrench. In strange villages he had encountered the hands of the children and learned that they were cruel to hurt. Also, he had once nearly had an eye poked out by a toddling papoose. From these experiences he became suspicious of all children. He could not tolerate them. When they came near with their ominous hands, he got up.

It was in a village at the Great Slave Lake, that, in the course of resenting the evil of the hands of the man-animals, he came to modify the law that he had learned from Grey Beaver: namely, that the unpardonable crime was to bite one of the gods. In this village, after the custom of all dogs in all villages, White Fang went foraging, for food. A boy was chopping frozen moose-meat

428

with an axe, and the chips were flying in the snow. White Fang, sliding by in quest of meat, stopped and began to eat the chips. He observed the boy lay down the axe and take up a stout club. White Fang sprang clear, just in time to escape the descending blow. The boy pursued him, and he, a stranger in the village, fled between two tepees to find himself cornered against a high earth bank.

There was no escape for White Fang. The only way out was between the two tepees, and this the boy guarded. Holding his club prepared to strike, he drew in on his cornered quarry. White Fang was furious. He faced the boy, bristling and snarling, his sense of justice outraged. He knew the law of forage. All the wastage of meat, such as the frozen chips, belonged to the dog that found it. He had done no wrong, broken no law, yet here was this boy preparing to give him a beating. White Fang scarcely knew what happened. He did it in a surge of rage. And he did it so quickly that the boy did not know either. All the boy knew was that he had in some unaccountable way been overturned into the snow, and that his club-hand had been ripped wide open by White Fang's teeth.

But White Fang knew that he had broken the law of the gods. He had driven his teeth into the sacred flesh of one of them, and could expect nothing but a most terrible punishment. He fled away to Grey Beaver, behind whose protecting legs he crouched when the bitten boy and the boy's family came, demanding vengeance. But they went away with vengeance unsatisfied. Grey Beaver defended White Fang. So did Mit-sah and Kloo-kooch. White Fang, listening to the wordy war and watching the angry gestures, knew that his act was justified. And so it came that he learned there were gods and gods. There were his gods, and there were other gods, and between them there was a difference. Justice or injustice, it was all the same, he must take all things from the hands of his own gods. But he was not compelled to take injustice from the other gods. It was his privilege to resent it with his teeth. And this also was a law of the gods.

Before the day was out, White Fang was to learn more about this law. Mit-sah, alone, gathering firewood in the forest, encountered the boy that had been bitten. With him were other boys. Hot words passed. Then all

429

the boys attacked Mit-sah. It was going hard with him. Blows were raining upon him from all sides. White Fang looked on at first. This was an affair of the gods, and no concern of his. Then he realised that this was Mit-sah, one of his own particular gods, who was being maltreated. It was no reasoned impulse that made White Fang do what he then did. A mad rush of anger sent him leaping in amongst the combatants. Five minutes later the landscape was covered with fleeing boys, many of whom dripped blood upon the snow in token that White Fang's teeth had not been idle. When Mit-sah told the story in camp, Grey Beaver ordered meat to be given to White Fang. He ordered much meat to be given, and White Fang, gorged and sleepy by the fire, knew that the law had received its verification.

It was in line with these experiences that White Fang came to learn the law of property and the duty of the defence of property. From the protection of his god's body to the protection of his god's possessions was a step, and this step he made. What was his god's was to be defended against all the world— even to the extent of biting other gods. Not only was such an act sacrilegious in its nature, but it was fraught with peril. The gods were all-powerful, and a dog was no match against them; yet White Fang learned to face them, fiercely belligerent and unafraid. Duty rose above fear, and thieving gods learned to leave Grey Beaver's property alone.

One thing, in this connection, White Fang quickly learnt, and that was that a thieving god was usually a cowardly god and prone to run away at the sounding of the alarm. Also, he learned that but brief time elapsed between his sounding of the alarm and Grey Beaver coming to his aid. He came to know that it was not fear of him that drove the thief away, but fear of Grey Beaver. White Fang did not give the alarm by barking. He never barked. His method was to drive straight at the intruder, and to sink his teeth in if he could. Because he was morose and solitary, having nothing to do with the other dogs, he was unusually fitted to guard his master's property; and in this he was encouraged and trained by Grey Beaver. One result of this was to make White Fang more ferocious and indomitable, and more solitary.

The months went by, binding stronger and stronger the covenant between dog and man. This was the ancient covenant that the first wolf that came in from the Wild entered into with man. And, like all succeeding wolves and wild dogs that had done likewise, White Fang worked the covenant out for himself. The terms were simple. For the possession of a flesh-and-blood god, he exchanged his own liberty. Food and fire, protection and companionship, were some of the things he received from the god. In return, he guarded the god's property, defended his body, worked for him, and obeyed him.

The possession of a god implies service. White Fang's was a service of duty and awe, but not of love. He did not know what love was. He had no experience of love. Kiche was a remote memory. Besides, not only had he abandoned the Wild and his kind when he gave himself up to man, but the terms of the covenant were such that if ever he met Kiche again he would not desert his god to go with her. His allegiance to man seemed somehow a law of his being greater than the love of liberty, of kind and kin.

CHAPTER VI—THE FAMINE

The spring of the year was at hand when Grey Beaver finished his long journey. It was April, and White Fang was a year old when he pulled into the home villages and was loosed from the harness by Mit-sah. Though a long way from his full growth, White Fang, next to Lip-lip, was the largest yearling in the village. Both from his father, the wolf, and from Kiche, he had inherited stature and strength, and already he was measuring up alongside the full-grown dogs. But he had not yet grown compact. His body was slender and rangy, and his strength more stringy than massive, His coat was the true wolf-grey, and to all appearances he was true wolf himself. The quarter-strain of dog he had inherited from Kiche had left no mark on him physically, though it had played its part in his mental make-up.

He wandered through the village, recognising with staid satisfaction the various gods he had known before the long journey. Then there were the dogs, puppies growing up like himself, and grown dogs that did not look so large and formidable as the memory pictures he retained of them. Also, he stood less in fear of them than formerly, stalking among them with a certain careless ease that was as new to him as it was enjoyable.

There was Baseek, a grizzled old fellow that in his younger days had but to uncover his fangs to send White Fang cringing and crouching to the right about. From him White Fang had learned much of his own insignificance; and from him he was now to learn much of the change and development that had taken place in himself. While Baseek had been growing weaker with age, White Fang had been growing stronger with youth.

It was at the cutting-up of a moose, fresh-killed, that White Fang learned of the changed relations in which he stood to the dog-world. He had got for himself a hoof and part of the shin-bone, to which quite a bit of meat was attached. Withdrawn from the immediate scramble of the other dogs—in fact out of sight behind a thicket—he was devouring his prize, when Baseek rushed in upon him. Before he knew what he was doing, he had slashed the intruder twice and sprung clear. Baseek was surprised by the other's temerity and swiftness of attack. He stood, gazing stupidly across at White Fang, the raw, red shin-bone between them.

Baseek was old, and already he had come to know the increasing valour of the dogs it had been his wont to bully. Bitter experiences these, which, perforce, he swallowed, calling upon all his wisdom to cope with them. In the old days he would have sprung upon White Fang in a fury of righteous wrath. But now his waning powers would not permit such a course. He bristled fiercely and looked ominously across the shin-bone at White Fang. And White Fang, resurrecting quite a deal of the old awe, seemed to wilt and to shrink in upon himself and grow small, as he cast about in his mind for a way to beat a retreat not too inglorious.

And right here Baseek erred. Had he contented himself with looking fierce and ominous, all would have been well. White Fang, on the verge of retreat, would have retreated, leaving the meat to him. But Baseek did not wait. He considered the victory already his and stepped forward to the meat. As he bent his head carelessly to smell it, White Fang bristled slightly. Even then it was not too late for Baseek to retrieve the situation. Had he merely stood over the meat, head up and glowering, White Fang would ultimately have slunk away. But the fresh meat was strong in Baseek's nostrils, and greed urged him to take a bite of it.

This was too much for White Fang. Fresh upon his months of mastery over his own team-mates, it was beyond his self-control to stand idly by while another devoured the meat that belonged to him. He struck, after his custom, without warning. With the first slash, Baseek's right ear was ripped into ribbons. He was astounded at the suddenness of it. But more things, and most grievous ones, were happening with equal suddenness. He was knocked off his feet. His throat was bitten. While he was struggling to his feet the young dog sank teeth twice into his shoulder. The swiftness of it was bewildering. He made a futile rush at White Fang, clipping the empty air with an outraged snap. The next moment his nose was laid open, and he was staggering backward away from the meat.

The situation was now reversed. White Fang stood over the shin-bone, bristling and menacing, while Baseek stood a little way off, preparing to retreat. He dared not risk a fight with this young lightning-flash, and again he knew, and more bitterly, the enfeeblement of oncoming age. His attempt to maintain his dignity was heroic. Calmly turning his back upon young dog and shin-bone, as though both were beneath his notice and unworthy of his consideration, he stalked grandly away. Nor, until well out of sight, did he stop to lick his bleeding wounds.

The effect on White Fang was to give him a greater faith in himself, and a greater pride. He walked less softly among the grown dogs; his attitude toward them was less compromising. Not that he went out of his way looking for trouble. Far from it. But upon his way he demanded consideration. He stood upon his right to go his way unmolested and to give trail to no dog. He had to be taken into account, that was all. He was no longer to be disregarded and ignored, as was the lot of puppies, and as continued to be the lot of the puppies that were his team-mates. They got out of the way, gave trail to the grown dogs, and gave up meat to them under compulsion. But White Fang, uncompanionable, solitary, morose, scarcely looking to right or left, redoubtable, forbidding of aspect, remote and alien, was accepted as an equal by his puzzled elders. They quickly learned to leave him alone, neither venturing hostile acts nor making overtures of friendliness. If they left him alone, he left them alone—a state of affairs that they found, after a few encounters, to be pre-eminently desirable.

In midsummer White Fang had an experience. Trotting along in his silent way to investigate a new tepee which had been erected on the edge of the village while he was away with the hunters after moose, he came full upon Kiche. He paused and looked at her. He *remembered* her vaguely, but he *remembered* her, and that was more than could be said for her. She lifted her lip at him in the old snarl of menace, and his memory became clear. His forgotten cubhood, all that was associated with that familiar snarl, rushed back to him. Before he had known the gods, she had been to him the centre-pin of the universe. The old familiar feelings of that time came back upon him, surged up within him. He bounded towards her joyously, and she met him with shrewd fangs that laid his cheek open to the bone. He did not understand. He backed away, bewildered and puzzled.

But it was not Kiche's fault. A wolf-mother was not made to remember her cubs of a year or so before. So she did not remember White Fang. He was a strange animal, an intruder; and her present litter of puppies gave her the right to resent such intrusion.

One of the puppies sprawled up to White Fang. They were half-brothers, only they did not know it. White Fang sniffed the puppy curiously, whereupon Kiche rushed upon him, gashing his face a second time. He backed farther away. All the old memories and associations died down again and passed into the grave from which they had been resurrected. He looked at Kiche licking her puppy and stopping now and then to snarl at him. She was without value to him. He had learned to get along without her. Her meaning was forgotten. There was no place for her in his scheme of things, as there was no place for him in hers.

He was still standing, stupid and bewildered, the memories forgotten, wondering what it was all about, when Kiche attacked him a third time, intent on driving him away altogether from the vicinity. And White Fang allowed himself to be driven away. This was a female of his kind, and it was a law of his kind that the males must not fight the females. He did not know anything about this law, for it was no generalisation of the mind, not a something acquired by experience of the world. He knew it as a secret prompting, as an urge of instinct—of the same instinct that made him howl at the moon and stars of nights, and that made him fear death and the unknown.

The months went by. White Fang grew stronger, heavier, and more compact, while his character was developing along the lines laid down by his heredity and his environment. His heredity was a life-stuff that may be likened to clay. It possessed many possibilities, was capable of being moulded into many different forms. Environment served to model the clay, to give it a particular form. Thus, had White Fang never come in to the fires of man, the Wild would have moulded him into a true wolf. But the gods had given him a different environment, and he was moulded into a dog that was rather wolfish, but that was a dog and not a wolf.

And so, according to the clay of his nature and the pressure of his surroundings, his character was being moulded into a certain particular shape. There was no escaping it. He was becoming more morose, more uncompanionable, more solitary, more ferocious; while the dogs were learning more and more that it was better to be at peace with him than at war, and Grey Beaver was coming to prize him more greatly with the passage of each day.

White Fang, seeming to sum up strength in all his qualities, nevertheless suffered from one besetting weakness. He could not stand being laughed at. The laughter of men was a hateful thing. They might laugh among themselves about anything they pleased except himself, and he did not mind. But the moment laughter was turned upon him he would fly into a most terrible rage. Grave, dignified, sombre, a laugh made him frantic to ridiculousness. It so outraged him and upset him that for hours he would behave like a demon. And woe to the dog that at such times ran foul of him. He knew the law too well to take it out of Grey Beaver; behind Grey Beaver were a club and godhead. But behind the dogs there was nothing but space, and into this space they flew when White Fang came on the scene, made mad by laughter.

In the third year of his life there came a great famine to the Mackenzie Indians. In the summer the fish failed. In the winter the cariboo forsook their accustomed track. Moose were scarce, the rabbits almost disappeared, hunting and preying animals perished. Denied their usual food-supply, weakened by hunger, they fell upon and devoured one another. Only the strong survived. White Fang's gods were always hunting animals. The old and the weak of them died of hunger. There was wailing in the village, where the women and children went without in order that what little they had might go into the bellies of the lean and hollow-eyed hunters who trod the forest in the vain pursuit of meat.

To such extremity were the gods driven that they ate the soft-tanned leather of their mocassins and mittens, while the dogs ate the harnesses off their backs and the very whip-lashes. Also, the dogs ate one another, and also the gods ate the dogs. The weakest and the more worthless were eaten first. The dogs that still lived, looked on and understood. A few of the boldest and wisest forsook the fires of the gods, which had now become a shambles, and fled into the forest, where, in the end, they starved to death or were eaten by wolves.

In this time of misery, White Fang, too, stole away into the woods. He was better fitted for the life than the other dogs, for he had the training of his cubhood to guide him. Especially adept did he become in stalking small living things. He would lie concealed for hours, following every movement of a cautious tree-squirrel, waiting, with a patience as huge as the hunger he suffered from, until the squirrel ventured out upon the ground. Even then, White Fang was not premature. He waited until he was sure of striking before the squirrel could gain a tree-refuge. Then, and not until then, would he flash from his hiding-place, a grey projectile, incredibly swift, never failing its mark—the fleeing squirrel that fled not fast enough.

Successful as he was with squirrels, there was one difficulty that prevented him from living and growing fat on them. There were not enough squirrels. So he was driven to hunt still smaller things. So acute did his hunger become at times that he was not above rooting out wood-mice from their burrows in the ground. Nor did he scorn to do battle with a weasel as hungry as himself and many times more ferocious.

In the worst pinches of the famine he stole back to the fires of the gods. But he did not go into the fires. He lurked in the forest, avoiding discovery and robbing the snares at the rare intervals when game was caught. He even robbed Grey Beaver's snare of a rabbit at a time when Grey Beaver staggered and tottered through the forest, sitting down often to rest, what of weakness and of shortness of breath.

One day While Fang encountered a young wolf, gaunt and scrawny, loose-jointed with famine. Had he not been hungry himself, White Fang might have gone with him and eventually found his way into the pack amongst his wild brethren. As it was, he ran the young wolf down and killed and ate him.

Fortune seemed to favour him. Always, when hardest pressed for food, he found something to kill. Again, when he was weak, it was his luck that none of the larger preying animals chanced upon him. Thus, he was strong from the two days' eating a lynx had afforded him when the hungry wolf-pack ran full tilt upon him. It was a long, cruel chase, but he was better nourished than they, and in the end outran them. And not only did he outrun them, but, circling widely back on his track, he gathered in one of his exhausted pursuers.

After that he left that part of the country and journeyed over to the valley wherein he had been born. Here, in the old lair, he encountered Kiche. Up to her old tricks, she, too, had fled the inhospitable fires of the gods and gone back to her old refuge to give birth to her young. Of this litter but one remained alive when White Fang came upon the scene, and this one was not destined to live long. Young life had little chance in such a famine.

Kiche's greeting of her grown son was anything but affectionate. But White Fang did not mind. He had outgrown his mother. So he turned tail philosophically and trotted on up the stream. At the forks he took the turning to the left, where he found the lair of the lynx with whom his mother and he had fought long before. Here, in the abandoned lair, he settled down and rested for a day.

During the early summer, in the last days of the famine, he met Lip-lip, who had likewise taken to the woods, where he had eked out a miserable existence.

White Fang came upon him unexpectedly. Trotting in opposite directions along the base of a high bluff, they rounded a corner of rock and found themselves face to face. They paused with instant alarm, and looked at each other suspiciously.

White Fang was in splendid condition. His hunting had been good, and for a week he had eaten his fill. He was even gorged from his latest kill. But in the moment he looked at Lip-lip his hair rose on end all along his back. It was an involuntary bristling on his part, the physical state that in the past had always accompanied the mental state produced in him by Lip-lip's bullying and persecution. As in the past he had bristled and snarled at sight of Lip-lip, so now, and automatically, he bristled and snarled. He did not waste any time. The thing was done thoroughly and with despatch. Lip-lip essayed to back away, but White Fang struck him hard, shoulder to shoulder. Lip-lip was overthrown and rolled upon his back. White Fang's teeth drove into the scrawny throat. There was a death-struggle, during which White Fang walked around, stiff-legged and observant. Then he resumed his course and trotted on along the base of the bluff.

One day, not long after, he came to the edge of the forest, where a narrow stretch of open land sloped down to the Mackenzie. He had been over this ground before, when it was bare, but now a village occupied it. Still hidden amongst the trees, he paused to study the situation. Sights and sounds and scents were familiar to him. It was the old village changed to a new place. But sights and sounds and smells were different from those he had last had when he fled away from it. There was no whimpering nor wailing. Contented sounds saluted his ear, and when he heard the angry voice of a woman he knew it to be the anger that proceeds from a full stomach. And there was a smell in the air of fish. There was food. The famine was gone. He came out boldly from the forest and trotted into camp straight to Grey Beaver's tepee. Grey Beaver was not there; but Kloo-kooch welcomed him with glad cries and the whole of a fresh-caught fish, and he lay down to wait Grey Beaver's coming.

PART IV

CHAPTER I—THE ENEMY OF HIS KIND

Had there been in White Fang's nature any possibility, no matter how remote, of his ever coming to fraternise with his kind, such possibility was irretrievably destroyed when he was made leader of the sled-team. For now the dogs hated him—hated him for the extra meat bestowed upon him by Mit-sah; hated him for all the real and fancied favours he received; hated him for that he fled always at the head of the team, his waving brush of a tail and his perpetually retreating hind-quarters for ever maddening their eyes.

And White Fang just as bitterly hated them back. Being sled-leader was anything but gratifying to him. To be compelled to run away before the yelling pack, every dog of which, for three years, he had thrashed and mastered, was almost more than he could endure. But endure it he must, or perish, and the life that was in him had no desire to perish out. The moment Mit-sah gave his order for the start, that moment the whole team, with eager, savage cries, sprang forward at White Fang.

There was no defence for him. If he turned upon them, Mit-sah would throw the stinging lash of the whip into his face. Only remained to him to run away. He could not encounter that howling horde with his tail and hind-quarters. These were scarcely fit weapons with which to meet the many merciless fangs. So run away he did, violating his own nature and pride with every leap he made, and leaping all day long.

One cannot violate the promptings of one's nature without having that nature recoil upon itself. Such a recoil is like that of a hair, made to grow out from the body, turning unnaturally upon the direction of its growth and growing into the body—a rankling, festering thing of hurt. And so with White Fang. Every urge of his being impelled him to spring upon the pack that cried at his heels, but it was the will of the gods that this should not be; and behind the will, to enforce it, was the whip of cariboo-gut with its biting thirty-foot lash. So White Fang could only eat his heart in bitterness and develop a hatred and malice commensurate with the ferocity and indomitability of his nature.

If ever a creature was the enemy of its kind, White Fang was that creature. He asked no quarter, gave none. He was continually marred and scarred by the teeth of the pack, and as continually he left his own marks upon the pack. Unlike most leaders, who, when camp was made and the dogs were unhitched, huddled near to the gods for protection, White Fang disdained such protection. He walked boldly about the camp, inflicting punishment in the night for what he had suffered in the day. In the time before he was made leader of the team, the pack had learned to get out of his way. But now it was different. Excited by the day-long pursuit of him, swayed subconsciously by the insistent iteration on their brains of the sight of him fleeing away, mastered by the feeling of mastery enjoyed all day, the dogs could not bring themselves to give way to him. When he appeared amongst them, there was always a squabble. His progress was marked by snarl and snap and growl. The very atmosphere he breathed was surcharged with hatred and malice, and this but served to increase the hatred and malice within him.

When Mit-sah cried out his command for the team to stop, White Fang obeyed. At first this caused trouble for the other dogs. All of them would spring upon the hated leader only to find the tables turned. Behind him would be Mit-sah, the great whip singing in his hand. So the dogs came to understand that when the team stopped by order, White Fang was to be let alone. But when White Fang stopped without orders, then it was allowed them to spring upon him and destroy him if they could. After several experiences, White Fang never stopped without orders. He learned quickly. It was in the nature of things, that he must learn quickly if he were to survive the unusually severe conditions under which life was vouchsafed him.

But the dogs could never learn the lesson to leave him alone in camp. Each day, pursuing him and crying defiance at him, the lesson of the previous night was erased, and that night would have to be learned over again, to be as immediately forgotten. Besides, there was a greater consistency in their dislike of him. They sensed between themselves and him a difference of kind—cause sufficient in itself for hostility. Like him, they were domesticated wolves. But they had been domesticated for generations. Much of the Wild had been lost, so that to them the Wild was the unknown, the terrible, the ever-menacing and ever warring. But to him, in appearance and action and impulse, still clung the Wild. He symbolised it, was its personification: so that when they showed their teeth to him they were defending themselves against the powers of destruction that lurked in the shadows of the forest and in the dark beyond the camp-fire.

But there was one lesson the dogs did learn, and that was to keep together. White Fang was too terrible for any of them to face single-handed. They met him with the mass-formation, otherwise he would have killed them, one by one, in a night. As it was, he never had a chance to kill them. He might roll a dog off its feet, but the pack would be upon him before he could follow up and deliver the deadly throat-stroke. At the first hint of conflict, the whole team drew together and faced him. The dogs had quarrels among themselves, but these were forgotten when trouble was brewing with White Fang.

On the other hand, try as they would, they could not kill White Fang. He was too quick for them, too formidable, too wise. He avoided tight places and always backed out of it when they bade fair to surround him. While, as for getting him off his feet, there was no dog among them capable of doing the trick. His feet clung to the earth with the same tenacity that he clung to life. For that matter, life and footing were synonymous in this unending warfare with the pack, and none knew it better than White Fang.

So he became the enemy of his kind, domesticated wolves that they were, softened by the fires of man, weakened in the sheltering shadow of man's strength. White Fang was bitter and implacable. The clay of him was so moulded. He declared a vendetta against all dogs. And so terribly did he live this vendetta that Grey Beaver, fierce savage himself, could not but marvel at White Fang's ferocity. Never, he swore, had there been the like of this animal; and the Indians in strange villages swore likewise when they considered the tale of his killings amongst their dogs.

When White Fang was nearly five years old, Grey Beaver took him on another great journey, and long *remembered* was the havoc he worked amongst the dogs of the many villages along the Mackenzie, across the Rockies, and down the Porcupine to the Yukon. He revelled in the vengeance he wreaked upon his kind. They were ordinary, unsuspecting dogs. They were not prepared for his swiftness and directness, for his attack without warning. They did not know him for what he was, a lightning-flash of slaughter. They bristled up to him, stiff-legged and challenging, while he, wasting no time on elaborate preliminaries, snapping into action like a steel spring, was at their throats and destroying them before they knew what was happening and while they were yet in the throes of surprise.

He became an adept at fighting. He economised. He never wasted his strength, never tussled. He was in too quickly for that, and, if he missed, was out again too quickly. The dislike of the wolf for close quarters was his to an unusual degree. He could not endure a prolonged contact with another body. It smacked of danger. It made him frantic. He must be away, free, on his own legs, touching no living thing. It was the Wild still clinging to him, asserting itself through him. This feeling had been accentuated by the Ishmaelite life he had led from his puppyhood. Danger lurked in contacts. It was the trap, ever the trap, the fear of it lurking deep in the life of him, woven into the fibre of him.

In consequence, the strange dogs he encountered had no chance against him. He eluded their fangs. He got them, or got away, himself untouched in either event. In the natural course of things there were exceptions to this. There were times when several dogs, pitching on to him, punished him before he could get away; and there were times when a single dog scored deeply on him. But these were accidents. In the main, so efficient a fighter had he become, he went his way unscathed.

Another advantage he possessed was that of correctly judging time and distance. Not that he did this consciously, however. He did not calculate such things. It was all automatic. His eyes saw correctly, and the nerves carried the vision correctly to his brain. The parts of him were better adjusted than those of the average dog. They worked together more smoothly and steadily.

His was a better, far better, nervous, mental, and muscular co-ordination. When his eyes conveyed to his brain the moving image of an action, his brain without conscious effort, knew the space that limited that action and the time required for its completion. Thus, he could avoid the leap of another dog, or the drive of its fangs, and at the same moment could seize the infinitesimal fraction of time in which to deliver his own attack. Body and brain, his was a more perfected mechanism. Not that he was to be praised for it. Nature had been more generous to him than to the average animal, that was all.

It was in the summer that White Fang arrived at Fort Yukon. Grey Beaver had crossed the great watershed between Mackenzie and the Yukon in the late winter, and spent the spring in hunting among the western outlying spurs of the Rockies. Then, after the break-up of the ice on the Porcupine, he had built a canoe and paddled down that stream to where it effected its junction with the Yukon just under the Artic circle. Here stood the old Hudson's Bay Company fort; and here were many Indians, much food, and unprecedented excitement. It was the summer of 1898, and thousands of gold-hunters were going up the Yukon to Dawson and the Klondike. Still hundreds of miles from their goal, nevertheless many of them had been on the way for a year, and the least any of them had travelled to get that far was five thousand miles, while some had come from the other side of the world.

Here Grey Beaver stopped. A whisper of the gold-rush had reached his ears, and he had come with several bales of furs, and another of gut-sewn mittens and moccasins. He would not have ventured so long a trip had he not expected generous profits. But what he had expected was nothing to what he realised. His wildest dreams had not exceeded a hundred per cent. profit; he made a thousand per cent. And like a true Indian, he settled down to trade carefully and slowly, even if it took all summer and the rest of the winter to dispose of his goods.

It was at Fort Yukon that White Fang saw his first white men. As compared with the Indians he had known, they were to him another race of beings, a race of superior gods. They impressed him as possessing superior power, and it is on power that godhead rests. White Fang did not reason it out, did not in his mind make the sharp generalisation that the white gods were more powerful. It was a feeling, nothing more, and yet none the less potent. As, in his puppyhood, the looming bulks of the tepees, man-reared, had affected him as manifestations of power, so was he affected now by the houses and the huge fort all of massive logs. Here was power. Those white gods were strong. They possessed greater mastery over matter than the gods he had known, most powerful among which was Grey Beaver. And yet Grey Beaver was as a child-god among these white-skinned ones.

To be sure, White Fang only felt these things. He was not conscious of them. Yet it is upon feeling, more often than thinking, that animals act; and every act White Fang now performed was based upon the feeling that the white men were the superior gods. In the first place he was very suspicious of them. There was no telling what unknown terrors were theirs, what unknown hurts they could administer. He was curious to observe them, fearful of being noticed by them. For the first few hours he was content with slinking around and watching them from a safe distance. Then he saw that no harm befell the dogs that were near to them, and he came in closer.

In turn he was an object of great curiosity to them. His wolfish appearance caught their eyes at once, and they pointed him out to one another. This act of pointing put White Fang on his guard, and when they tried to approach him he showed his teeth and backed away. Not one succeeded in laying a hand on him, and it was well that they did not.

White Fang soon learned that very few of these gods—not more than a dozen—lived at this place. Every two or three days a steamer (another and colossal manifestation of power) came into the bank and stopped for several hours. The white men came from off these steamers and went away on them again. There seemed untold numbers of these white men. In the first day or so, he saw more of them than he had seen Indians in all his life; and as the days went by they continued to come up the river, stop, and then go on up the river out of sight.

But if the white gods were all-powerful, their dogs did not amount to much. This White Fang quickly discovered by mixing with those that came ashore with their masters. They were irregular shapes and sizes. Some were short-legged—too short; others were long-legged—too long. They had hair instead of fur, and a few had very little hair at that. And none of them knew how to fight.

As an enemy of his kind, it was in White Fang's province to fight with them. This he did, and he quickly achieved for them a mighty contempt. They were soft and helpless, made much noise, and floundered around clumsily trying to accomplish by main strength what he accomplished by dexterity and cunning. They rushed bellowing at him. He sprang to the side. They did not know what had become of him; and in that moment he struck them on the shoulder, rolling them off their feet and delivering his stroke at the throat.

Sometimes this stroke was successful, and a stricken dog rolled in the dirt, to be pounced upon and torn to pieces by the pack of Indian dogs that waited. White Fang was wise. He had long since learned that the gods were made angry when their dogs were killed. The white men were no exception to this. So he was content, when he had overthrown and slashed wide the throat of one of their dogs, to drop back and let the pack go in and do the cruel finishing work. It was then that the white men rushed in, visiting their wrath heavily on the pack, while White Fang went free. He would stand off at a little distance and look on, while stones, clubs, axes, and all sorts of weapons fell upon his fellows. White Fang was very wise.

But his fellows grew wise in their own way; and in this White Fang grew wise with them. They learned that it was when a steamer first tied to the bank that they had their fun. After the first two or three strange dogs had been downed and destroyed, the white men hustled their own animals back on board and wrecked savage vengeance on the offenders. One white man, having seen his dog, a setter, torn to pieces before his eyes, drew a revolver. He fired rapidly, six times, and six of the pack lay dead or dying—another manifestation of power that sank deep into White Fang's consciousness.

White Fang enjoyed it all. He did not love his kind, and he was shrewd enough to escape hurt himself. At first, the killing of the white men's dogs had been a diversion. After a time it became his occupation. There was no work for him to do. Grey Beaver was busy trading and getting wealthy. So White Fang hung around the landing with the disreputable gang of Indian dogs, waiting for steamers. With the arrival of a steamer the fun began. After a few minutes, by the time the white men had got over their surprise, the gang scattered. The fun was over until the next steamer should arrive.

But it can scarcely be said that White Fang was a member of the gang. He did not mingle with it, but remained aloof, always himself, and was even feared by it. It is true, he worked with it. He picked the quarrel with the strange dog while the gang waited. And when he had overthrown the strange dog the gang went in to finish it. But it is equally true that he then withdrew, leaving the gang to receive the punishment of the outraged gods.

It did not require much exertion to pick these quarrels. All he had to do, when the strange dogs came ashore, was to show himself. When they saw him they rushed for him. It was their instinct. He was the Wild—the unknown, the terrible, the ever-menacing, the thing that prowled in the darkness around the fires of the primeval world when they, cowering close to the fires, were reshaping their instincts, learning to fear the Wild out of which they had come, and which they had deserted and betrayed. Generation by generation, down all the generations, had this fear of the Wild been stamped into their natures. For centuries the Wild had stood for terror and destruction. And during all this time free licence had been theirs, from their masters, to kill the things of the Wild. In doing this they had protected both themselves and the gods whose companionship they shared.

And so, fresh from the soft southern world, these dogs, trotting down the gang-plank and out upon the Yukon shore had but to see White Fang to experience the irresistible impulse to rush upon him and destroy him. They might be town-reared dogs, but the instinctive fear of the Wild was theirs just the same. Not alone with their own eyes did they see the wolfish creature in the clear light of day, standing before them. They saw him with the eyes of their ancestors, and by their inherited memory they knew White Fang for the wolf, and they *remembered* the ancient feud.

All of which served to make White Fang's days enjoyable. If the sight of him drove these strange dogs upon him, so much the better for him, so much the worse for them. They looked upon him as legitimate prey, and as legitimate prey he looked upon them.

Not for nothing had he first seen the light of day in a lonely lair and fought his first fights with the ptarmigan, the weasel, and the lynx. And not for nothing had his puppyhood been made bitter by the persecution of Lip-lip and the whole puppy pack. It might have been otherwise, and he would then have been otherwise. Had Lip-lip not existed, he would have passed his puppyhood with the other puppies and grown up more doglike and with more liking for dogs. Had Grey Beaver possessed the plummet of affection and love, he might have sounded the deeps of White Fang's nature and brought up to the surface all manner of kindly qualities. But these things had not been so. The clay of White Fang had been moulded until he became what he was, morose and lonely, unloving and ferocious, the enemy of all his kind.

CHAPTER II—THE MAD GOD

A small number of white men lived in Fort Yukon. These men had been long in the country. They called themselves Sour-doughs, and took great pride in so classifying themselves. For other men, new in the land, they felt nothing but disdain. The men who came ashore from the steamers were newcomers. They were known as *chechaquos*, and they always wilted at the application of the name. They made their bread with baking-powder. This was the invidious distinction between them and the Sour-doughs, who, forsooth, made their bread from sour-dough because they had no baking-powder.

All of which is neither here nor there. The men in the fort disdained the newcomers and enjoyed seeing them come to grief. Especially did they enjoy the havoc worked amongst the newcomers' dogs by White Fang and his disreputable gang. When a steamer arrived, the men of the fort made it a point always to come down to the bank and see the fun. They looked forward to it with as much anticipation as did the Indian dogs, while they were not slow to appreciate the savage and crafty part played by White Fang.

But there was one man amongst them who particularly enjoyed the sport. He would come running at the first sound of a steamboat's whistle; and when the last fight was over and White Fang and the pack had scattered, he would return slowly to the fort, his face heavy with regret. Sometimes, when a soft southland dog went down, shrieking its death-cry under the fangs of the pack, this man would be unable to contain himself, and would leap into the air and cry out with delight. And always he had a sharp and covetous eye for White Fang.

This man was called "Beauty" by the other men of the fort. No one knew his first name, and in general he was known in the country as Beauty Smith. But he was anything save a beauty. To antithesis was due his naming. He was pre-eminently unbeautiful. Nature had been niggardly with him. He was a small man to begin with; and upon his meagre frame was deposited an even more strikingly meagre head. Its apex might be likened to a point. In fact, in his boyhood, before he had been named Beauty by his fellows, he had been called "Pinhead."

Backward, from the apex, his head slanted down to his neck and forward it slanted uncompromisingly to meet a low and remarkably wide forehead. Beginning here, as though regretting her parsimony, Nature had spread his features with a lavish hand. His eyes were large, and between them was the distance of two eyes. His face, in relation to the rest of him, was prodigious. In order to discover the necessary area, Nature had given him an enormous prognathous jaw. It was wide and heavy, and protruded outward and down until it seemed to rest on his chest. Possibly this appearance was due to the weariness of the slender neck, unable properly to support so great a burden.

This jaw gave the impression of ferocious determination. But something lacked. Perhaps it was from excess. Perhaps the jaw was too large. At any rate, it was a lie. Beauty Smith was known far and wide as the weakest of weak-kneed and snivelling cowards. To complete his description, his teeth were large and yellow, while the two eye-teeth, larger than their fellows, showed under his lean lips like fangs. His eyes were yellow and muddy, as though Nature had run short on pigments and squeezed together the dregs of all her tubes. It was the same with his hair, sparse and irregular of growth, muddy-yellow and dirty-yellow, rising on his head and sprouting out of his face in unexpected tufts and bunches, in appearance like clumped and wind-blown grain.

In short, Beauty Smith was a monstrosity, and the blame of it lay elsewhere. He was not responsible. The clay of him had been so moulded in the making. He did the cooking for the other men in the fort, the dish-washing and the drudgery. They did not despise him. Rather did they tolerate him in a broad human way, as one tolerates any creature evilly treated in the making. Also, they feared him. His cowardly rages made them dread a shot in the back or poison in their coffee. But somebody had to do the cooking, and whatever else his shortcomings, Beauty Smith could cook.

This was the man that looked at White Fang, delighted in his ferocious prowess, and desired to possess him. He made overtures to White Fang from the first. White Fang began by ignoring him. Later on, when the overtures became more insistent, White Fang bristled and bared his teeth and backed away. He did not like the man. The feel of him was bad. He sensed the evil in him, and feared the extended hand and the attempts at soft-spoken speech. Because of all this, he hated the man.

With the simpler creatures, good and bad are things simply understood. The good stands for all things that bring easement and satisfaction and surcease from pain. Therefore, the good is liked. The bad stands for all things that are fraught with discomfort, menace, and hurt, and is hated accordingly. White Fang's feel of Beauty Smith was bad. From the man's distorted body and twisted mind, in occult ways, like mists rising from malarial marshes, came emanations of the unhealth within. Not by reasoning, not by the five senses alone, but by other and remoter and uncharted senses, came the feeling to White Fang that the man was ominous with evil, pregnant with hurtfulness, and therefore a thing bad, and wisely to be hated.

White Fang was in Grey Beaver's camp when Beauty Smith first visited it. At the faint sound of his distant feet, before he came in sight, White Fang knew who was coming and began to bristle. He had been lying down in an abandon of comfort, but he arose quickly, and, as the man arrived, slid away in true wolf-fashion to the edge of the camp. He did not know what they said, but he could see the man and Grey Beaver talking together. Once, the man pointed at him, and White Fang snarled back as though the hand were just descending upon him instead of being, as it was, fifty feet away. The man laughed at this; and White Fang slunk away to the sheltering woods, his head turned to observe as he glided softly over the ground.

Grey Beaver refused to sell the dog. He had grown rich with his trading and stood in need of nothing. Besides, White Fang was a valuable animal, the strongest sled-dog he had ever owned, and the best leader. Furthermore, there was no dog like him on the Mackenzie nor the Yukon. He could fight. He killed other dogs as easily as men killed mosquitoes. (Beauty Smith's eyes lighted up at this, and he licked his thin lips with an eager tongue). No, White Fang was not for sale at any price.

But Beauty Smith knew the ways of Indians. He visited Grey Beaver's camp often, and hidden under his coat was always a black bottle or so. One of the potencies of whisky is the breeding of thirst. Grey Beaver got the thirst. His fevered membranes and burnt stomach began to clamour for more and more of the scorching fluid; while his brain, thrust all awry by the unwonted stimulant, permitted him to go any length to obtain it. The money he had received for his furs and mittens and moccasins began to go. It went faster and faster, and the shorter his money-sack grew, the shorter grew his temper.

In the end his money and goods and temper were all gone. Nothing remained to him but his thirst, a prodigious possession in itself that grew more prodigious with every sober breath he drew. Then it was that Beauty Smith had talk with him again about the sale of White Fang; but this time the price offered was in bottles, not dollars, and Grey Beaver's ears were more eager to hear.

"You ketch um dog you take um all right," was his last word.

The bottles were delivered, but after two days. "You ketch um dog," were Beauty Smith's words to Grey Beaver.

White Fang slunk into camp one evening and dropped down with a sigh of content. The dreaded white god was not there. For days his manifestations of desire to lay hands on him had been growing more insistent, and during that time White Fang had been compelled to avoid the camp. He did not know what evil was threatened by those insistent hands. He knew only that they did threaten evil of some sort, and that it was best for him to keep out of their reach.

But scarcely had he lain down when Grey Beaver staggered over to him and tied a leather thong around his neck. He sat down beside White Fang, holding the end of the thong in his hand. In the other hand he held a bottle, which, from time to time, was inverted above his head to the accompaniment of gurgling noises.

An hour of this passed, when the vibrations of feet in contact with the ground foreran the one who approached. White Fang heard it first, and he was bristling with recognition while Grey Beaver still nodded stupidly. White Fang tried to draw the thong softly out of his master's hand; but the relaxed fingers closed tightly and Grey Beaver roused himself.

Beauty Smith strode into camp and stood over White Fang. He snarled softly up at the thing of fear, watching keenly the deportment of the hands. One hand extended outward and began to descend upon his head. His soft snarl grew tense and harsh. The hand continued slowly to descend, while he crouched beneath it, eyeing it malignantly, his snarl growing shorter and shorter as, with quickening breath, it approached its culmination. Suddenly he snapped, striking with his fangs like a snake. The hand was jerked back, and the teeth came together emptily with a sharp click. Beauty Smith was frightened and angry. Grey Beaver clouted White Fang alongside the head, so that he cowered down close to the earth in respectful obedience.

White Fang's suspicious eyes followed every movement. He saw Beauty Smith go away and return with a stout club. Then the end of the thong was given over to him by Grey Beaver. Beauty Smith started to walk away. The thong grew taut. White Fang resisted it. Grey Beaver clouted him right and left to make him get up and follow. He obeyed, but with a rush, hurling himself upon the stranger who was dragging him away. Beauty Smith did not jump away. He had been waiting for this. He swung the club smartly, stopping the rush midway and smashing White Fang down upon the ground. Grey Beaver laughed and nodded approval. Beauty Smith tightened the thong again, and White Fang crawled limply and dizzily to his feet.

He did not rush a second time. One smash from the club was sufficient to convince him that the white god knew how to handle it, and he was too wise to fight the inevitable. So he followed morosely at Beauty Smith's heels, his tail between his legs, yet snarling softly under his breath. But Beauty Smith kept a wary eye on him, and the club was held always ready to strike.

At the fort Beauty Smith left him securely tied and went in to bed. White Fang waited an hour. Then he applied his teeth to the thong, and in the space of ten seconds was free. He had wasted no time with his teeth. There had been no useless gnawing. The thong was cut across, diagonally, almost as clean as though done by a knife. White Fang looked up at the fort, at the same time bristling and growling. Then he turned and trotted back to Grey Beaver's camp. He owed no allegiance to this strange and terrible god. He had given himself to Grey Beaver, and to Grey Beaver he considered he still belonged.

But what had occurred before was repeated—with a difference. Grey Beaver again made him fast with a thong, and in the morning turned him over to Beauty Smith. And here was where the difference came in. Beauty Smith gave him a beating. Tied securely, White Fang could only rage futilely and endure the punishment. Club and whip were both used upon him, and he experienced the worst beating he had ever received in his life. Even the big beating given him in his puppyhood by Grey Beaver was mild compared with this.

Beauty Smith enjoyed the task. He delighted in it. He gloated over his victim, and his eyes flamed dully, as he swung the whip or club and listened to White Fang's cries of pain and to his helpless bellows and snarls. For Beauty Smith was cruel in the way that cowards are cruel. Cringing and snivelling himself before the blows or angry speech of a man, he revenged himself, in turn, upon creatures weaker than he. All life likes power, and Beauty Smith was no exception. Denied the expression of power amongst his own kind, he fell back upon the lesser creatures and there vindicated the life that was in him. But Beauty Smith had not created himself, and no blame was to be attached to him. He had come into the world with a twisted body and a brute intelligence. This had constituted the clay of him, and it had not been kindly moulded by the world.

White Fang knew why he was being beaten. When Grey Beaver tied the thong around his neck, and passed the end of the thong into Beauty Smith's keeping, White Fang knew that it was his god's will for him to go with Beauty Smith. And when Beauty Smith left him tied outside the fort, he knew that it was Beauty Smith's will that he should remain there. Therefore, he had disobeyed the will of both the gods, and earned the consequent punishment. He had seen dogs change owners in the past, and he had seen the runaways beaten as he was being beaten. He was wise, and yet in the nature of him there were forces greater than wisdom. One of these was fidelity. He did not love Grey Beaver, yet, even in the face of his will and his anger, he was faithful to him. He could not help it. This faithfulness was a quality of the clay that composed him. It was the quality that was peculiarly the possession of his kind; the quality that set apart his species from all other species; the quality that has enabled the wolf and the wild dog to come in from the open and be the companions of man.

After the beating, White Fang was dragged back to the fort. But this time Beauty Smith left him tied with a stick. One does not give up a god easily, and so with White Fang. Grey Beaver was his own particular god, and, in spite of Grey Beaver's will, White Fang still clung to him and would not give him up. Grey Beaver had betrayed and forsaken him, but that had no effect upon him. Not for nothing had he surrendered himself body and soul to Grey Beaver. There had been no reservation on White Fang's part, and the bond was not to be broken easily.

So, in the night, when the men in the fort were asleep, White Fang applied his teeth to the stick that held him. The wood was seasoned and dry, and it was tied so closely to his neck that he could scarcely get his teeth to it. It was only by the severest muscular exertion and neck-arching that he succeeded in getting the wood between his teeth, and barely between his teeth at that; and it was only by the exercise of an immense patience, extending through many hours, that he succeeded in gnawing through the stick. This was something that dogs were not supposed to do. It was unprecedented. But White Fang did it, trotting away from the fort in the early morning, with the end of the stick hanging to his neck.

He was wise. But had he been merely wise he would not have gone back to Grey Beaver who had already twice betrayed him. But there was his faithfulness, and he went back to be betrayed yet a third time. Again he yielded to the tying of a thong around his neck by Grey Beaver, and again Beauty Smith came to claim him. And this time he was beaten even more severely than before.

Grey Beaver looked on stolidly while the white man wielded the whip. He gave no protection. It was no longer his dog. When the beating was over White Fang was sick. A soft southland dog would have died under it, but not he. His school of life had been sterner, and he was himself of sterner stuff. He had too great vitality. His clutch on life was too strong. But he was very sick. At first he was unable to drag himself along, and Beauty Smith had to wait half-an-hour for him. And then, blind and reeling, he followed at Beauty Smith's heels back to the fort.

But now he was tied with a chain that defied his teeth, and he strove in vain, by lunging, to draw the staple from the timber into which it was driven. After a few days, sober and bankrupt, Grey Beaver departed up the Porcupine on his long journey to the Mackenzie. White Fang remained on the Yukon, the property of a man more than half mad and all brute. But what is a dog to know in its consciousness of madness? To White Fang, Beauty Smith was a veritable, if terrible, god. He was a mad god at best, but White Fang knew nothing of madness; he knew only that he must submit to the will of this new master, obey his every whim and fancy.

CHAPTER III—THE REIGN OF HATE

Under the tutelage of the mad god, White Fang became a fiend. He was kept chained in a pen at the rear of the fort, and here Beauty Smith teased and irritated and drove him wild with petty torments. The man early discovered White Fang's susceptibility to laughter, and made it a point after painfully tricking him, to laugh at him. This laughter was uproarious and scornful, and at the same time the god pointed his finger derisively at White Fang. At such times reason fled from White Fang, and in his transports of rage he was even more mad than Beauty Smith.

Formerly, White Fang had been merely the enemy of his kind, withal a ferocious enemy. He now became the enemy of all things, and more ferocious than ever. To such an extent was he tormented, that he hated blindly and without the faintest spark of reason. He hated the chain that bound him, the men who peered in at him through the slats of the pen, the dogs that accompanied the men and that snarled malignantly at him in his helplessness. He hated the very wood of the pen that confined him. And, first, last, and most of all, he hated Beauty Smith.

But Beauty Smith had a purpose in all that he did to White Fang. One day a number of men gathered about the pen. Beauty Smith entered, club in hand, and took the chain off from White Fang's neck. When his master had gone out, White Fang turned loose and tore around the pen, trying to get at the men outside. He was magnificently terrible. Fully five feet in length, and standing two and one-half feet at the shoulder, he far outweighed a wolf of corresponding size. From his mother he had inherited the heavier proportions of the dog, so that he weighed, without any fat and without an ounce of superfluous flesh, over ninety pounds. It was all muscle, bone, and sinew-fighting flesh in the finest condition.

The door of the pen was being opened again. White Fang paused. Something unusual was happening. He waited. The door was opened wider. Then a huge dog was thrust inside, and the door was slammed shut behind him. White Fang had never seen such a dog (it was a mastiff); but the size and fierce aspect of the intruder did not deter him. Here was some thing, not wood nor iron, upon which to wreak his hate. He leaped in with a flash of fangs that ripped down the side of the mastiff's neck. The mastiff shook his head, growled hoarsely, and plunged at White Fang. But White Fang was here, there, and everywhere, always evading and eluding, and always leaping in and slashing with his fangs and leaping out again in time to escape punishment.

The men outside shouted and applauded, while Beauty Smith, in an ecstasy of delight, gloated over the ripping and mangling performed by White Fang. There was no hope for the mastiff from the first. He was too ponderous and slow. In the end, while Beauty Smith beat White Fang back with a club, the mastiff was dragged out by its owner. Then there was a payment of bets, and money clinked in Beauty Smith's hand.

White Fang came to look forward eagerly to the gathering of the men around his pen. It meant a fight; and this was the only way that was now vouchsafed him of expressing the life that was in him. Tormented, incited to hate, he was kept a prisoner so that there was no way of satisfying that hate except at the times his master saw fit to put another dog against him. Beauty Smith had estimated his powers well, for he was invariably the victor. One day, three dogs were turned in upon him in succession. Another day a full-grown wolf, fresh-caught from the Wild, was shoved in through the door of the pen. And on still another day two dogs were set against him at the same time. This was his severest fight, and though in the end he killed them both he was himself half killed in doing it.

In the fall of the year, when the first snows were falling and mush-ice was running in the river, Beauty Smith took passage for himself and White Fang on a steamboat bound up the Yukon to Dawson. White Fang had now achieved a reputation in the land. As "the Fighting Wolf" he was known far and wide, and the cage in which he was kept on the steam-boat's deck was usually surrounded by curious men. He raged and snarled at them, or lay quietly and studied them with cold hatred. Why should he not hate them? He never asked himself the question. He knew only hate and lost himself in the passion of it. Life had become a hell to him. He had not been made for the close confinement wild beasts endure at the hands of men. And yet it was in precisely this way that he was treated. Men stared at him, poked sticks between the bars to make him snarl, and then laughed at him.

They were his environment, these men, and they were moulding the clay of him into a more ferocious thing than had been intended by Nature. Nevertheless, Nature had given him plasticity. Where many another animal would have died or had its spirit broken, he adjusted himself and lived, and at no expense of the spirit. Possibly Beauty Smith, arch-fiend and tormentor, was capable of breaking White Fang's spirit, but as yet there were no signs of his succeeding.

If Beauty Smith had in him a devil, White Fang had another; and the two of them raged against each other unceasingly. In the days before, White Fang had had the wisdom to cower down and submit to a man with a club in his hand; but this wisdom now left him. The mere sight of Beauty Smith was sufficient to send him into transports of fury. And when they came to close quarters, and he had been beaten back by the club, he went on growling and snarling, and showing his fangs. The last growl could never be extracted from him. No matter how terribly he was beaten, he had always another growl; and when Beauty Smith gave up and withdrew, the defiant growl followed after him, or White Fang sprang at the bars of the cage bellowing his hatred.

When the steamboat arrived at Dawson, White Fang went ashore. But he still lived a public life, in a cage, surrounded by curious men. He was exhibited as "the Fighting Wolf," and men paid fifty cents in gold dust to see him. He was given no rest. Did he lie down to sleep, he was stirred up by a sharp stick—so that the audience might get its money's worth. In order to make the exhibition interesting, he was kept in a rage most of the time. But worse than all this, was the atmosphere in which he lived. He was regarded as the most fearful of wild beasts, and this was borne in to him through the bars of the cage. Every word, every cautious action, on the part of the men, impressed upon him his own terrible ferocity. It was so much added fuel to the flame of his fierceness. There could be but one result, and that was that his ferocity fed upon itself and increased. It was another instance of the plasticity of his clay, of his capacity for being moulded by the pressure of environment.

In addition to being exhibited he was a professional fighting animal. At irregular intervals, whenever a fight could be arranged, he was taken out of his cage and led off into the woods a few miles from town. Usually this occurred at night, so as to avoid interference from the mounted police of the Territory. After a few hours of waiting, when daylight had come, the audience and the dog with which he was to fight arrived. In this manner it came about that he fought all sizes and breeds of dogs. It was a savage land, the men were savage, and the fights were usually to the death.

Since White Fang continued to fight, it is obvious that it was the other dogs that died. He never knew defeat. His early training, when he fought with Lip-lip and the whole puppy-pack, stood him in good stead. There was the tenacity with which he clung to the earth. No dog could make him lose his footing. This was the favourite trick of the wolf breeds—to rush in upon him, either directly or with an unexpected swerve, in the hope of striking his shoulder and overthrowing him. Mackenzie hounds, Eskimo and Labrador dogs, huskies and Malemutes—all tried it on him, and all failed. He was never known to lose his footing. Men told this to one another, and looked each time to see it happen; but White Fang always disappointed them.

Then there was his lightning quickness. It gave him a tremendous advantage over his antagonists. No matter what their fighting experience, they had never encountered a dog that moved so swiftly as he. Also to be reckoned with, was the immediateness of his attack. The average dog was accustomed to the preliminaries of snarling and bristling and growling, and the average dog was knocked off his feet and finished before he had begun to fight or recovered from his surprise. So often did this happen, that it became the custom to hold White Fang until the other dog went through its preliminaries, was good and ready, and even made the first attack.

But greatest of all the advantages in White Fang's favour, was his experience. He knew more about fighting than did any of the dogs that faced him. He had fought more fights, knew how to meet more tricks and methods, and had more tricks himself, while his own method was scarcely to be improved upon.

As the time went by, he had fewer and fewer fights. Men despaired of matching him with an equal, and Beauty Smith was compelled to pit wolves against him. These were trapped by the Indians for the purpose, and a fight between White Fang and a wolf was always sure to draw a crowd. Once, a full-grown female lynx was secured, and this time White Fang fought for his life. Her quickness matched his; her ferocity equalled his; while he fought with his fangs alone, and she fought with her sharp-clawed feet as well.

But after the lynx, all fighting ceased for White Fang. There were no more animals with which to fight—at least, there was none considered worthy of fighting with him. So he remained on exhibition until spring, when one Tim Keenan, a faro-dealer, arrived in the land. With him came the first bull-dog that had ever entered the Klondike. That this dog and White Fang should come together was inevitable, and for a week the anticipated fight was the mainspring of conversation in certain quarters of the town.

CHAPTER IV—THE CLINGING DEATH

Beauty Smith slipped the chain from his neck and stepped back.

For once White Fang did not make an immediate attack. He stood still, ears pricked forward, alert and curious, surveying the strange animal that faced him. He had never seen such a dog before. Tim Keenan shoved the bull-dog forward with a muttered "Go to it." The animal waddled toward the centre of the circle, short and squat and ungainly. He came to a stop and blinked across at White Fang.

There were cries from the crowd of, "Go to him, Cherokee! Sick 'm, Cherokee! Eat 'm up!"

But Cherokee did not seem anxious to fight. He turned his head and blinked at the men who shouted, at the same time wagging his stump of a tail good-naturedly. He was not afraid, but merely lazy. Besides, it did not seem to him that it was intended he should fight with the dog he saw before him. He was not used to fighting with that kind of dog, and he was waiting for them to bring on the real dog.

Tim Keenan stepped in and bent over Cherokee, fondling him on both sides of the shoulders with hands that rubbed against the grain of the hair and that made slight, pushing-forward movements. These were so many suggestions. Also, their effect was irritating, for Cherokee began to growl, very softly, deep down in his throat. There was a correspondence in rhythm between the growls and the movements of the man's hands. The growl rose in the throat with the culmination of each forward-pushing movement, and ebbed down to start up afresh with the beginning of the next movement. The end of each movement was the accent of the rhythm, the movement ending abruptly and the growling rising with a jerk.

This was not without its effect on White Fang. The hair began to rise on his neck and across the shoulders. Tim Keenan gave a final shove forward and stepped back again. As the impetus that carried Cherokee forward died down, he continued to go forward of his own volition, in a swift, bow-legged run. Then White Fang struck. A cry of startled admiration went up. He had covered the distance and gone in more like a cat than a dog; and with the same cat-like swiftness he had slashed with his fangs and leaped clear.

The bull-dog was bleeding back of one ear from a rip in his thick neck. He gave no sign, did not even snarl, but turned and followed after White Fang. The display on both sides, the quickness of the one and the steadiness of the other, had excited the partisan spirit of the crowd, and the men were making new bets and increasing original bets. Again, and yet again, White Fang sprang in, slashed, and got away untouched, and still his strange foe followed after him, without too great haste, not slowly, but deliberately and determinedly, in a businesslike sort of way. There was purpose in his method—something for him to do that he was intent upon doing and from which nothing could distract him.

His whole demeanour, every action, was stamped with this purpose. It puzzled White Fang. Never had he seen such a dog. It had no hair protection. It was soft, and bled easily. There was no thick mat of fur to baffle White Fang's teeth as they were often baffled by dogs of his own breed. Each time that his teeth struck they sank easily into the yielding flesh, while the animal did not seem able to defend itself. Another disconcerting thing was that it made no outcry, such as he had been accustomed to with the other dogs he had fought. Beyond a growl or a grunt, the dog took its punishment silently. And never did it flag in its pursuit of him.

Not that Cherokee was slow. He could turn and whirl swiftly enough, but White Fang was never there. Cherokee was puzzled, too. He had never fought before with a dog with which he could not close. The desire to close had always been mutual. But here was a dog that kept at a distance, dancing and dodging here and there and all about. And when it did get its teeth into him, it did not hold on but let go instantly and darted away again.

But White Fang could not get at the soft underside of the throat. The bull-dog stood too short, while its massive jaws were an added protection. White Fang darted in and out unscathed, while Cherokee's wounds increased.

Both sides of his neck and head were ripped and slashed. He bled freely, but showed no signs of being disconcerted. He continued his plodding pursuit, though once, for the moment baffled, he came to a full stop and blinked at the men who looked on, at the same time wagging his stump of a tail as an expression of his willingness to fight.

In that moment White Fang was in upon him and out, in passing ripping his trimmed remnant of an ear. With a slight manifestation of anger, Cherokee took up the pursuit again, running on the inside of the circle White Fang was making, and striving to fasten his deadly grip on White Fang's throat. The bull-dog missed by a hair's-breadth, and cries of praise went up as White Fang doubled suddenly out of danger in the opposite direction.

The time went by. White Fang still danced on, dodging and doubling, leaping in and out, and ever inflicting damage. And still the bull-dog, with grim certitude, toiled after him. Sooner or later he would accomplish his purpose, get the grip that would win the battle. In the meantime, he accepted all the punishment the other could deal him. His tufts of ears had become tassels, his neck and shoulders were slashed in a score of places, and his very lips were cut and bleeding—all from these lightning snaps that were beyond his foreseeing and guarding.

Time and again White Fang had attempted to knock Cherokee off his feet; but the difference in their height was too great. Cherokee was too squat, too close to the ground. White Fang tried the trick once too often. The chance came in one of his quick doublings and counter-circlings. He caught Cherokee with head turned away as he whirled more slowly. His shoulder was exposed. White Fang drove in upon it: but his own shoulder was high above, while he struck with such force that his momentum carried him on across over the other's body. For the first time in his fighting history, men saw White Fang lose his footing. His body turned a half-somersault in the air, and he would have landed on his back had he not twisted, catlike, still in the air, in the effort to bring his feet to the earth. As it was, he struck heavily on his side. The next instant he was on his feet, but in that instant Cherokee's teeth closed on his throat.

It was not a good grip, being too low down toward the chest; but Cherokee held on. White Fang sprang to his feet and tore wildly around, trying to shake off the bull-dog's body. It made him frantic, this clinging, dragging weight. It bound his movements, restricted his freedom. It was like the trap, and all his instinct resented it and revolted against it. It was a mad revolt. For several minutes he was to all intents insane. The basic life that was in him took charge of him. The will to exist of his body surged over him. He was dominated by this mere flesh-love of life. All intelligence was gone. It was as though he had no brain. His reason was unseated by the blind yearning of the flesh to exist and move, at all hazards to move, to continue to move, for movement was the expression of its existence.

Round and round he went, whirling and turning and reversing, trying to shake off the fifty-pound weight that dragged at his throat. The bull-dog did little but keep his grip. Sometimes, and rarely, he managed to get his feet to the earth and for a moment to brace himself against White Fang. But the next moment his footing would be lost and he would be dragging around in the whirl of one of White Fang's mad gyrations. Cherokee identified himself with his instinct. He knew that he was doing the right thing by holding on, and there came to him certain blissful thrills of satisfaction. At such moments he even closed his eyes and allowed his body to be hurled hither and thither, willy-nilly, careless of any hurt that might thereby come to it. That did not count. The grip was the thing, and the grip he kept.

White Fang ceased only when he had tired himself out. He could do nothing, and he could not understand. Never, in all his fighting, had this thing happened. The dogs he had fought with did not fight that way. With them it was snap and slash and get away, snap and slash and get away. He lay partly on his side, panting for breath. Cherokee still holding his grip, urged against him, trying to get him over entirely on his side. White Fang resisted, and he could feel the jaws shifting their grip, slightly relaxing and coming together again in a chewing movement. Each shift brought the grip closer to his throat. The bull-dog's method was to hold what he had, and when opportunity favoured to work in for more. Opportunity favoured when White Fang remained quiet. When White Fang struggled, Cherokee was content merely to hold on.

The bulging back of Cherokee's neck was the only portion of his body that White Fang's teeth could reach. He got hold toward the base where the neck comes out from the shoulders; but he did not know the chewing method of fighting, nor were his jaws adapted to it. He spasmodically ripped and tore with his fangs for a space. Then a change in their position diverted him. The bull-dog had managed to roll him over on his back, and still hanging on to his throat, was on top of him. Like a cat, White Fang bowed his hind-quarters in, and, with the feet digging into his enemy's abdomen above him, he began to claw with long tearing-strokes. Cherokee might well have been disembowelled had he not quickly pivoted on his grip and got his body off of White Fang's and at right angles to it.

There was no escaping that grip. It was like Fate itself, and as inexorable. Slowly it shifted up along the jugular. All that saved White Fang from death was the loose skin of his neck and the thick fur that covered it. This served to form a large roll in Cherokee's mouth, the fur of which well-nigh defied his teeth. But bit by bit, whenever the chance offered, he was getting more of the loose skin and fur in his mouth. The result was that he was slowly throttling White Fang. The latter's breath was drawn with greater and greater difficulty as the moments went by.

It began to look as though the battle were over. The backers of Cherokee waxed jubilant and offered ridiculous odds. White Fang's backers were correspondingly depressed, and refused bets of ten to one and twenty to one, though one man was rash enough to close a wager of fifty to one. This man was Beauty Smith. He took a step into the ring and pointed his finger at White Fang. Then he began to laugh derisively and scornfully. This produced the desired effect. White Fang went wild with rage. He called up his reserves of strength, and gained his feet. As he struggled around the ring, the fifty pounds of his foe ever dragging on his throat, his anger passed on into panic. The basic life of him dominated him again, and his intelligence fled before the will of his flesh to live. Round and round and back again, stumbling and falling and rising, even uprearing at times on his hind-legs and lifting his foe clear of the earth, he struggled vainly to shake off the clinging death.

At last he fell, toppling backward, exhausted; and the bull-dog promptly shifted his grip, getting in closer, mangling more and more of the fur-folded flesh, throttling White Fang more severely than ever. Shouts of applause went up for the victor, and there were many cries of "Cherokee!" "Cherokee!" To this Cherokee responded by vigorous wagging of the stump of his tail. But the clamour of approval did not distract him. There was no sympathetic relation between his tail and his massive jaws. The one might wag, but the others held their terrible grip on White Fang's throat.

It was at this time that a diversion came to the spectators. There was a jingle of bells. Dog-mushers' cries were heard. Everybody, save Beauty Smith, looked apprehensively, the fear of the police strong upon them. But they saw, up the trail, and not down, two men running with sled and dogs. They were evidently coming down the creek from some prospecting trip. At sight of the crowd they stopped their dogs and came over and joined it, curious to see the cause of the excitement. The dog-musher wore a moustache, but the other, a taller and younger man, was smooth-shaven, his skin rosy from the pounding of his blood and the running in the frosty air.

White Fang had practically ceased struggling. Now and again he resisted spasmodically and to no purpose. He could get little air, and that little grew less and less under the merciless grip that ever tightened. In spite of his armour of fur, the great vein of his throat would have long since been torn open, had not the first grip of the bull-dog been so low down as to be practically on the chest. It had taken Cherokee a long time to shift that grip upward, and this had also tended further to clog his jaws with fur and skin-fold.

In the meantime, the abysmal brute in Beauty Smith had been rising into his brain and mastering the small bit of sanity that he possessed at best. When he saw White Fang's eyes beginning to glaze, he knew beyond doubt that the fight was lost. Then he broke loose. He sprang upon White Fang and began savagely to kick him. There were hisses from the crowd and cries of protest, but that was all. While this went on, and Beauty Smith continued to kick White Fang, there was a commotion in the crowd. The tall young newcomer was forcing his way through, shouldering men right and left without ceremony or gentleness. When he broke through into the ring, Beauty Smith was just in the act of delivering another kick. All his weight was on one foot, and he was in a state of unstable equilibrium. At that moment the newcomer's fist landed a smashing blow full in his face. Beauty Smith's remaining leg left the ground, and his whole body seemed to lift into the air as he turned over backward and struck the snow. The newcomer turned upon the crowd.

"You cowards!" he cried. "You beasts!"

He was in a rage himself—a sane rage. His grey eyes seemed metallic and steel-like as they flashed upon the crowd. Beauty Smith regained his feet and came toward him, sniffling and cowardly. The new-comer did not understand. He did not know how abject a coward the other was, and thought he was coming back intent on fighting. So, with a "You beast!" he smashed Beauty Smith over backward with a second blow in the face. Beauty Smith decided that the snow was the safest place for him, and lay where he had fallen, making no effort to get up.

"Come on, Matt, lend a hand," the newcomer called the dog-musher, who had followed him into the ring.

Both men bent over the dogs. Matt took hold of White Fang, ready to pull when Cherokee's jaws should be loosened. This the younger man endeavoured to accomplish by clutching the bulldog's jaws in his hands and trying to spread them. It was a vain undertaking. As he pulled and tugged and wrenched, he kept exclaiming with every expulsion of breath, "Beasts!"

The crowd began to grow unruly, and some of the men were protesting against the spoiling of the sport; but they were silenced when the newcomer lifted his head from his work for a moment and glared at them.

"You damn beasts!" he finally exploded, and went back to his task.

"It's no use, Mr. Scott, you can't break 'm apart that way," Matt said at last.

The pair paused and surveyed the locked dogs.

"Ain't bleedin' much," Matt announced. "Ain't got all the way in yet."

"But he's liable to any moment," Scott answered. "There, did you see that! He shifted his grip in a bit."

The younger man's excitement and apprehension for White Fang was growing. He struck Cherokee about the head savagely again and again. But that did not loosen the jaws. Cherokee wagged the stump of his tail in advertisement that he understood the meaning of the blows, but that he knew he was himself in the right and only doing his duty by keeping his grip.

"Won't some of you help?" Scott cried desperately at the crowd.

But no help was offered. Instead, the crowd began sarcastically to cheer him on and showered him with facetious advice.

"You'll have to get a pry," Matt counselled.

The other reached into the holster at his hip, drew his revolver, and tried to thrust its muzzle between the bull-dog's jaws. He shoved, and shoved hard, till the grating of the steel against the locked teeth could be distinctly heard. Both men were on their knees, bending over the dogs. Tim Keenan strode into the ring. He paused beside Scott and touched him on the shoulder, saying ominously:

"Don't break them teeth, stranger."

"Then I'll break his neck," Scott retorted, continuing his shoving and wedging with the revolver muzzle.

"I said don't break them teeth," the faro-dealer repeated more ominously than before.

But if it was a bluff he intended, it did not work. Scott never desisted from his efforts, though he looked up coolly and asked:

"Your dog?"

The faro-dealer grunted.

"Then get in here and break this grip."

"Well, stranger," the other drawled irritatingly, "I don't mind telling you that's something I ain't worked out for myself. I don't know how to turn the trick."

"Then get out of the way," was the reply, "and don't bother me. I'm busy."

Tim Keenan continued standing over him, but Scott took no further notice of his presence. He had managed to get the muzzle in between the jaws on one side, and was trying to get it out between the jaws on the other side. This accomplished, he pried gently and carefully, loosening the jaws a bit at a time, while Matt, a bit at a time, extricated White Fang's mangled neck.

"Stand by to receive your dog," was Scott's peremptory order to Cherokee's owner.

The faro-dealer stooped down obediently and got a firm hold on Cherokee.

"Now!" Scott warned, giving the final pry.

The dogs were drawn apart, the bull-dog struggling vigorously.

"Take him away," Scott commanded, and Tim Keenan dragged Cherokee back into the crowd.

White Fang made several ineffectual efforts to get up. Once he gained his feet, but his legs were too weak to sustain him, and he slowly wilted and sank back into the snow. His eyes were half closed, and the surface of them was glassy. His jaws were apart, and through them the tongue protruded, draggled and limp. To all appearances he looked like a dog that had been strangled to death. Matt examined him.

"Just about all in," he announced; "but he's breathin' all right."

Beauty Smith had regained his feet and come over to look at White Fang.

"Matt, how much is a good sled-dog worth?" Scott asked.

The dog-musher, still on his knees and stooped over White Fang, calculated for a moment.

"Three hundred dollars," he answered.

"And how much for one that's all chewed up like this one?" Scott asked, nudging White Fang with his foot.

"Half of that," was the dog-musher's judgment. Scott turned upon Beauty Smith.

"Did you hear, Mr. Beast? I'm going to take your dog from you, and I'm going to give you a hundred and fifty for him."

He opened his pocket-book and counted out the bills.

Beauty Smith put his hands behind his back, refusing to touch the proffered money.

"I ain't a-sellin'," he said.

"Oh, yes you are," the other assured him. "Because I'm buying. Here's your money. The dog's mine."

Beauty Smith, his hands still behind him, began to back away.

Scott sprang toward him, drawing his fist back to strike. Beauty Smith cowered down in anticipation of the blow.

"I've got my rights," he whimpered.

"You've forfeited your rights to own that dog," was the rejoinder. "Are you going to take the money? or do I have to hit you again?"

"All right," Beauty Smith spoke up with the alacrity of fear. "But I take the money under protest," he added. "The dog's a mint. I ain't a-goin' to be robbed. A man's got his rights."

"Correct," Scott answered, passing the money over to him. "A man's got his rights. But you're not a man. You're a beast."

471

"Wait till I get back to Dawson," Beauty Smith threatened. "I'll have the law on you."

"If you open your mouth when you get back to Dawson, I'll have you run out of town. Understand?"

Beauty Smith replied with a grunt.

"Understand?" the other thundered with abrupt fierceness.

"Yes," Beauty Smith grunted, shrinking away.

"Yes what?"

"Yes, sir," Beauty Smith snarled.

"Look out! He'll bite!" some one shouted, and a guffaw of laughter went up.

Scott turned his back on him, and returned to help the dog-musher, who was working over White Fang.

Some of the men were already departing; others stood in groups, looking on and talking. Tim Keenan joined one of the groups.

"Who's that mug?" he asked.

"Weedon Scott," some one answered.

"And who in hell is Weedon Scott?" the faro-dealer demanded.

"Oh, one of them crackerjack minin' experts. He's in with all the big bugs. If you want to keep out of trouble, you'll steer clear of him, that's my talk. He's all hunky with the officials. The Gold Commissioner's a special pal of his."

"I thought he must be somebody," was the faro-dealer's comment. "That's why I kept my hands offen him at the start."

CHAPTER V—THE INDOMITABLE

"It's hopeless," Weedon Scott confessed.

He sat on the step of his cabin and stared at the dog-musher, who responded with a shrug that was equally hopeless.

Together they looked at White Fang at the end of his stretched chain, bristling, snarling, ferocious, straining to get at the sled-dogs. Having received sundry lessons from Matt, said lessons being imparted by means of a club, the sled-dogs had learned to leave White Fang alone; and even then they were lying down at a distance, apparently oblivious of his existence.

"It's a wolf and there's no taming it," Weedon Scott announced.

"Oh, I don't know about that," Matt objected. "Might be a lot of dog in 'm, for all you can tell. But there's one thing I know sure, an' that there's no gettin' away from."

The dog-musher paused and nodded his head confidentially at Moosehide Mountain.

"Well, don't be a miser with what you know," Scott said sharply, after waiting a suitable length of time. "Spit it out. What is it?"

The dog-musher indicated White Fang with a backward thrust of his thumb.

"Wolf or dog, it's all the same—he's ben tamed 'ready."

"No!"

"I tell you yes, an' broke to harness. Look close there. D'ye see them marks across the chest?"

"You're right, Matt. He was a sled-dog before Beauty Smith got hold of him."

"And there's not much reason against his bein' a sled-dog again."

"What d'ye think?" Scott queried eagerly. Then the hope died down as he added, shaking his head, "We've had him two weeks now, and if anything he's wilder than ever at the present moment."

"Give 'm a chance," Matt counselled. "Turn 'm loose for a spell."

The other looked at him incredulously.

"Yes," Matt went on, "I know you've tried to, but you didn't take a club."

"You try it then."

The dog-musher secured a club and went over to the chained animal. White Fang watched the club after the manner of a caged lion watching the whip of its trainer.

"See 'm keep his eye on that club," Matt said. "That's a good sign. He's no fool. Don't dast tackle me so long as I got that club handy. He's not clean crazy, sure."

As the man's hand approached his neck, White Fang bristled and snarled and crouched down. But while he eyed the approaching hand, he at the same time contrived to keep track of the club in the other hand, suspended threateningly above him. Matt unsnapped the chain from the collar and stepped back.

White Fang could scarcely realise that he was free. Many months had gone by since he passed into the possession of Beauty Smith, and in all that period he had never known a moment of freedom except at the times he had been loosed to fight with other dogs. Immediately after such fights he had always been imprisoned again.

He did not know what to make of it. Perhaps some new devilry of the gods was about to be perpetrated on him. He walked slowly and cautiously, prepared to be assailed at any moment. He did not know what to do, it was all so unprecedented. He took the precaution to sheer off from the two watching gods, and walked carefully to the corner of the cabin. Nothing happened. He was plainly perplexed, and he came back again, pausing a dozen feet away and regarding the two men intently.

"Won't he run away?" his new owner asked.

Matt shrugged his shoulders. "Got to take a gamble. Only way to find out is to find out."

"Poor devil," Scott murmured pityingly. "What he needs is some show of human kindness," he added, turning and going into the cabin.

He came out with a piece of meat, which he tossed to White Fang. He sprang away from it, and from a distance studied it suspiciously.

"Hi-yu, Major!" Matt shouted warningly, but too late.

Major had made a spring for the meat. At the instant his jaws closed on it, White Fang struck him. He was overthrown. Matt rushed in, but quicker than he was White Fang. Major staggered to his feet, but the blood spouting from his throat reddened the snow in a widening path.

"It's too bad, but it served him right," Scott said hastily.

But Matt's foot had already started on its way to kick White Fang. There was a leap, a flash of teeth, a sharp exclamation. White Fang, snarling fiercely, scrambled backward for several yards, while Matt stooped and investigated his leg.

"He got me all right," he announced, pointing to the torn trousers and undercloths, and the growing stain of red.

"I told you it was hopeless, Matt," Scott said in a discouraged voice. "I've thought about it off and on, while not wanting to think of it. But we've come to it now. It's the only thing to do."

As he talked, with reluctant movements he drew his revolver, threw open the cylinder, and assured himself of its contents.

"Look here, Mr. Scott," Matt objected; "that dog's ben through hell. You can't expect 'm to come out a white an' shinin' angel. Give 'm time."

"Look at Major," the other rejoined.

The dog-musher surveyed the stricken dog. He had sunk down on the snow in the circle of his blood and was plainly in the last gasp.

"Served 'm right. You said so yourself, Mr. Scott. He tried to take White Fang's meat, an' he's dead-O. That was to be expected. I wouldn't give two whoops in hell for a dog that wouldn't fight for his own meat."

"But look at yourself, Matt. It's all right about the dogs, but we must draw the line somewhere."

"Served me right," Matt argued stubbornly. "What'd I want to kick 'm for? You said yourself that he'd done right. Then I had no right to kick 'm."

"It would be a mercy to kill him," Scott insisted. "He's untamable."

"Now look here, Mr. Scott, give the poor devil a fightin' chance. He ain't had no chance yet. He's just come through hell, an' this is the first time he's ben loose. Give 'm a fair chance, an' if he don't deliver the goods, I'll kill 'm myself. There!"

"God knows I don't want to kill him or have him killed," Scott answered, putting away the revolver. "We'll let him run loose and see what kindness can do for him. And here's a try at it."

He walked over to White Fang and began talking to him gently and soothingly.

"Better have a club handy," Matt warned.

Scott shook his head and went on trying to win White Fang's confidence.

White Fang was suspicious. Something was impending. He had killed this god's dog, bitten his companion god, and what else was to be expected than some terrible punishment? But in the face of it he was indomitable. He bristled and showed his teeth, his eyes vigilant, his whole body wary and prepared for anything. The god had no club, so he suffered him to approach quite near. The god's hand had come out and was descending upon his head. White Fang shrank together and grew tense as he crouched under it. Here was danger, some treachery or something. He knew the hands of the gods, their proved mastery, their cunning to hurt. Besides, there was his old antipathy to being touched. He snarled more menacingly, crouched still lower, and still the hand descended. He did not want to bite the hand, and he endured the peril of it until his instinct surged up in him, mastering him with its insatiable yearning for life.

Weedon Scott had believed that he was quick enough to avoid any snap or slash. But he had yet to learn the remarkable quickness of White Fang, who struck with the certainty and swiftness of a coiled snake.

Scott cried out sharply with surprise, catching his torn hand and holding it tightly in his other hand. Matt uttered a great oath and sprang to his side. White Fang crouched down, and backed away, bristling, showing his fangs, his eyes malignant with menace. Now he could expect a beating as fearful as any he had received from Beauty Smith.

"Here! What are you doing?" Scott cried suddenly.

Matt had dashed into the cabin and come out with a rifle.

"Nothin'," he said slowly, with a careless calmness that was assumed, "only goin' to keep that promise I made. I reckon it's up to me to kill 'm as I said I'd do."

"No you don't!"

"Yes I do. Watch me."

As Matt had pleaded for White Fang when he had been bitten, it was now Weedon Scott's turn to plead.

"You said to give him a chance. Well, give it to him. We've only just started, and we can't quit at the beginning. It served me right, this time. And—look at him!"

White Fang, near the corner of the cabin and forty feet away, was snarling with blood-curdling viciousness, not at Scott, but at the dog-musher.

"Well, I'll be everlastingly gosh-swoggled!" was the dog-musher's expression of astonishment.

"Look at the intelligence of him," Scott went on hastily. "He knows the meaning of firearms as well as you do. He's got intelligence and we've got to give that intelligence a chance. Put up the gun."

"All right, I'm willin'," Matt agreed, leaning the rifle against the woodpile.

"But will you look at that!" he exclaimed the next moment.

White Fang had quieted down and ceased snarling. "This is worth investigatin'. Watch."

Matt, reached for the rifle, and at the same moment White Fang snarled. He stepped away from the rifle, and White Fang's lifted lips descended, covering his teeth.

"Now, just for fun."

Matt took the rifle and began slowly to raise it to his shoulder. White Fang's snarling began with the movement, and increased as the movement approached its culmination. But the moment before the rifle came to a level on him, he leaped sidewise behind the corner of the cabin. Matt stood staring along the sights at the empty space of snow which had been occupied by White Fang.

The dog-musher put the rifle down solemnly, then turned and looked at his employer.

"I agree with you, Mr. Scott. That dog's too intelligent to kill."

CHAPTER VI—THE LOVE-MASTER

As White Fang watched Weedon Scott approach, he bristled and snarled to advertise that he would not submit to punishment. Twenty-four hours had passed since he had slashed open the hand that was now bandaged and held up by a sling to keep the blood out of it. In the past White Fang had experienced delayed punishments, and he apprehended that such a one was about to befall him. How could it be otherwise? He had committed what was to him sacrilege, sunk his fangs into the holy flesh of a god, and of a white-skinned superior god at that. In the nature of things, and of intercourse with gods, something terrible awaited him.

The god sat down several feet away. White Fang could see nothing dangerous in that. When the gods administered punishment they stood on their legs. Besides, this god had no club, no whip, no firearm. And furthermore, he himself was free. No chain nor stick bound him. He could escape into safety while the god was scrambling to his feet. In the meantime he would wait and see.

The god remained quiet, made no movement; and White Fang's snarl slowly dwindled to a growl that ebbed down in his throat and ceased. Then the god spoke, and at the first sound of his voice, the hair rose on White Fang's neck and the growl rushed up in his throat. But the god made no hostile movement, and went on calmly talking. For a time White Fang growled in unison with him, a correspondence of rhythm being established between growl and voice. But the god talked on interminably. He talked to White Fang as White Fang had never been talked to before. He talked softly and soothingly, with a gentleness that somehow, somewhere, touched White Fang. In spite of himself and all the pricking warnings of his instinct, White Fang began to have confidence in this god. He had a feeling of security that was belied by all his experience with men.

After a long time, the god got up and went into the cabin. White Fang scanned him apprehensively when he came out. He had neither whip nor club nor weapon. Nor was his uninjured hand behind his back hiding something. He sat down as before, in the same spot, several feet away. He held out a small piece of meat. White Fang pricked his ears and investigated it suspiciously, managing to look at the same time both at the meat and the god, alert for any overt act, his body tense and ready to spring away at the first sign of hostility.

Still the punishment delayed. The god merely held near to his nose a piece of meat. And about the meat there seemed nothing wrong. Still White Fang suspected; and though the meat was proffered to him with short inviting thrusts of the hand, he refused to touch it. The gods were all-wise, and there was no telling what masterful treachery lurked behind that apparently harmless piece of meat. In past experience, especially in dealing with squaws, meat and punishment had often been disastrously related.

In the end, the god tossed the meat on the snow at White Fang's feet. He smelled the meat carefully; but he did not look at it. While he smelled it he kept his eyes on the god. Nothing happened. He took the meat into his mouth and swallowed it. Still nothing happened. The god was actually offering him another piece of meat. Again he refused to take it from the hand, and again it was tossed to him. This was repeated a number of times. But there came a time when the god refused to toss it. He kept it in his hand and steadfastly proffered it.

The meat was good meat, and White Fang was hungry. Bit by bit, infinitely cautious, he approached the hand. At last the time came that he decided to eat the meat from the hand. He never took his eyes from the god, thrusting his head forward with ears flattened back and hair involuntarily rising and cresting on his neck. Also a low growl rumbled in his throat as warning that he was not to be trifled with. He ate the meat, and nothing happened. Piece by piece, he ate all the meat, and nothing happened. Still the punishment delayed.

He licked his chops and waited. The god went on talking. In his voice was kindness—something of which White Fang had no experience whatever. And within him it aroused feelings which he had likewise never experienced before. He was aware of a certain strange satisfaction, as though some need were being gratified, as though some void in his being were being filled. Then again came the prod of his instinct and the warning of past experience. The gods were ever crafty, and they had unguessed ways of attaining their ends.

Ah, he had thought so! There it came now, the god's hand, cunning to hurt, thrusting out at him, descending upon his head. But the god went on talking. His voice was soft and soothing. In spite of the menacing hand, the voice inspired confidence. And in spite of the assuring voice, the hand inspired distrust. White Fang was torn by conflicting feelings, impulses. It seemed he would fly to pieces, so terrible was the control he was exerting, holding together by an unwonted indecision the counter-forces that struggled within him for mastery.

He compromised. He snarled and bristled and flattened his ears. But he neither snapped nor sprang away. The hand descended. Nearer and nearer it came. It touched the ends of his upstanding hair. He shrank down under it. It followed down after him, pressing more closely against him. Shrinking, almost shivering, he still managed to hold himself together. It was a torment, this hand that touched him and violated his instinct. He could not forget in a day all the evil that had been wrought him at the hands of men. But it was the will of the god, and he strove to submit.

The hand lifted and descended again in a patting, caressing movement. This continued, but every time the hand lifted, the hair lifted under it. And every time the hand descended, the ears flattened down and a cavernous growl surged in his throat. White Fang growled and growled with insistent warning. By this means he announced that he was prepared to retaliate for any hurt he might receive. There was no telling when the god's ulterior motive might be disclosed. At any moment that soft, confidence-inspiring voice might break forth in a roar of wrath, that gentle and caressing hand transform itself into a vice-like grip to hold him helpless and administer punishment.

But the god talked on softly, and ever the hand rose and fell with non-hostile pats. White Fang experienced dual feelings. It was distasteful to his instinct. It restrained him, opposed the will of him toward personal liberty.

And yet it was not physically painful. On the contrary, it was even pleasant, in a physical way. The patting movement slowly and carefully changed to a rubbing of the ears about their bases, and the physical pleasure even increased a little. Yet he continued to fear, and he stood on guard, expectant of unguessed evil, alternately suffering and enjoying as one feeling or the other came uppermost and swayed him.

"Well, I'll be gosh-swoggled!"

So spoke Matt, coming out of the cabin, his sleeves rolled up, a pan of dirty dish-water in his hands, arrested in the act of emptying the pan by the sight of Weedon Scott patting White Fang.

At the instant his voice broke the silence, White Fang leaped back, snarling savagely at him.

Matt regarded his employer with grieved disapproval.

"If you don't mind my expressin' my feelin's, Mr. Scott, I'll make free to say you're seventeen kinds of a damn fool an' all of 'em different, an' then some."

Weedon Scott smiled with a superior air, gained his feet, and walked over to White Fang. He talked soothingly to him, but not for long, then slowly put out his hand, rested it on White Fang's head, and resumed the interrupted patting. White Fang endured it, keeping his eyes fixed suspiciously, not upon the man that patted him, but upon the man that stood in the doorway.

"You may be a number one, tip-top minin' expert, all right all right," the dog-musher delivered himself oracularly, "but you missed the chance of your life when you was a boy an' didn't run off an' join a circus."

White Fang snarled at the sound of his voice, but this time did not leap away from under the hand that was caressing his head and the back of his neck with long, soothing strokes.

It was the beginning of the end for White Fang—the ending of the old life and the reign of hate. A new and incomprehensibly fairer life was dawning. It required much thinking and endless patience on the part of

Weedon Scott to accomplish this. And on the part of White Fang it required nothing less than a revolution. He had to ignore the urges and promptings of instinct and reason, defy experience, give the lie to life itself.

Life, as he had known it, not only had had no place in it for much that he now did; but all the currents had gone counter to those to which he now abandoned himself. In short, when all things were considered, he had to achieve an orientation far vaster than the one he had achieved at the time he came voluntarily in from the Wild and accepted Grey Beaver as his lord. At that time he was a mere puppy, soft from the making, without form, ready for the thumb of circumstance to begin its work upon him. But now it was different. The thumb of circumstance had done its work only too well. By it he had been formed and hardened into the Fighting Wolf, fierce and implacable, unloving and unlovable. To accomplish the change was like a reflux of being, and this when the plasticity of youth was no longer his; when the fibre of him had become tough and knotty; when the warp and the woof of him had made of him an adamantine texture, harsh and unyielding; when the face of his spirit had become iron and all his instincts and axioms had crystallised into set rules, cautions, dislikes, and desires.

Yet again, in this new orientation, it was the thumb of circumstance that pressed and prodded him, softening that which had become hard and remoulding it into fairer form. Weedon Scott was in truth this thumb. He had gone to the roots of White Fang's nature, and with kindness touched to life potencies that had languished and well-nigh perished. One such potency was *love*. It took the place of *like*, which latter had been the highest feeling that thrilled him in his intercourse with the gods.

But this love did not come in a day. It began with *like* and out of it slowly developed. White Fang did not run away, though he was allowed to remain loose, because he liked this new god. This was certainly better than the life he had lived in the cage of Beauty Smith, and it was necessary that he should have some god. The lordship of man was a need of his nature. The seal of his dependence on man had been set upon him in that early day when he turned his back on the Wild and crawled to Grey Beaver's feet to receive the expected beating. This seal had been stamped upon him again, and ineradicably, on his second return from the Wild, when the long famine was over and there was fish once more in the village of Grey Beaver.

And so, because he needed a god and because he preferred Weedon Scott to Beauty Smith, White Fang remained. In acknowledgment of fealty, he proceeded to take upon himself the guardianship of his master's property. He prowled about the cabin while the sled-dogs slept, and the first night-visitor to the cabin fought him off with a club until Weedon Scott came to the rescue. But White Fang soon learned to differentiate between thieves and honest men, to appraise the true value of step and carriage. The man who travelled, loud-stepping, the direct line to the cabin door, he let alone—though he watched him vigilantly until the door opened and he received the endorsement of the master. But the man who went softly, by circuitous ways, peering with caution, seeking after secrecy—that was the man who received no suspension of judgment from White Fang, and who went away abruptly, hurriedly, and without dignity.

Weedon Scott had set himself the task of redeeming White Fang—or rather, of redeeming mankind from the wrong it had done White Fang. It was a matter of principle and conscience. He felt that the ill done White Fang was a debt incurred by man and that it must be paid. So he went out of his way to be especially kind to the Fighting Wolf. Each day he made it a point to caress and pet White Fang, and to do it at length.

At first suspicious and hostile, White Fang grew to like this petting. But there was one thing that he never outgrew—his growling. Growl he would, from the moment the petting began till it ended. But it was a growl with a new note in it. A stranger could not hear this note, and to such a stranger the growling of White Fang was an exhibition of primordial savagery, nerve-racking and blood-curdling. But White Fang's throat had become harsh-fibred from the making of ferocious sounds through the many years since his first little rasp of anger in the lair of his cubhood, and he could not soften the sounds of that throat now to express the gentleness he felt. Nevertheless, Weedon Scott's ear and sympathy were fine enough to catch the new note all but drowned in the fierceness—the note that was the faintest hint of a croon of content and that none but he could hear.

As the days went by, the evolution of *like* into *love* was accelerated. White Fang himself began to grow aware of it, though in his consciousness he knew not what love was. It manifested itself to him as a void in his being—a hungry, aching, yearning void that clamoured to be filled. It was a pain and an unrest; and it received easement only by the touch of the new god's presence. At such times love was joy to him, a wild, keen-thrilling satisfaction. But when away from his god, the pain and the unrest returned; the void in him sprang up and pressed against him with its emptiness, and the hunger gnawed and gnawed unceasingly.

White Fang was in the process of finding himself. In spite of the maturity of his years and of the savage rigidity of the mould that had formed him, his nature was undergoing an expansion. There was a burgeoning within him of strange feelings and unwonted impulses. His old code of conduct was changing. In the past he had liked comfort and surcease from pain, disliked discomfort and pain, and he had adjusted his actions accordingly. But now it was different. Because of this new feeling within him, he ofttimes elected discomfort and pain for the sake of his god. Thus, in the early morning, instead of roaming and foraging, or lying in a sheltered nook, he would wait for hours on the cheerless cabin-stoop for a sight of the god's face. At night, when the god returned home, White Fang would leave the warm sleeping-place he had burrowed in the snow in order to receive the friendly snap of fingers and the word of greeting. Meat, even meat itself, he would forego to be with his god, to receive a caress from him or to accompany him down into the town.

Like had been replaced by *love*. And love was the plummet dropped down into the deeps of him where like had never gone. And responsive out of his deeps had come the new thing—love. That which was given unto him did he return. This was a god indeed, a love-god, a warm and radiant god, in whose light White Fang's nature expanded as a flower expands under the sun.

But White Fang was not demonstrative. He was too old, too firmly moulded, to become adept at expressing himself in new ways. He was too self-possessed, too strongly poised in his own isolation. Too long had he cultivated reticence, aloofness, and moroseness. He had never barked in his life, and he could not now learn to bark a welcome when his god approached. He was never in the way, never extravagant nor foolish in the expression of his love. He never ran to meet his god. He waited at a distance; but he always waited, was always there. His love partook of the nature of worship, dumb, inarticulate, a silent adoration. Only by the steady regard of his eyes did he express his love, and by the unceasing following with his eyes of his god's every movement. Also, at times, when his god looked at him and spoke to him, he betrayed an awkward self-consciousness, caused by the struggle of his love to express itself and his physical inability to express it.

He learned to adjust himself in many ways to his new mode of life. It was borne in upon him that he must let his master's dogs alone. Yet his dominant nature asserted itself, and he had first to thrash them into an acknowledgment of his superiority and leadership. This accomplished, he had little trouble with them. They gave trail to him when he came and went or walked among them, and when he asserted his will they obeyed.

In the same way, he came to tolerate Matt—as a possession of his master. His master rarely fed him. Matt did that, it was his business; yet White Fang divined that it was his master's food he ate and that it was his master who thus fed him vicariously. Matt it was who tried to put him into the harness and make him haul sled with the other dogs. But Matt failed. It was not until Weedon Scott put the harness on White Fang and worked him, that he understood. He took it as his master's will that Matt should drive him and work him just as he drove and worked his master's other dogs.

Different from the Mackenzie toboggans were the Klondike sleds with runners under them. And different was the method of driving the dogs. There was no fan-formation of the team. The dogs worked in single file, one behind another, hauling on double traces. And here, in the Klondike, the leader was indeed the leader. The wisest as well as strongest dog was the leader, and the team obeyed him and feared him. That White Fang should quickly gain this post was inevitable. He could not be satisfied with less, as Matt learned after much inconvenience and trouble. White Fang picked out the post for himself, and Matt backed his judgment with strong language after the experiment had been tried. But, though he worked in the sled in the day, White Fang did not forego the guarding of his master's property in the night. Thus he was on duty all the time, ever vigilant and faithful, the most valuable of all the dogs.

"Makin' free to spit out what's in me," Matt said one day, "I beg to state that you was a wise guy all right when you paid the price you did for that dog. You clean swindled Beauty Smith on top of pushin' his face in with your fist."

A recrudescence of anger glinted in Weedon Scott's grey eyes, and he muttered savagely, "The beast!"

In the late spring a great trouble came to White Fang. Without warning, the love-master disappeared. There had been warning, but White Fang was unversed in such things and did not understand the packing of a grip. He *remembered* afterwards that his packing had preceded the master's disappearance; but at the time he suspected nothing. That night he waited for the master to return. At midnight the chill wind that blew drove him to shelter at the rear of the cabin. There he drowsed, only half asleep, his ears keyed for the first sound of the familiar step. But, at two in the morning, his anxiety drove him out to the cold front stoop, where he crouched, and waited.

But no master came. In the morning the door opened and Matt stepped outside. White Fang gazed at him wistfully. There was no common speech by which he might learn what he wanted to know. The days came and went, but never the master. White Fang, who had never known sickness in his life, became sick. He became very sick, so sick that Matt was finally compelled to bring him inside the cabin. Also, in writing to his employer, Matt devoted a postscript to White Fang.

Weedon Scott reading the letter down in Circle City, came upon the following:

"That dam wolf won't work. Won't eat. Aint got no spunk left. All the dogs is licking him. Wants to know what has become of you, and I don't know how to tell him. Mebbe he is going to die."

It was as Matt had said. White Fang had ceased eating, lost heart, and allowed every dog of the team to thrash him. In the cabin he lay on the floor near the stove, without interest in food, in Matt, nor in life. Matt might talk gently to him or swear at him, it was all the same; he never did more than turn his dull eyes upon the man, then drop his head back to its customary position on his fore-paws.

And then, one night, Matt, reading to himself with moving lips and mumbled sounds, was startled by a low whine from White Fang. He had got upon his feet, his ears cocked towards the door, and he was listening intently. A moment later, Matt heard a footstep. The door opened, and Weedon Scott stepped in. The two men shook hands. Then Scott looked around the room.

"Where's the wolf?" he asked.

Then he discovered him, standing where he had been lying, near to the stove. He had not rushed forward after the manner of other dogs. He stood, watching and waiting.

"Holy smoke!" Matt exclaimed. "Look at 'm wag his tail!"

Weedon Scott strode half across the room toward him, at the same time calling him. White Fang came to him, not with a great bound, yet quickly. He was awakened from self-consciousness, but as he drew near, his eyes took on a strange expression. Something, an incommunicable vastness of feeling, rose up into his eyes as a light and shone forth.

"He never looked at me that way all the time you was gone!" Matt commented.

Weedon Scott did not hear. He was squatting down on his heels, face to face with White Fang and petting him—rubbing at the roots of the ears, making long caressing strokes down the neck to the shoulders, tapping the spine gently with the balls of his fingers. And White Fang was growling responsively, the crooning note of the growl more pronounced than ever.

But that was not all. What of his joy, the great love in him, ever surging and struggling to express itself, succeeded in finding a new mode of expression. He suddenly thrust his head forward and nudged his way in between the master's arm and body. And here, confined, hidden from view all except his ears, no longer growling, he continued to nudge and snuggle.

The two men looked at each other. Scott's eyes were shining.

"Gosh!" said Matt in an awe-stricken voice.

A moment later, when he had recovered himself, he said, "I always insisted that wolf was a dog. Look at 'm!"

With the return of the love-master, White Fang's recovery was rapid. Two nights and a day he spent in the cabin. Then he sallied forth. The sled-dogs had forgotten his prowess. They *remembered* only the latest, which was his weakness and sickness. At the sight of him as he came out of the cabin, they sprang upon him.

"Talk about your rough-houses," Matt murmured gleefully, standing in the doorway and looking on.

"Give 'm hell, you wolf! Give 'm hell!—an' then some!"

White Fang did not need the encouragement. The return of the love-master was enough. Life was flowing through him again, splendid and indomitable. He fought from sheer joy, finding in it an expression of much that he felt and that otherwise was without speech. There could be but one ending. The team dispersed in ignominious defeat, and it was not until after dark that the dogs came sneaking back, one by one, by meekness and humility signifying their fealty to White Fang.

Having learned to snuggle, White Fang was guilty of it often. It was the final word. He could not go beyond it. The one thing of which he had always been particularly jealous was his head. He had always disliked to have it touched. It was the Wild in him, the fear of hurt and of the trap, that had given rise to the panicky impulses to avoid contacts. It was the mandate of his instinct that that head must be free. And now, with the love-master, his snuggling was the deliberate act of putting himself into a position of hopeless helplessness. It was an expression of perfect confidence, of absolute self-surrender, as though he said: "I put myself into thy hands. Work thou thy will with me."

One night, not long after the return, Scott and Matt sat at a game of cribbage preliminary to going to bed. "Fifteen-two, fifteen-four an' a pair makes six," Mat was pegging up, when there was an outcry and sound of snarling without. They looked at each other as they started to rise to their feet.

"The wolf's nailed somebody," Matt said.

A wild scream of fear and anguish hastened them.

"Bring a light!" Scott shouted, as he sprang outside.

Matt followed with the lamp, and by its light they saw a man lying on his back in the snow. His arms were folded, one above the other, across his face and throat. Thus he was trying to shield himself from White Fang's teeth. And there was need for it. White Fang was in a rage, wickedly making his attack on the most vulnerable spot. From shoulder to wrist of the crossed arms, the coat-sleeve, blue flannel shirt and undershirt were ripped in rags, while the arms themselves were terribly slashed and streaming blood.

All this the two men saw in the first instant. The next instant Weedon Scott had White Fang by the throat and was dragging him clear. White Fang struggled and snarled, but made no attempt to bite, while he quickly quieted down at a sharp word from the master.

Matt helped the man to his feet. As he arose he lowered his crossed arms, exposing the bestial face of Beauty Smith. The dog-musher let go of him precipitately, with action similar to that of a man who has picked up live fire. Beauty Smith blinked in the lamplight and looked about him. He caught sight of White Fang and terror rushed into his face.

At the same moment Matt noticed two objects lying in the snow. He held the lamp close to them, indicating them with his toe for his employer's benefit—a steel dog-chain and a stout club.

Weedon Scott saw and nodded. Not a word was spoken. The dog-musher laid his hand on Beauty Smith's shoulder and faced him to the right about. No word needed to be spoken. Beauty Smith started.

In the meantime the love-master was patting White Fang and talking to him.

"Tried to steal you, eh? And you wouldn't have it! Well, well, he made a mistake, didn't he?"

"Must 'a' thought he had hold of seventeen devils," the dog-musher sniggered.

White Fang, still wrought up and bristling, growled and growled, the hair slowly lying down, the crooning note remote and dim, but growing in his throat.

PART V

CHAPTER I—THE LONG TRAIL

It was in the air. White Fang sensed the coming calamity, even before there was tangible evidence of it. In vague ways it was borne in upon him that a change was impending. He knew not how nor why, yet he got his feel of the oncoming event from the gods themselves. In ways subtler than they knew, they betrayed their intentions to the wolf-dog that haunted the cabin-stoop, and that, though he never came inside the cabin, knew what went on inside their brains.

"Listen to that, will you!" the dog-musher exclaimed at supper one night.

Weedon Scott listened. Through the door came a low, anxious whine, like a sobbing under the breath that had just grown audible. Then came the long sniff, as White Fang reassured himself that his god was still inside and had not yet taken himself off in mysterious and solitary flight.

"I do believe that wolf's on to you," the dog-musher said.

Weedon Scott looked across at his companion with eyes that almost pleaded, though this was given the lie by his words.

"What the devil can I do with a wolf in California?" he demanded.

"That's what I say," Matt answered. "What the devil can you do with a wolf in California?"

But this did not satisfy Weedon Scott. The other seemed to be judging him in a non-committal sort of way.

"White man's dogs would have no show against him," Scott went on. "He'd kill them on sight. If he didn't bankrupt me with damaged suits, the authorities would take him away from me and electrocute him."

"He's a downright murderer, I know," was the dog-musher's comment.

Weedon Scott looked at him suspiciously.

"It would never do," he said decisively.

"It would never do!" Matt concurred. "Why you'd have to hire a man 'specially to take care of 'm."

The other suspicion was allayed. He nodded cheerfully. In the silence that followed, the low, half-sobbing whine was heard at the door and then the long, questing sniff.

"There's no denyin' he thinks a hell of a lot of you," Matt said.

The other glared at him in sudden wrath. "Damn it all, man! I know my own mind and what's best!"

"I'm agreein' with you, only . . . "

"Only what?" Scott snapped out.

"Only . . . " the dog-musher began softly, then changed his mind and betrayed a rising anger of his own. "Well, you needn't get so all-fired het up about it. Judgin' by your actions one'd think you didn't know your own mind."

Weedon Scott debated with himself for a while, and then said more gently: "You are right, Matt. I don't know my own mind, and that's what's the trouble."

"Why, it would be rank ridiculousness for me to take that dog along," he broke out after another pause.

"I'm agreein' with you," was Matt's answer, and again his employer was not quite satisfied with him.

"But how in the name of the great Sardanapolis he knows you're goin' is what gets me," the dog-musher continued innocently.

"It's beyond me, Matt," Scott answered, with a mournful shake of the head.

Then came the day when, through the open cabin door, White Fang saw the fatal grip on the floor and the love-master packing things into it. Also, there were comings and goings, and the erstwhile placid atmosphere of the cabin was vexed with strange perturbations and unrest. Here was indubitable evidence. White Fang had already scented it. He now reasoned it. His god was preparing for another flight. And since he had not taken him with him before, so, now, he could look to be left behind.

That night he lifted the long wolf-howl. As he had howled, in his puppy days, when he fled back from the Wild to the village to find it vanished and naught but a rubbish-heap to mark the site of Grey Beaver's tepee, so now he pointed his muzzle to the cold stars and told to them his woe.

Inside the cabin the two men had just gone to bed.

"He's gone off his food again," Matt remarked from his bunk.

There was a grunt from Weedon Scott's bunk, and a stir of blankets.

"From the way he cut up the other time you went away, I wouldn't wonder this time but what he died."

The blankets in the other bunk stirred irritably.

"Oh, shut up!" Scott cried out through the darkness. "You nag worse than a woman."

"I'm agreein' with you," the dog-musher answered, and Weedon Scott was not quite sure whether or not the other had snickered.

The next day White Fang's anxiety and restlessness were even more pronounced. He dogged his master's heels whenever he left the cabin, and haunted the front stoop when he remained inside. Through the open door he could catch glimpses of the luggage on the floor. The grip had been joined by two large canvas bags and a box. Matt was rolling the master's blankets and fur robe inside a small tarpaulin. White Fang whined as he watched the operation.

Later on two Indians arrived. He watched them closely as they shouldered the luggage and were led off down the hill by Matt, who carried the bedding and the grip. But White Fang did not follow them. The master was still in the cabin. After a time, Matt returned. The master came to the door and called White Fang inside.

"You poor devil," he said gently, rubbing White Fang's ears and tapping his spine. "I'm hitting the long trail, old man, where you cannot follow. Now give me a growl—the last, good, good-bye growl."

But White Fang refused to growl. Instead, and after a wistful, searching look, he snuggled in, burrowing his head out of sight between the master's arm and body.

"There she blows!" Matt cried. From the Yukon arose the hoarse bellowing of a river steamboat. "You've got to cut it short. Be sure and lock the front door. I'll go out the back. Get a move on!"

The two doors slammed at the same moment, and Weedon Scott waited for Matt to come around to the front. From inside the door came a low whining and sobbing. Then there were long, deep-drawn sniffs.

"You must take good care of him, Matt," Scott said, as they started down the hill. "Write and let me know how he gets along."

"Sure," the dog-musher answered. "But listen to that, will you!"

Both men stopped. White Fang was howling as dogs howl when their masters lie dead. He was voicing an utter woe, his cry bursting upward in great heart-breaking rushes, dying down into quavering misery, and bursting upward again with a rush upon rush of grief.

The *Aurora* was the first steamboat of the year for the Outside, and her decks were jammed with prosperous adventurers and broken gold seekers, all equally as mad to get to the Outside as they had been originally to get to the Inside. Near the gang-plank, Scott was shaking hands with Matt, who was preparing to go ashore. But Matt's hand went limp in the other's grasp as his gaze shot past and remained fixed on something behind him. Scott turned to see. Sitting on the deck several feet away and watching wistfully was White Fang.

495

The dog-musher swore softly, in awe-stricken accents. Scott could only look in wonder.

"Did you lock the front door?" Matt demanded. The other nodded, and asked, "How about the back?"

"You just bet I did," was the fervent reply.

White Fang flattened his ears ingratiatingly, but remained where he was, making no attempt to approach.

"I'll have to take 'm ashore with me."

Matt made a couple of steps toward White Fang, but the latter slid away from him. The dog-musher made a rush of it, and White Fang dodged between the legs of a group of men. Ducking, turning, doubling, he slid about the deck, eluding the other's efforts to capture him.

But when the love-master spoke, White Fang came to him with prompt obedience.

"Won't come to the hand that's fed 'm all these months," the dog-musher muttered resentfully. "And you—you ain't never fed 'm after them first days of gettin' acquainted. I'm blamed if I can see how he works it out that you're the boss."

Scott, who had been patting White Fang, suddenly bent closer and pointed out fresh-made cuts on his muzzle, and a gash between the eyes.

Matt bent over and passed his hand along White Fang's belly.

"We plump forgot the window. He's all cut an' gouged underneath. Must 'a' butted clean through it, b'gosh!"

But Weedon Scott was not listening. He was thinking rapidly. The *Aurora's* whistle hooted a final announcement of departure. Men were scurrying down the gang-plank to the shore. Matt loosened the bandana from his own neck and started to put it around White Fang's. Scott grasped the dog-musher's hand.

"Good-bye, Matt, old man. About the wolf—you needn't write. You see, I've . . . !"

"What!" the dog-musher exploded. "You don't mean to say . . .?"

"The very thing I mean. Here's your bandana. I'll write to you about him."

Matt paused halfway down the gang-plank.

"He'll never stand the climate!" he shouted back. "Unless you clip 'm in warm weather!"

The gang-plank was hauled in, and the *Aurora* swung out from the bank. Weedon Scott waved a last good-bye. Then he turned and bent over White Fang, standing by his side.

"Now growl, damn you, growl," he said, as he patted the responsive head and rubbed the flattening ears.

CHAPTER II—THE SOUTHLAND

White Fang landed from the steamer in San Francisco. He was appalled. Deep in him, below any reasoning process or act of consciousness, he had associated power with godhead. And never had the white men seemed such marvellous gods as now, when he trod the slimy pavement of San Francisco. The log cabins he had known were replaced by towering buildings. The streets were crowded with perils—waggons, carts, automobiles; great, straining horses pulling huge trucks; and monstrous cable and electric cars hooting and clanging through the midst, screeching their insistent menace after the manner of the lynxes he had known in the northern woods.

All this was the manifestation of power. Through it all, behind it all, was man, governing and controlling, expressing himself, as of old, by his mastery over matter. It was colossal, stunning. White Fang was awed. Fear sat upon him. As in his cubhood he had been made to feel his smallness and puniness on the day he first came in from the Wild to the village of Grey Beaver, so now, in his full-grown stature and pride of strength, he was made to feel small and puny. And there were so many gods! He was made dizzy by the swarming of them. The thunder of the streets smote upon his ears. He was bewildered by the tremendous and endless rush and movement of things. As never before, he felt his dependence on the love-master, close at whose heels he followed, no matter what happened never losing sight of him.

But White Fang was to have no more than a nightmare vision of the city—an experience that was like a bad dream, unreal and terrible, that haunted him for long after in his dreams. He was put into a baggage-car by the master, chained in a corner in the midst of heaped trunks and valises. Here a squat and brawny god held sway, with much noise, hurling trunks and boxes about, dragging them in through the door and tossing them into the piles, or flinging them out of the door, smashing and crashing, to other gods who awaited them.

And here, in this inferno of luggage, was White Fang deserted by the master. Or at least White Fang thought he was deserted, until he smelled out the master's canvas clothes-bags alongside of him, and proceeded to mount guard over them.

"'Bout time you come," growled the god of the car, an hour later, when Weedon Scott appeared at the door. "That dog of yourn won't let me lay a finger on your stuff."

White Fang emerged from the car. He was astonished. The nightmare city was gone. The car had been to him no more than a room in a house, and when he had entered it the city had been all around him. In the interval the city had disappeared. The roar of it no longer dinned upon his ears. Before him was smiling country, streaming with sunshine, lazy with quietude. But he had little time to marvel at the transformation. He accepted it as he accepted all the unaccountable doings and manifestations of the gods. It was their way.

There was a carriage waiting. A man and a woman approached the master. The woman's arms went out and clutched the master around the neck—a hostile act! The next moment Weedon Scott had torn loose from the embrace and closed with White Fang, who had become a snarling, raging demon.

"It's all right, mother," Scott was saying as he kept tight hold of White Fang and placated him. "He thought you were going to injure me, and he wouldn't stand for it. It's all right. It's all right. He'll learn soon enough."

"And in the meantime I may be permitted to love my son when his dog is not around," she laughed, though she was pale and weak from the fright.

She looked at White Fang, who snarled and bristled and glared malevolently.

"He'll have to learn, and he shall, without postponement," Scott said.

He spoke softly to White Fang until he had quieted him, then his voice became firm.

"Down, sir! Down with you!"

This had been one of the things taught him by the master, and White Fang obeyed, though he lay down reluctantly and sullenly.

"Now, mother."

Scott opened his arms to her, but kept his eyes on White Fang.

"Down!" he warned. "Down!"

White Fang, bristling silently, half-crouching as he rose, sank back and watched the hostile act repeated. But no harm came of it, nor of the embrace from the strange man-god that followed. Then the clothes-bags were taken into the carriage, the strange gods and the love-master followed, and White Fang pursued, now running vigilantly behind, now bristling up to the running horses and warning them that he was there to see that no harm befell the god they dragged so swiftly across the earth.

At the end of fifteen minutes, the carriage swung in through a stone gateway and on between a double row of arched and interlacing walnut trees. On either side stretched lawns, their broad sweep broken here and there by great sturdy-limbed oaks. In the near distance, in contrast with the young-green of the tended grass, sunburnt hay-fields showed tan and gold; while beyond were the tawny hills and upland pastures. From the head of the lawn, on the first soft swell from the valley-level, looked down the deep-porched, many-windowed house.

Little opportunity was given White Fang to see all this. Hardly had the carriage entered the grounds, when he was set upon by a sheep-dog, bright-eyed, sharp-muzzled, righteously indignant and angry. It was between him and the master, cutting him off. White Fang snarled no warning, but his hair bristled as he made his silent and deadly rush. This rush was never completed. He halted with awkward abruptness, with stiff fore-legs bracing himself against his momentum, almost sitting down on his haunches, so desirous was he of avoiding contact with the dog he was in the act of attacking. It was a female, and the law of his kind thrust a barrier between. For him to attack her would require nothing less than a violation of his instinct.

But with the sheep-dog it was otherwise. Being a female, she possessed no such instinct. On the other hand, being a sheep-dog, her instinctive fear of the Wild, and especially of the wolf, was unusually keen. White Fang was to her a wolf, the hereditary marauder who had preyed upon her flocks from the time sheep were first herded and guarded by some dim ancestor of hers. And so, as he abandoned his rush at her and braced himself to avoid the contact, she sprang upon him. He snarled involuntarily as he felt her teeth in his shoulder, but beyond this made no offer to hurt her. He backed away, stiff-legged with self-consciousness, and tried to go around her. He dodged this way and that, and curved and turned, but to no purpose. She remained always between him and the way he wanted to go.

"Here, Collie!" called the strange man in the carriage.

Weedon Scott laughed.

"Never mind, father. It is good discipline. White Fang will have to learn many things, and it's just as well that he begins now. He'll adjust himself all right."

The carriage drove on, and still Collie blocked White Fang's way. He tried to outrun her by leaving the drive and circling across the lawn but she ran on the inner and smaller circle, and was always there, facing him with her two rows of gleaming teeth. Back he circled, across the drive to the other lawn, and again she headed him off.

The carriage was bearing the master away. White Fang caught glimpses of it disappearing amongst the trees. The situation was desperate. He essayed another circle. She followed, running swiftly. And then, suddenly, he turned upon her. It was his old fighting trick. Shoulder to shoulder, he struck her squarely. Not only was she overthrown. So fast had she been running that she rolled along, now on her back, now on her side, as she struggled to stop, clawing gravel with her feet and crying shrilly her hurt pride and indignation.

White Fang did not wait. The way was clear, and that was all he had wanted. She took after him, never ceasing her outcry. It was the straightaway now, and when it came to real running, White Fang could teach her things.

501

She ran frantically, hysterically, straining to the utmost, advertising the effort she was making with every leap: and all the time White Fang slid smoothly away from her silently, without effort, gliding like a ghost over the ground.

As he rounded the house to the *porte-cochère*, he came upon the carriage. It had stopped, and the master was alighting. At this moment, still running at top speed, White Fang became suddenly aware of an attack from the side. It was a deer-hound rushing upon him. White Fang tried to face it. But he was going too fast, and the hound was too close. It struck him on the side; and such was his forward momentum and the unexpectedness of it, White Fang was hurled to the ground and rolled clear over. He came out of the tangle a spectacle of malignancy, ears flattened back, lips writhing, nose wrinkling, his teeth clipping together as the fangs barely missed the hound's soft throat.

The master was running up, but was too far away; and it was Collie that saved the hound's life. Before White Fang could spring in and deliver the fatal stroke, and just as he was in the act of springing in, Collie arrived. She had been out-manoeuvred and out-run, to say nothing of her having been unceremoniously tumbled in the gravel, and her arrival was like that of a tornado—made up of offended dignity, justifiable wrath, and instinctive hatred for this marauder from the Wild. She struck White Fang at right angles in the midst of his spring, and again he was knocked off his feet and rolled over.

The next moment the master arrived, and with one hand held White Fang, while the father called off the dogs.

"I say, this is a pretty warm reception for a poor lone wolf from the Arctic," the master said, while White Fang calmed down under his caressing hand. "In all his life he's only been known once to go off his feet, and here he's been rolled twice in thirty seconds."

The carriage had driven away, and other strange gods had appeared from out the house. Some of these stood respectfully at a distance; but two of them, women, perpetrated the hostile act of clutching the master around the neck. White Fang, however, was beginning to tolerate this act. No harm seemed to come of it, while the noises the gods made were certainly not threatening. These gods also made overtures to White Fang, but he warned them off with a snarl, and the master did likewise with word of mouth. At such times White Fang leaned in close against the master's legs and received reassuring pats on the head.

The hound, under the command, "Dick! Lie down, sir!" had gone up the steps and lain down to one side of the porch, still growling and keeping a sullen watch on the intruder. Collie had been taken in charge by one of the woman-gods, who held arms around her neck and petted and caressed her; but Collie was very much perplexed and worried, whining and restless, outraged by the permitted presence of this wolf and confident that the gods were making a mistake.

All the gods started up the steps to enter the house. White Fang followed closely at the master's heels. Dick, on the porch, growled, and White Fang, on the steps, bristled and growled back.

"Take Collie inside and leave the two of them to fight it out," suggested Scott's father. "After that they'll be friends."

"Then White Fang, to show his friendship, will have to be chief mourner at the funeral," laughed the master.

The elder Scott looked incredulously, first at White Fang, then at Dick, and finally at his son.

"You mean . . .?"

Weedon nodded his head. "I mean just that. You'd have a dead Dick inside one minute—two minutes at the farthest."

He turned to White Fang. "Come on, you wolf. It's you that'll have to come inside."

White Fang walked stiff-legged up the steps and across the porch, with tail rigidly erect, keeping his eyes on Dick to guard against a flank attack, and at the same time prepared for whatever fierce manifestation of the unknown that might pounce out upon him from the interior of the house. But no thing of fear pounced out, and when he had gained the inside he scouted carefully around, looking at it and finding it not. Then he lay down with a contented grunt at the master's feet, observing all that went on, ever ready to spring to his feet and fight for life with the terrors he felt must lurk under the trap-roof of the dwelling.

CHAPTER III—THE GOD'S DOMAIN

Not only was White Fang adaptable by nature, but he had travelled much, and knew the meaning and necessity of adjustment. Here, in Sierra Vista, which was the name of Judge Scott's place, White Fang quickly began to make himself at home. He had no further serious trouble with the dogs. They knew more about the ways of the Southland gods than did he, and in their eyes he had qualified when he accompanied the gods inside the house. Wolf that he was, and unprecedented as it was, the gods had sanctioned his presence, and they, the dogs of the gods, could only recognise this sanction.

Dick, perforce, had to go through a few stiff formalities at first, after which he calmly accepted White Fang as an addition to the premises. Had Dick had his way, they would have been good friends. All but White Fang was averse to friendship. All he asked of other dogs was to be let alone. His whole life he had kept aloof from his kind, and he still desired to keep aloof. Dick's overtures bothered him, so he snarled Dick away. In the north he had learned the lesson that he must let the master's dogs alone, and he did not forget that lesson now. But he insisted on his own privacy and self-seclusion, and so thoroughly ignored Dick that that good-natured creature finally gave him up and scarcely took as much interest in him as in the hitching-post near the stable.

Not so with Collie. While she accepted him because it was the mandate of the gods, that was no reason that she should leave him in peace. Woven into her being was the memory of countless crimes he and his had perpetrated against her ancestry. Not in a day nor a generation were the ravaged sheepfolds to be forgotten. All this was a spur to her, pricking her to retaliation. She could not fly in the face of the gods who permitted him, but that did not prevent her from making life miserable for him in petty ways. A feud, ages old, was between them, and she, for one, would see to it that he was reminded.

So Collie took advantage of her sex to pick upon White Fang and maltreat him. His instinct would not permit him to attack her, while her persistence would not permit him to ignore her. When she rushed at him he turned his fur-protected shoulder to her sharp teeth and walked away stiff-legged and stately. When she forced him too hard, he was compelled to go about in a circle, his shoulder presented to her, his head turned from her, and on his face and in his eyes a patient and bored expression. Sometimes, however, a nip on his hind-quarters hastened his retreat and made it anything but stately. But as a rule he managed to maintain a dignity that was almost solemnity. He ignored her existence whenever it was possible, and made it a point to keep out of her way. When he saw or heard her coming, he got up and walked off.

There was much in other matters for White Fang to learn. Life in the Northland was simplicity itself when compared with the complicated affairs of Sierra Vista. First of all, he had to learn the family of the master. In a way he was prepared to do this. As Mit-sah and Kloo-kooch had belonged to Grey Beaver, sharing his food, his fire, and his blankets, so now, at Sierra Vista, belonged to the love-master all the denizens of the house.

But in this matter there was a difference, and many differences. Sierra Vista was a far vaster affair than the tepee of Grey Beaver. There were many persons to be considered. There was Judge Scott, and there was his wife. There were the master's two sisters, Beth and Mary. There was his wife, Alice, and then there were his children, Weedon and Maud, toddlers of four and six. There was no way for anybody to tell him about all these people, and of blood-ties and relationship he knew nothing whatever and never would be capable of knowing. Yet he quickly worked it out that all of them belonged to the master. Then, by observation, whenever opportunity offered, by study of action, speech, and the very intonations of the voice, he slowly learned the intimacy and the degree of favour they enjoyed with the master. And by this ascertained standard, White Fang treated them accordingly. What was of value to the master he valued; what was dear to the master was to be cherished by White Fang and guarded carefully.

Thus it was with the two children. All his life he had disliked children. He hated and feared their hands. The lessons were not tender that he had learned of their tyranny and cruelty in the days of the Indian villages.

When Weedon and Maud had first approached him, he growled warningly and looked malignant. A cuff from the master and a sharp word had then compelled him to permit their caresses, though he growled and growled under their tiny hands, and in the growl there was no crooning note. Later, he observed that the boy and girl were of great value in the master's eyes. Then it was that no cuff nor sharp word was necessary before they could pat him.

Yet White Fang was never effusively affectionate. He yielded to the master's children with an ill but honest grace, and endured their fooling as one would endure a painful operation. When he could no longer endure, he would get up and stalk determinedly away from them. But after a time, he grew even to like the children. Still he was not demonstrative. He would not go up to them. On the other hand, instead of walking away at sight of them, he waited for them to come to him. And still later, it was noticed that a pleased light came into his eyes when he saw them approaching, and that he looked after them with an appearance of curious regret when they left him for other amusements.

All this was a matter of development, and took time. Next in his regard, after the children, was Judge Scott. There were two reasons, possibly, for this. First, he was evidently a valuable possession of the master's, and next, he was undemonstrative. White Fang liked to lie at his feet on the wide porch when he read the newspaper, from time to time favouring White Fang with a look or a word—untroublesome tokens that he recognised White Fang's presence and existence. But this was only when the master was not around. When the master appeared, all other beings ceased to exist so far as White Fang was concerned.

White Fang allowed all the members of the family to pet him and make much of him; but he never gave to them what he gave to the master. No caress of theirs could put the love-croon into his throat, and, try as they would, they could never persuade him into snuggling against them. This expression of abandon and surrender, of absolute trust, he reserved for the master alone. In fact, he never regarded the members of the family in any other light than possessions of the love-master.

Also White Fang had early come to differentiate between the family and the servants of the household. The latter were afraid of him, while he merely refrained from attacking them. This because he considered that they were likewise possessions of the master. Between White Fang and them existed a neutrality and no more. They cooked for the master and washed the dishes and did other things just as Matt had done up in the Klondike. They were, in short, appurtenances of the household.

Outside the household there was even more for White Fang to learn. The master's domain was wide and complex, yet it had its metes and bounds. The land itself ceased at the county road. Outside was the common domain of all gods—the roads and streets. Then inside other fences were the particular domains of other gods. A myriad laws governed all these things and determined conduct; yet he did not know the speech of the gods, nor was there any way for him to learn save by experience. He obeyed his natural impulses until they ran him counter to some law. When this had been done a few times, he learned the law and after that observed it.

But most potent in his education was the cuff of the master's hand, the censure of the master's voice. Because of White Fang's very great love, a cuff from the master hurt him far more than any beating Grey Beaver or Beauty Smith had ever given him. They had hurt only the flesh of him; beneath the flesh the spirit had still raged, splendid and invincible. But with the master the cuff was always too light to hurt the flesh. Yet it went deeper. It was an expression of the master's disapproval, and White Fang's spirit wilted under it.

In point of fact, the cuff was rarely administered. The master's voice was sufficient. By it White Fang knew whether he did right or not. By it he trimmed his conduct and adjusted his actions. It was the compass by which he steered and learned to chart the manners of a new land and life.

In the Northland, the only domesticated animal was the dog. All other animals lived in the Wild, and were, when not too formidable, lawful spoil for any dog. All his days White Fang had foraged among the live things for food. It did not enter his head that in the Southland it was otherwise. But this he was to learn early in his residence in Santa Clara Valley. Sauntering around the corner of the house in the early morning, he came upon a chicken that had escaped from the chicken-yard. White Fang's natural impulse was to eat it. A couple of bounds, a flash of teeth and a frightened squawk, and he had scooped in the adventurous fowl. It was farm-bred and fat and tender; and White Fang licked his chops and decided that such fare was good.

Later in the day, he chanced upon another stray chicken near the stables. One of the grooms ran to the rescue. He did not know White Fang's breed, so for weapon he took a light buggy-whip. At the first cut of the whip, White Fang left the chicken for the man. A club might have stopped White Fang, but not a whip. Silently, without flinching, he took a second cut in his forward rush, and as he leaped for the throat the groom cried out, "My God!" and staggered backward. He dropped the whip and shielded his throat with his arms. In consequence, his forearm was ripped open to the bone.

The man was badly frightened. It was not so much White Fang's ferocity as it was his silence that unnerved the groom. Still protecting his throat and face with his torn and bleeding arm, he tried to retreat to the barn. And it would have gone hard with him had not Collie appeared on the scene. As she had saved Dick's life, she now saved the groom's. She rushed upon White Fang in frenzied wrath. She had been right. She had known better than the blundering gods. All her suspicions were justified. Here was the ancient marauder up to his old tricks again.

The groom escaped into the stables, and White Fang backed away before Collie's wicked teeth, or presented his shoulder to them and circled round and round. But Collie did not give over, as was her wont, after a decent interval of chastisement. On the contrary, she grew more excited and angry every moment, until, in the end, White Fang flung dignity to the winds and frankly fled away from her across the fields.

"He'll learn to leave chickens alone," the master said. "But I can't give him the lesson until I catch him in the act."

Two nights later came the act, but on a more generous scale than the master had anticipated. White Fang had observed closely the chicken-yards and the habits of the chickens. In the night-time, after they had gone to roost, he climbed to the top of a pile of newly hauled lumber. From there he gained the roof of a chicken-house, passed over the ridgepole and dropped to the ground inside. A moment later he was inside the house, and the slaughter began.

In the morning, when the master came out on to the porch, fifty white Leghorn hens, laid out in a row by the groom, greeted his eyes. He whistled to himself, softly, first with surprise, and then, at the end, with admiration. His eyes were likewise greeted by White Fang, but about the latter there were no signs of shame nor guilt. He carried himself with pride, as though, forsooth, he had achieved a deed praiseworthy and meritorious. There was about him no consciousness of sin. The master's lips tightened as he faced the disagreeable task. Then he talked harshly to the unwitting culprit, and in his voice there was nothing but godlike wrath. Also, he held White Fang's nose down to the slain hens, and at the same time cuffed him soundly.

White Fang never raided a chicken-roost again. It was against the law, and he had learned it. Then the master took him into the chicken-yards. White Fang's natural impulse, when he saw the live food fluttering about him and under his very nose, was to spring upon it. He obeyed the impulse, but was checked by the master's voice. They continued in the yards for half an hour. Time and again the impulse surged over White Fang, and each time, as he yielded to it, he was checked by the master's voice. Thus it was he learned the law, and ere he left the domain of the chickens, he had learned to ignore their existence.

"You can never cure a chicken-killer." Judge Scott shook his head sadly at luncheon table, when his son narrated the lesson he had given White Fang. "Once they've got the habit and the taste of blood . . ." Again he shook his head sadly.

But Weedon Scott did not agree with his father. "I'll tell you what I'll do," he challenged finally. "I'll lock White Fang in with the chickens all afternoon."

"But think of the chickens," objected the judge.

"And furthermore," the son went on, "for every chicken he kills, I'll pay you one dollar gold coin of the realm."

"But you should penalise father, too," interpose Beth.

Her sister seconded her, and a chorus of approval arose from around the table. Judge Scott nodded his head in agreement.

"All right." Weedon Scott pondered for a moment. "And if, at the end of the afternoon White Fang hasn't harmed a chicken, for every ten minutes of the time he has spent in the yard, you will have to say to him, gravely and with deliberation, just as if you were sitting on the bench and solemnly passing judgment, 'White Fang, you are smarter than I thought.'"

From hidden points of vantage the family watched the performance. But it was a fizzle. Locked in the yard and there deserted by the master, White Fang lay down and went to sleep. Once he got up and walked over to the trough for a drink of water. The chickens he calmly ignored. So far as he was concerned they did not exist. At four o'clock he executed a running jump, gained the roof of the chicken-house and leaped to the ground outside, whence he sauntered gravely to the house. He had learned the law. And on the porch, before the delighted family, Judge Scott, face to face with White Fang, said slowly and solemnly, sixteen times, "White Fang, you are smarter than I thought."

But it was the multiplicity of laws that befuddled White Fang and often brought him into disgrace. He had to learn that he must not touch the chickens that belonged to other gods. Then there were cats, and rabbits, and turkeys; all these he must let alone. In fact, when he had but partly learned the law, his impression was that he must leave all live things alone. Out in the back-pasture, a quail could flutter up under his nose unharmed. All tense and trembling with eagerness and desire, he mastered his instinct and stood still. He was obeying the will of the gods.

And then, one day, again out in the back-pasture, he saw Dick start a jackrabbit and run it. The master himself was looking on and did not interfere. Nay, he encouraged White Fang to join in the chase. And thus he learned that there was no taboo on jackrabbits. In the end he worked out the complete law. Between him and all domestic animals there must be no hostilities. If not amity, at least neutrality must obtain. But the other animals—the squirrels, and quail, and cottontails, were creatures of the Wild who had never yielded allegiance to man. They were the lawful prey of any dog. It was only the tame that the gods protected, and between the tame deadly strife was not permitted. The gods held the power of life and death over their subjects, and the gods were jealous of their power.

Life was complex in the Santa Clara Valley after the simplicities of the Northland. And the chief thing demanded by these intricacies of civilisation was control, restraint—a poise of self that was as delicate as the fluttering of gossamer wings and at the same time as rigid as steel. Life had a thousand faces, and White Fang found he must meet them all—thus, when he went to town, in to San Jose, running behind the carriage or loafing about the streets when the carriage stopped. Life flowed past him, deep and wide and varied, continually impinging upon his senses, demanding of him instant and endless adjustments and correspondences, and compelling him, almost always, to suppress his natural impulses.

There were butcher-shops where meat hung within reach. This meat he must not touch. There were cats at the houses the master visited that must be let alone. And there were dogs everywhere that snarled at him and that he must not attack. And then, on the crowded sidewalks there were persons innumerable whose attention he attracted. They would stop and look at him, point him out to one another, examine him, talk of him, and, worst of all, pat him. And these perilous contacts from all these strange hands he must endure. Yet this endurance he achieved. Furthermore, he got over being awkward and self-conscious. In a lofty way he received the attentions of the multitudes of strange gods. With condescension he accepted their condescension. On the other hand, there was something about him that prevented great familiarity. They patted him on the head and passed on, contented and pleased with their own daring.

But it was not all easy for White Fang. Running behind the carriage in the outskirts of San Jose, he encountered certain small boys who made a practice of flinging stones at him. Yet he knew that it was not permitted him to pursue and drag them down. Here he was compelled to violate his instinct of self-preservation, and violate it he did, for he was becoming tame and qualifying himself for civilisation.

Nevertheless, White Fang was not quite satisfied with the arrangement. He had no abstract ideas about justice and fair play. But there is a certain sense of equity that resides in life, and it was this sense in him that resented the unfairness of his being permitted no defence against the stone-throwers. He forgot that in the covenant entered into between him and the gods they were pledged to care for him and defend him. But one day the master sprang from the carriage, whip in hand, and gave the stone-throwers a thrashing. After that they threw stones no more, and White Fang understood and was satisfied.

One other experience of similar nature was his. On the way to town, hanging around the saloon at the cross-roads, were three dogs that made a practice of rushing out upon him when he went by. Knowing his deadly method of fighting, the master had never ceased impressing upon White Fang the law that he must not fight. As a result, having learned the lesson well, White Fang was hard put whenever he passed the cross-roads saloon. After the first rush, each time, his snarl kept the three dogs at a distance but they trailed along behind, yelping and bickering and insulting him. This endured for some time. The men at the saloon even urged the dogs on to attack White Fang. One day they openly sicked the dogs on him. The master stopped the carriage.

"Go to it," he said to White Fang.

But White Fang could not believe. He looked at the master, and he looked at the dogs. Then he looked back eagerly and questioningly at the master.

The master nodded his head. "Go to them, old fellow. Eat them up."

White Fang no longer hesitated. He turned and leaped silently among his enemies. All three faced him. There was a great snarling and growling, a clashing of teeth and a flurry of bodies. The dust of the road arose in a cloud and screened the battle. But at the end of several minutes two dogs were struggling in the dirt and the third was in full flight. He leaped a ditch, went through a rail fence, and fled across a field. White Fang followed, sliding over the ground in wolf fashion and with wolf speed, swiftly and without noise, and in the centre of the field he dragged down and slew the dog.

With this triple killing his main troubles with dogs ceased. The word went up and down the valley, and men saw to it that their dogs did not molest the Fighting Wolf.

CHAPTER IV—THE CALL OF KIND

The months came and went. There was plenty of food and no work in the Southland, and White Fang lived fat and prosperous and happy. Not alone was he in the geographical Southland, for he was in the Southland of life. Human kindness was like a sun shining upon him, and he flourished like a flower planted in good soil.

And yet he remained somehow different from other dogs. He knew the law even better than did the dogs that had known no other life, and he observed the law more punctiliously; but still there was about him a suggestion of lurking ferocity, as though the Wild still lingered in him and the wolf in him merely slept.

He never chummed with other dogs. Lonely he had lived, so far as his kind was concerned, and lonely he would continue to live. In his puppyhood, under the persecution of Lip-lip and the puppy-pack, and in his fighting days with Beauty Smith, he had acquired a fixed aversion for dogs. The natural course of his life had been diverted, and, recoiling from his kind, he had clung to the human.

Besides, all Southland dogs looked upon him with suspicion. He aroused in them their instinctive fear of the Wild, and they greeted him always with snarl and growl and belligerent hatred. He, on the other hand, learned that it was not necessary to use his teeth upon them. His naked fangs and writhing lips were uniformly efficacious, rarely failing to send a bellowing on-rushing dog back on its haunches.

But there was one trial in White Fang's life—Collie. She never gave him a moment's peace. She was not so amenable to the law as he. She defied all efforts of the master to make her become friends with White Fang. Ever in his ears was sounding her sharp and nervous snarl. She had never forgiven him the chicken-killing episode, and persistently held to the belief that his intentions were bad. She found him guilty before the act, and treated him accordingly. She became a pest to him, like a policeman following him around the stable and the hounds, and, if he even so much as glanced curiously at a pigeon or chicken, bursting into an outcry of indignation and wrath. His favourite way of ignoring her was to lie down, with his head on his fore-paws, and pretend sleep. This always dumfounded and silenced her.

With the exception of Collie, all things went well with White Fang. He had learned control and poise, and he knew the law. He achieved a staidness, and calmness, and philosophic tolerance. He no longer lived in a hostile environment. Danger and hurt and death did not lurk everywhere about him. In time, the unknown, as a thing of terror and menace ever impending, faded away. Life was soft and easy. It flowed along smoothly, and neither fear nor foe lurked by the way.

He missed the snow without being aware of it. "An unduly long summer," would have been his thought had he thought about it; as it was, he merely missed the snow in a vague, subconscious way. In the same fashion, especially in the heat of summer when he suffered from the sun, he experienced faint longings for the Northland. Their only effect upon him, however, was to make him uneasy and restless without his knowing what was the matter.

White Fang had never been very demonstrative. Beyond his snuggling and the throwing of a crooning note into his love-growl, he had no way of expressing his love. Yet it was given him to discover a third way. He had always been susceptible to the laughter of the gods. Laughter had affected him with madness, made him frantic with rage. But he did not have it in him to be angry with the love-master, and when that god elected to laugh at him in a good-natured, bantering way, he was nonplussed. He could feel the pricking and stinging of the old anger as it strove to rise up in him, but it strove against love. He could not be angry; yet he had to do something. At first he was dignified, and the master laughed the harder. Then he tried to be more dignified, and the master laughed harder than before. In the end, the master laughed him out of his dignity. His jaws slightly parted, his lips lifted a little, and a quizzical expression that was more love than humour came into his eyes. He had learned to laugh.

Likewise he learned to romp with the master, to be tumbled down and rolled over, and be the victim of innumerable rough tricks. In return he feigned anger, bristling and growling ferociously, and clipping his teeth together in snaps that had all the seeming of deadly intention. But he never forgot himself. Those snaps were always delivered on the empty air. At the end of such a romp, when blow and cuff and snap and snarl were fast and furious, they would break off suddenly and stand several feet apart, glaring at each other. And then, just as suddenly, like the sun rising on a stormy sea, they would begin to laugh. This would always culminate with the master's arms going around White Fang's neck and shoulders while the latter crooned and growled his love-song.

But nobody else ever romped with White Fang. He did not permit it. He stood on his dignity, and when they attempted it, his warning snarl and bristling mane were anything but playful. That he allowed the master these liberties was no reason that he should be a common dog, loving here and loving there, everybody's property for a romp and good time. He loved with single heart and refused to cheapen himself or his love.

The master went out on horseback a great deal, and to accompany him was one of White Fang's chief duties in life. In the Northland he had evidenced his fealty by toiling in the harness; but there were no sleds in the Southland, nor did dogs pack burdens on their backs. So he rendered fealty in the new way, by running with the master's horse. The longest day never played White Fang out. His was the gait of the wolf, smooth, tireless and effortless, and at the end of fifty miles he would come in jauntily ahead of the horse.

It was in connection with the riding, that White Fang achieved one other mode of expression—remarkable in that he did it but twice in all his life. The first time occurred when the master was trying to teach a spirited thoroughbred the method of opening and closing gates without the rider's dismounting. Time and again and many times he ranged the horse up to the gate in the effort to close it and each time the horse became frightened and backed and plunged away. It grew more nervous and excited every moment. When it reared, the master put the spurs to it and made it drop its fore-legs back to earth, whereupon it would begin kicking with its hind-legs. White Fang watched the performance with increasing anxiety until he could contain himself no longer, when he sprang in front of the horse and barked savagely and warningly.

Though he often tried to bark thereafter, and the master encouraged him, he succeeded only once, and then it was not in the master's presence. A scamper across the pasture, a jackrabbit rising suddenly under the horse's feet, a violent sheer, a stumble, a fall to earth, and a broken leg for the master, was the cause of it. White Fang sprang in a rage at the throat of the offending horse, but was checked by the master's voice.

"Home! Go home!" the master commanded when he had ascertained his injury.

White Fang was disinclined to desert him. The master thought of writing a note, but searched his pockets vainly for pencil and paper. Again he commanded White Fang to go home.

The latter regarded him wistfully, started away, then returned and whined softly. The master talked to him gently but seriously, and he cocked his ears, and listened with painful intentness.

"That's all right, old fellow, you just run along home," ran the talk. "Go on home and tell them what's happened to me. Home with you, you wolf. Get along home!"

White Fang knew the meaning of "home," and though he did not understand the remainder of the master's language, he knew it was his will that he should go home. He turned and trotted reluctantly away. Then he stopped, undecided, and looked back over his shoulder.

"Go home!" came the sharp command, and this time he obeyed.

The family was on the porch, taking the cool of the afternoon, when White Fang arrived. He came in among them, panting, covered with dust.

"Weedon's back," Weedon's mother announced.

The children welcomed White Fang with glad cries and ran to meet him. He avoided them and passed down the porch, but they cornered him against a rocking-chair and the railing. He growled and tried to push by them. Their mother looked apprehensively in their direction.

"I confess, he makes me nervous around the children," she said. "I have a dread that he will turn upon them unexpectedly some day."

Growling savagely, White Fang sprang out of the corner, overturning the boy and the girl. The mother called them to her and comforted them, telling them not to bother White Fang.

"A wolf is a wolf!" commented Judge Scott. "There is no trusting one."

"But he is not all wolf," interposed Beth, standing for her brother in his absence.

"You have only Weedon's opinion for that," rejoined the judge. "He merely surmises that there is some strain of dog in White Fang; but as he will tell you himself, he knows nothing about it. As for his appearance—"

He did not finish his sentence. White Fang stood before him, growling fiercely.

"Go away! Lie down, sir!" Judge Scott commanded.

White Fang turned to the love-master's wife. She screamed with fright as he seized her dress in his teeth and dragged on it till the frail fabric tore away. By this time he had become the centre of interest.

He had ceased from his growling and stood, head up, looking into their faces. His throat worked spasmodically, but made no sound, while he struggled with all his body, convulsed with the effort to rid himself of the incommunicable something that strained for utterance.

"I hope he is not going mad," said Weedon's mother. "I told Weedon that I was afraid the warm climate would not agree with an Arctic animal."

"He's trying to speak, I do believe," Beth announced.

At this moment speech came to White Fang, rushing up in a great burst of barking.

"Something has happened to Weedon," his wife said decisively.

They were all on their feet now, and White Fang ran down the steps, looking back for them to follow. For the second and last time in his life he had barked and made himself understood.

After this event he found a warmer place in the hearts of the Sierra Vista people, and even the groom whose arm he had slashed admitted that he was a wise dog even if he was a wolf. Judge Scott still held to the same opinion, and proved it to everybody's dissatisfaction by measurements and descriptions taken from the encyclopaedia and various works on natural history.

The days came and went, streaming their unbroken sunshine over the Santa Clara Valley. But as they grew shorter and White Fang's second winter in the Southland came on, he made a strange discovery. Collie's teeth were no longer sharp. There was a playfulness about her nips and a gentleness that prevented them from really hurting him. He forgot that she had made life a burden to him, and when she disported herself around him he responded solemnly, striving to be playful and becoming no more than ridiculous.

One day she led him off on a long chase through the back-pasture land into the woods. It was the afternoon that the master was to ride, and White Fang knew it. The horse stood saddled and waiting at the door. White Fang hesitated. But there was that in him deeper than all the law he had learned, than the customs that had moulded him, than his love for the master, than the very will to live of himself; and when, in the moment of his indecision, Collie nipped him and scampered off, he turned and followed after. The master rode alone that day; and in the woods, side by side, White Fang ran with Collie, as his mother, Kiche, and old One Eye had run long years before in the silent Northland forest.

CHAPTER V—THE SLEEPING WOLF

It was about this time that the newspapers were full of the daring escape of a convict from San Quentin prison. He was a ferocious man. He had been ill-made in the making. He had not been born right, and he had not been helped any by the moulding he had received at the hands of society. The hands of society are harsh, and this man was a striking sample of its handiwork. He was a beast—a human beast, it is true, but nevertheless so terrible a beast that he can best be characterised as carnivorous.

In San Quentin prison he had proved incorrigible. Punishment failed to break his spirit. He could die dumb-mad and fighting to the last, but he could not live and be beaten. The more fiercely he fought, the more harshly society handled him, and the only effect of harshness was to make him fiercer. Strait-jackets, starvation, and beatings and clubbings were the wrong treatment for Jim Hall; but it was the treatment he received. It was the treatment he had received from the time he was a little pulpy boy in a San Francisco slum—soft clay in the hands of society and ready to be formed into something.

It was during Jim Hall's third term in prison that he encountered a guard that was almost as great a beast as he. The guard treated him unfairly, lied about him to the warden, lost his credits, persecuted him. The difference between them was that the guard carried a bunch of keys and a revolver. Jim Hall had only his naked hands and his teeth. But he sprang upon the guard one day and used his teeth on the other's throat just like any jungle animal.

After this, Jim Hall went to live in the incorrigible cell. He lived there three years. The cell was of iron, the floor, the walls, the roof. He never left this cell. He never saw the sky nor the sunshine. Day was a twilight and night was a black silence. He was in an iron tomb, buried alive. He saw no human face, spoke to no human thing. When his food was shoved in to him, he growled like a wild animal. He hated all things. For days and nights he bellowed his rage at the universe. For weeks and months he never made a sound, in the black silence eating his very soul. He was a man and a monstrosity, as fearful a thing of fear as ever gibbered in the visions of a maddened brain.

And then, one night, he escaped. The warders said it was impossible, but nevertheless the cell was empty, and half in half out of it lay the body of a dead guard. Two other dead guards marked his trail through the prison to the outer walls, and he had killed with his hands to avoid noise.

He was armed with the weapons of the slain guards—a live arsenal that fled through the hills pursued by the organised might of society. A heavy price of gold was upon his head. Avaricious farmers hunted him with shot-guns. His blood might pay off a mortgage or send a son to college. Public-spirited citizens took down their rifles and went out after him. A pack of bloodhounds followed the way of his bleeding feet. And the sleuth-hounds of the law, the paid fighting animals of society, with telephone, and telegraph, and special train, clung to his trail night and day.

Sometimes they came upon him, and men faced him like heroes, or stampeded through barbed-wire fences to the delight of the commonwealth reading the account at the breakfast table. It was after such encounters that the dead and wounded were carted back to the towns, and their places filled by men eager for the man-hunt.

And then Jim Hall disappeared. The bloodhounds vainly quested on the lost trail. Inoffensive ranchers in remote valleys were held up by armed men and compelled to identify themselves. While the remains of Jim Hall were discovered on a dozen mountain-sides by greedy claimants for blood-money.

In the meantime the newspapers were read at Sierra Vista, not so much with interest as with anxiety. The women were afraid. Judge Scott pooh-poohed and laughed, but not with reason, for it was in his last days on the bench that Jim Hall had stood before him and received sentence. And in open court-room, before all men, Jim Hall had proclaimed that the day would come when he would wreak vengeance on the Judge that sentenced him.

For once, Jim Hall was right. He was innocent of the crime for which he was sentenced. It was a case, in the parlance of thieves and police, of "rail-roading." Jim Hall was being "rail-roaded" to prison for a crime he had not committed. Because of the two prior convictions against him, Judge Scott imposed upon him a sentence of fifty years.

Judge Scott did not know all things, and he did not know that he was party to a police conspiracy, that the evidence was hatched and perjured, that Jim Hall was guiltless of the crime charged. And Jim Hall, on the other hand, did not know that Judge Scott was merely ignorant. Jim Hall believed that the judge knew all about it and was hand in glove with the police in the perpetration of the monstrous injustice. So it was, when the doom of fifty years of living death was uttered by Judge Scott, that Jim Hall, hating all things in the society that misused him, rose up and raged in the court-room until dragged down by half a dozen of his blue-coated enemies. To him, Judge Scott was the keystone in the arch of injustice, and upon Judge Scott he emptied the vials of his wrath and hurled the threats of his revenge yet to come. Then Jim Hall went to his living death . . . and escaped.

Of all this White Fang knew nothing. But between him and Alice, the master's wife, there existed a secret. Each night, after Sierra Vista had gone to bed, she rose and let in White Fang to sleep in the big hall. Now White Fang was not a house-dog, nor was he permitted to sleep in the house; so each morning, early, she slipped down and let him out before the family was awake.

On one such night, while all the house slept, White Fang awoke and lay very quietly. And very quietly he smelled the air and read the message it bore of a strange god's presence. And to his ears came sounds of the strange god's movements. White Fang burst into no furious outcry. It was not his way. The strange god walked softly, but more softly walked White Fang, for he had no clothes to rub against the flesh of his body. He followed silently. In the Wild he had hunted live meat that was infinitely timid, and he knew the advantage of surprise.

The strange god paused at the foot of the great staircase and listened, and White Fang was as dead, so without movement was he as he watched and waited. Up that staircase the way led to the love-master and to the love-master's dearest possessions. White Fang bristled, but waited. The strange god's foot lifted. He was beginning the ascent.

Then it was that White Fang struck. He gave no warning, with no snarl anticipated his own action. Into the air he lifted his body in the spring that landed him on the strange god's back. White Fang clung with his fore-paws to the man's shoulders, at the same time burying his fangs into the back of the man's neck. He clung on for a moment, long enough to drag the god over backward. Together they crashed to the floor. White Fang leaped clear, and, as the man struggled to rise, was in again with the slashing fangs.

Sierra Vista awoke in alarm. The noise from downstairs was as that of a score of battling fiends. There were revolver shots. A man's voice screamed once in horror and anguish. There was a great snarling and growling, and over all arose a smashing and crashing of furniture and glass.

But almost as quickly as it had arisen, the commotion died away. The struggle had not lasted more than three minutes. The frightened household clustered at the top of the stairway. From below, as from out an abyss of blackness, came up a gurgling sound, as of air bubbling through water. Sometimes this gurgle became sibilant, almost a whistle. But this, too, quickly died down and ceased. Then naught came up out of the blackness save a heavy panting of some creature struggling sorely for air.

Weedon Scott pressed a button, and the staircase and downstairs hall were flooded with light. Then he and Judge Scott, revolvers in hand, cautiously descended. There was no need for this caution. White Fang had done his work. In the midst of the wreckage of overthrown and smashed furniture, partly on his side, his face hidden by an arm, lay a man. Weedon Scott bent over, removed the arm and turned the man's face upward. A gaping throat explained the manner of his death.

"Jim Hall," said Judge Scott, and father and son looked significantly at each other.

Then they turned to White Fang. He, too, was lying on his side. His eyes were closed, but the lids slightly lifted in an effort to look at them as they bent over him, and the tail was perceptibly agitated in a vain effort to wag. Weedon Scott patted him, and his throat rumbled an acknowledging growl. But it was a weak growl at best, and it quickly ceased. His eyelids drooped and went shut, and his whole body seemed to relax and flatten out upon the floor.

"He's all in, poor devil," muttered the master.

"We'll see about that," asserted the Judge, as he started for the telephone.

"Frankly, he has one chance in a thousand," announced the surgeon, after he had worked an hour and a half on White Fang.

Dawn was breaking through the windows and dimming the electric lights. With the exception of the children, the whole family was gathered about the surgeon to hear his verdict.

"One broken hind-leg," he went on. "Three broken ribs, one at least of which has pierced the lungs. He has lost nearly all the blood in his body. There is a large likelihood of internal injuries. He must have been jumped upon. To say nothing of three bullet holes clear through him. One chance in a thousand is really optimistic. He hasn't a chance in ten thousand."

"But he mustn't lose any chance that might be of help to him," Judge Scott exclaimed. "Never mind expense. Put him under the X-ray—anything. Weedon, telegraph at once to San Francisco for Doctor Nichols. No reflection on you, doctor, you understand; but he must have the advantage of every chance."

The surgeon smiled indulgently. "Of course I understand. He deserves all that can be done for him. He must be nursed as you would nurse a human being, a sick child. And don't forget what I told you about temperature. I'll be back at ten o'clock again."

White Fang received the nursing. Judge Scott's suggestion of a trained nurse was indignantly clamoured down by the girls, who themselves undertook the task. And White Fang won out on the one chance in ten thousand denied him by the surgeon.

The latter was not to be censured for his misjudgment. All his life he had tended and operated on the soft humans of civilisation, who lived sheltered lives and had descended out of many sheltered generations. Compared with White Fang, they were frail and flabby, and clutched life without any strength in their grip. White Fang had come straight from the Wild, where the weak perish early and shelter is vouchsafed to none. In neither his father nor his mother was there any weakness, nor in the generations before them. A constitution of iron and the vitality of the Wild were White Fang's inheritance, and he clung to life, the whole of him and every part of him, in spirit and in flesh, with the tenacity that of old belonged to all creatures.

Bound down a prisoner, denied even movement by the plaster casts and bandages, White Fang lingered out the weeks. He slept long hours and dreamed much, and through his mind passed an unending pageant of Northland visions. All the ghosts of the past arose and were with him. Once again he lived in the lair with Kiche, crept trembling to the knees of Grey Beaver to tender his allegiance, ran for his life before Lip-lip and all the howling bedlam of the puppy-pack.

He ran again through the silence, hunting his living food through the months of famine; and again he ran at the head of the team, the gut-whips of Mit-sah and Grey Beaver snapping behind, their voices crying "Ra! Raa!" when they came to a narrow passage and the team closed together like a fan to go through. He lived again all his days with Beauty Smith and the fights he had fought. At such times he whimpered and snarled in his sleep, and they that looked on said that his dreams were bad.

But there was one particular nightmare from which he suffered— the clanking, clanging monsters of electric cars that were to him colossal screaming lynxes. He would lie in a screen of bushes, watching for a squirrel to venture far enough out on the ground from its tree-refuge. Then, when he sprang out upon it, it would transform itself into an electric car, menacing and terrible, towering over him like a mountain, screaming and clanging and spitting fire at him. It was the same when he challenged the hawk down out of the sky. Down out of the blue it would rush, as it dropped upon him changing itself into the ubiquitous electric car. Or again, he would be in the pen of Beauty Smith. Outside the pen, men would be gathering, and he knew that a fight was on. He watched the door for his antagonist to enter. The door would open, and thrust in upon him would come the awful electric car. A thousand times this occurred, and each time the terror it inspired was as vivid and great as ever.

Then came the day when the last bandage and the last plaster cast were taken off. It was a gala day. All Sierra Vista was gathered around. The master rubbed his ears, and he crooned his love-growl. The master's wife called him the "Blessed Wolf," which name was taken up with acclaim and all the women called him the Blessed Wolf.

He tried to rise to his feet, and after several attempts fell down from weakness. He had lain so long that his muscles had lost their cunning, and all the strength had gone out of them. He felt a little shame because of his weakness, as though, forsooth, he were failing the gods in the service he owed them. Because of this he made heroic efforts to arise and at last he stood on his four legs, tottering and swaying back and forth.

"The Blessed Wolf!" chorused the women.

Judge Scott surveyed them triumphantly.

"Out of your own mouths be it," he said. "Just as I contended right along. No mere dog could have done what he did. He's a wolf."

"A Blessed Wolf," amended the Judge's wife.

"Yes, Blessed Wolf," agreed the Judge. "And henceforth that shall be my name for him."

"He'll have to learn to walk again," said the surgeon; "so he might as well start in right now. It won't hurt him. Take him outside."

And outside he went, like a king, with all Sierra Vista about him and tending on him. He was very weak, and when he reached the lawn he lay down and rested for a while.

Then the procession started on, little spurts of strength coming into White Fang's muscles as he used them and the blood began to surge through them. The stables were reached, and there in the doorway, lay Collie, a half-dozen pudgy puppies playing about her in the sun.

White Fang looked on with a wondering eye. Collie snarled warningly at him, and he was careful to keep his distance. The master with his toe helped one sprawling puppy toward him. He bristled suspiciously, but the master warned him that all was well. Collie, clasped in the arms of one of the women, watched him jealously and with a snarl warned him that all was not well.

The puppy sprawled in front of him. He cocked his ears and watched it curiously. Then their noses touched, and he felt the warm little tongue of the puppy on his jowl. White Fang's tongue went out, he knew not why, and he licked the puppy's face.

Hand-clapping and pleased cries from the gods greeted the performance. He was surprised, and looked at them in a puzzled way. Then his weakness asserted itself, and he lay down, his ears cocked, his head on one side, as he watched the puppy. The other puppies came sprawling toward him, to Collie's great disgust; and he gravely permitted them to clamber and tumble over him. At first, amid the applause of the gods, he betrayed a trifle of his old self-consciousness and awkwardness. This passed away as the puppies' antics and mauling continued, and he lay with half-shut patient eyes, drowsing in the sun.

About Author

John Griffith London (born **John Griffith Chaney**; January 12, 1876 – November 22, 1916) was an American novelist, journalist, and social activist. A pioneer in the world of commercial magazine fiction, he was one of the first writers to become a worldwide celebrity and earn a large fortune from writing. He was also an innovator in the genre that would later become known as science fiction.

His most famous works include The Call of the Wild and White Fang, both set in the Klondike Gold Rush, as well as the short stories "To Build a Fire", "An Odyssey of the North", and "Love of Life". He also wrote about the South Pacific in stories such as "The Pearls of Parlay", and "The Heathen".

London was part of the radical literary group "The Crowd" in San Francisco and a passionate advocate of unionization, workers' rights, socialism, and eugenics. He wrote several works dealing with these topics, such as his dystopian novel The Iron Heel, his non-fiction exposé The People of the Abyss, The War of the Classes, and Before Adam.

Family

Jack London's mother, Flora Wellman, was the fifth and youngest child of Pennsylvania Canal builder Marshall Wellman and his first wife, Eleanor Garrett Jones. Marshall Wellman was descended from Thomas Wellman, an early Puritan settler in the Massachusetts Bay Colony. Flora left Ohio and moved to the Pacific coast when her father remarried after her mother died. In San Francisco, Flora worked as a music teacher and spiritualist, claiming to channel the spirit of a Sauk chief, Black Hawk.

Biographer Clarice Stasz and others believe London's father was astrologer William Chaney. Flora Wellman was living with Chaney in San Francisco when she became pregnant. Whether Wellman and Chaney were legally married is unknown. Stasz notes that in his memoirs, Chaney refers to London's mother Flora Wellman as having been his "wife"; he also cites an advertisement in which Flora called herself "Florence Wellman Chaney".

According to Flora Wellman's account, as recorded in the San Francisco Chronicle of June 4, 1875, Chaney demanded that she have an abortion. When she refused, he disclaimed responsibility for the child. In desperation, she shot herself. She was not seriously wounded, but she was temporarily deranged. After giving birth, Flora turned the baby over for care to Virginia Prentiss, an African-American woman and former slave. She was a major maternal figure throughout London's life. Late in 1876, Flora Wellman married John London, a partially disabled Civil War veteran, and brought her baby John, later known as Jack, to live with the newly married couple. The family moved around the San Francisco Bay Area before settling in Oakland, where London completed public grade school.

In 1897, when he was 21 and a student at the University of California, Berkeley, London searched for and read the newspaper accounts of his mother's suicide attempt and the name of his biological father. He wrote to William Chaney, then living in Chicago. Chaney responded that he could not be London's father because he was impotent; he casually asserted that London's mother had relations with other men and averred that she had slandered him when she said he insisted on an abortion. Chaney concluded by saying that he was more to be pitied than London. London was devastated by his father's letter; in the months following, he quit school at Berkeley and went to the Klondike during the gold rush boom.

Early life

London was born near Third and Brannan Streets in San Francisco. The house burned down in the fire after the 1906 San Francisco earthquake; the California Historical Society placed a plaque at the site in 1953. Although the family was working class, it was not as impoverished as London's later accounts claimed. London was largely self-educated.

In 1885, London found and read Ouida's long Victorian novel Signa. He credited this as the seed of his literary success. In 1886, he went to the Oakland Public Library and found a sympathetic librarian, Ina Coolbrith, who encouraged his learning. (She later became California's first poet laureate and an important figure in the San Francisco literary community).

In 1889, London began working 12 to 18 hours a day at Hickmott's Cannery. Seeking a way out, he borrowed money from his foster mother Virginia Prentiss, bought the sloop Razzle-Dazzle from an oyster pirate named French Frank, and became an oyster pirate himself. In his memoir, John Barleycorn, he claims also to have stolen French Frank's mistress Mamie. After a few months, his sloop became damaged beyond repair. London hired on as a member of the California Fish Patrol.

In 1893, he signed on to the sealing schooner Sophie Sutherland, bound for the coast of Japan. When he returned, the country was in the grip of the panic of '93 and Oakland was swept by labor unrest. After grueling jobs in a jute mill and a street-railway power plant, London joined Coxey's Army and began his career as a tramp. In 1894, he spent 30 days for vagrancy in the Erie County Penitentiary at Buffalo, New York. In The Road, he wrote:

> Man-handling was merely one of the very minor unprintable horrors of the Erie County Pen. I say 'unprintable'; and in justice I must also say undescribable. They were unthinkable to me until I saw them, and I was no spring chicken in the ways of the world and the awful abysses of human degradation. It would take a deep plummet to reach bottom in the Erie County Pen, and I do but skim lightly and facetiously the surface of things as I there saw them.
>
> — Jack London, The Road

After many experiences as a hobo and a sailor, he returned to Oakland and attended Oakland High School. He contributed a number of articles to the high school's magazine, The Aegis. His first published work was "Typhoon off the Coast of Japan", an account of his sailing experiences.

As a schoolboy, London often studied at Heinold's First and Last Chance Saloon, a port-side bar in Oakland. At 17, he confessed to the bar's owner, John Heinold, his desire to attend university and pursue a career as a writer. Heinold lent London tuition money to attend college.

London desperately wanted to attend the University of California, located in Berkeley. In 1896, after a summer of intense studying to pass certification exams, he was admitted. Financial circumstances forced him to leave in 1897 and he never graduated. No evidence has surfaced that he ever wrote for student publications while studying at Berkeley.

While at Berkeley, London continued to study and spend time at Heinold's saloon, where he was introduced to the sailors and adventurers who would influence his writing. In his autobiographical novel, John Barleycorn, London mentioned the pub's likeness seventeen times. Heinold's was the place where London met Alexander McLean, a captain known for his cruelty at sea. London based his protagonist Wolf Larsen, in the novel The Sea-Wolf, on McLean.

Heinold's First and Last Chance Saloon is now unofficially named Jack London's Rendezvous in his honor.

Gold rush and first success

On July 12, 1897, London (age 21) and his sister's husband Captain Shepard sailed to join the Klondike Gold Rush. This was the setting for some of his first successful stories. London's time in the harsh Klondike, however, was detrimental to his health. Like so many other men who were malnourished in the goldfields, London developed scurvy. His gums became swollen, leading to the loss of his four front teeth. A constant gnawing pain affected his hip and leg muscles, and his face was stricken with marks that always reminded him of the struggles he faced in the Klondike. Father William Judge, "The Saint of Dawson", had a facility in Dawson that provided shelter, food and any available medicine to London and others. His struggles there inspired London's short story, "To Build a Fire" (1902, revised in 1908), which many critics assess as his best.

His landlords in Dawson were mining engineers Marshall Latham Bond and Louis Whitford Bond, educated at Yale and Stanford, respectively. The brothers' father, Judge Hiram Bond, was a wealthy mining investor. The Bonds, especially Hiram, were active Republicans. Marshall Bond's diary mentions friendly sparring with London on political issues as a camp pastime.

London left Oakland with a social conscience and socialist leanings; he returned to become an activist for socialism. He concluded that his only hope of escaping the work "trap" was to get an education and "sell his brains". He saw his writing as a business, his ticket out of poverty, and, he hoped, a means of beating the wealthy at their own game. On returning to California in 1898, London began working to get published, a struggle described in his novel, Martin Eden (serialized in 1908, published in 1909). His first published story since high school was "To the Man On Trail", which has frequently been collected in anthologies. When The Overland Monthly offered him only five dollars for it—and was slow paying—London came close to abandoning his writing career. In his words, "literally and literarily I was saved" when The Black Cat accepted his story "A Thousand Deaths", and paid him $40—the "first money I ever received for a story".

London began his writing career just as new printing technologies enabled lower-cost production of magazines. This resulted in a boom in popular magazines aimed at a wide public audience and a strong market for short fiction. In 1900, he made $2,500 in writing, about $77,000 in today's currency. Among the works he sold to magazines was a short story known as either "Diable" (1902) or "Bâtard" (1904), two editions of the same basic story; London received $141.25 for this story on May 27, 1902. In the text, a cruel French Canadian brutalizes his dog, and the dog retaliates and kills the man. London told some of his critics that man's actions are the main cause of the behavior of their animals, and he would show this in another story, The Call of the Wild.

In early 1903, London sold The Call of the Wild to The Saturday Evening Post for $750, and the book rights to Macmillan for $2,000. Macmillan's promotional campaign propelled it to swift success.

While living at his rented villa on Lake Merritt in Oakland, California, London met poet George Sterling; in time they became best friends. In 1902, Sterling helped London find a home closer to his own in nearby Piedmont. In his letters London addressed Sterling as "Greek", owing to Sterling's aquiline nose and classical profile, and he signed them as "Wolf". London was later to depict Sterling as Russ Brissenden in his autobiographical novel Martin Eden (1910) and as Mark Hall in The Valley of the Moon (1913).

In later life London indulged his wide-ranging interests by accumulating a personal library of 15,000 volumes. He referred to his books as "the tools of my trade".

First marriage (1900–04)

London married Elizabeth "Bessie" Maddern on April 7, 1900, the same day The Son of the Wolf was published. Bess had been part of his circle of friends for a number of years. She was related to stage actresses Minnie Maddern Fiske and Emily Stevens. Stasz says, "Both acknowledged publicly that they were not marrying out of love, but from friendship and a belief that they would produce sturdy children." Kingman says, "they were comfortable together... Jack had made it clear to Bessie that he did not love her, but that he liked her enough to make a successful marriage."

London met Bessie through his friend at Oakland High School, Fred Jacobs; she was Fred's fiancée. Bessie, who tutored at Anderson's University Academy in Alameda California, tutored Jack in preparation for his entrance exams for the University of California at Berkeley in 1896. Jacobs was killed aboard the USAT Scandia in 1897, but Jack and Bessie continued their friendship, which included taking photos and developing the film together. This was the beginning of Jack's passion for photography.

During the marriage, London continued his friendship with Anna Strunsky, co-authoring The Kempton-Wace Letters, an epistolary novel contrasting two philosophies of love. Anna, writing "Dane Kempton's" letters, arguing for a romantic view of marriage, while London, writing "Herbert Wace's" letters, argued for a scientific view, based on Darwinism and eugenics. In the novel, his fictional character contrasted two women he had known.

London's pet name for Bess was "Mother-Girl" and Bess's for London was "Daddy-Boy". Their first child, Joan, was born on January 15, 1901, and their second, Bessie (later called Becky), on October 20, 1902. Both children were born in Piedmont, California. Here London wrote one of his most celebrated works, The Call of the Wild.

While London had pride in his children, the marriage was strained. Kingman says that by 1903 the couple were close to separation as they were "extremely incompatible". "Jack was still so kind and gentle with Bessie that when Cloudsley Johns was a house guest in February 1903 he didn't suspect a breakup of their marriage."

London reportedly complained to friends Joseph Noel and George Sterling:

> [Bessie] is devoted to purity. When I tell her morality is only evidence of low blood pressure, she hates me. She'd sell me and the children out for her damned purity. It's terrible. Every time I come back after being away from home for a night she won't let me be in the same room with her if she can help it.

Stasz writes that these were "code words for fear that was consorting with prostitutes and might bring home venereal disease."

On July 24, 1903, London told Bessie he was leaving and moved out. During 1904, London and Bess negotiated the terms of a divorce, and the decree was granted on November 11, 1904.

War correspondent (1904)

London accepted an assignment of the San Francisco Examiner to cover the Russo-Japanese War in early 1904, arriving in Yokohama on January 25, 1904. He was arrested by Japanese authorities in Shimonoseki, but released through the intervention of American ambassador Lloyd Griscom. After travelling to Korea, he was again arrested by Japanese authorities for straying too close to the border with Manchuria without official permission, and was sent back to Seoul. Released again, London was permitted to travel with the Imperial Japanese Army to the border, and to observe the Battle of the Yalu.

London asked William Randolph Hearst, the owner of the San Francisco Examiner, to be allowed to transfer to the Imperial Russian Army, where he felt that restrictions on his reporting and his movements would be less severe. However, before this could be arranged, he was arrested for a third time in four months, this time for assaulting his Japanese assistants, whom he accused of stealing the fodder for his horse. Released through the personal intervention of President Theodore Roosevelt, London departed the front in June 1904.

Bohemian Club

On August 18, 1904, London went with his close friend, the poet George Sterling, to "Summer High Jinks" at the Bohemian Grove. London was elected to honorary membership in the Bohemian Club and took part in many activities. Other noted members of the Bohemian Club during this time included Ambrose Bierce, Gelett Burgess, Allan Dunn, John Muir, Frank Norris, and Herman George Scheffauer.

Beginning in December 1914, London worked on The Acorn Planter, A California Forest Play, to be performed as one of the annual Grove Plays, but it was never selected. It was described as too difficult to set to music. London published The Acorn Planter in 1916.

Second marriage

After divorcing Maddern, London married Charmian Kittredge in 1905. London had been introduced to Kittredge in 1900 by her aunt Netta Eames, who was an editor at Overland Monthly magazine in San Francisco. The two met prior to his first marriage but became lovers years later after Jack and Bessie London visited Wake Robin, Netta Eames' Sonoma County resort, in 1903. London was injured when he fell from a buggy, and Netta arranged for Charmian to care for him. The two developed a friendship, as Charmian, Netta, her husband Roscoe, and London were politically aligned with socialist causes. At some point the relationship became romantic, and Jack divorced his wife to marry Charmian, who was five years his senior.

Biographer Russ Kingman called Charmian "Jack's soul-mate, always at his side, and a perfect match." Their time together included numerous trips, including a 1907 cruise on the yacht Snark to Hawaii and Australia. Many of London's stories are based on his visits to Hawaii, the last one for 10 months beginning in December 1915.

The couple also visited Goldfield, Nevada, in 1907, where they were guests of the Bond brothers, London's Dawson City landlords. The Bond brothers were working in Nevada as mining engineers.

London had contrasted the concepts of the "Mother Girl" and the "Mate Woman" in The Kempton-Wace Letters. His pet name for Bess had been "Mother-Girl;" his pet name for Charmian was "Mate-Woman."Charmian's aunt and foster mother, a disciple of Victoria Woodhull, had raised her without prudishness.Every biographer alludes to Charmian's uninhibited sexuality.

Joseph Noel calls the events from 1903 to 1905 "a domestic drama that would have intrigued the pen of an Ibsen.... London's had comedy relief in it and a sort of easy-going romance." In broad outline, London was restless in his first marriage, sought extramarital sexual affairs, and found, in Charmian Kittredge, not only a sexually active and adventurous partner, but his future life-companion. They attempted to have children; one child died at birth, and another pregnancy ended in a miscarriage.

In 1906, London published in Collier's magazine his eye-witness report of the San Francisco earthquake.

Beauty Ranch (1905–16)

In 1905, London purchased a 1,000 acres (4.0 km2) ranch in Glen Ellen, Sonoma County, California, on the eastern slope of Sonoma Mountain.He wrote: "Next to my wife, the ranch is the dearest thing in the world to me." He desperately wanted the ranch to become a successful business enterprise. Writing, always a commercial enterprise with London, now became even more a means to an end: "I write for no other purpose than to add to the beauty that now belongs to me. I write a book for no other reason than to add three or four hundred acres to my magnificent estate."

Stasz writes that London "had taken fully to heart the vision, expressed in his agrarian fiction, of the land as the closest earthly version of Eden ... he educated himself through the study of agricultural manuals and scientific tomes. He conceived of a system of ranching that today would be praised for its ecological wisdom." He was proud to own the first concrete silo in California, a circular piggery that he designed. He hoped to adapt the wisdom of Asian sustainable agriculture to the United States. He hired both Italian and Chinese stonemasons, whose distinctly different styles are obvious.

The ranch was an economic failure. Sympathetic observers such as Stasz treat his projects as potentially feasible, and ascribe their failure to bad luck or to being ahead of their time. Unsympathetic historians such as Kevin Starr suggest that he was a bad manager, distracted by other concerns and impaired by his alcoholism. Starr notes that London was absent from his ranch about six months a year between 1910 and 1916 and says, "He liked the show of managerial power, but not grinding attention to detail .... London's workers laughed at his efforts to play big-time rancher the operation a rich man's hobby."

London spent $80,000 ($2,280,000 in current value) to build a 15,000-square-foot (1,400 m2) stone mansion called Wolf House on the property. Just as the mansion was nearing completion, two weeks before the Londons planned to move in, it was destroyed by fire.

London's last visit to Hawaii, beginning in December 1915, lasted eight months. He met with Duke Kahanamoku, Prince Jonah Kūhiō Kalaniana'ole, Queen Lili'uokalani and many others, before returning to his ranch in July 1916. He was suffering from kidney failure, but he continued to work.

The ranch (abutting stone remnants of Wolf House) is now a National Historic Landmark and is protected in Jack London State Historic Park.

Animal activism

London witnessed animal cruelty in the training of circus animals, and his subsequent novels Jerry of the Islands and Michael, Brother of Jerry included a foreword entreating the public to become more informed about this practice. In 1918, the Massachusetts Society for the Prevention of Cruelty to Animals and the American Humane Education Society teamed up to create the Jack London Club, which sought to inform the public about cruelty to circus animals and encourage them to protest this establishment. Support from Club members led to a temporary cessation of trained animal acts at Ringling-Barnum and Bailey in 1925.

Death

London died November 22, 1916, in a sleeping porch in a cottage on his ranch. London had been a robust man but had suffered several serious illnesses, including scurvy in the Klondike. Additionally, during travels on the Snark, he and Charmian picked up unspecified tropical infections, and diseases, including yaws. At the time of his death, he suffered from dysentery, late-stage alcoholism, and uremia; he was in extreme pain and taking morphine.

London's ashes were buried on his property not far from the Wolf House. London's funeral took place on November 26, 1916, attended only by close friends, relatives, and workers of the property. In accordance with his wishes, he was cremated and buried next to some pioneer children, under a rock that belonged to the Wolf House. After Charmian's death in 1955, she was also cremated and then buried with her husband in the same spot that her husband chose. The grave is marked by a mossy boulder. The buildings and property were later preserved as Jack London State Historic Park, in Glen Ellen, California.

Suicide debate

Because he was using morphine, many older sources describe London's death as a suicide, and some still do. This conjecture appears to be a rumor, or speculation based on incidents in his fiction writings. His death certificate gives the cause as uremia, following acute renal colic.

The biographer Stasz writes, "Following London's death, for a number of reasons, a biographical myth developed in which he has been portrayed as an alcoholic womanizer who committed suicide. Recent scholarship based upon firsthand documents challenges this caricature." Most biographers, including Russ Kingman, now agree he died of uremia aggravated by an accidental morphine overdose.

London's fiction featured several suicides. In his autobiographical memoir John Barleycorn, he claims, as a youth, to have drunkenly stumbled overboard into the San Francisco Bay, "some maundering fancy of going out with the tide suddenly obsessed me". He said he drifted and nearly succeeded in drowning before sobering up and being rescued by fishermen. In the dénouement of The Little Lady of the Big House, the heroine, confronted by the pain of a mortal gunshot wound, undergoes a physician-assisted suicide by morphine. Also, in Martin Eden, the principal protagonist, who shares certain characteristics with London, drowns himself.

Plagiarism accusations

London was vulnerable to accusations of plagiarism, both because he was such a conspicuous, prolific, and successful writer and because of his methods of working. He wrote in a letter to Elwyn Hoffman, "expression, you see—with me—is far easier than invention." He purchased plots and novels from the young Sinclair Lewis and used incidents from newspaper clippings as writing material.

In July 1901, two pieces of fiction appeared within the same month: London's "Moon-Face", in the San Francisco Argonaut, and Frank Norris' "The Passing of Cock-eye Blacklock", in Century Magazine. Newspapers showed the similarities between the stories, which London said were "quite different in manner of treatment, patently the same in foundation and motive." London explained both writers based their stories on the same newspaper account. A year later, it was discovered that Charles Forrest McLean had published a fictional story also based on the same incident.

Egerton Ryerson Young claimed The Call of the Wild (1903) was taken from Young's book My Dogs in the Northland (1902). London acknowledged using it as a source and claimed to have written a letter to Young thanking him.

In 1906, the New York World published "deadly parallel" columns showing eighteen passages from London's short story "Love of Life" side by side with similar passages from a nonfiction article by Augustus Biddle and J. K. Macdonald, titled "Lost in the Land of the Midnight Sun". London noted the World did not accuse him of "plagiarism", but only of "identity of time and situation", to which he defiantly "pled guilty".

542

The most serious charge of plagiarism was based on London's "The Bishop's Vision", Chapter 7 of his novel The Iron Heel (1908). The chapter is nearly identical to an ironic essay that Frank Harris published in 1901, titled "The Bishop of London and Public Morality". Harris was incensed and suggested he should receive 1/60th of the royalties from The Iron Heel, the disputed material constituting about that fraction of the whole novel. London insisted he had clipped a reprint of the article, which had appeared in an American newspaper, and believed it to be a genuine speech delivered by the Bishop of London.

Views

Atheism

London was an atheist. He is quoted as saying, "I believe that when I am dead, I am dead. I believe that with my death I am just as much obliterated as the last mosquito you and I squashed."

Socialism

London wrote from a socialist viewpoint, which is evident in his novel The Iron Heel. Neither a theorist nor an intellectual socialist, London's socialism grew out of his life experience. As London explained in his essay, "How I Became a Socialist", his views were influenced by his experience with people at the bottom of the social pit. His optimism and individualism faded, and he vowed never to do more hard physical work than necessary. He wrote that his individualism was hammered out of him, and he was politically reborn. He often closed his letters "Yours for the Revolution."

London joined the Socialist Labor Party in April 1896. In the same year, the San Francisco Chronicle published a story about the twenty-year-old London's giving nightly speeches in Oakland's City Hall Park, an activity he was arrested for a year later. In 1901, he left the Socialist Labor Party and joined the new Socialist Party of America. He ran unsuccessfully as the high-profile Socialist candidate for mayor of Oakland in 1901 (receiving 245 votes) and 1905 (improving to 981 votes), toured the country lecturing on socialism in 1906, and published two collections of essays about socialism: The War of the Classes (1905) and Revolution, and other Essays (1906).

Stasz notes that "London regarded the Wobblies as a welcome addition to the Socialist cause, although he never joined them in going so far as to recommend sabotage." Stasz mentions a personal meeting between London and Big Bill Haywood in 1912.

In his late (1913) book The Cruise of the Snark, London writes about appeals to him for membership of the Snark's crew from office workers and other "toilers" who longed for escape from the cities, and of being cheated by workmen.

In his Glen Ellen ranch years, London felt some ambivalence toward socialism and complained about the "inefficient Italian labourers" in his employ. In 1916, he resigned from the Glen Ellen chapter of the Socialist Party, but stated emphatically he did so "because of its lack of fire and fight, and its loss of emphasis on the class struggle." In an unflattering portrait of London's ranch days, California cultural historian Kevin Starr refers to this period as "post-socialist" and says "... by 1911 ... London was more bored by the class struggle than he cared to admit."

Race

London shared common concerns among many European Americans in California about Asian immigration, described as "the yellow peril"; he used the latter term as the title of a 1904 essay. This theme was also the subject of a story he wrote in 1910 called "The Unparalleled Invasion". Presented as an historical essay set in the future, the story narrates events between 1976 and 1987, in which China, with an ever-increasing population, is taking over and colonizing its neighbors with the intention of taking over the entire Earth. The western nations respond with biological warfare and bombard China with dozens of the most infectious diseases. On his fears about China, he admits, "it must be taken into consideration that the above postulate is itself a product of Western race-egotism, urged by our belief in our own righteousness and fostered by a faith in ourselves which may be as erroneous as are most fond race fancies."

By contrast, many of London's short stories are notable for their empathetic portrayal of Mexican ("The Mexican"), Asian ("The Chinago"), and Hawaiian ("Koolau the Leper") characters. London's war correspondence from the Russo-Japanese War, as well as his unfinished novel Cherry, show he admired much about Japanese customs and capabilities. London's writings have been popular among the Japanese, who believe he portrayed them positively.

In "Koolau the Leper", London describes Koolau, who is a Hawaiian leper—and thus a very different sort of "superman" than Martin Eden—and who fights off an entire cavalry troop to elude capture, as "indomitable spiritually—a ... magnificent rebel". This character is based on Hawaiian leper Kaluaikoolau, who in 1893 revolted and resisted capture from forces of the Provisional Government of Hawaii in the Kalalau Valley.

An amateur boxer and avid boxing fan, London reported on the 1910 Johnson–Jeffries fight, in which the black boxer Jack Johnson vanquished Jim Jeffries, known as the "Great White Hope". In 1908, London had reported on an earlier fight of Johnson's, contrasting the black boxer's coolness and intellectual style, with the apelike appearance and fighting style of his Canadian opponent, Tommy Burns:

> [What won] on Saturday was bigness, coolness, quickness, cleverness, and vast physical superiority ... Because a white man wishes a white man to win, this should not prevent him from giving absolute credit to the best man, even when that best man was black. All hail to Johnson. ... superb. He was impregnable ... as inaccessible as Mont Blanc.

Those who defend London against charges of racism cite the letter he wrote to the Japanese-American Commercial Weekly in 1913:

> In reply to yours of August 16, 1913. First of all, I should say by stopping the stupid newspaper from always fomenting race prejudice. This of course, being impossible, I would say, next, by educating the people of Japan so that they will be too intelligently tolerant to respond to any call to race prejudice. And, finally, by realizing, in industry and

545

government, of socialism—which last word is merely a word that stands for the actual application of in the affairs of men of the theory of the Brotherhood of Man.

In the meantime the nations and races are only unruly boys who have not yet grown to the stature of men. So we must expect them to do unruly and boisterous things at times. And, just as boys grow up, so the races of mankind will grow up and laugh when they look back upon their childish quarrels.

In 1996, after the City of Whitehorse, Yukon, renamed a street in honor of London, protests over London's alleged racism forced the city to change the name of "Jack London Boulevard"[failed verification] back to "Two-mile Hill".

Eugenics

London supported eugenics, including forced sterilization of criminals or those deemed feeble minded. His novel Before Adam(1906–07) has been described as having pro-eugenic themes.

London wrote to Frederick H. Robinson of the periodical Medical Review of Reviews, stating, "I believe the future belongs to eugenics, and will be determined by the practice of eugenics."

Works

Short stories

Western writer and historian Dale L. Walker writes:

London's true métier was the short story ... London's true genius lay in the short form, 7,500 words and under, where the flood of images in his teeming brain and the innate power of his narrative gift were at once constrained and freed. His stories that run longer than the magic 7,500 generally—but certainly not always—could have benefited from self-editing.

London's "strength of utterance" is at its height in his stories, and they are painstakingly well-constructed. "To Build a Fire" is the best known of all his stories. Set in the harsh Klondike, it recounts the haphazard trek of a new arrival who has ignored an old-timer's warning about the risks of traveling alone. Falling through the ice into a creek in seventy-five-below weather, the unnamed man is keenly aware that survival depends on his untested skills at quickly building a fire to dry his clothes and warm his extremities. After publishing a tame version of this story—with a sunny outcome—in The Youth's Companion in 1902, London offered a second, more severe take on the man's predicament in The Century Magazine in 1908. Reading both provides an illustration of London's growth and maturation as a writer. As Labor (1994) observes: "To compare the two versions is itself an instructive lesson in what distinguished a great work of literary art from a good children's story."

Other stories from the Klondike period include: "All Gold Canyon", about a battle between a gold prospector and a claim jumper; "The Law of Life", about an aging American Indian man abandoned by his tribe and left to die; "Love of Life", about a trek by a prospector across the Canadian tundra; "To the Man on Trail," which tells the story of a prospector fleeing the Mounted Police in a sled race, and raises the question of the contrast between written law and morality; and "An Odyssey of the North," which raises questions of conditional morality, and paints a sympathetic portrait of a man of mixed White and Aleut ancestry.

London was a boxing fan and an avid amateur boxer. "A Piece of Steak" is a tale about a match between older and younger boxers. It contrasts the differing experiences of youth and age but also raises the social question of the treatment of aging workers. "The Mexican" combines boxing with a social theme, as a young Mexican endures an unfair fight and ethnic prejudice to earn money with which to aid the revolution.

Several of London's stories would today be classified as science fiction. "The Unparalleled Invasion" describes germ warfare against China; "Goliath" is about an irresistible energy weapon; "The Shadow and the Flash" is a tale about two brothers who take different routes to achieving invisibility; "A

Relic of the Pliocene" is a tall tale about an encounter of a modern-day man with a mammoth. "The Red One" is a late story from a period when London was intrigued by the theories of the psychiatrist and writer Jung. It tells of an island tribe held in thrall by an extraterrestrial object.

Some nineteen original collections of short stories were published during London's brief life or shortly after his death. There have been several posthumous anthologies drawn from this pool of stories. Many of these stories were located in the Klondike and the Pacific. A collection of Jack London's San Francisco Stories was published in October 2010 by Sydney Samizdat Press.

Novels

London's most famous novels are The Call of the Wild, White Fang, The Sea-Wolf, The Iron Heel, and Martin Eden.

In a letter dated December 27, 1901, London's Macmillan publisher George Platt Brett, Sr., said "he believed Jack's fiction represented 'the very best kind of work' done in America."

Critic Maxwell Geismar called The Call of the Wild "a beautiful prose poem"; editor Franklin Walker said that it "belongs on a shelf with Walden and Huckleberry Finn"; and novelist E.L. Doctorow called it "a mordant parable ... his masterpiece."

The historian Dale L. Walker commented:

Jack London was an uncomfortable novelist, that form too long for his natural impatience and the quickness of his mind. His novels, even the best of them, are hugely flawed.

Some critics have said that his novels are episodic and resemble linked short stories. Dale L. Walker writes:

The Star Rover, that magnificent experiment, is actually a series of short stories connected by a unifying device ... Smoke Bellew is a series of stories bound together in a novel-like form by their reappearing protagonist, Kit Bellew; and John Barleycorn ... is a synoptic series of short episodes.

Ambrose Bierce said of The Sea-Wolf that "the great thing—and it is among the greatest of things—is that tremendous creation, Wolf Larsen ... the hewing out and setting up of such a figure is enough for a man to do in one lifetime. "However, he noted, "The love element, with its absurd suppressions, and impossible proprieties, is awful."

The Iron Heel is an example of a dystopian novel that anticipates and influenced George Orwell's Nineteen Eighty-Four. London's socialist politics are explicitly on display here. The Iron Heel meets the contemporary definition of soft science fiction. The Star Rover (1915) is also science fiction.

Apocrypha

Jack London Credo

London's literary executor, Irving Shepard, quoted a Jack London Credo in an introduction to a 1956 collection of London stories:

I would rather be ashes than dust!

I would rather that my spark should burn out in a brilliant blaze than it should be stifled by dry-rot.

I would rather be a superb meteor, every atom of me in magnificent glow, than a sleepy and permanent planet.

The function of man is to live, not to exist.

I shall not waste my days in trying to prolong them.

I shall use my time.

The biographer Stasz notes that the passage "has many marks of London's style" but the only line that could be safely attributed to London was the first. The words Shepard quoted were from a story in the San Francisco Bulletin, December 2, 1916, by journalist Ernest J. Hopkins, who visited the ranch just weeks before London's death. Stasz notes, "Even more so than today journalists' quotes were unreliable or even sheer inventions," and says no direct source in London's writings has been found. However, at least one line, according to Stasz, is authentic, being referenced by London and written in his own hand in the autograph book of Australian suffragette Vida Goldstein:

Dear Miss Goldstein:–

Seven years ago I wrote you that I'd rather be ashes than dust. I still subscribe to that sentiment.

Sincerely yours,

Jack London

Jan. 13, 1909

In his short story "By The Turtles of Tasman", a character, defending her "ne'er-do-well grasshopperish father" to her "antlike uncle", says: "... my father has been a king. He has lived .... Have you lived merely to live? Are you afraid to die? I'd rather sing one wild song and burst my heart with it, than live a thousand years watching my digestion and being afraid of the wet. When you are dust, my father will be ashes."

"The Scab"

A short diatribe on "The Scab" is often quoted within the U.S. labor movement and frequently attributed to London. It opens:

After God had finished the rattlesnake, the toad, and the vampire, he had some awful substance left with which he made a scab. A scab is a two-legged animal with a corkscrew soul, a water brain, a combination backbone of jelly and glue. Where others have hearts, he carries a tumor of rotten principles. When a scab comes down the street, men turn their backs and Angels weep in Heaven, and the Devil shuts the gates of hell to keep him out....

In 1913 and 1914, a number of newspapers printed the first three sentences with varying terms used instead of "scab", such as "knocker","stool pigeon"or "scandal monger"

This passage as given above was the subject of a 1974 Supreme Court case, Letter Carriers v. Austin, in which Justice Thurgood Marshall referred to it as "a well-known piece of trade union literature, generally attributed to author Jack London". A union newsletter had published a "list of scabs," which was granted to be factual and therefore not libelous, but then went on to quote the passage as the "definition of a scab". The case turned on the question of whether the "definition" was defamatory. The court ruled that "Jack London's... 'definition of a scab' is merely rhetorical hyperbole, a lusty and imaginative expression of the contempt felt by union members towards those who refuse to join", and as such was not libelous and was protected under the First Amendment.

Despite being frequently attributed to London, the passage does not appear at all in the extensive collection of his writings at Sonoma State University's website. However, in his book The War of the Classes he published a 1903 speech entitled "The Scab", which gave a much more balanced view of the topic:

> The laborer who gives more time or strength or skill for the same wage than another, or equal time or strength or skill for a less wage, is a scab. The generousness on his part is hurtful to his fellow-laborers, for it compels them to an equal generousness which is not to their liking, and which gives them less of food and shelter. But a word may be said for the scab. Just as his act makes his rivals compulsorily generous, so do they, by fortune of birth and training, make compulsory his act of generousness.
>
> [...]
>
> Nobody desires to scab, to give most for least. The ambition of every individual is quite the opposite, to give least for most; and, as a result, living in a tooth-and-nail society, battle royal is waged by the ambitious individuals. But in its most salient aspect, that of the struggle over the division of the joint product, it is no longer a battle between individuals, but between groups of individuals. Capital and labor apply

themselves to raw material, make something useful out of it, add to its value, and then proceed to quarrel over the division of the added value. Neither cares to give most for least. Each is intent on giving less than the other and on receiving more.

Legacy and honors

Mount London, also known as Boundary Peak 100, on the Alaska-British Columbia boundary, in the Boundary Ranges of the Coast Mountains of British Columbia, is named for him.

Jack London Square on the waterfront of Oakland, California was named for him.

He was honored by the United States Postal Service with a 25¢ Great Americans series postage stamp released on January 11, 1986.

Jack London Lake (Russian), a mountain lake located in the upper reaches of the Kolyma River in Yagodninsky district of Magadan Oblast.

Fictional portrayals of London include Michael O'Shea in the 1943 film Jack London, Jeff East in the 1980 film Klondike Fever, Aaron Ashmore in the Murdoch Mysteries episode "Murdoch of the Klondike" from 2012, and Johnny Simmons in the 2014 miniseries Klondike. (Source: Wikipedia)

NOTABLE WORKS

NOVELS

The Cruise of the Dazzler (1902)

A Daughter of the Snows (1902)

The Call of the Wild (1903)

The Kempton-Wace Letters (1903) (published anonymously, co-authored with Anna Strunsky)

The Sea-Wolf (1904)

The Game (1905)

White Fang (1906)

Before Adam (1907)

The Iron Heel (1908)

Martin Eden (1909)

Burning Daylight (1910)

Adventure (1911)

The Scarlet Plague (1912)

A Son of the Sun (1912)

The Abysmal Brute (1913)

The Valley of the Moon (1913)

The Mutiny of the Elsinore (1914)

The Star Rover (1915) (published in England as The Jacket)

The Little Lady of the Big House (1916)

Jerry of the Islands (1917)

Michael, Brother of Jerry (1917)

Hearts of Three (1920) (novelization of a script by Charles Goddard)

The Assassination Bureau, Ltd (1963) (left half-finished, completed by Robert L. Fish)

SHORT STORIES

"An Old Soldier's Story" (1894)

"Who Believes in Ghosts!" (1895)

"And 'FRISCO Kid Came Back" (1895)

"Night's Swim In Yeddo Bay" (1895)

"One More Unfortunate" (1895)

"Sakaicho, Hona Asi And Hakadaki" (1895)

"A Klondike Christmas" (1897)

"Mahatma's Little Joke" (1897)

"O Haru" (1897)

"Plague Ship" (1897)

"The Strange Experience Of A Misogynist" (1897)

"Two Gold Bricks" (1897)

"The Devil's Dice Box" (1898)

"A Dream Image" (1898)

"The Test: A Clondyke Wooing" (1898)

"To the Man on Trail" (1898)

"In a Far Country" (1899)

"The King of Mazy May" (1899)

"The End Of The Chapter" (1899)

"The Grilling Of Loren Ellery" (1899)

"The Handsome Cabin Boy" (1899)

"In The Time Of Prince Charley" (1899)

"Old Baldy" (1899)

"The Men of Forty Mile" (1899)

"Pluck and Pertinacity" (1899)

"The Rejuvenation of Major Rathbone" (1899)

"The White Silence" (1899)

"A Thousand Deaths" (1899)

"Wisdom of the Trail" (1899)

"An Odyssey of the North" (1900)

"The Son of the Wolf" (1900)

"Even unto Death" (1900)

"The Man with the Gash" (1900)

"A Lesson in Heraldry" (1900)

"A Northland Miracle" (1900)

"Proper "GIRLIE"" (1900)

"Thanksgiving on Slav Creek" (1900)

"Their Alcove" (1900)

"Housekeeping in the Klondike" (1900)

"Dutch Courage" (1900)

"Where the Trail Forks" (1900)

"Hyperborean Brew" (1901)

"A Relic of the Pliocene" (1901)

"The Lost Poacher" (1901)

"The God of His Fathers" (1901)

""FRISCO Kid's" Story" (1901)

"The Law of Life" (1901)

"The Minions of Midas" (1901)

"In the Forests of the North" (1902)

"The "Fuzziness" of Hoockla-Heen" (1902)

"The Story of Keesh" (1902)

"Keesh, Son of Keesh" (1902)

"Nam-Bok, the Unveracious" (1902)

"Li Wan the Fair" (1902)

"Lost Face"

"Master of Mystery" (1902)

"The Sunlanders" (1902)

"The Death of Ligoun" (1902)

"Moon-Face" (1902)

"Diable—A Dog" (1902), renamed Bâtard in 1904

"To Build a Fire" (1902, revised 1908)

"Samuel" (1909)

"South of the Slot" (1909)

"The Chinago" (1909)

"The Dream of Debs" (1909)

"The Madness of John Harned" (1909)

"The Seed of McCoy" (1909)

"A Piece of Steak" (1909)

"Mauki" (1909)

"The Whale Tooth" (1909)

"Goliath" (1910)

"The Unparalleled Invasion" (1910)

"Told in the Drooling Ward" (1910)

"When the World was Young" (1910)

"The Terrible Solomons" (1910)

"The Inevitable White Man" (1910)

"The Heathen" (1910)

"Yah! Yah! Yah!" (1910)

"By the Turtles of Tasman" (1911)

"The Mexican" (1911)

"War" (1911)

"The Unmasking of the Cad" (1911)

"The Scarlet Plague" (1912)

"The Captain of the Susan Drew" (1912)

"The Sea-Farmer" (1912)

"The Feathers of the Sun" (1912)

"The Prodigal Father" (1912)

"Samuel" (1913)

"The Sea-Gangsters" (1913)

"The Strength of the Strong" (1914)

"Told in the Drooling Ward" (1914)

"The Hussy" (1916)

"Like Argus of the Ancient Times" (1917)

"Jerry of the Islands" (1917)

"The Red One" (1918)

"Shin-Bones" (1918)

"The Bones of Kahekili" (1919)

SHORT STORY COLLECTIONS

Son of the Wolf (1900)

Chris Farrington, Able Seaman (1901)

The God of His Fathers & Other Stories (1901)

Children of the Frost (1902)

The Faith of Men and Other Stories (1904)

Tales of the Fish Patrol (1906)

Moon-Face and Other Stories (1906)

Love of Life and Other Stories (1907)

Lost Face (1910)

South Sea Tales (1911)

When God Laughs and Other Stories (1911)

The House of Pride & Other Tales of Hawaii (1912)

Smoke Bellew (1912)

A Son of the Sun (1912)

The Night Born (1913)

The Strength of the Strong (1914)

The Turtles of Tasman (1916)

The Human Drift (1917)

The Red One (1918)

On the Makaloa Mat (1919)

Dutch Courage and Other Stories (1922)

AUTOBIOGRAPHICAL MEMOIRS

The Road (1907)

The Cruise of the Snark (1911)

John Barleycorn (1913)

NON-FICTION AND ESSAYS

Through the Rapids on the Way to the Klondike (1899)

From Dawson to the Sea (1899)

What Communities Lose by the Competitive System (1900)

The Impossibility of War (1900)

Phenomena of Literary Evolution (1900)

A Letter to Houghton Mifflin Co. (1900)

Husky, Wolf Dog of the North (1900)

Editorial Crimes –- A Protest (1901)

Again the Literary Aspirant (1902)

The People of the Abyss (1903)

How I Became a Socialist (1903)

The War of the Classes (1905)

The Story of an Eyewitness (1906)

A Letter to Woman's Home Companion (1906)

Revolution, and other Essays (1910)

Mexico's Army and Ours (1914)

Lawgivers (1914)

Our Adventures in Tampico (1914)

Stalking the Pestilence (1914)

The Red Game of War (1914)

The Trouble Makers of Mexico (1914)

With Funston's Men (1914)

POETRY

Of Man of the Future (1915)

Oh You Everybody's Girl (19)

On the Face of the Earth You are the One (1915)

Rainbows End (1914)

Republican Rallying Song (1916)

Sonnet (1901)

The Gift of God (1905)

The Klondyker's Dream (1914)

The Lover's Liturgy (1913)

The Mammon Worshippers (1911)

The Republican Battle-Hymn (1905)

The Return of Ulysses (1915)

The Sea Sprite and the Shooting Star (1916)

The Socialist's Dream (1912)

The Song of the Flames (1903)

The Way of War (1906)

The Worker and the Tramp (1911)

Tick! Tick! Tick! (1915)

Too Late (1912)

Weasel Thieves (1913)

When All the World Shouted my Name (1905)

Where the Rainbow Fell (1902)

Your Kiss (1914)

PLAYS

Theft (1910)

Daughters of the Rich: A One Act Play (1915)

The Acorn Planter: A California Forest Play (1916)

CPSIA information can be obtained
at www.ICGtesting.com
Printed in the USA
LVHW052040021120
670493LV00002B/115